RETURN TO REICHENBACH

BY

GERI SCHEAR

Paperback ISBN 978-1-78705-006-8
ePub ISBN 978-1-78705-007-5
PDF ISBN 978-1-78705-008-2
Published in the UK by MX Publishing
335 Princess Park Manor, Royal Drive,
London, N11 3GX
www.mxpublishing.co.uk
Cover design by Brian Belanger

Grateful acknowledgment to Conan Doyle Estate Ltd. for the use of the
Sherlock Holmes characters created by Sir Arthur Conan Doyle.

1

FROM THE DIARY OF MR SHERLOCK HOLMES

Friday, 21ˢᵗ October, 1898

The telegram said only, "Man found on moor in nightshirt. Please come."

On the train, Watson said, "What on earth could have possessed a man to go wandering around the moors in such a state, Holmes? Can he be a lunatic?"

"You know my process, Watson. It is a capital mistake to theorise in advance of the facts. Even I cannot be expected to develop a reasonable hypothesis based on six words."

He fell silent, but I knew he was merely framing his next question. As the train pulled into Clapham Junction station, it came. "You must have formed a theory, Holmes," he said.

My frown did nothing to discourage him. He is too used to me by now, I suppose, to take my aloofness at face value. I said, "I have formed seven hypotheses that broadly cover the little that we know. Until I have facts I cannot determine which is the most likely."

"For instance?"

Sometimes the man is like a child. His need for entertainment is really very immature.

Crowds alighted from the train and dispersed on the platform. They were replaced with another crowd who waved goodbye, and puffed and panted through the carriage in search of their compartments. I have never seen a duller group of travellers.

Were I a criminal instead of a detective, no form of public transport would be safe from me. It is such fertile ground for the picking of pockets and the taking of lives.

"Holmes?" Watson urged, again.

"For instance, I cannot determine how the man came to the moors until I know where, exactly, he was found. All I can determine is that he is alive and incapacitated."

Watson's face fell into that comically bewildered expression that usually irritates me, only because I know that most of the time he pretends an ignorance he does not, in fact, possess. In this case, I knew I had truly amazed him. I wrapped my coat closer around me and buried my head in my scarf.

"Wait a minute," he cried. "You cannot leave it like that. Holmes!"

"Come, my dear Watson. You have as much information as I. You can draw your own conclusions, surely?"

Silence reigned for ten delicious minutes and then he said, "If the man were capable of speaking rationally, he would have given the police some sort of explanation. If that were so, they would not have consulted you."

"Precisely."

Another few moments and then, "But how can you be sure he isn't dead?"

"My dear Watson," I said, exasperated, "If the man were dead they would have said they had found a corpse or a body. They describe him as a man; ergo, he is still alive."

"So he may prove to be a mental patient, if he is unable to give an account of himself."

"Possibly, but I think not."

"There are several mental hospitals in Devonshire, most of them around the Exeter area, if memory serves. Isn't it possible this poor fellow escaped from one of them?"

"Unlikely." At his continued bewilderment, I added, "For two reasons: In the first place, the police would surely have checked the local institutions to determine if a patient were missing. In the second, it is customary in such facilities, I believe, to dress the inmates in institutional clothing. This fellow was found in his nightshirt."

"Oh."

I deterred him from further speculation by ruminating on the mathematical probabilities of being struck by lightening. Within twenty minutes, my oratory had the desired effect.

Doctor Watson was asleep.

Inspector Pendleton met us at St David's station in Exeter. A short, stout man with the skin of a former tin miner, he seemed greatly relieved by our presence.

"Would you like to see the man first, Mr Holmes?" he said, "Or should I take you to the area where he was found?"

"I would like to see the man," I replied. "What is his condition?"

"He is gibbering, I am afraid. He makes no sense. He cannot even tell us his name."

"Is he a lunatic, escaped from one of the asylums?" Watson said.

"No; I have asked. He is not from a hospital, nor is he from the gaol."

"Where is the man now?" I asked.

"I brought him to the station. He's in one of the cells."

The station in Waterbeer Street was about ten years old and felt cleaner and less jaded than most of its London counterparts. Watson put this, bewilderingly, to the proximity of the sea.

Pendleton led us down to the cells. Though clean, these were still as horrifying as any other gaol. The walls were white. Several feet above the floor was an arc-shaped window paned with thick glass. Beneath this, a man lay upon a cot, tightly confined in leather straps. He tugged and pulled this way and that.

"Good heavens," Watson said. He stepped forward and examined the unfortunate. "Has a doctor seen him?"

"Yes, sir," Pendleton said. "That was the first thing we did. I have his report on my desk."

"Get it," Watson said.

When we were alone, he said, "This is grotesque, Holmes. This fellow is suffering from a drug of some sort. A great deal of it, if I'm not mistaken. Look at his pupils."

"I agree. Pin-point."

"Help me remove these restraints."

It took us considerable time and effort to complete this task. The prisoner cowered and cried, he pulled against us, sobbing bitterly, and flailed as soon as his hands were released. Truly a dreadful sight.

"Here, what are you doing?" the policeman said, as he returned. "It took four of my men to get him into those things."

"They are barbaric," Watson snapped.

"They are for his own protection," Pendleton said. "He was trying to hurt himself. He would have succeeded, too, if we had not tied him down."

"I have to be able to examine him," I said, "if I am to learn anything. I cannot see through these restraints. If need be, we shall put them back on when we have finished our observations."

4

I undid the last of the leather straps that bound the man's legs, and removed the straight-jacket.

Watson crooned at the unfortunate, called him 'lad', and patted his back.

The fellow continued to sob, but no longer fought against us.

"There now," Watson said, "That's better isn't it? We have taken those nasty straps off. Are you hungry? Would you like something to eat?"

The man said nothing but continued to wail. After the third time of being asked, he made a motion that may have been a nod.

"See if you can find him some food," Watson said to the policeman, "Meat or even a biscuit. It will help him understand that we mean him no harm."

Pendleton hurried away and returned some minutes later with a plate of cold chicken.

The patient-prisoner ate ravenously.

"He's been starved for several days," I said.

"How can you tell that, Mr Holmes?" the policeman asked.

"His breath smells like fruit. The unmistakable odour of ketones… I have frequently observed it in people who have been starved. I should write a paper."

"Poor beggar," Pendleton said.

The man ate, but could not answer any questions. His speech was entirely gibberish. "The snakes," he cried at one point, "Get them off me! The snakes!"

His name he had forgotten; his reasons for being in Exeter, his family, all were locked in the confused jumble of his brain.

He pointed at an indefinable spot on the floor and screamed. "The snakes, the snakes!" His screams were piercing, terrible, and they went on and on.

"I shall have to sedate him, Holmes," Watson said.

I agreed. There was no sense to be had from the fellow in his current state.

Twenty minutes later when he slept, I was able to conduct my examination. The man's flesh was striped with long, savage welts. They covered his back, his thighs, and even his genitalia. A dozen cigarette burns covered his feet and ankles. The undamaged parts of his soles were well-maintained and spoke of affluence. These feet had worn only the finest leather.

His right hand was well developed and there were calluses on his index and middle fingers suggesting he had spent a great amount of time writing.

The pinches on the side of his nose indicated he customarily wore spectacles. He looked like any of thousands of English businessmen. However, despite these signs of a sedentary occupation, his physique was excellent. His arms and legs suggested he spent a great deal of time in a wide range of exercises. Mountain-climbing, walking, and, yes, swimming. Curious.

"What was he wearing when you found him? These trousers and jumper he's in now are a poor fit; and your telegram referred to a nightshirt."

"You are right, Mr Holmes. These clothes were brought by one of the local charities. The cells are cold and I did not want the man to suffer any more than he already had."

"That was kind," Watson said, "but why keep him here? Surely he'd be better in a hospital?"

"I had hopes that his family would claim him… But you're right; he cannot stay here."

I examined the nightshirt. It was expensive and bore an Italian label.

"He has been abroad," I said, examining the garment. "This tailor has a reputation for precision in his measurements. Judging by the size of the garment and the man's frame, I would judge he has lost at least ten pounds since its purchase. He is a man of means. Tell me, Inspector, has no one reported anyone missing over the past week?"

"No, Mr Holmes. I sent word all over. I have not yet heard back from London, but I'm sure this man is not a local."

"Have you asked the local railway staff if they recognise him?" I said.

Pendleton's face lit. "No, I have not. That is an excellent suggestion, Mr Holmes. If he is a frequent visitor to Exeter they might know his name. I shall ask the station master to come and take a look at the fellow, while he is still quiet."

After Pendleton left, Watson said, "Surely the railwaymen will not know this man, Holmes."

"It is unlikely, I agree, but they may know when our nameless friend came to Exeter and if he travelled with a companion. If we are exceedingly fortunate, they may recall where he boarded the train."

Watson, hungry as usual, asked if we might have lunch while we awaited the railwayman. Leaving a constable in charge of the patient, we went to the local alehouse and I had a cup of coffee while my friend sampled the meat pie.

By the time we returned to the station, Mr Mafeking, the station master, had arrived with one of his porters, a man called Burke.

"Don't know his name," the porter said, "but he arrived about a week ago. He was with a few other men. They seemed in merry spirits."

"You did not catch the names of any of these gentlemen?" I said.

The porter's face scrunched into a ball, as if all his muscles pulled inwards. "No," he said. "I'm sorry. A couple of them looked like foreigners. Dark. One of them was a toff, by the way he was dressed. Tall, he was. About as tall as yourself, sir. Black hair and black eyes. This poor chap here was generous. He was paying for everything. That's why I remember him. Good tip, he gave me."

"Do you remember which train they arrived on?"

More frowning. "One of the afternoon trains from Paddington, I think. It was busy that day and there was a right crowd of people on the platform. I called a cab for these gentlemen."

"Do you know whose cab?"

"No. I'm sorry, sir. It was just too busy. I reckon I wouldn't have remembered the gent at all if he hadn't handed me that sovereign. Poor bugger. Begging your pardon, sir. What happened to him?"

"We do not know," Pendleton said.

The two men turned to leave and I was on the point of asking for the names of local cabbies, when the porter stopped and turned back.

"The man had a trunk," he said. "A big yellow trunk with foreign stamps all over it. I helped him load it into the back of the cab."

"Then the cab was large enough to take four men in addition to luggage?"

Another pause while he considered. The wait was vexing, but the fellow was doing his best so I forced myself to be patient.

"They took a Clarence cab, what they call a 'growler', sir. Don't remember who was driving… Come about, it had to be either Murray or Sheppy. Any of the other growler drivers would give you a hand, like, but not that pair."

"Where can we find these fellows?"

"They'll be at the station at some point during the day, waiting for a fare."

"Excellent. Then with your permission, we will return there with you."

Back we went to St David's. There were a couple of cabs outside, but both were Hansoms.

"You're welcome to sit in my waiting room, if you like, gents," the stationmaster said.

And so we sat. The policeman asked a number of inane questions to which I did not listen. A babble of conversation ensued between him and Watson, with occasional interjections from one of the railway workers. Now and then, I caught my name, but I was not paying heed. I was tracking the arrival of this man to Exeter. A man no one knew. A paradoxical fellow: physically active yet sedentary. Much-travelled and wealthy. Why had he come to Devonshire? Who were the men who accompanied him? Why had no one reported him missing? The rumble of trains on the track outside made for a comforting sort of background noise for my thoughts.

All the while, I stared out the window. After almost half an hour, a growler arrived.

"That's Mr Murray," Burke said.

"Ask him to join us, would you, Mr Burke?" said the inspector.

The porter hurried out and returned moments later with a sulky-looking cabby.

"I 'ope this won't take long," he said. "I'm losing customers."

"The length of time depends how long it takes you to tell us what we need to know," Pendleton said with spirit. I confess I was surprised to find him capable of such energy. "This gentleman is Mr Sherlock Holmes, you'll have heard that name, I warrant. Be so good as to answer his questions."

"Well?" Murray said.

"Four men arrived about a week ago. We are looking for the cabby who took them to their destination. Two of the men were gentlemen; two seemed like foreigners. One of the gentlemen had a large yellow trunk with a great many stamps from other countries on it. He was about five foot ten inches, well dressed, with dark brown hair. He was wearing spectacles."

"A week ago, you say?" He shook his head. "Not ringing no bells."

"It was late afternoon, if I remember right," Burke added, helpfully. "I think they came on the London train."

"Not me. I'll ask the other lads, if you like, though, your honour."

"Very well. Report to Inspector Pendleton," I said. "Have you seen a cabby by the name of Sheppy this morning?"

"Yes, sir. He should be along shortly. Just stopped to wet his whistle, so to speak."

The fellow left us and we sat back to wait. It was not long before another growler arrived. "That's Sheppy now," said Burke. He ran out and brought the fellow back to meet with us. A small, greasy man who reeked of gin and had rotten teeth. The tattoo on his left arm told of a stretch in Pentonville.

"I remember," he said. "Four fellows. One of them gave me a hand, I remember. Dark looking chap. Maybe a foreigner, though he sounded like an Englishman. The rest of 'em were useless. One of the fellows seemed a toff, smart coat he had. Made free with the coppers."

"You didn't catch any of their names?"

He frowned. "It's been a while," he said. "And I've had a lot of fares since then."

"There's a shilling in it if you can take us to the place where you left these gentlemen."

At that, his greedy eyes lit up. "Updike!" he exclaimed. "That was it. Mr Updike. He was the toff. I didn't catch any of the other names, though."

"Do you remember where you took them?"

"Aye, we took Longdown Road a way out to the moor. There's a farmhouse."

"Who owns it?"

"Some farmer. Didn't catch his name."

"Can you take us there?"

He hesitated.

"We will, of course, pay you," I added.

At that, he brightened. "Aye, I can indeed, gents."

An hour later, we arrived at a forlorn farm on the moor. The curtains were drawn and the land lay fallow. There were no animals in sight. Whatever this place was being used for, it was not farm work. An air of decay lay over land almost like an acrid smoke. I sniffed. Watson glanced at me and nodded.

"Stay here," I said to the cabby. "Inspector, I am afraid you must prepare yourself."

The first body was lying on the hall floor just a few feet from the door. She, for it was a middle-aged woman, lay face down with a gunshot wound in her back.

Watson briefly examined her. "Dead two or three days," he said.

There were two sets of bloody footprints in the hallway. The first set appeared just before the corpse. A tall man, approximately six foot two, and left-handed. The left foot was decidedly the more decisive. There were two steps and then nothing. A closer examination revealed a bloody smear on the dead woman's skirt. Interesting. So the left-handed man had accidentally stepped in the victim's blood and wiped his shoes in her clothing.

The second set of footprints came from a room on our left. They led us to the body of man perhaps sixty years of age, lying in an armchair. The right side of his head had been shot off. A teacup lay broken on the floor beside him

The room was alive with flies. Watson opened the window to let them out.

Pendleton stood in the doorway, a handkerchief to his mouth. I feared he might vomit.

"Perhaps you should go and fetch your constables, Inspector," I said.

"Yes... Yes, Mr Holmes. I'll do that." He turned to leave, but hesitated. "I should examine the premises."

"Let Holmes do that," Watson said. "If you have an expert at hand, why not use him?"

"I shall let you know everything we discover, Inspector," I said. "Ah, you might also see if you can find out who owns this farm."

The man left and I resumed my exploration of the murder house.

"He shot the man first, as you would expect," I said. "The fellow wasn't expecting it; he had a teacup in his hand. The woman ran to the door. Gunman followed; his footsteps are tracked in blood, as you see. He shot her where she stood."

"Poor devils," Watson said. "I don't understand, Holmes. Why come to a farmhouse in the middle of nowhere and slaughter two people?"

"They did not want to leave any witnesses."

We explored the bedrooms. One was where the murdered couple had slept. Their clothing and belongings mutely protested their deaths. Two of the other rooms showed signs of being recently occupied and abandoned. Nothing was left. Only the unmade beds gave any indication that anyone had been here. I sniffed the bedlinen but too many days had passed for them to reveal anything of use.

I found more of interest in the last room. Here was a large yellow trunk covered in stamps from most of the countries in Europe. It was full of men's clothing. Expensive shirts, silk ties, impeccably tailored suits. These were neatly packed. It seemed our unfortunate victim had come to Exeter expecting a holiday.

"Curious they did not take the time to remove these," I mused.

In the wardrobe hung an expensive coat. The lapel was decorated with a silver tiepin in the shape of a lamp.

"I've seen that somewhere before," Watson said.

"Yes. I have one. So does Mycroft. This is the symbol of the Diogenes Club."

2

Watson stared at me. "Then the poor wretch in Exeter's police station works for the government."

"It would seem so…" I was busy rummaging through the coat pockets. "Aha!" I cried as my fingers found a wallet.

I drew it out and opened it. "Augustus Updike," I read. "I do not know the name. No doubt Mycroft will be able to tell us more."

We made our way through the rest of the farmhouse, but there was little of interest until we arrived in the kitchen. There we found a broken kerosene lamp beside a charred dresser.

"See here, Watson," I said. "This is why they did not bother to remove the trunk or Updike's belongings. They expected all the evidence to be destroyed in an inferno." I examined the damage. "Yes, they set fire to the dresser. It is badly charred. The damage could have been considerable if the weather had stayed clement."

"But the window was open and the torrent doused the flames…" Watson said, following my reasoning. "Why leave the window open, Holmes?"

"Because the murders were committed before the weather broke. No doubt they thought the breeze would fan the flames. Nothing worked out the way these fellows planned. A result of hubris or poor planning: who can say? First, Updike escaped onto the moor. One of the gang shot the farmer and his wife. There was a chance a neighbour might show up at any moment… The fiends had to flee and with all haste. They set the fire and fled. Unfortunately for them, the weather turned before the flames took hold. I believe it was clement enough in the area until Wednesday night. I deduce, therefore, that it was on Wednesday that all these events occurred: Updike's flight and the murder of the farmer and his wife."

"Poor creatures," Watson said. "But how did the killers manage to escape? It's a long walk back to Exeter."

"I suspect we shall find the stables empty. Our quarry will have stolen the horses."

Other than a singed ledger in the dresser drawer, we could learn no more from the house. I led the way to the ancient stables at the back.

"Good God," Watson cried, "It looks like an abattoir."

The sight that met us was one of the most horrifying I have ever seen. From the ancient stone walls hung new iron chains and manacles. These were ghastly enough, but it was the blood that made my stomach churn. Every surface was spattered. Blood stained the ground, all of the walls, and even the ceiling. Gobbets of the stuff covered with flies hung from the manacles and the chains.

"Marks of a flogging," I noted. "More than one, in fact. That explains the state of the unfortunate gentleman in the inspector's gaol." I knelt down and sniffed at the ghastly stains on the ground beneath the chains. "Urine and faeces," I said. "They kept him here for days while they tortured him."

I continued to examine the stables. Flies buzzed and dined upon the blood. The stench was noxious. Still, the ground here was revealing.

Two men had left footprints. One set were the gunman's, the second probably belonged to the third member of the gang. I also found the footprints of the farmer's wife.

My inspection complete, Watson and I went outside to breathe the clean air.

"This is a case to give a man nightmares, Holmes," Watson said.

"It is distressing," I agreed.

"What do you make of it?"

"Our victim is a government official. Given the quality of his clothing and the number of exotic stamps on his luggage, I surmise his work is connected with the Foreign Office.

"He was brought here by three men under some pretext, probably a holiday. His companions, however, had other plans and, once here, subjected him to torture."

"Poor beggar," Watson said. "But why? What on earth did they want of him?"

"Most likely government information. A man like that must know many secrets."

"Then, did he tell them what they wanted to know? Is that why they let him go?"

"They did not release him. He was found in his shift on the moor, after all. No, I suspect he managed to escape, almost certainly with the aid of the farmer's wife. Her footprints are clearly visible in the stables. There are also the tentative footprints of another man. Slender, mid-forties, unused to exercise. He was one of the three who brought Updike here, but there are signs that he and the woman stood near Updike for some time."

"Threatening him?"

"Or trying to free him. Updike could not have escaped from those manacles unaided.

"I must send a telegram to London. Mycroft needs to know about this with all haste."

Night was drifting over the moor behind thick oily clouds. The waxing gibbous moon emerged from time to time, plating the lonely land with silver. In the distance, a dog howled and Watson jumped.

"It is just a dog, Watson," I said. "The Baskerville estate is many miles away. Besides, that beast is dead."

"All the same, it's pretty unsettling here. Dead bodies, evidence of torture, and who knows what. I hope the horses did not witness that brutality."

"Indeed." I glanced at him. Saw his distress. "I am sure they have been found by a neighbour and are being well looked after."

"Do you think Updike took one of them? The horses, I mean."

"I doubt he could have managed to ride in his condition."

"I cannot remember a worse case, Holmes." He shuddered. "It is loathsome, just to be here, even in the open air. The entire farm seems ghastly."

"I share your revulsion, Watson," I agreed, "but we shall not have to remain here much longer. Observe: Inspector Pendleton is returning."

To our east coming along the winding road, came the lights of approaching carriages. Watson's relief hissed out of him in a long sigh.

3

Monday, 24ᵗʰ October

This morning we returned to London.

Augustus Updike, still gibbering, was accompanied to his home by two burly caretakers who had been hired by Mycroft. Updike's manservant, a bulldog of a fellow called Townsend, gasped in horror at his master's appearance.

"Good God," he cried. "What has happened to you, sir?"

Updike wept.

Once the caretakers took their charge to his room, I asked the servant for information.

"I have worked with Mr Updike for ten years, sir," he said. "He is a good master and has a kind heart."

"Do you know what he was doing in Dartmoor?"

"No, sir, I do not. He told me he had an important job coming up and decided to take a few days holiday before getting started. I had the impression he would not be travelling alone, but I cannot tell you why I thought so, or with whom he was travelling."

"What can you tell me about his family and friends?"

"Well, Mrs Updike lives in Italy. She and the master have lived apart for several years. Even before that, they were not close. Mr Updike travelled a great deal, you see, and the mistress preferred to stay in one place. There's no other family."

"And his friends and acquaintances?"

"Just work colleagues, but I have not met them. He's not a man for socialising, is Mr Updike." He frowned. "The only person I've heard him mention once or twice is another Mr Holmes."

"Mycroft Holmes?"

"That's it, sir. I wouldn't say he thought of Mr Holmes as a friend, but he certainly admired him. Called him the Queen's linchpin."

The fellow could not, or would not, tell us more. He seemed too distressed by his master's condition to offer much information. Well, we can call upon him again if need be.

Watson and I went on to Whitehall. Mycroft flopped down in his great armchair and closed his eyes. This was my invitation to begin.

"The facts," I said, "are these: In the early hours of Thursday last, a man was discovered by a horse rider on the moor. The eastern side, some thirty-five miles from Exeter. The man was conscious but deranged. He could not answer any questions, not even regarding his name. After local investigations proved fruitless, the local policeman, an inspector named Pendleton, asked for my help.

"I learned that the man is Augustus Updike. A pin on his coat revealed he was a member of the Diogenes Club."

Mycroft grunted, but did not comment.

"I then discovered the fellow's wallet, which I have here." I handed it to him.

"His identification papers and a hundred pounds," Mycroft said, examining the calf's leather object. "The motive was not robbery, then."

"No, indeed. Did Updike tell you he was going on holiday?"

"No, we were not in the habit of sharing confidences. He was responsible for his own schedule."

"His manservant told me that Updike said he had serious work lying ahead and decided to take a short break before beginning. Did he?"

"Yes. Updike was responsible for securing the anti-anarchist conference that will take place in Rome this December. He was to gather information about who would be attending, what their recommendations would be, and report to me so I could pass on my analysis to the Prime Minister. It's a nuisance that he's taken himself out of commission."

"Taken himself...?" Watson sputtered. "The man was tortured. He is fortunate to be alive."

"Is he?" Mycroft said. "Fortunate to be alive, I mean. By all accounts, he is an imbecile. I am not indifferent to the man's fate, Doctor, I assure you."

I shook my head and Watson fell silent. One would have to know my brother extremely well to perceive the degree of distress and anger that burned behind his indolent exterior.

"How well did you know him?" I asked.

"Not as well as I should have liked. He spent most of his time out in the field and only returned to England a few months ago. I had perhaps half a dozen conversations with him."

"What sort of a man was he?"

"He has – or, rather, had – a formidable mind," Mycroft said. "He had a brain to match your own, Sherlock. Possibly even mine." His eyes twinkled but there was no real mirth there. "He could speak several languages, was a chess grand-master, and authored several books on Imperial Rome. Moreover, his understanding of international politics was extraordinary. A brilliant man." He released a long sigh. "Did you learn anything about his kidnappers?"

"Three men accompanied him to Exeter. Two were described as foreigners, whatever that means. From my examination of the farmhouse, I can say that one is approximately six feet two inches tall, is fastidious in his manners, and has almost certainly killed before. I suspect he is the leader of this group, but that is open to debate."

"Why do you think so, Holmes?" Watson said.

"The trail of blood leading to the door..." To Mycroft, I added, "The two people who lived in the house, a Mr Tolliver and his wife, were shot to death. The gunman shot the male first. He then walked to the hallway and killed the woman. Someone, not the gunman, stepped into the blood in the hallway, and wiped it off his boot on the dead woman's frock. That suggests a particularly callous nature and, from it, I infer that he, and not the gunman, led the group. Of the third man, I could find no traces other than his footprints in the stables. He and the farmer's wife helped Updike escape. I am sure of it.

"Updike's flight threw their plans awry and they panicked. They left his belongings behind, and made a bad show of covering the crime with fire."

"Could they not have murdered the Tollivers as soon as they arrived?" Watson said.

"And leave the bodies cluttering up the living room and the hallway? I think not. No, more likely one of the couple realised Updike was being tortured and remonstrated. In any case, the kidnappers did not dare let them live; they were doomed from the beginning."

"I agree," Mycroft said. "Only Updike's refusal to talk and his escape were not factored into their equations."

"How can we be sure he did not talk?" Watson said.

"Because they would have killed him as soon as they got what they wanted," I said.

"Poor wretch," Watson said. "At least there seems to be money for his care. I should hate to think of so brave a man spending the rest of his days in a place like Bedlam or Coney Hatch."

"I cannot imagine a greater agony," I said, "than to be locked in a horror of one's own mind and be unable to escape."

"His wife is in Italy," Mycroft said. "I sent word to her as soon as I heard. I assume she is on her way back to London. There is no other family. Updike's staff seem competent enough. That fellow, Townsend, is devoted to his master.

"Sherlock, you must get to the bottom of this. You must find out all you can about these people. I do not think the conference is at risk, but I cannot take any chances. There are too many sensitive issues at stake."

When we finally arrived back at Baker Street, we were greeted by the aroma of roast duck. Watson sniffed the air and said, "I deduce, my dear Holmes, that Beatrice is coming to dinner."

"Her ladyship telephoned to ask if you were back from Devonshire, Mr Holmes," Mrs Hudson confirmed. "I did not think you'd mind her dining with you and the doctor this evening."

"No, not at all," I said, ignoring Watson's poor attempts at containing his mirth.

"It is such an honour, Mrs Hudson," he said with hardly a smirk, "To have the Queen's own goddaughter dine upon your food."

If Mrs H perceived Watson's teasing, she ignored it. "It is, indeed," she said.

The duck was excellent, but I think B hardly tasted it. She was utterly engrossed in my narration of the 'Case of the Man on the Moor', as Watson has taken to calling it.

"How barbaric," she said. "Do you have any idea who these men are, Sherlock?"

"None," I said. "I spent some time questioning the railway staff, not only in Exeter, but on the London to Devonshire trains. They are an exceedingly dull and unobservant lot."

"Oh, come, Holmes," Watson said. "Given the sheer volume of passengers, and the time that has passed since Updike made the journey, it is hardly surprising."

"I suppose you're right," I said. "In any case, there is little to go on. Most of the evidence at the scene was obliterated by rain or contaminated by the flies and the maggots."

B looked a little queasy and set down her fork. "How will you proceed?" she said.

"Go back to the beginning. I shall see what I can learn of Updike's movements in the days before he was kidnapped."

Friday, 11th November

Augustus Updike's condition has not changed. The best medical minds in the country have been consulted, but they do not agree with one another. Mycroft has been to visit him. It is a measure of his respect for the unfortunate fellow that he should do so.

"If a man like Updike can be mentally deranged, Sherlock," he told me, "I hold no hope for any of us."

Every avenue I have travelled in these last weeks has led me to a brick wall. None of Updike's acquaintances or even his colleagues seem to know anything about him. His time abroad served to make him a cypher among his English associates. I am met with comments about his intelligence and his generosity, but no one knew the *man*. Yesterday, I was struck by the thought that he and my brother seem cast in the same mould. I had the chilling realisation that if Mycroft should ever be kidnapped, no one save myself could claim to know anything of his habits. Indeed, I myself know little enough of his daily activities.

The thought seemed to poison my mind for I had the dream again. This time, however, while I struggled with Moriarty on the Falls, it was Mycroft who fell into the chasm. I awoke soaked in perspiration. I spent some time in meditation. By the time Watson awoke, I was in my usual state of calm.

Monday, 21st November

I returned Updike's home and spoke with Townsend, the unfortunate fellow's manservant. Tried, at any rate. The man is exhausted by his efforts to care for his employer. Updike rambles, he screams, he fights. He cannot be trusted with utensils and so must be spoon-fed. Even then, he clamps his mouth shut and struggles against those who would help him. Townsend kept watch over the unfortunate as I asked my questions. In these circumstances, my process was badly compromised.

"Do you not have nurses to care for Mr Updike?" Watson asked.

"I had to discharge them," Townsend replied. "I found one of them hitting the master. Striking him because he refused to eat. Dreadful people."

"You cannot do this work on your own. You must sleep sometimes."

"I sleep when he sleeps."

"Well, we shall not long detain you," I said. "I wondered if you had any ideas what brought your master to Devonshire."

"A holiday… He said he was going on holiday."

"Do you know with whom?"

"No, I am sorry."

Updike shouted, "Snakes! Snakes!" and cowered from something none of us could see.

"Did he ever speak of any enemies? Someone who might have wanted to harm him?"

"No one, Mr Holmes, unless it was someone connected to his work, and I know nothing about that. He kept those matters strictly confidential."

At that, Updike began to scream. Watson and I rose to leave. Townsend apologised for being distracted, but we could hardly blame him. I did not envy him his dreadful work.

As I put on my hat I said, "Tell me, Townsend, can you think of any significance snakes may have for your unfortunate master?"

"Snakes?" he said, and shuddered. "Hates them, he does. One of the reasons he spent so little time in Italy was because he is mortally afraid of the creatures."

Did his kidnappers know of his terror and use it to torment him? Were the burns on his feet meant to simulate snakebites?

I still have nothing to report to Mycroft. He has spoken with the Prime Minister and they have decided to proceed with the conference as planned.

4

Friday, 25th November

Augustus Updike is dead. Despite a full staff of servants led by the devoted Townsend, he somehow managed to secure a knife and cut his throat.

I cannot think when I last saw Mycroft so distressed or so angry.

"His wife is utterly indifferent," he told me, "and refuses to return to England because 'it is not convenient at present.' Not convenient! I have little sympathy for the so-called fair sex, as you know, Sherlock. Other than Beatrice, there are few worthy of notice. But, this petticoat who calls herself Updike's wife – or, rather, widow – is as cold and unfeeling a creature as I have ever encountered. I sent a telegram informing her of Updike's condition when he was first discovered, and received no response whatever. This morning I sent another telling her of her husband's death. Here is her reply—" He thrust the telegram at me. Before I had a chance to read it he paraphrased, "I may make whatever funeral arrangements I choose. She is too busy at present. Too busy. Damned vixen."

Spleen vented, he sank back in his chair. After several moments of head-shaking, he said, "Have you learned anything?"

"Nothing of any value. I have not given up."

"See that you don't."

Tuesday, 13th December

The anti-anarchy conference continues without any difficulties. Mycroft assures me they have laid on extra security and remain vigilant.

In the meantime, I make little progress on the case. I have been back to Devonshire and again interviewed the railway staff. I met the farmer's neighbours. It seems Peter and Mary Tolliver used to keep sheep and grow vegetables until two years ago when their only son died suddenly. After that, they lost interest in everything. A few months ago they advertised rooms for rent. I surmise this was how they meant to earn their living.

Pendleton and I combed the moor for several miles around the farmhouse. It added nothing to my investigation, beyond renewing my admiration for Updike's endurance.

The singed ledger I found was an incomplete record of the Tolliver's previous customers. Unfortunately, most of the pages had been ripped out. The only names that remained were a couple of newlyweds from Ealing. I went to see them, but they could tell me nothing of any great interest. They were troubled to hear that the Tollivers had been murdered, but had spent little time with them. Most of their holiday was spent travelling around the moor.

Friday, 16th December

This evening, Watson and I were surprised by a visit from Peter Huggins.

Huggins is one of the finest QCs in the land. Though I have the greatest respect for him, we do not often socialise. His schedule and mine preclude such niceties. I was pleased, if surprised, to see him. More, I was intrigued by the agitated man who accompanied him.

"Mr Huggins," I said, as he entered our rooms. "What a great pleasure it is to see you. May I wish you the compliments of the season? You remember my friend Doctor Watson?"

"Of course," he said. "I am glad to find you at home, Mr Holmes. This is Mr Hardwicke."

"Mr Hardwicke," I said, shaking his hand. "Congratulations on taking the silk."

"Oh," said the man. "You have heard of me, then?"

"Not at all," I replied. "But your attire is specific to members of your profession and no more than a few weeks old. Given your comparative youth, I surmise these are the first such garments you have worn. Ergo, you have but recently joined the lofty ranks of Queen's Counsel. But, you are in distress, I perceive. Is that why you are planning to go to Ireland?"

The fellow stared at me in astonishment. "Good gracious, Mr Holmes, you are all Huggins said and more. You are correct in every particular. It is hardly two months since I was elevated to my current rank. I was a junior barrister for seventeen years prior to this. How did you know about Ireland?"

"Your tickets are sticking out of your pocket," Watson said, smiling. He poured brandy for our guests. The two sat before the fire, warming their legs.

"You may speak to Mr Holmes in complete confidence, Edgar," Huggins said. "If there is any man in the Kingdom who can help you, it is he."

"Thank you, Mr Huggins," I said, "Please, Mr Hardwicke, tell us everything. You may trust to my discretion as well as that of Doctor Watson."

"Well, then," said the fellow. "I am afraid, very afraid, that my life may be in danger.

"Over the past month, I have been plagued with something of a most perplexing and disquieting nature. At first I put the matter down to childish pranks, but recent developments… Forgive me. Huggins tells me you dislike an illogically told tale; it is an opinion I share and yet, here I am doing it myself. Let me begin at the beginning.

"I am married with an eight-year-old daughter Jane and a six-year-old son Nigel. Our lives are mundane and have never been touched by anything outré or disturbing.

"On Guy Fawkes Night I took my children to see the bonfire on Hampstead Heath. They had a splendid time and were in high spirits, as you can imagine. But even as I ran around and played their children's games, I observed a figure standing in the shadows. I could not shake the feeling that he was watching me."

"What did he look like?" I asked.

"He wore a mask in the form of a skull. He was otherwise dressed entirely in black, with a black cape and a hood pulled down low over the mask. There were other people wearing costumes and I can think of no reason why I should be alarmed. And yet… I could not shake a sense of malice that emanated from the fellow."

His hand shook as he sipped his brandy.

"I know it sounds absurd for an intelligent man, well-educated and secure in the legal profession, to balk at such nonsense and yet, for reasons I cannot explain, the fellow filled me with deep disquiet."

Our guest met my eye and said, "No doubt you think me a fool, Mr Holmes. It is no less than I felt myself after I had returned to the warmth and security of my home.

"By the following morning I was quite myself again and set off to work as usual. It was a long and busy day. I was occupied with a difficult case. Then, after court recessed, I had a great deal of paperwork to complete and briefs to review before I was able to leave for home. It was somewhat after ten o'clock by the time I left chambers.

"I made my way down Gray's Inn Road and caught a Hansom. As I said, I was weary, and I suppose my attention was still upon my case and my work. I alighted from the cab and went to pay the fare. To my astonishment, when the cabbie turned around I was horrified to see he was wearing that same skull mask. The fellow slapped the coins out of my hand and took off at high speed. I was shaken, as you can imagine."

"I take it you have seen this fellow since?" I said.

"Several times. Once I saw him standing across the street from my chambers. I ran down to challenge him, but he had gone by the time I arrived. Another time I saw him outside my home. Sometimes I think I catch sight of him in the street, but I can no longer trust my own wits."

"And something happened today that compelled you to seek my counsel," I said. "Pray, what was it?"

He dabbed his brow, which was clammy, and said, "Today was a light day for me in chambers. The docket is being cleared in preparation for the Christmas holidays and my own case came to a successful conclusion several days ago. I therefore decided to leave work early. I was home before five o'clock and my daughter Jane said her little brother had been crying. He's not a lad for crying as a rule. I went to the nursery and sure enough, the lad was fair trembling. I asked him what had happened and he said a strange man had met him on the heath and given him something that he was to give to me."

Hardwicke handed me the item.

"A card from the tarot," I said. "The Death card."

"May I?" Watson said. He took the card and peered at it. "There are dozens of different tarot cards designs. I think this one comes from a common Italian deck. The 'Death' card doesn't necessarily mean death. It can represent a loss of some sort, or a change. Unsettling for the boy, of course."

I stared my friend in amazement. Huggins and Hardwicke seemed equally astonished. After a moment, Watson became aware of our surprise and said, "I once had a patient who read the cards." He handed the item back to me and said no more.

"I had not spoken of this matter with my wife," Hardwicke continued, "I did not wish to alarm her. She is very superstitious and she has a mortal terror of the Death card. Indeed, she became quite hysterical when I spoke of it, but I could keep quiet no longer. I had to reveal the whole dreadful saga to her. As you can imagine, it has thrown a pall over our holiday preparations and we are all sick with worry. I am not concerned for myself, Mr Holmes, I can take care of myself, but how am I to protect after my wife and children?"

"Be assured, my dear Mr Hardwicke, we shall get to the bottom of this mystery. I take it there have been no direct threats made against you or your family?"

"Not direct, no, but I believe threat is implied."

"And you have arranged to go to Ireland for the holidays?"

"We had originally planned to stay at home, but when my son was approached I decided London was not safe. We will stay with my wife's family in Kells. You may reach me at this address." He handed me a sheet of paper containing the particulars.

"I think it might ease your mind to get away," I said. "I am sure you and your family will be safe enough in Ireland. In the meantime, leave this card with me and give me as complete a description of this skull mask and its wearer as you can."

"I am afraid I cannot tell you much, Mr Holmes," he replied. He frowned in recollection. "The fellow seems a giant, but you cannot trust that appraisal. I fear my anxiety has exaggerated his proportions. He is tall, however, and sprightly. His build is slender. Nigel said the fellow's voice was peculiar. Raspy. That suggests something to you?"

"Just that he may have disguised his voice as well as his face."

"Yes, that is possible, but why?"

"The only reason for him to alter his voice would be if your son had met him." I replied.

"I had not thought of that. Yes, you are quite right. However, I still cannot conceive of any of my acquaintances who might behave in so unworthy a manner."

"Your son never accompanies you to work? He has never attended a trial, for instance?"

"No, indeed. He is a bright lad for a six-year-old, but such places are not suitable for children."

"Have you dismissed any servants recently?"

"No," he said. "Our servants have been with us for many years. If there had been an issue with a tradesperson, my wife would have mentioned it, I am sure."

"You have colleagues at the office. You must have brought a few of them home to dinner on occasion?"

"That is true. We had a dinner to celebrate my elevation in rank. Many of my colleagues attended."

At this, Huggins interjected, "I should say, Mr Holmes, that Hardwicke is highly esteemed in chambers. As a junior, he was punctilious and exceptionally hard-working. We were all delighted when he took silk. I really cannot imagine any of our peers behaving in so shameful a manner. To threaten a man is bad enough, but only a bounder would involve a man's child."

I smiled at this. "I am afraid I do not share your esteem of your colleagues, Huggins. I have known rather too many villains in the legal profession. They, like doctors, are ideally placed to prey upon the vulnerable."

"You realise, Holmes," Watson said, "You have managed to insult every man in the room."

I was surprised and said so. "I meant no disrespect to any of you; I am merely stating a fact. But we must not lose sight of our topic. You, Mr Hardwicke, are certain you have no enemies among your peers. Huggins concurs. I must be content with that."

Hardwicke replied, "I realise these questions are essential, Mr Holmes, but I have given the matter a great deal of thought already. It may sound... well, unscientific, but I believe that if I knew this fellow, I'd have a sense of familiarity from him, disguised though he may be. However, I have no such impression."

"And when the fellow spoke with your son, I assume he wore the mask?"

"Yes, he did. The boy was alarmed, but managed to stay calm."

"And what of your wife? Does she have any enemies?"

"Good heavens, no! Anna is the kindest of women with a sweet temperament. She is loved by all who know her."

"Even women of virtue can have enemies," I said. "Just a few months ago, a woman of my... acquaintance was hounded by a deadly creature through no fault of her own."

Huggins continued to shake his head. "No, Mr Holmes. Not Anna."

"I see. May I speak to your wife before you travel?"

"It's out of the question, I am afraid. Our decision to leave London was made rather suddenly and she is busy with preparations. You can certainly speak to her when we return."

"Well, that will have to do. How long will your family remain in Ireland?"

"I am due to return to chambers on the fourth of January."

"Very well. You leave in the morning?"

"Yes, we take the train to Holyhead and the boat from there."

"I shall certainly endeavour to look into the matter, Mr Hardwicke. I should add that I am currently engaged on another case of considerable importance. However, I see no reason why I cannot make inquiries on your behalf. Do, please, let me know at once if there are any further developments."

"Thank you, Mr Holmes. I am already much relieved in my mind."

I rose and walked him to the door. "Very well," I said, "I will be in touch. You may telephone or send a telegram if you need me urgently."

5

After our guests left, I sat staring at the tarot card. It was a curious looking thing. I might even say sinister. It depicted a skeleton wielding a sickle standing upon a jumble of skulls and bones. The word '*morte*' was written above the skeleton's head.

"I bow to your expertise, Watson," I said. "What else can you tell me about this card?"

"Not much more than I already told you," he said.

For all the nonchalance of his demeanour, I perceived there was something he was not saying. I could not have been more astounded. There is no more guileless, honest man in all the Empire than John Watson.

He flushed at my expression and said, "Oh very well. I'll tell you. Just, please, Holmes, try not to read too much into it, will you?"

Without waiting for my reply, he continued: "Several years ago, I was... well, I was unhappy. Several things had happened and I was as low in spirit as I have ever been.

"As I already told you, I had a patient who read the tarot and other devices, the crystal ball, the palm, and so forth. One day she came to see me regarding a problem with her eyesight. After I examined her and wrote a prescription, she told me she read a great darkness on my heart. You know I do not believe in this sort of mysticism as a rule, but she seemed... well, astute. She offered to do a reading for me and I agreed."

I snorted. "Oh, really, Watson, I am astonished. I would have declared you the last man in all of Christendom to fall for such chicanery. Why did you not tell me what you were doing? Were you worried I'd mock you?"

35

He turned to the fire and poked it with undue attention, then piled on more coal. He would not meet my eye. This behaviour was so unlike my friend that I found myself unsettled. Was it simple fear of being mocked that rendered him silent? When had he ever been so low in spirit? I would have known, surely.

Then I realised and felt a fool. A wretched fool.

"Watson," I said, "Was this when I was… I mean, was it after Reichenbach?"

He refilled his scotch before saying, "Well, Mary had died… There were a lot of things."

"Including my absence."

He downed his glass, rose, and said, "Good night, Holmes."

For a long time I sat alone. For once, my thoughts were not occupied with a case, a splendid case, but with the pain I had thoughtlessly inflicted upon my dearest friend. In the five years since my return, not once has Watson berated me or even spoken of what he endured. We alluded to the matter in oblique references. I thought we were beyond needing to discuss such things, but I now realised such thinking was merely a sop to my conscience.

It was a long time before I felt able to sleep, and when I did my dreams were full of savage brutes and falling. Always falling.

Saturday, 17th December

This morning, Watson took me to an address in Golders Green to meet his former patient, Mme Bronski. She lived in a redbrick house on Templar's Avenue. The garden was well tended and the house suggested a vigorous housekeeper. Before we knocked on the door, Watson clutched my arm.

"Holmes," he said, "I know you will find her odd. Ludicrous, even. She looks strange and her behaviour is stranger still. But I have seen her perform extraordinary things and give great comfort to people in distress. She is peculiar, certainly, but she has a kind heart, and she was a friend to me when I needed one."

"I am not sure what you are asking of me, Watson."

"Just… try not to be too harsh with her."

I gave my word. This, it transpired, was fortunate or else I would have cried with laughter at the sight of the ridiculous old woman.

"Doctor Watson," she said, rising from an oversized chair with difficulty. She was one of the largest women I've ever encountered, larger even than Mycroft. She stood at least six feet tall and was nearly as wide. Her eyes were almost invisible, tiny raisins in the pastry-white flesh of her face. Her many chins rolled over and over, forming something of a collar around her neck, and these rested on the collar of a black silk gown. Her lips were small and pink and her cheeks glowed an unnatural rouge. She wore her grey hair in a nest of gravity-defying ringlets. In short, she was grotesque.

Her welcome was warm enough, however, and she seemed genuinely pleased to see my friend. She held him in a warm embrace for several moments. At length, she released him and invited us to sit. She insisted upon serving us tea and scones. I sucked in my irritation. I wanted to get down to business, but the whole wearying matter of social niceties must first be endured.

"You are much happier now, I ween, my old friend," she said to Watson as she poured the tea. "You see, my dear, I told you it would all come right in the end. And love isn't done with you, you know. Not by a long chalk. It is all around you in shades of green. You'll see."

Then, turning to me, she said, "Not nice to play dead, is it, dearie? You'll see, too."

"What does that mean?" I asked. I do not believe my tone was unpleasant but Watson shot me a disapproving glance anyway.

"You'll find out. The universe has a way of balancing the scales. Yes, my dear, you'll see." She stared at me and the tiny eyes were sharp as steel and twice as hard. "Someone has misled you. You congratulate yourself on your wits; think you're so much cleverer than anyone else. You think that you can't be fooled, but you'll learn."

"Learn what?"

"That no one can fool a man as well as he can himself. Sometimes we believe the things we do because it's easier."

I gave Watson an irritated look, but the woman wasn't through with me yet.

"Someone you fear casts a long shadow. You think you are done with him but he is not done with you. It's not a good idea to retrace old steps, *mon cher*... Patience," she said. "This coming year will test you in ways you cannot conceive. It will teach you humility. But if you survive, you will discover a happiness you never before imagined."

"Mme Bronski," Watson said, "We wanted to consult with you about a tarot card." He handed it to her.

She took the card in her hand then, with a cry of horror, flung it onto the table. "This is evil," she cried. "It belongs to a man of great power and great malice. Oh, take it away, take it away..."

38

She held her head in her hands and rocked. Her breath came in shallow jerks and her brow glistened with great pearls of perspiration.

"Who?" I said. "Who is he?"

"Holmes," Watson hissed.

He sat beside the corpulent woman and gently massaged her temples. "There now," he crooned. "There's nothing to fear, nothing to worry about. It's all right."

The woman's colour was ghastly. All the blood seemed to have sunk from her face to her bosom and there it settled in great angry blotches. She said nothing, but rocked back and forth, making a queer noise like a low-pitched hum.

Watson poured tea, held the cup to her lips, and helped her drink. As he did so, he said, "Holmes, put that wretched thing away." He nodded towards the card.

I would have said the woman's reaction was an elaborate charade for our entertainment, but there was no denying her ghastly colour. Whether her response was merely that of a hysteric, I cannot say, but there was no question she was in deep distress. I put the card in my pocket.

After several minutes, the woman seemed to calm down. She drank her tea and her breathing gradually became more regular.

"There now," Watson said. "Holmes has put it away. There is nothing to distress you."

She nodded, still rocking. She seemed like a grotesque child. Vulnerable. Enormous.

"I apologise for upsetting you, Mme Bronski," I said.

She clutched my hand. "You must get rid of it, Mr Holmes. Now. At once. It is evil. Oh, it is wholly evil. Death it says, and death it is. Oh, for mercy sake destroy it."

"I assure you, I have no intention of keeping it," I said. "But what can you tell me about it? About the man who owns it? What is his name?"

She said nothing but made a low noise of distress. 'Keening', Watson later called it, and that is as good a description as any.

She refused to eat and managed to drink her tea only with Watson's help. Eventually, her colour improved and her breathing seemed less laboured.

"Madame?" Watson said, gently. "We need your help. Please."

She squeezed his hand and I was again struck by the genuine affection they seemed to share.

"I do not know his name," she whispered. "He is known only as the Sorcerer. He has an evil reputation. The fakers avoid him because he is ruthless. Among those of us with the Gift, we dare not speak of him, save in whispers." She leaned forward and hissed, "If he is your enemy there is only one thing you can do."

"What is that?" I said.

"Buy a coffin."

Forty minutes later, Watson and I stepped out into the cleaner, colder air of London. The city danced with shoppers preparing for the Yuletide celebration. Though we had walked only a few steps, I felt we had covered great vistas, not only of miles but of centuries. I gulped in the London fog. Vile though it was, it tasted sweet after Mme Bronski's suffocating room.

"I'm sorry that wasn't more helpful, Holmes," Watson said as we hailed a cab. "I've never seen her like that."

"No? I must say I am greatly surprised that you would have spent any time in that creature's company. What benefit could you get from her ramblings?"

"Comfort," he said. Then he turned his face to the window and said nothing more for the rest of our journey back to Baker Street.

6

This evening, I dined with B in Wimpole Street.

"Do you think this woman could really have some sort of special talent, Sherlock?" she asked when I told her about the events of the past few days.

"I do not doubt that she believes this nonsense," I said, "Or she may merely be somewhat more observant than others. You know, I could have made a perfectly comfortable living if I had chosen to set myself up as a mystic instead of a consulting detective. The skills are not dissimilar."

"You have too much honour to making your living by defrauding people. But you say Watson visited this woman when you were... That is, after your disappearance?"

"With some regularity, I believe. I could not be more surprised."

"Why?"

I set down my fork and said, "What do you mean?"

"I do not understand why you are so astonished. As I understand it, in the space of less than a twelvemonth, he lost his beloved wife and his dearest friend. Even one such loss must distress a man. The two coming so closely together must have been very painful. The religion of his childhood is not a comforting thing; no wonder he sought solace elsewhere."

For several moments, I said nothing. I have never fully acknowledged the impact my disappearance had on the people I left behind. B's words forced me to think back to my sudden appearance in Watson's consulting rooms, how I threw off my disguise to delight him, as I thought. I believed myself so clever, such a master of the dramatic. In hindsight, my behaviour merely seems cruel. Watson fainted at the sight of me.

I was suddenly and heartily ashamed of myself.

"I did it to protect him. There was no other way to ensure his safety... Do you think he will ever forgive me?"

"I believe he already has. He takes your fondness for him on trust but..."

"Go on," I said.

"Trust is rather the issue, isn't it? He must feel you had no faith in him. I am not saying that is a correct assessment, only that it may be his perception. Well, it is good that you appreciate how he must have felt. The thing is you and he are such men."

"Well, of course we are men. What sort of a statement is that?"

"I mean in your behaviour. Women will talk, you see. They might even shout and cry, but they will tell the whole ghastly truth to one another. Then the matter is done and we can go on. Men, though... You always have to be so stoic, to preserve your air of indifference. I cannot think it is healthy."

I said nothing and we continued to dine in silence. It seems that ever since I first met B, my previous ideas have been challenged almost daily. I may have married her for purely pragmatic reasons, but I have never had cause to regret the decision. Quite the reverse, in fact.

She said, "What of the Updike case? There is no news?"

"Nothing. It is frustrating. Mycroft is anxious for answers, but I have learned nothing of substance yet."

"Even the great Sherlock Holmes cannot construct clues out of thin air," B said, "Although it probably seems that way to most people."

"Yes, indeed. Mycroft is concerned that there may be some risk to the government, but I can find nothing to support that theory."

"Is there anything I can do?"

"If I cannot find the answers I doubt you can. Forgive me, I did not mean…"

"Do not apologise," she said. "I understand."

The servants removed the plates of beef and replaced them with dishes of Italian ice. B said, "How shall you proceed? With this new case, I mean."

"I have made inquiries about this 'Sorcerer' character. Unfortunately, the title is not uncommon amongst people who make their living swindling the gullible masses. I have nothing to distinguish this individual from the thousands of others of the sort. I have spoken with Lestrade, and the Irregulars will see what they can learn. I should hate to fail in not one but two cases. It is a wretched end to a wretched year."

She squeezed my hand. I know she shares my grief at the loss of our young friend this past summer. At least I find comfort in knowing his killer paid the price.

I filled her glass with Madeira and she sipped without apparently tasting the excellent vintage. I said nothing. I recognise that focused look. My patience was rewarded, for some moments later she said,

"I have a vague recollection that my father was acquainted with a man who was considered something of an expert in the esoteric arts."

"Do you remember the expert's name?"

"No, I have been trying to remember. There may be something in the files. Father's interests were broad, as I've told you, and he was acquainted with people from a wide range of circles." Grinning at me she added, "*Mit Geistesstärke tu ich Wunder auch.*"

It took me a moment to place the quote. "Goethe," I said. "From *Der Zauberlehrling*, 'The Sorcerer's Apprentice'. *With my powers of will I can do some witching, too*. Very apt."

44

"Do you think he is at risk?" she said, "This Mr Hardwicke, I mean. I would not like to think of harm befalling any friend of Mr Huggins. He is such a kind gentleman. He was so good to the boys during the summer when they had to testify."

"Yes. That is, yes, he was kind. He is a decent fellow and seems fond of his junior colleague. As to Hardwicke's safety, I cannot theorise with so little evidence. Still, I will not be sanguine in my mind until we have learned as much as we can about this alleged Sorcerer."

"And though you try to be patient, you will not rest easy until I have searched my father's papers. If you are finished with your meal, we might look now."

Two hours later, B found the letter. It was from a retired major by the name of Sir Christopher Carandini. In it, he described himself as a former Royal Engineer who had spent many years studying the occult arts, if 'art' is the word. Despite this curious interest, he struck me as highly intelligent and not without a degree of sophistication in his thought.

"I would like to meet Sir Christopher," I said. "He seems to bring a scientific curiosity to the subject. It is possible he has at least heard of this Sorcerer."

"I shall send him a message, shall I?" B said. "We might visit him tomorrow. Given his interest in the occult, I cannot imagine he will mind meeting us on the Sabbath, though, of course, he might be occupied with Christmas preparations."

"Bah, Christmas," I said.

"Why, Sherlock," she said, laughing, "Have you been reading Mr Dickens's *A Christmas Carol*? Have fear lest the ghosts of the season, past, present and future, dog your sleep."

I laughed, too. "I have no objection to the season, per se, but it does interfere with the course of my investigations. I do not see why all normal activity must cease just because of one celebration. Do you mean to accompany me?"

"If I may," she said. "Since he was an acquaintance of my father's, I may be of use."

"Your presence is always welcome."

The message was dispatched. Sir Christopher replied by return, agreeing to meet with us at eleven o'clock tomorrow morning.

Sunday, 18th December

Sir Christopher Carandini lived in Warwick Square, a stone's throw from St Gabriel's Church in Pimlico. B and I were admitted by a bored manservant and led into a comfortable room that was part library, part clock-maker's shop.

Our host rose to greet us. He was exceedingly tall, and so thin as to be almost cadaveric. Despite his considerable age, his posture was excellent, as befit the former soldier. His black hair had no more than a sprinkling of silver. Only his withered features and the economy of his movements acknowledged his years. His dark eyes pierced into mine, intensely curious.

"Mr Sherlock Holmes," he said in a deep, rich voice. "This is an honour, a great honour indeed. And Lady Beatrice, how do you do? I was acquainted with your late father."

"I know, Sir Christopher," said B. "My father had friends and acquaintances from so many walks of life. I understand that you and he were interested in the late Mme Blavatsky."

"The so-called medium or spiritualist," he replied. "That must be fifteen years ago, or more. There is enough genuine mystery in the world; we have no need of frauds. Please, sit down. How can I help you?"

He eased himself back into his armchair with a little difficulty. He must be at least eighty years old, I thought, though far more spry than others of his years.

"I understand you are well versed in matters of the occult?" I said.

"I am considered something of an expert," he replied without any false humility.

"And your specific areas of expertise?"

"Vast. I have, over the years, delved into the *Egyptian Book of the Dead*; the holiday known as *Dia de los Muertos*; and the Celtic rituals of Hallowe'en and Samhain. I have explored cases of alleged hauntings, witches, and the undead. I flatter myself that no one in England, perhaps the world, can match my knowledge. It is not much of a legacy, I fear. I might serve you better, Mr Holmes, if I knew the focus of your inquiry. You will forgive me, but occult matters seem beyond the purview of the detective."

I took the tarot card from my pocket and handed it to him. "A certain gentleman of my acquaintance is being followed by a masked figure. The man's son was given this card. I wonder if you might be able to tell me something about it."

Sir Christopher studied it. His mouth pursed.

"Ah, the Death card," he said, "This one is from the Visconti-Sforza deck. The original dates back to fifteenth century Milan, but there are many variations. It is one of the most popular decks and frequently reproduced in one form or another." His eyes flickered to the bookcase on his right. He rose, waving away our attempts to assist him. His fingers lightly skimmed the books and rested on a large tome, briefly, before moving on to another, smaller volume. He brought this to his desk and thumbed through the pages. "Ah, yes," he said, after a moment, "here it is."

Sir Christopher handed me the book, an encyclopaedia of the tarot, and I looked at the picture he indicated. It was an exact match for the Death card that had been given to the unfortunate young Hardwicke. Sir Christopher said, "This card is based on a design that goes back about two hundred years, though, as I said, the original is even older still. This particular version differs by the skulls and bones at the feet of the skeleton. Rather macabre."

"I do not suppose you can tell me who might have owned it?"

His black eyes bore into mine. After several moments he said, "I have been engaged in esoteric studies for many years, Mr Holmes. I do not believe in angels or fairies or ghosts. Frankly, I am not convinced in the existence of either God or the Devil. Very little frightens me. But the man who owned this card..." He poured a glass of water from a crystal carafe and downed it before continuing. "He is known as the Sorcerer. No doubt there is some prosaic explanation for his accomplishments, but many people, people whose opinions I trust, fear him. We have never been able to expose him as a fraud."

"But fraud he must be," I replied. "There are no such things as magical arts or practitioners."

"Perhaps," Sir Christopher replied. "Let me tell you something about this fellow and you can judge for yourself.

"I had a friend by the name of Barton. Like me, he was interested in the study of the dark arts purely as an intellectual pursuit. He shared my scepticism and, like me, was devoted to exposing frauds among these so-called spiritualists. Barton's studies led him to this fellow, the Sorcerer, and he was granted an audience."

"An audience?" B said. Her mirth and scepticism mirrored my own. "Does the fellow think of himself as king or pope?"

"Either. Both." Sir Christopher took another drink of water before continuing. "I had dinner with my friend the following day. Even though it had been several hours since his meeting with the Sorcerer, Barton was still shaken. At first he did not want to speak about it. He looked over his shoulder repeatedly through our conversation and seemed on the brink of a nervous collapse. This was most uncharacteristic. Barton, though serious in his work, had a keen sense of humour. This often helped him deal with the more unsettling aspects of our inquiries. I should add that while most of the people we studied were obvious frauds, there was a small number whose talent defied explanation. These were the ones we found unsettling.

"I was surprised to find my friend in such a state of agitation. I tried to cheer him. He and I had investigated many frauds together and exposed any number of charlatans. Barton was the last man I would have expected to become unhinged, and yet there was no denying his terror. 'I shall die,' he hissed at me before he left. 'The fellow has put a hex on me and I am done for. For the love of God, Chris, have nothing to do with the fellow. Save yourself.'

"Those were the last words he ever spoke to me. Two days later he was dead."

"Dead? How?" I asked.

"An accident, they said. He was run over by a Hansom in Oxford Street. The driver of the vehicle was never apprehended."

"You do not believe it was an accident?" I asked.

"I do not believe in coincidences, Mr Holmes. Neither, I think, do you. No, my friend was hounded to death by this so-called Sorcerer."

"If he had been intimidated enough," B said, "perhaps he was too agitated to pay close attention to where he trod. It might still be an unfortunate accident."

Our host smiled. "You are indeed your father's daughter, Lady Beatrice. That is precisely what he would have said. You may be right. Who can say?"

"But you do not think so?" I said.

"After my friend's death I decided to see what I could learn about this so-called Sorcerer. What I discovered was chilling. A litany of victims. I began a file but never completed it. I was warned off and I took the hint."

"I should like to see your file."

"It has been years," he said. "I am not sure where it is. I shall look for it and send it to you. This man must be stopped."

"Can you remember anything about him?"

"He was using the name Frankall at the time. Angel Frankall. Almost certainly an alias."

"Do you know where I can find him?"

"I am afraid not."

"What about the people who you believe were his victims? Do you remember their names?"

"No. The information would be in my file. It may take me some time to find, I'm afraid. I do not always remember where I put things, but I will look."

"Perhaps you need an assistant," B said gently. "Is there no one who can help you?"

He suddenly looked every one of his many years. He was frail, melancholy, a man who walked in the shadow of death. "Only my servants." The amused tone suggested these were inadequate. His dark eyes looked up at the painting to his left. It depicted a young man in an army uniform.

"Your son?" B said. "Is he abroad?"

"He is dead, killed in the opening hours of the Boer conflict. He had no military ambitions. He joined the army because I wished it."

"He must have loved you very much."

"He did, and it cost him his life. I could have prevented his death and I did not. It was Paul's death that sparked my interest in the occult. I began to visit mediums, hoping one of them would put me in touch with him. None ever did. Eventually, I came to accept there is nothing beyond this world. My rage sparked my determination to expose fraudsters. Alas, I have lost even that fire. If there is a more loathsome existence than to be old and alone, I hope never to discover it. To be old is to be ignored, to be rendered silent and invisible. These days I spend my time making clocks. Perhaps I am hoping to turn back time." He smiled and indicated the table beneath the window strewn with cogs and pendants and fine instruments. "I was an engineer. I suppose I like tinkering. Please, take one with you. You, too, Mr Holmes." He handed us each a small, well-crafted carriage clock.

"Thank you." B said. She gave him her card. "You must come to tea, Sir Christopher. You need not be alone, you know."

"I never leave the house. The world outside frightens me. It moves so quickly."

She seemed distressed. "If you need anything, I hope you will let me know."

"You are kind, Lady Beatrice. I hope you will be careful, Mr Holmes. This fellow does not care for interference."

"I have encountered his ilk before," I replied, "yet I live on."

"Your client, the man who received the card: he is safe?"

"He is for the present. He has left the country for the holidays. I have hopes to resolve this matter before he returns." I paused. "One other matter, Sir Christopher, have you ever encountered a woman by the name of Mme Bronski?"

"Yes, I know her. She seems to be one of the rare true talents."

"You mean you believe she is a genuine mystic?"

He hesitated. "If she is a fraud, she is an exceedingly good one. I was never able to catch her in a deception. When I attended one of her readings, she knew at once why I was there. Most of these alleged mediums refuse to work when there is a sceptic present. They claim that doubt hinders their talent. Mme Bronski did no such thing. Furthermore, she not only told me many extremely private things from my past, but she offered a five-year prediction which, in all but one case, has come true."

"What was the exception"? I asked.

"My death. But she has until my birthday in June before I can claim she is wrong."

I left B at Wimpole Street and spent the afternoon in the city. I felt tainted by Sir Christopher's melancholy and London has a way of lifting my spirits.

I did not return to Baker Street until after four o'clock. I was back no more than half an hour when Mrs Hudson brought me a large envelope. Sir Christopher's file. The attached note read,

Some papers are missing, Mr Holmes, but I thought you would prefer to begin with these rather than waiting for the rest.

Your servant, C.L. Carandini

I sat at the table and spread the contents out before me. These were half a dozen hand-written reports from people who related their encounters with the so-called Sorcerer, and a handful of newspaper cuttings about a variety of disparate events. They made for chilling reading. If Carandini's information was correct, there was unquestionably a pattern. This series of apparent accidents or illnesses involved people who seemed to have nothing in common, save they had recently crossed paths with this Sorcerer.

The genius of the thing lay in its diversity. The victims were men and women; they were clerks, and cooks, and knights of the realm. The causes of death ranged from the banal – fever or accidents – to the outré. There was one case, for instance, of a man who flung himself off Tower Bridge screaming that the birds were plotting against him. The newspaper report said the man acted in full view of dozens of people. There was no evidence he was coerced in any way. Sir Christopher wrote that the man had recently attended a séance with the Sorcerer. He did not, however, cite his source of information. This was a failing through all the records. The comments were anecdotal, largely unattributed, and undated. The curse of age, I suppose.

I was still reading when Watson arrived home. He seemed a little embarrassed by the previous evening's conversation and so I decided not to mention it. B might take issue with the way men do things, but we are men. What can we do?

Instead, I told my friend about Sir Christopher Carandini and all I had learned from him. Well, I omitted his comments about Mme Bronski.

Watson sat on the chair next to mine and examined the papers.

"Well, what a clever devil he is, to be sure," my friend exclaimed. "If any of these cases came to my table as a police surgeon, I should not hesitate to attribute the cause of death to disease or accident or self-harm."

"Rather like the man who was 'accidentally' run over on Oxford Street? That's the genius of it, Watson."

"A terrible genius. "But there is one big question that comes to my mind."

"You mean why," I said. "Yes, that is the same question that perplexes me. Why were any of these people killed? A few were wealthy, titled, but many seemed to be ordinary, unassuming citizens. This one," I said, picking up a specific cutting. "She was nothing more than a housewife. Who would want her dead?"

Watson was silent for a moment, and then said, "Husbands do sometimes tire of their wives, Holmes. Very few men have the luxury of keeping their spouses in a separate home from themselves, and being able to call upon said spouse at their own convenience."

"Murder for hire. My thoughts exactly. That is the only thing that makes sense. On the other hand, few of the victims were wealthy. I have never heard of a murder for hire where the murderer was not paid."

"Gain of some other sort, perhaps?"

"Perhaps. Then again, perhaps there is no real link with these cases at all. Sir Christopher makes a persuasive argument, but he is undoubtedly influenced by his own revulsion."

A moment later the door opened and Mrs Hudson entered carrying a tray. "It is dinnertime, Mr Holmes. Do you think you might move all these… things."

She could not have sounded more disapproving if the table were strewn with putrefying body parts.

Watson helped me scoop up all the files and return them to their folder. Our housekeeper waited with no great patience.

"I do have other things to do, you know, Mr Holmes," she said. "Or have you forgotten Christmas?"

"I forget nothing, Mrs Hudson. I apologise for the clutter, but it is a matter of great importance."

Table cleared, she and the maid laid out the food, and then she swept from the room in a manner I can only describe as regal.

As we ate, Watson said, "Well, Holmes, how shall you proceed?"

"This Sorcerer chap seems something of a will-o-the-wisp, Watson. I shall see what the Irregulars and my other spies on the streets can tell me."

7

Tuesday, 20ᵗʰ December

I slept late and was awakened by the delivery of a telegram.

"Watson, come quickly. We are needed," I cried.

"What is it, Holmes?" he said, yawning and rubbing his eyes.

"We must go to Ireland. Now. At once. Check the Bradshaw for the time of the next train."

He found the book. "The boat-train leaves at eleven o'clock," he said, "and arrives at half-past eight tonight. What is going on, Holmes?"

"Hardwicke's son has been kidnapped."

We caught the train just seconds before the whistle blew. Given the season, every compartment was full. Watson and I were compelled to share our carriage with a bishop and a young priest. Watson muttered that the vows of poverty apparently do not prevent the clergy from travelling first class. I chortled, much to the consternation of the other passengers.

At Holyhead, we disembarked the train and boarded the boat headed to the Dublin port at the North Wall. This would be a wearisome journey at the best of times, but travelling just a few days before Christmas made it almost intolerable. There was not one square foot of space on either the train or the boat. Noisy parents and their even noisier children were everywhere I looked. For a time I stood on the deck. Even the rain and spume were preferable to the chaos within. The biggest disadvantage was that the weather made it impossible to smoke.

Watson joined me and said, "You'll catch your death out here, Holmes."

"And I shall run mad if I have to sit with my screaming, malodourous fellow-travellers. Let me be, Watson."

He said nothing, but stood at my side. After several minutes, he checked his watch. "We should be landing in an hour."

I checked my own watch. "Less than half an hour by my reckoning, Watson. It is eight o'clock now and we land at eight thirty, do we not?"

"Yes, eight thirty, but local time. Ireland is twenty-five minutes behind Greenwich."

I groaned.

"Tell you what, old thing, I shall stand you dinner in Dublin. A good meal and a pint of stout in a quiet hotel will set you to rights."

"A child is missing, Watson. We cannot delay. We must make haste to Kells."

He was silent. I recognised that silence.

"Well?" I demanded.

"I am afraid it isn't a matter of getting a train to Kells, Holmes. We have to go to Amiens Street Station in Dublin and take the train to Drogheda. From there we go to Kells."

"And how long does the train to Drogheda take?"

He studied the waves. "Well, it takes a rather convoluted route along the coast for a time. The train to Kells, though, should be much shorter."

"Please leave me, Watson."

"Yes, Holmes."

I am not in general a bad traveller, but by the time we made landfall I was utterly weary and out of sorts. The thought of spending another age on not one, but two more trains was almost more than I could bear.

We stumbled off the boat amid a crowd of holiday-makers and stood perplexed. As I pondered the probability of getting a cab, I heard someone call my name.

"Mr Holmes, sir!" he cried. "Mr Sherlock Holmes!"

The voice belonged to a small, weathered man in a heavy overcoat and a bowler hat.

"You'd be Mr Sherlock Holmes and Doctor Watson?" he said in a heavy Irish accent. "Lorcan is my name. Mr Hardwicke sent me to collect ye, and convey ye with all haste to Kells."

"Oh that is good news," Watson said. "You have a carriage?"

"I do, and it's just outside, if ye'll follow me."

A few moments later, Watson and I settled in the Brougham. Lorcan handed us a basket of food and a couple of bottles of Irish porter. "We've a wee while on the road," he said, "And I'm sure you're famished after that awful journey. Put those blankets over ye, now. 'Tis fierce cold, the night."

"It's a shame you had to come all this way," Watson said. "We could have taken the train."

"Well," said the man, "you could go by train, right enough. That is to say trains, for wouldn't you need two of them?"

"I should have thought the train would be a much quicker journey," Watson said. "Quicker than a carriage, I mean. Not that we're ungrateful."

"Ah, now, if you could get a train in Dublin and go directly to Kells you'd be there in a flash, so you would. But 'tis not that easy. No, the train takes you all around the houses. First, you'd need to get to Drogheda. That line travels through Clontarf, and then Raheny, and Portmarknock... Wait, now, I'm missing one. That's right, Baldoyle... Aye, and who knows where else? Then, when you arrive in Drogheda with your eyes falling out of your head, you'd need to change for the train to Kells and face another hour and a half. With the waiting and the stopping at the stations and the good Lord knows what, wouldn't you walk it faster? Besides," he paused for effect. "Ye've already missed the last train from Drogheda, and there won't be another till morning."

"I see," I said. "In that case, we're very grateful to you for collecting us, Lorcan."

"Sure and you're welcome," he said. "Sit back, now, me boyos, I'll have you there in no time. You're in safe hands. I haven't lost a passenger yet." He cackled.

"What news of Mr Hardwicke's son?" I asked.

He shook his head and his sadness was genuine, "Snatched from his bed, poor lad," he said. "His mammy and daddy are beside themselves. Good people they are, Mr Holmes. Christian people, for all they're not Cat'lic. I hope you'll be able to help them."

The man could tell me nothing about when the boy had been taken, or if any strangers had been seen in the area.

"The neighbours have been all kindness, sir," he said. "There's no one like the Irish when there's a crisis. Combed the countryside, they have, looking for the lad, and word sent throughout the whole county. Aye, and Dublin, too. Please God, they'll have found him safe and well by the time we get back."

Although I seldom eat much when I am on a case, the long journey had whetted my appetite. Watson and I ate our meal with relish. Whether because of our hunger, or the excellence of the meal, I cannot say, but I have seldom dined better. We washed down the cold meats, bread, and cheese with the excellent porter. Thus invigorated, Watson engaged our coachman in conversation.

The two discussed Irish geography and history at great length. Eventually, the topic turned to folklore. I half-listened to their low hum of voices. After the bedlam on the boat and the train, this journey through the dark Irish countryside was blessedly soothing. Quiet and tobacco were all I needed. I am a man of simple tastes.

The carriage trundled over lonely country roads heading north and to the west. Now and then, the quarter moon peeked from behind the clouds revealing long fields that stretched for miles, but for most of the journey the only light was the yellow glow of Lorcan's lamp. The journey felt surreal, as if I was asleep and in the middle of a strange dream from which I could not awaken.

We seemed to travel for hours. Once, the lamp caught the pink eyes of a rabbit that leaped out from behind a hedge. In the distance, I could hear the cry of an owl. For the rest of the journey, though, we might have been the last living creatures left on the earth. This eerie feeling was compounded by Lorcan's conversation, which was full of the banshee, and ghosts, and other such macabre topics.

Eventually, even Watson's interest waned in fatigue. He fell asleep and the carriage trundled on through the night.

"That would be Tara over there," Lorcan said, about two hours into our journey. "'Tis the ancient home of the High Kings of Ireland. We're not far from Kells, now, me lads. I'm sure they'll have the kettle on. I could murder a nice cup of tea, meself."

By the time we reached Kells it was almost eleven o'clock and the town already seemed asleep. That was not the case with our destination, Aisling House. Light shone from every window. The front door flew open as soon as our carriage pulled into the driveway, and Hardwicke came running to meet us.

"Mr Holmes," he cried, "Thank God you've come."

We followed him into a large, comfortable living room. The Christmas wreaths and decorations made a harsh contrast to the grief and despair of the inhabitants. From the mantle hung two Christmas stockings embroidered with the names Jane and Nigel.

A young woman sat by the great hearth in a pitiable state of grief. An older woman, her mother, I perceived, tried in vain to comfort her. A man with the air of a country squire, unquestionably Mrs Hardwicke's father, stood helplessly beside them.

Less readily identifiable was the sickly-looking man with a gaunt face and poor colouring who sat on the other side of the hearth. The only sounds were the crackling of the fire, the ticking of the clock, and the mother's muffled sobbing.

"This is Mr Sherlock Holmes and his friend, Doctor Watson," Hardwicke announced. He introduced the occupants of the house to us.

"My wife, Anna, and her parents Simon and Ana-Marie Jefferson."

We shook hands. Mr Jefferson said, "We have heard a great deal about your skills, Mr Holmes. I hope you will be able to bring our boy back to us."

The sickly-looking man was introduced as Brian McKenna, an old friend of the family. He was too ill to rise and his handshake was damp, limp. It was the hand of a dying man. "Thank heavens you've come," he said. "Anna is at her wits end."

"Indeed, we are all in such a state," Jefferson said. "Where are my manners? You have been travelling all day and I am sure you would like something to eat."

"We saved you some supper, Mr Holmes, Doctor," Mrs Jefferson said. "It is such a long journey from London."

"We ate on the way," I replied. "Lorcan saw we were well looked after."

"Oh, we couldn't greet you without giving you a meal," the woman replied.

Hardwicke added, with a smile, "The Irish take hospitality very seriously, Mr Holmes."

"Indeed and we do," his mother-in-law said. "You'll come, now, and eat. I won't hear a word of refusal."

Watson shot me a sympathetic look. However, while I itched to start work on the case, I was fatigued. We had, by this time, been travelling for a full twelve hours. Sitting and resting for a few minutes seemed an excellent idea. Besides, there was not much I could accomplish in the dark. I would have to make do with asking questions and forming a plan.

We all trooped into an elegant dining room and sat at the long table. Watson and I were served thick stew and crusty bread. My friend ate ravenously; I drank the strong tea and did enough justice to the meal not to offend our hostess. As I picked at the food, I asked for a detailed account of the boy's disappearance.

"We arrived in Kells on Monday evening," Hardwicke said. "Yesterday. I cannot believe it was only yesterday. We stayed in Dublin on Sunday to break up the journey. On Monday, we did our Christmas shopping, and so by the time we arrived in Kells it was almost six o'clock. We had dinner and sent the children to bed at eight. Anna and I were tired, and so retired about ten o'clock."

"That is very clear," I said. "Continue."

"We slept soundly. Kells is a quiet town and Aisling House has no immediate neighbours. It is my custom to sleep late when we are here. My wife is an early riser, however. Around six, she got up and went to check on the children."

"Excuse me," I interrupted. "Is that your practice, Mrs Hardwicke, or did something compel you?"

"I always check on them," the woman said in a hoarse voice, "any time I get up. Nigel tends to throw off his covers and I worry…" She held a handkerchief to her mouth. Her husband squeezed her hand.

"The boy was not in his bed," Hardwicke continued, "and his window was open."

"He was gone," Mrs Hardwicke cried. "Someone took him."

"Hush, *alanna*," Mrs Jefferson said. "Isn't Mr Holmes here now? He'll find the boy. Don't worry, child, we'll find him."

Hardwicke said, "At first we thought he simply woke early and went out. Nigel has an adventurous spirit and an abundance of energy. He loves coming to Kells. He has many friends here. I told myself he had gone on a lark."

"But the boy would not ordinarily leave the house via the window, surely?" I said. "Or was there some reason he might not use the door?"

"No reason at all," Hardwicke said. "The door is just on the latch and he could open it easily enough. I did not think of it before, but there would have been no reason for him to leave the window open. It was a cold night and the wind was high."

"Did it rain?"

"Not then, no, but later, when we were looking…" His voice broke and he squeezed his wife's hand.

63

"What has been done to find your son?"

"We all of us searched the immediate area," Hardwicke replied. "Even his sister helped. We examined the house from top to bottom, and the grounds, and the fields beyond. When the search failed and we confirmed that none of his friends had seen him, we alerted the authorities and I sent you a telegram. In light of recent events..." He could not bring himself to say more.

His wife made a sudden sobbing noise.

"We are cursed," she cried. "What can we do? We are cursed."

"Hush, child," her mother said. "Let me give you a posset and you can go to bed."

"I'll not lie in a bed until my son is found."

Although he was obviously distressed, Jefferson forced himself to focus. "The local constable sent word around Meath and the neighbouring counties," he said. "The police in Dublin were alerted. Our neighbours joined in the search of the area and there isn't an inch of Kells they did not examine."

"Pray be specific. Where did they look?"

Jefferson said, "Well, as Edgar says, we began by searching the house, the orchard, and all the fields around. We brought the dogs, but they could not pick up the scent. We searched every building in the town as well as..." he glanced nervously at his daughter, "ditches and the Blackwater River. Edgar and I examined the old round tower, the Spire of Lloyd, and St Colmcille's house."

"What is the significance of these places?" I said.

"They are curious buildings. Exactly the sort of places to entice a small boy," McKenna put in, speaking for the first time. "I remember the allure."

"They are all locked up," Hardwicke added, "but boys being what they are… In any case, there was no sign Nigel had ever been in any of them."

I pondered this information in silence. Hardwicke, demonstrating extraordinary patience and sensitivity, held his peace and let me think.

"Show me the boy's room," I said.

"Should you not finish your meal first?" McKenna said.

"Holmes seldom eats very much when he is working on a case," Watson said. He half-rose and said, "Do you need me?"

"Not yet," I said. "Mr Jefferson, get me a map of the area and mark all the places that have been searched."

"I shall do so at once," he said.

Hardwicke led me to a small room on the first floor. It was on the east side of the house and overlooked the orchard. There were no other houses nearby. A kidnapper would have gone wholly unnoticed.

The house did not have gas laid on and I was compelled to examine the room by lamplight. Given the time since the boy had vanished, and the poor light source, I was not optimistic of finding anything of worth.

"Has the room been cleaned since you discovered the boy was missing?" I said.

"No, it has not," Hardwicke replied. "I gave instructions that no one was to go in. I had hopes the boy would show up on his own accord, but in case he did not I wanted to give you as much to work with as possible."

The man's voice broke.

"Forgive me," he said. "But he is just a small boy. Who would want to do such a thing? Did a monster follow me all the way from London? I thought we would be safe here…"
His voice drowned in a wave of tears.

"There, now," I said, more optimistically than I felt. "You have done everything right. It was an excellent thought to preserve the room. Who knows what we may learn?"

"What can I do, Mr Holmes?" he said. "Give me some task, or I shall run mad."

"Bring me as many lamps and candles you can find," I replied.

"At once."

I could have managed well enough with one lantern; still, it gave the man something to do. It also gave me time alone to think, to focus.

There was no doubt that the boy had been snatched, almost certainly by the same fellow who had terrorised his father in London. I fought down my certainty. Best keep an open mind while I began my examination.

I scanned the room. A cot flanked the left wall. The covers had been pulled back but revealed no sign of a struggle. A toy soldier lay beside the pillow. To my right stood a dresser; and directly ahead, a casement window of leaded glass.

I began at the casement. The hinges were well oiled and the window swung open easily and silently. It was secured by a simple latch. An easy matter to slide it open from the outside. The windowsill revealed a muddy footprint. In addition, the wooden frame had a small crack at the base, a result of taking a man's weight. Well, whoever had taken the boy entered the house via the window. So far, so obvious.

Outside, a mature hawthorn tree spread its branches around the window. I spotted a thread of light-coloured wool caught on a twig. I plucked it and put it into an envelope for later examination. I leaned out of the window and examined the scene below me. It would be an easy thing for an agile man to ascend that tree, open the window, and snatch the sleeping child.

I turned my attention to the rest of the room.

The rug beneath the window captured the outline of a man's muddy footprint. A size thirteen, I estimated, although the imprint was too indistinct for me to be precise. The boy's bed stood on the other side of the narrow room. Two strides, and the man would have him. But why?

That it might be coincidental, nothing to do with the threats Hardwicke received in London, was altogether implausible. I do not believe in coincidence. No, this was part of a plan.

All the way here on trains, boats and carriages, I pondered the problem. My throat was raw from the amount of tobacco I had inhaled. The entire, wearisome journey, I wrestled with this question: If a man is being threatened in London, and seeks refuge in Ireland, why is the threat enacted here, in the middle of the Irish countryside? Was the kidnapper merely tenacious, or was there another explanation?

If kidnap – or worse – were intended, surely that could have been accomplished just as easily in London as here in County Meath?

Unless…

A glimmer of an explanation occurred to me. Yes! Why not? It made perfect sense. Still, certainty was premature. I must conduct my investigation and see where the facts lead me.

I looked at the boy's cot and frowned. Sheets, a blanket, and a patchwork quilt. A minute pinprick of blood, I thought it must be blood, on the bottom sheet.

A few moments later, Hardwicke returned with two maids and they handed me a dozen lit lanterns and candles.

I said, "Is there anything missing from the room, other than the boy, I mean?"

"No," Hardwicke said, "Nothing."

"You are certain?"

One of the maids said, "The crocheted blanket is missing from the bed. Mrs Jefferson made it herself, so she did. Young Nigel always likes to have it on top of his quilt to snuggle against. There, now, how did I miss that?"

"What does it mean?" Hardwicke said.

"That the man who took your son did not want him to waken in the cold."

"Oh."

He missed the point, so I explained: "He is taking care of the boy, Hardwicke. He has not harmed him."

The man fairly sagged with relief. "Oh, thank God, thank God," he said.

"What of the boy's clothes?" I asked, "Are any of those missing?"

"No, Mr Holmes," the other maid replied. "I checked that myself. I helped the young master get ready for bed last eve and I laid out his clothes for the morning. They're still there, on top of the dresser."

"Well done," I said. "That is helpful."

"How?" Hardwicke said.

"It confirms my theory that the boy did not leave of his own accord. Tell me," I continued, "have there been any strangers in town this week?"

The same maid replied, "There are always visitors at this time of year, sir. New faces as well as old."

"Where would they stay?"

"With their families, for the most part," Hardwicke replied.

"There are a few inns, sir," the maid said. "My sister works in The Heights and she says it's packed with visitors."

"Chief Constable Henderson went to all these places asking about Nigel," Hardwicke said.

I tsked. "He should be searching for the kidnapper; find the man and you find the boy. I think you should visit all these inns yourself, Hardwicke."

"I shall go at once," he replied. He turned to leave then hesitated.

I said, "You are looking for a tall man, at least six foot two. He is slender, and has black hair. He will probably have an English accent, though he might try to disguise it."

"Is that the villain who took my son?" Hardwicke said. "By God I'll have him!"

"Ask Doctor Watson to accompany you," I said. "You must be calm. If the fellow is there and if he has taken the boy, you will need him to tell you where Nigel is. Let Watson do all the talking, Hardwicke. I mean it. You must say and do nothing. If the fellow is there, Watson will know what to do. Say nothing to the others. I do not want to raise hopes only to dash them. We must deal with facts."

"I understand. I shall do exactly as you ask, Mr Holmes."

A few minutes later, I heard the front door close. I thought it exceedingly unlikely the kidnapper would take a room in so public place as an inn. He would not want to draw attention to himself. Besides, he could hardly carry the boy to his room without being observed. Then again, if the aim were murder perhaps he had killed the child and merely deposited the remains.

I shook my head. No, if murder were the aim, why not simply kill the boy as he slept? This game was far more subtle. I believed the boy was alive, at least for now. If that were so, the kidnapper had private accommodation near town. Somewhere he could keep the boy prisoner without rousing suspicions.

Still, the inns were worth checking and, besides, it gave Hardwicke something to do. In the unlikely event that they found the fellow, Watson would ensure our friend did not act rashly.

I finished my search of the room. There was little else to see even with the additional lamps and candles. I went outside to examine the grounds.

Old Lorcan held the lantern and tried unsuccessfully to suppress a yawn as I examined the earth beneath the boy's window. Whatever secrets the kidnapper may have left, they had been silenced by the rain and the feet of the search party.

With little difficulty, I climbed the tree outside the boy's window. I found two more threads of wool in the branches.

"Is this how he got in?" Lorcan asked.

"I believe so," I said.

He shook his head and spat on the ground. "May the divil take him. 'Tis bad luck to turn a fairy 'thorn to evil use."

"A fairy 'thorn?"

"'This what we call it when there's a single hawthorn tree. They're meant to be a protection over special places. This one has been here many a year. It's older than meself, and me mammy, too. Great misfortune befalls a man who has abused the fairy 'thorn."

I paid scant heed. No doubt Watson would be delighted at this piece of folklore, but I had other concerns.

The house was about fifty feet back from the road and there were no immediate neighbours. There would be no difficulty in carrying the boy to a nearby cart or horse. That pinprick of blood suggested the boy had been injected with a drug to ensure he did not waken and cry out.

I returned to the living room. The Jeffersons and McKenna were eager to hear my news, as was the child's mother, but I did not want to say too much. Not yet. We made idle conversation until Watson and Hardwicke returned an hour or so later, dispirited and cold.

"There are no visitors who match the kidnapper's description, I'm afraid," Watson said. "The inn keepers were eager to help, but they can vouch for all their guests. There are no strangers."

"Well," I said, "I suggest you get some sleep and we shall start again early in the morning."

"Yes, that's probably the best thing to do," Jefferson said. "Come, Anna, you must go to bed. A good night's sleep will do you a world of good."

"I saw the magpie when I opened the door," she said. "Oh daddy, daddy, my baby is lost. 'Tis a sure sign of death when you see a magpie at the door. He looked straight at me, so he did."

"Do not give up hope, my dear," said her husband. "I have every faith in Mr Holmes."

"Brian, will you stay?" said Mrs Hardwicke. "It is very late."

"Thank you, Mrs Jefferson," McKenna replied, "but you need the beds for Mr Holmes and the doctor. I shall have Lorcan take me home."

"Oh, let Lorcan rest," I said. "I shall take you. I should like to get a look at the town."

I had a quiet word with Jefferson, and the family retired. Watson, protesting that he would gladly assist me if I needed him, also was persuaded to go to bed. Lorcan brought around a trap and I assisted the frail McKenna onto the seat beside me, and off we went.

"I'm up at the other end of town, along Balrath Road," he said. "Just head up towards the round tower and I'll direct you from there. That's it yonder. The tower, I mean."

Indeed, the tower loomed tall against the now clear night sky. I hoped Watson would not be too diverted by the thing. It takes little to engage his imagination.

"Is it accessible?" I said.

"No, indeed. It is not safe. It is in the Church of Ireland's grounds, St Columba's, that is. The caretaker looks after everything. It is hundreds of years old."

"It is just a shell, I suppose?"

"There are steps, I believe. I have never been inside it myself. It is not easy access. The doorway is a few feet over the base. They did search it, if that's what you were wondering." He stopped and coughed. He coughed hard for a long time and I began to wonder if he would vomit with the effort. Eventually, the coughing stopped and he sank back, exhausted.

"You should not talk," I said. "Tell me how to get to your home and then you can rest."

I maintained a steady pace as we travelled along the country roads. After a short time, McKenna rallied enough to say, "Will you be able to help them, Mr Holmes? Poor Anna is in such an agony of despair."

"I mean to try. Have you known her for long?" I asked.

"All our lives," he said. "We grew up together."

"You seem very close."

"I had hopes to marry her," he said, "when I was a young man."

"You proposed?" I said.

"Yes, on Christmas Eve fifteen years ago. I had a ring… She had just met Hardwicke a few weeks before in Dublin. I missed my opportunity by such a slender margin. Is there anything worse than seeing your heart's desire snatched away at the last instant?"

"And now you are ill," I said. "Is it serious?"

"Terminal. I'll not live to see another daffodil. The medicine the doctor gives me makes the pain manageable, but as time passes, I need more and more of the stuff."

"Do you have family?"

"A distant cousin, but I have not seen him in years. My parents died several years ago. I never married or had children. I am entirely alone in the world."

"But you have good friends. You cannot underestimate their value."

"Oh, yes. I know how lucky I am."

He began to cough again and said no more.

I continued along Balrath Road. The land rolled in gently undulating rises and falls. On a clear day, I thought, one could see for the miles. Other than the occasional cottage and some straggling trees and bushes, the view was unbroken. No doubt it was alluring enough during daylight hours. In the dead of night it had an inhospitable feeling. The farther we travelled, the fewer the buildings became.

After a long stretch of nothing but farmland, the dying man said, "Here, this is it."

The house was a squat two stories. It stood back from the road by a distance of perhaps a quarter mile. It was in darkness.

I pulled the trap up outside the house and helped McKenna out. "I shall take you in," I said. "Please, take my arm."

"No," he said. "Thank you, Mr Holmes, I appreciate your kindness, but I wish to stand on my own two feet for as long as I'm able."

"You're sure you can manage?" I said.

"Quite sure. Please."

"Very well," I said.

He stumbled into the house, nodded again his thanks, and then shut the door. I climbed into the trap and headed back to the road.

8

Wednesday, 21ˢᵗ December

For a long time I waited in the grass, watching. It was a chilly night and I could not even stand up for fear of being seen. Weary hours passed and the house remained in darkness. I debated with myself on my best course of action. I wished I had Watson with me, but there had been no way of bringing him without raising suspicion.

I am a patient man and I believe that my stamina has few equals, but I confess that it was as weary and miserable night as I can remember. Unproductive, too, for nothing happened save the rain fell and the sky eventually cleared to a leaden dawn. It was soon daylight and I could lie in the grass no longer.

At length, I devised a plan. I was not completely satisfied with it, but even I cannot be in two places at once.

I hurried back to Aisling House and arrived in time for breakfast. Watson exclaimed when he saw my appearance, which was, I am sure, rather the worse for wear. I quickly bathed and changed. I said nothing to the family of my nocturnal exploits but only commented that it was a sad thing to see the unfortunate McKenna all alone over Christmas.

"We have invited him to stay with us," Hardwicke said, "But he feels himself a burden, I suppose."

"I think he might be more willing if Mrs Hardwicke were to ask him. Will you not do so?" I asked the lady. "Surely it is not too much for an old friend?"

The woman stared at me without comprehension for several minutes. Around her neck she wore a silver pendant of a four-leafed clover. She twisted it around and around.

"Anna," her husband said, "An act of charity at Christmas time. I think Mr Holmes is right."

"Cast your bread upon the waters and they shall come back to you," Mrs Jefferson said. "Go comb your hair like a good girl, and remember what a fine friend Brian has been to you."

The woman stared at her mother and then at her husband. Whatever she read in their eyes, she seemed appeased. "Very well, Mr Holmes," she said, "If you wish it. I fear I am a poor Christian at present."

"You are preoccupied with your concern for your son. It is perfectly understandable. But I must ask you to trust me. Will you?"

"Can it help Nigel?"

"It may."

"Well, then," she said, with considerable effort. "Of course I shall."

"Have Lorcan drive you in the barouche, my dear," Jefferson said. "It will be much more comfortable for Brian than the trap."

"And stay with your friend while he packs," I said. "Be insistent. Men do tend to forget important things if they do not have a woman to remind them."

"Besides, his medication might make it difficult for him to remember things," Watson said, just beginning to comprehend what I had planned.

As Hardwicke helped his wife into the carriage, I said, "Please do not talk to Mr McKenna about your son, Mrs Hardwicke. I know it is uppermost in your thoughts, but the man is so ill…"

She swallowed and said, "I shall be good, and speak to him about his paintings. He likes talking about art."

As soon as the lady left, I downed a speedy cup of coffee while I stood.

"Your appearance suggests news, Mr Holmes," Hardwicke said. "You have found my son?"

"Perhaps," I said. "Perhaps. You must indulge me a little longer. I need to use the trap again."

"Of course. We can leave at once."

"No, you must stay here. I beg you will not argue. You must trust me, Hardwicke. Watson, you are with me. So long as we take care, we may be successful. Say nothing to your wife or McKenna, I beg you."

"You have my word."

Watson and I hurried away in the trap at a high rate of speed but making sure we did not overtake the barouche.

As we raced through Kells, I told Watson what I suspected.

"Good God," he cried. "I have never heard anything more fiendish. Surely there must be some other explanation, Holmes?"

"I wish that were true, my good fellow, but I have no doubt."

"Is the boy still alive?"

I hesitated. "For the present, I believe. I suspect they plan to keep him alive until Christmas."

"And then? Holmes, what are you suggesting?"

"I believe they plan to give the dead child to his mother as a ghastly Yuletide gift."

"Good God, Holmes! That is an appalling thought," Watson cried.

"They are appalling people."

We passed the tower and it was a measure of Watson's outrage that he did not notice, nor did he pay heed to the Celtic crosses.

I said, "Last night, I was worried that my arrival might compel our quarry to flee. I kept watch, but there was no sign of activity. These are cool customers, Watson. They will not be deterred from their plan."

"They could have left this morning after you returned to Aisling House."

"They would not get far if they did. I spoke with Simon Jefferson last night. At my behest, he arranged with the chief constable to close all the roads leading out of town, just as a precaution. In any case, if our birds were to flee, it would be under cover of darkness. They would not wait until morning. These fellows know the streets are being watched and everyone is on the alert for the boy. No, I think we have an excellent chance of catching them."

In light of sullen day, Balrath Road revealed a bleak sort of beauty. No wonder Ireland breeds so many poets with such inspiration on their doorsteps.

"Do you have your revolver?" I said as we neared our destination.

"Yes." Watson glanced at me, his face pale and smudged with fatigue. "I am surprised you did not storm the house on your own last night, Holmes. Knowing what is at stake."

"It was knowing the stakes that compelled me to wait, Watson. I cannot be sure how many men there are in that house. At least two. Perhaps more. I could not risk the boy being slain while I tussled with one or other of these brutes."

At length we arrived back at the spot I had so recently vacated. We left the trap hidden in a grove of trees, and continued the last several yards on foot.

"Down here, Watson," I said.

We squatted down in a ditch and waited.

After an interminable age, Mrs Hardwicke appeared with McKenna leaning heavily upon her arm. She and Lorcan helped him into the carriage and off they went, headed back towards town.

"Make haste, Watson!" I hissed as soon as they were out of sight, and I ran towards the house.

At the back door, I said, softly, "We must be quiet as mice if we are to catch this fellow."

With the help of my burglar's kit, I unlocked the door and we stepped inside.

The house was still and yet my instincts told me we were not alone. A moment later, we heard a scraping sound come from directly above us.

I pointed up the stairs and Watson nodded. All was going well until we were almost at the landing. Watson trod on a loose floorboard. It creaked. We froze.

Several things happened in the next instant. A dark masked figure suddenly sprang upon us with a terrible cry. A liquid burned my face and my eyes screamed in agony. Then I felt a mighty blow to my chest and fell backwards, tumbling down the stairs.

I fought against pain and struggled to my feet, I could not see. *I could not see.*

Footsteps rushed passed me. I grabbed with my blind hands but could not hold the villain. There was a blast of cold as the door was flung open and, moments later, the thunder of horses' hooves. I heard the crack of a pistol.

I could not move. I lay on the staircase and cried out, "Watson, Watson, are you there?"

"Here, Holmes. I am right here. Do not move and do not touch your face, for the love of God." I felt his hands undo my shirt and examine my wounds.

"Nothing too bad," he said. "Lean on me. This way. Keep your eyes closed."

My face and eyes burned. It took all my will not to rub at the liquid that blistered my skin.

Watson led me outside and had me place my head beneath the water pump. He started at once to work the handle and washed the filthy stuff off my face and neck with cold, fresh water.

"Did you get him?" I said. "The kidnapper?"

"No, I didn't. He was on that horse and away before I got outside. One thing, though, Holmes. He was alone, no accomplice. And he did not have the boy with him."

"We ought to try to catch him," I began, though I knew it was hopeless. He had a head start, and was on horseback, to boot. He was long gone, not through the barricaded roads but over the fields. Damnation!

"First things first," Watson said.

He examined my face and said, "There is some redness and swelling, but it has already improved. At least we got it in time to prevent any serious damage. Can you see?"

"My vision is blurred, but it is improving. My God, Watson, if you hadn't been here. I shudder to think—"

"Do not dwell on it, Holmes."

"What was it he sprayed at us?"

"A pepper of some sort, I think."

"You are not hurt, Watson?"

"No, I was a little behind you. You gave me quite a start when I saw you fall, I can tell you."

His hands moved methodically over my shoulders and spine, examining me for injuries. I winced when he pressed on my ribs.

"You've cracked a few, I'm afraid," he said. "Can you manage until we get back to Aisling House?"

"Yes, yes. But first, we must find the boy."

"You stay here. I'll go."

Before I could protest, he was off, running through the house, banging doors and crying, "Nigel? Where are you, lad?"

I followed more slowly, still struggling to see. A few moments later, Watson cried, "Here! Holmes, I've found him."

The boy was lying on the floor of a cupboard under the stairs wrapped in a pale blue crocheted blanket. I feared the worst but it appeared he was merely unconscious.

"He's still breathing, at least," Watson said. He patted the boy's face and called his name, but the child remained in a deep sleep.

"Are you all right to stay here for a moment, Holmes?" Watson said. "I shall bring the cart around."

"Yes, do. Be careful, Watson. That fellow may have crept back and could be lurking out there, ready to pounce again."

"I have my pistol," he said. "Do not worry. I shall be alert."

I confess I was in considerable discomfort. It was Watson who carried the boy to the trap, and it was Watson who drove us back to Aisling House.

We travelled more slowly this time and I felt every jolt of the bumpy road. By the time we reached sight of the tower, the boy started to waken. The cold air and the soft rain roused him. He cried in alarm when he found himself in a cart with two strange men.

"Hush," I said. "You are quite safe. I am Sherlock Holmes and this is Doctor John Watson. We are friends of your father's and are taking you home."

He was still in his nightgown. Even with the woollen blanket wrapped around him, he shivered in the cold.

"I'm hungry," he said.

Watson chuckled. "Well, that's a good sign."

Lorcan was in the driveway when we clattered back to the Aisling estate.

"Mr Hardwicke! Mr Jefferson! They've found him! The young master is found!"

We were not even able to get into the house for we were immediately surrounded by the family. The unfortunate child was clutched to various bosoms. Watson's hand and mine were shaken to the point of agony.

"My son, my darling boy," Hardwicke cried. "Oh thank God. And thank you, too, Mr Holmes, Doctor, for restoring him to us. Are you all right, Nigel?"

"I'm hungry," the boy said, again.

We all bundled into the living room. The boy, other than being hungry and sleepy, seemed none the worst for his experience.

Only one man was silent.

"Well, Mr McKenna," I said, "What have you to say for yourself?"

"Brian?" Mrs Hardwicke said, turning to her old friend. "Why, what is this? What does Mr Holmes mean?"

"Would you care to tell Mr and Mrs Hardwicke where I found their son?" I said.

Hardwicke leaped at the fellow, clutching him by the throat.

"Don't, Edgar, oh, please don't," his wife said, weeping. "There must be a mistake. Brian would never harm Nigel."

But one look at the man's face was enough to reveal the truth.

"Dear God, why? Do you hate me so much? Brian? Brian, answer me."

"Hate," he spat. "You do not even know the meaning of the world. You go through the world convinced that everyone loves you and they do. To their great cost, they do. You crush a man's heart so easily and still expect him to be your friend. Well, I'm no friend to you, Anna Hardwicke. My curse is all you'll get from me. I'll see you suffer yet."

He spat at her and made to leave the room.

"Hold there," Jefferson said. "Lorcan, send for the constable. Do not let that man leave."

"You have no right to detain me," McKenna said, but there was no power in his words.

"You kidnapped my grandson," Jefferson said. "That's a hanging offense."

"I'm a dead man, anyway. Do what you please."

Two hours later, something resembling normalcy returned to Aisling House. The boy, fed and restored to his usual youthful spirits, played in his room with his gentle sister, closely watched by the maids. McKenna was under lock and key pending trial. Watson had tended my wounds so I was as comfortable as I could reasonably expect. The family insisted on settling me on their sofa and I was not permitted to move for any reason.

"Now, Mr Holmes," said Hardwicke, "You have more than justified every tale I have ever heard of you. It is a wonder to me how you found our dear boy and returned him to us. Please, will you not tell us how you managed it?"

"Ah, yes. Well, it was a case of a plot being far too elaborate for common sense. Let us begin with Guy Fawkes Night. That is when you first noticed that you were being watched by a masked man. By all accounts, the fellow made no effort to conceal himself. Indeed, he made great effort to be seen. He meant to be intimidating.

"A sinister, masked figure appeared several more times over the next few weeks. These visitations culminated in the Death card that was given to your young son.

"Why would he do such a thing? What was the purpose for this strange action? You were already uneasy. Why give the boy that sinister card? I was, I confess, greatly puzzled by the seemingly irrational behaviour of the antagonist."

"But now you are not?" Jefferson said. "I must admit it makes no sense to me, even now."

"When we heard the boy had been kidnapped, and in Ireland, not London, I knew there was a dangerous plan afoot. I was reminded of an old story." I tried to sit up a little more and winced. Anna Hardwicke hurried to reposition my pillow for me.

"A story?" she said.

"Thank you. Yes. Some time ago, a friend of mine, Rabbi Steinmetz, gave me a book, a collection of stories about logic and philosophy. In it, there is a tale about King Solomon.

"It seems Solomon had two servants of whom he was particularly fond. These men came from the land of Cush. One day the king came upon the Angel of Death and was surprised to find him looking sad. The King asked why and Death replied, 'Because I am ordered to take your two beloved servants, the men from Cush.' Solomon, in order to protect the men, sent them away to the land of Luz, a legendary place where no man dies. However, as the servants came within reach of the gates they fell down dead.

"The next day, Solomon again encountered Death, and this time he saw that he was happy. He asked why and the other replied, 'Because you sent the two men to the very place where they were meant to die.'"

"I'm not sure I follow, Holmes," Watson said.

"No? Well, I am not about to discuss the intricacies of the myth, but it did suggest that sometimes fate can lead us to our destiny. The decisions we make have consequences we can never anticipate.

"You were hounded in London, Mr Hardwicke, and yet no harm befell you or your family. It was not until your son was given the tarot card that you became seriously alarmed. Your response was twofold: you consulted me, and you arranged to leave England for the holidays.

"You come here to Kells and it is only now that the threat is realised. It is evident that your masked adversary meant for you to flee to Ireland. That he intended you to meet your fate here.

"That raised the question: why would anyone want you to come here? Why kidnap the boy here, in Ireland, rather than in London?"

"Because McKenna could not, himself, travel," Simon Jefferson replied.

"Yes, that is true," Hardwicke said, "But it was not he who followed me around London. Who was it? Who gave Nigel that card?"

"A cohort hired by McKenna," I said. "It was he who appeared at the Guy Fawkes event and who dogged your footsteps. It was he who snatched your son from his bed. Once

85

I met McKenna, I realised he was the only person who could not have come to you in London, but needed you to come to him."

"But why?" Anna Hardwicke cried, "For what reason? Just to terrorise my family?"

"To injure you in the most brutal way possible," I said. I sipped the tea that Ana-Marie Hardwicke handed me before continuing. "I insisted on taking McKenna home last night and in the course of the journey I asked about his history with you, Mrs Hardwicke. He told me how he offered marriage to you on a Christmas Day many years ago. You rejected him. Though he spoke the words casually enough, I sensed a deep resentment lay beneath them."

"And he hated me," Hardwicke said, "For being the father of Anna's children. I suppose he thought I robbed him of that joy."

"Exactly so."

"And that is how he chose to injure you," Watson added, "By attacking your family."

Simon Jefferson said, "But could he not have arranged that in London? Why the elaborate deception? Why lure my family here?"

"It was not enough to cause pain," I replied, "He wanted to witness it first-hand. He needed to see your grief and despair, to wallow in your misery."

"Good God," Hardwicke exclaimed. "I remember McKenna once said that my children ought to have been his. That he would die without an heir because of me. I thought it was a jest in poor taste, but a jest nonetheless. I did not take it seriously."

"I fear he has been harbouring his resentment for a long time," I said.

Watson added, "It is possible these perceived slights were magnified by his illness. Men face death in such unique ways."

I did not mention my suspicion that McKenna and his agent intended for the body of Hardwicke's son to be discovered on Christmas Day. Under the tree with the gifts, perhaps. Appalling. .

"How did you confirm your theory, Mr Holmes?" Jefferson asked. "It is a leap of logic from suspecting a man, and another thing entirely to discover where the boy was hidden."

"You are quite correct. I knew it was McKenna. Only a person with knowledge of the household would know where the boy slept. My priority was the boy's safe return. Your son had been snatched alive from his bed, so I believed the kidnappers had no plans to immediately harm him. Later, in my conversation with McKenna, he told me how close he came to winning Mrs Hardwicke's hand. 'I missed my opportunity by such a slender margin. Is there anything worse than seeing your heart's desire snatched away at the last instant?' he said. Those words made me hope that he and his cohort would keep the boy alive up to the last minute. He wanted you, too, to feel the bitterness of a last-minute loss.

"I spent the rest of the night watching McKenna's home. I had taken the trap a short distance down the road so he would think I had left. I then returned and lay in the grass, keeping watch. It was a long, wretched night. I did not see another person, neither man nor boy.

"I could not remain there lying on the wet grass once daylight returned. I would have charged into the house on my own, but I could not be sure that one man alone, even I, would be able to ensure the boy's safety, assuming he was still alive.

Nor could I be sure that McKenna did not have other allies lying in wait. Therefore, I returned here and asked your wife to persuade McKenna to leave that house. I suspect McKenna wanted to be present when the boy's life was snuffed out."

Mrs Hardwicke cried out and fled from the room. Watson frowned.

"Forgive me," I said. "I spoke too bluntly."

"You are being truthful, Mr Holmes," Jefferson said, "And to my mind, that never needs an apology. I am afraid this entire affair has weighed rather heavily upon my daughter."

"Quite understandable," Watson said.

"Pray continue, Mr Holmes," Hardwicke said.

"I wanted to be sure McKenna was out of the way. Frankly, I suspect he had planned to take your son's life with his own hands."

"But surely McKenna was too ill to harm Nigel?" Hardwicke said. "I mean, could he not have meant to hold the boy to worry us and release him later?"

"A man who has gone to such elaborate lengths to exact revenge is the last person I would trust, Mr Hardwicke. Besides, as Watson will tell you, fury and hate can give unimagined strength to even the weakest of men. At any rate, it was a chance I was not prepared to take."

"Quite right," Jefferson said.

"I agonised over leaving that house to return here, but I had to risk it. If I had entered the building on my own, I might have placed your son in grave jeopardy. There was too great a risk that McKenna would kill the boy while I tangled with his accomplice, or accomplices. No, I knew that I needed assistance, and no man is more reliable than Doctor Watson. With his help, I knew we had a chance to recover your son alive."

"We are forever in your debt for bringing about such a happy conclusion to such a dreadful business," Hardwicke said.

"Not entirely happy," I replied. "The accomplice managed to escape."

9

Tuesday, 27th December

This morning I spoke with Anna Hardwicke about her history with fortune tellers.

"When we married, I gave my word to Edgar that I should have nothing more to do with them," she said. "I kept my promise."

"Come, Mrs Hardwicke, you owe me the truth, surely? I shall say nothing to your husband."

"I am telling the truth... That is, I have not sought them out, but one found me."

"Ah. This was recently?"

"Yes, a few months ago. September or October, I think. I was walking around the Heath with my children and a tall man stopped me and said I had dropped my glove. As he handed it back to me, he stared at me intently and said, 'Oh, you are a long way from home...' and he proceeded to tell me all sorts of things that no one knew, not even Edgar. I saw he had a great talent. I invited him to come to my home to give me a full reading."

"Did you suggest it or did he?"

"Oh, I did. Yes, I am sure I did... Before I could ask him what sort of method he used, he said, 'You need not fear, Mrs Hardwicke, I will not use the tarot.'" She leaned forward, eyes as bright as a zealot's, and said, "There, Mr Holmes. Does that not prove he was a genuine mystic?"

"You had not mentioned the tarot?"

"Oh, no, I am in mortal terror of it. A gypsy woman told me when I was a young girl that if I ever saw the Death card I would die a terrible death."

"I see. Did the man came to your house?"

"Yes, a week later. Oh, he was quite amazing. He called my beloved grandmother to speak to me and we had a wonderful session."

"Your son saw you talking to this man?"

"Yes, he was with me on the heath, and in the house when the man called."

"Did the man give you a name?"

"He said I should call him Angel. A blessed name. What does this have to do with Nigel, Mr Holmes?"

"I believe he is a dangerous man, Mrs Hardwicke. I think it was he who gave your son that card. You must promise me you'll have nothing more to do with him."

"Oh, oh, that is too dreadful! You have my word, Mr Holmes."

This afternoon, over Watsons' protests, I went to see McKenna in his gaol cell. "It is not a task I undertake with any great enthusiasm, Watson, but it must be done. I must learn everything I can about this Sorcerer fellow. He has damaged enough lives."

I was not optimistic that McKenna would tell me much, and in that I was, sadly, correct.

"Ask me whatever you like, Mr Holmes," he said. "I shall not feel obliged to answer."

I said, "The plan was very clever, Mr McKenna. Was it yours?"

"No. I should like to take credit for it, but it was not mine."

"The Sorcerer's?" I said, watching him closely.

McKenna's waxy face blanched still further. He said, "I told him I wanted to see Anna suffer before I died. It was not enough to know she was in agony; I wanted to see it. He devised the plan and it worked perfectly. Would have worked perfectly if you had not shown up."

"You know, if you reveal the name of your ally, this so-called Sorcerer, the judge might be persuaded to leniency."

"What is the point? I am a dead man in any case. Likely I will not live long enough to see the rope. Even if I do…" He coughed and sank back on his cot.

"This man who helped you is dangerous. Other lives may be at risk. Come. I do not believe you are wholly evil. Tell me his name."

But he would say no more.

Wednesday, 28th December

We have been wined and feted beyond all endurance. The Hardwickes and the Jeffersons went to considerable pains to ensure our comfort and included us in all their Christmas celebrations. I was obliged to rest, and be lauded, and recover from my injuries. The journey back to London is so onerous, even when one is in good health; in my current condition with three broken ribs and a great many bruises, it would be in all ways detestable. At least my eyes have recovered and my normal vision restored. The delay in our return has one advantage, at least: the trains and the boat should not be so busy now the Christmas holiday is over.

After so much solicitude and inactivity, I was becoming restive and finally persuaded Watson to let me take a walk. "Not far, and we'll return the minute you become fatigued," he said. "You really should rest and let those injuries heal."

We walked the short distance to the grounds of St Columba's Church and I stared at the ancient tower rising up above us.

"This is rather splendid, is it not?" Watson said. "Jefferson tells me it is almost a thousand years old. He said a chieftain was murdered here."

"Recently?"

"Oh, Holmes, it is scandalous how you thrill at the word 'murder'. No, it was not recent. It was in 1076. It is mentioned in the annals."

"Oh."

"What a pity it is locked up, but I suppose it is not very safe. The book was found here, you know. The *Book of Kells*."

"Yes, I have heard of the *Book of Kells*."

"They took it to Dublin many years ago for safekeeping. It's rather a shame it did not remain here."

"Quite," I said, not really listening. Watson really does find pleasure in the most extraordinary things.

I sat on a gravestone as he scurried about. "How are you feeling, Holmes?" he called, at one juncture. "You are not overdoing it?"

"My dear Watson, I think I can sit for a time without ill effect."

Truth to tell, I was feeling rather less well than I cared to admit. My ribs hurt considerably and I was unable to take more than shallow breaths due to the bindings Watson had wrapped around my chest. Still, I could not endure another minute indoors with the relentlessly grateful Hardwickes. The solitude was worth some discomfort.

Watson ambled around the churchyard pointing out any manner of fascinating things. Celtic crosses and crumbling headstones. Such fun. I managed not to yawn.

"Many of these stones are hundreds of years old. Isn't that fascinating?"

"Why? People died hundreds of years ago."

"And look at this sundial. It is quite splendid. Can you see it, Holmes?"

"Yes, yes, I see."

He returned after twenty minutes and sat beside me. "Enough of this entertainment," he said. "What do you say to stopping somewhere for a drink?"

I was compelled to lean on his arm as we strolled back down the gentle hill. The five-minute walk took almost half an hour. It was a relief to step into an inn and sit in a comfortable chair by the fire. Watson ordered Irish whiskey for both us. The waiter brought it to the table a few moments later and refused payment. The locals, knowing who we are and why we are in town, have gone out of their way to be hospitable. We raised our glasses to them and they applauded.

"The Irish welcome is no myth, I see," Watson said to a chorus of cheers.

I sipped and fell silent. After several minutes Watson said, "She'll understand, Holmes." At my surprise, he smiled and said, "Beatrice gave you that tiepin a few months ago and you tend to caress it whenever you think of her. We have just celebrated Christmas. You had planned to spend the day with her, but were unable to do so."

"It is most disconcerting when you read me so easily, my dear Watson. Why do you never write your fictional self as wise as you really are?"

"Because I do not want anything to distract the reader from the real brilliance that is you."

I chinked his glass in acknowledgement of the compliment.

He continued, "Beatrice will appreciate that you had no choice but to come and rescue that unfortunate child. She is not unreasonable."

"I know. She never makes any demands of me. I can count on her to understand."

"Then why…? Ah, because you rather wish she would make demands. You are worried that if she does not protest your absence, perhaps she has no real affection for you."

I said nothing, but sipped the excellent whiskey.

"Holmes," Watson persisted. "I am right, am I not?"

"It would be completely irrational to take issue with Beatrice's independence when it is one of the things that drew me to her in the first place."

He merely looked at me with what I can only describe as a smug expression.

"I am not so irrational, surely?" I said.

"You are a man. You might have the world convinced you are no more than a reasoning machine; I made that mistake myself when I did not know you so well. Now…"

"Now?"

"Let us say that now I know you much better."

"I did not even send her a message telling her I was going away," I said. I was conscious that my voice sounded peevish, but I could not seem to snap myself out of my gloom. Those ancient Celtic crosses and battered tombstones were undoubtedly affecting my mood.

"We shall be home in time for New Year," I said. "I suppose we can celebrate, then."

"If you are quite sure you will be able to travel. It is not a comfortable journey and a very long one."

"What is that old saying, what cannot be cured must be endured? I shall feel better once we are back in London. Charming though Kells may be, it is not home. Well, the compliments of the season to you, my dear Watson. This would have been a wretched business entirely if you had not been at my side."

He turned his head slightly, but not before I saw the huge beam of pleasure on his face.

Friday, 31st December

Baker Street: Joy! With trains, boats, and carriages, we did not arrive home until last night. I cannot understand why one is so fatigued from travel when all one does is sit. In any event, Watson and I arrived exhausted and we both slept late.

With our breakfast, Mrs Hudson brought up several parcels, all neatly wrapped. She placed them on the table along with our kippers and coffee.

"What is this, Mrs Hudson?" I asked.

"I think you should open them, Mr Holmes," she said.

She left us alone and Watson and I began our happy investigation.

"I say, Holmes," the doctor said, "Isn't this splendid?" He held up a cashmere dressing gown and read the card. "With warmest affection, B. What a generous present."

I grunted and turned my attention to my own gift. I folded back the wrapping to reveal a first edition copy of Kreutzer's *42 Études ou Caprices*. I am rather fond of Kreutzer's bowing technique and his philosophy of control before action. I read the card: "I hope you have a splendid holiday, dear Sherlock, and that I will see you again soon. Affectionately, B."

There were other, smaller gifts, too. A packet of shag from the Irregulars, a knitted scarf from Mrs Hudson, dark green for Watson; mine was blue. At the top of the pile lay a letter from Mycroft:

Seasons Greetings, my dear brother.

I gather you and the unfortunate doctor have been fetched off to Ireland for reasons I care not to imagine. Something to do with a lurid crime, I have no doubt. I hope it is a crime and not some Fenian affair.

You have nothing to report vis-à-vis Augustus Updike, I suppose? There are matters abroad on which I should like your thoughts, if you can tear yourself away from these squalid murders that you seem to find so entertaining.

I dined with your good wife over the holidays. I think she was disappointed by your absence, not that she would admit to such a thing. As your brother, I believe I have certain rights, and one of these is telling you unpleasant truths. Well, this truth is that the way you are treating that unfortunate woman is shameful. Really, Sherlock, running off to Ireland – Ireland! – without even telling your wife you were leaving. I hope it was worth it.

Please come and see me at your earliest convenience.

M

As we finished breakfast, I announced my intention of visiting my beleaguered wife. "Will you accompany me, my dear fellow?" I asked Watson. "I would like to take you both to dinner."

"If you think Beatrice will not object to my presence, I would be delighted, my dear Holmes. I shall have Mrs Hudson call a cab. No, you absolutely cannot walk."

A few minutes later, we stepped out onto Baker Street. As we climbed ungracefully into the waiting Hansom, Kevin came running up with some of the younger Irregulars in tow.

"Watcher, Mr 'olmes," he said. "Ta for the Christmas grub. We 'ad a proper knees up."

"Knees up?" I said, baffled. "What Christmas treat do you mean, Kevin?"

"The one with Billy and Ma and Da Davenport. We 'uz all there, all us Irregulars and lots of our mums and dads, too. Lady Beatrice made sure we had so much to eat we fair waddled home, didn't we, Mikey?"

"It were a proper feast," Mikey said.

"I am glad you enjoyed it. I hope you remembered your manners and said thank you."

"'Ere, watcher take us for, Mr H? 'ooligans?"

As we rode the Hansom to Wimpole Street, Watson said, "That was very good of Beatrice to make sure the children were fed. She has a good heart."

"Yes," I said, "She does."

Beatrice herself made little of the matter when I mentioned it. "It was really Davenport and his wife who arranged it," she said. "Billy made sure everyone was invited and no one was left out. We called it Tommy's Christmas Feast."

She also made little of my absence over the holidays. "Your brother came and we had a perfectly delightful dinner," she said. "We drank a toast to you both. I invited Sir Christopher, but he would not leave his home."

Despite her chatter, I sensed she was upset about something.

"I was just worried," she said, when I pressed her. "It was not that you left in such a hurry, but that you left no word. You were supposed to dine with me on Christmas and I did not even know you had left the country until I telephoned Mrs Hudson." She smiled, but I read the same pain in her eyes that had been so recently in Watson's.

"Forgive me," I said, "Time was of the essence. A child had been kidnapped…"

She raised her hand to forestall my explanation, "You need not explain," she said. "I only ask that you send word to me when you next leave in a hurry."

"I shall," I replied. "You have my word."

"And you are hurt, I see. I should not scold you when you are in pain."

"Was that a scolding?" I said, lightly.

The Strand was charming. The Savoy had a large Christmas tree in their foyer decorated with electric fairy lights. It drew quite a crowd of admirers. We strolled on to Simpson's. Their décor was a little less elaborate but no less charming. We sat at our usual table and dined upon a goose of the highest quality.

It was not until much later, after we had left Watson at Baker Street and returned to Wimpole Street that I told B the details of Nigel Hardwicke's kidnapping and how I had recovered him.

"Oh, thank goodness you were in time," B said. "No wonder you left in such haste. Please forgive my earlier irritability, Sherlock. I know the importance of your work. I have no right to make demands of you."

"No, you are perfectly correct. Were our situation reversed, you would never have disappeared without sending some word to me. I fear I am still learning behaviour that other men seem to know instinctively."

"I do not want you to be as other men. Other men are two a penny, but there is only one Sherlock Holmes."

Later, she observed, "You have resolved your quarrel with Watson, I see. He was quite his old self this evening."

"All the same," I said, "I know what pain I caused him. I should like to make amends. I just do not know how."

"You will think of something, I am sure."

10

Sunday, 1ˢᵗ January, 1899

Although it is Sunday and most of the country is celebrating the New Year, I found Mycroft hard at work in his office. The building was otherwise deserted. Even Gillespie was absent. Without the usual hum of voices and the thundering steps of the pages, the place felt even more silent and desolate than usual.

I let myself in through the side door with the key Mycroft gave me several years ago, and began the meandering trek through the building to his chambers. It is irksome that he does not give me the key to the entrance on the Horse Guards Avenue side that is directly beneath his office, but Mycroft deems that doorway too conspicuous and a security risk. I am therefore obliged to enter on the opposite side of the building and walk almost a mile of corridors and staircases in order to reach him. Such a waste of time. More to the point, I had to stop to catch my breath three times, and that is not including the climb up the interminable staircases.

Mycroft ignored my complaints, of course, though for once he did not chastise me for making them. He joined me by the fire and we shared a pot of coffee. It was good to see him. I thought he seemed far healthier than he was during the summer and I said so.

"The leg is a bother," he admitted, "But it seems to be doing quite well at present. I see you have had adventures of your own. What is it, a broken rib?"+

"Three broken ribs, in fact. Watson has me taped up tighter than a drum; it is difficult to breathe. He is concerned that I could puncture a lung. But you did not want to discuss health, Mycroft."

101

"No, indeed. It is a relief to have the anti-anarchy conference over and done with. Still, the business of the country goes on. Now, Sherlock, about Ireland…"

For the next two hours we discussed all of Europe, much of the Americas, and a considerable portion of Africa.

"Nothing new regarding Updike, then?" Mycroft said when we finished dissecting the world.

"Not yet. I have not forgotten the case, Mycroft, but there is so little to go on. I cannot make bricks without straw."

He yawned and stretched. "I suppose not," he said. "Well, here is something that may help: Updike's doting wife has returned from Italy."

"Odd that it has taken her so long," I said. "Even an indifferent wife must surely be sensitive to the appearance of things. I shall pay her a visit. Do you know anything about her?"

"Nothing at all. However, her refusal to return when her husband was discovered in such a state, nor even to attend his funeral, suggests a nature of unusual callousness, even for a woman."

Monday, 2nd January

This morning Watson and I called upon Mrs Updike. The maid showed us into the dead man's study. The widow, dressed in blue, rose to greet us. So, she did not even care enough for her late spouse to don mourning garb. Interesting.

Nothing I had heard of the woman led me to expect warmth, but her indifference to the death of her husband, a man who had shared her bed, a man, one presumes, she once loved, was disgusting. A finer example of the unfair sex, I cannot imagine.

I explained the reason for my visit, but she hardly seemed to be listening.

"I doubt I can help you," she said. She seemed more interested in the papers before her.

"I am trying to learn what happened to your husband, Mrs Updike. The circumstances of his illness and subsequent death were… unusual."

"I do not know what you mean, Mr Holmes."

"Come, Madame, it is hardly common for grown men to be found wandering the moors in their nightshirts."

She did not answer.

"Do you know why he was in Devonshire?" I persisted.

"I have no idea." She drew a diary from the desk drawer and flicked through the pages. "He carried his secrecy even into his journal. There is no entry for the date. You may keep this if you think it will help." She handed the book to me. An attempt to speed my departure rather than a desire to assist, I thought.

"My husband has been almost a stranger to me these past several years, Mr Holmes," she continued. "He lived his life and I lived mine. I can tell you nothing of his recent activities. He was a hard man to live with. Then, to cap it all, he takes his own life. Selfish to the end. He could not even stay his hand to preserve his family from the shame of suicide."

"I realise this is painful," I said. "But I believe he was driven to take his own life. Any information you can give us would be helpful."

"Even when we lived together my husband was a stranger to me. He stayed away for months at a time and when he came home he refused to tell me what he had been doing." Her eyes gleamed with a vengeful fire. "I was nothing to him. I was only his wife. Chattel." She all but spat this last word.

"You must have loved him once," Watson said.

"With all my heart," she said, "but that was a long time ago. He snuffed it out of me, and now I love nothing. I love only my hate."

The icy façade cracked and I glimpsed the depth of her feeling. "Marriage to Augustus brought me nothing, not even children. No, one thing: he gave me the house in Italy. When I have settled his estate, I shall return there and never come back to England."

She rose and rang the bell for the servant. "I do not wish to discuss the matter further, Mr Holmes. The police investigated my husband's death and were satisfied that it was nothing more than a suicide. This is my shame."

A maid came into the room and bobbed in an abbreviated curtsey.

The widow said, "These gentlemen are leaving, Rose. Please see them out."

In the vestibule, I asked, "Is Townsend available? I should like to speak with him."

"No, sir," the maid replied. "The mistress sent him home for a day or two. There weren't much needed doing here and he were that upset about the master. He'll be back tomorrow. I'll tell him you were asking for him, sir."

As I climbed into the cab to return to Baker Street, I said, "It is tiresome to become fatigued so easily. Still, I know you can manage on your own, Watson. You know what to do?"

"Leave it to me, Holmes."

The maid came out of the house before I was settled in my seat. Watson joined her. By the time she turned the corner, the girl was giggling at something he said.

He did not return to Baker Street until eight o'clock.

"You look pleased with yourself," I observed. "Did you enjoy the meat pie?"

It took him only a moment. He examined his clothing and rubbed at the remnants of his meal on his coat with a handkerchief.

"I take it the young woman has romantic interests elsewhere?" I added.

"There, now, how could you tell that?"

"Because you have great allure for the fair sex. Few women are impervious to your charms unless they are already attached. A woman whose affections are engaged will tell a man when he has a stain on his clothing. If she is very interested, she might make so bold as to try to remove the stain herself. Rose did neither; ergo, her affections lie elsewhere."

"You're perfectly correct, Holmes," he replied. "And I thank you for the compliment."

"Well, what did you learn?"

He made himself comfortable in his chair, lit a cigarette, and said, "Rose is a perfectly amiable young woman and I enjoyed her company. A bit of a chatterbox, perhaps: very happy to discuss her former employer, though she'd rather speak of her young man. That's a fellow she calls 'Dilly'. He's a valet for a gentleman in Pimlico."

"Yes, yes, but what did you learn about the Updikes?"

"You know, Holmes, patience is deemed a virtue."

"So is coming to the point."

He chuckled. "Very well. Rose tells me the marriage was an unhappy one. Updike was, as we know, away from home for long periods at a time. His wife suspected him of engaging in dalliances and demanded an explanation upon his return. He, of course, would say nothing."

"Because he had been on the Queen's business. Yes, that must have caused some resentment."

"Despite that, Rose insists Updike loved his wife deeply. It broke his heart when she asked him for a divorce. He refused to give it to her. Perhaps he thought she would come around. In any case, he was generous. He gave her the house in Italy for her sole use, as well as a substantial monthly allowance."

"Did she take a lover?"

"Rose knows nothing of Mrs Updike's activities since the marriage broke down. She – Rose, I mean – and Townsend returned to England with their master; the rest of the servants stayed in Italy with their mistress."

"And there was no communication between the Updikes thereafter?"

"Augustus wrote to his wife pretty regularly but she seldom replied."

I relit my pipe and drew a lungful of smoke; I coughed for several minutes, and then sipped the water Watson silently handed to me.

"How did the staff like Mr Updike?" I said when I recovered my speech.

"Holmes, I do wish—"

"Yes, yes, I know. I have put the pipe away. Updike?"

"He was a favourite with the staff. He was affable to all, regardless of their station."

"A household with no mistress and a master who is gone for months at a time must be very pleasant for the servants. No wonder they liked him. I suppose none of them knew anything of his activities?"

"Rose says the staff believed that he was a spy. The resolute manservant, Townsend, accompanied Updike on many of his travels. He may know more than he has told us thus far."

"My last conversation with him was under trying circumstances. Updike demanded every moment of the poor fellow's attention and energy. I should dearly like to speak to him again. I assume Mrs Updike inherited everything when her husband died?"

"It seems so. It was a matter of some gossip below stairs. Townsend in particular was outraged. Of course, he and all the other servants have been given notice. Rose said that Mrs Updike gave each of them ten pounds as a thank-you gift."

He cruelly lit another cigarette. "Rose believes they would have been much happier if they'd had offspring."

"Sentimentality," I said, dismissing the notion.

"Like it or not, Holmes, children do make a difference. I, ah, I suppose you and Beatrice have talked about the possibility?"

I tossed more coal on the fire and then said, "As with so much in life, procreation is not entirely within our control. I would like to have a child. That surprises you, does it not? It surprises me. Yes, I rather think I would; but the lack of one would not make me despondent."

"What of Beatrice?"

"What of her?"

"Would she not like to become a mother?"

"We have not discussed it. I would like to see her books."

"Beatrice has books?"

"Not B, Watson, do pay attention. Mrs Updike. I would like to see the contents of Augustus Updike's will. More to the point, I would like to find out if Mrs Updike made a large payment to someone upon her husband's death."

Tuesday, 3rd January

This evening, Byron Townsend called upon us in response to Watson's carefully worded invitation. I was again struck by his physique. He is a bulldog of a man. Were it not for his elegant tailoring, I should put him down as a dock worker. His neck and shoulders are most unusual for a manservant.

"Thank you, Mr Townsend," I said, "I appreciate you coming here. Some of our questions may seem impertinent, but my only interest is learning what happened to your unfortunate master."

"I am happy to tell you anything you wish, Mr Holmes. He was a good man. Broke my heart to see the state of him when you returned him to us. God rest his soul."

"Indeed. Most distressing. I know we have spoken before, but I hoped you may have had time to reflect since then."

"It was difficult to remember things and answer your questions when the master was in such straits, sir. Ask me anything you like. I will help any way I can."

"Excellent. The last time we spoke, you said Mr Updike was going to Devonshire for a holiday. Can you add anything to that?"

"I fear not, Mr Holmes. I have wracked my brain. He said only that he was taking a short holiday and would see me in a few days."

"He did not want you to accompany him?"

"No, but that was not unusual. Mr Updike's work often took him away on his own and he was used to fending for himself. 'Self-sufficiency,' he called it. Don't think his wife would have seen it the same way, but there you are."

"It would not please your mistress if she knew you were helping us, I am sure."

"It is of no matter to me," he replied. "She may go to the devil."

"How well do you know her?"

"The mistress? Not very. I was hired by Mr Updike about ten years ago. Back then, they had been married at least five years. They were still living together as man and wife, but things had already soured between them."

"How so?" Watson asked.

"Well, he was gone, wasn't he? Weeks at a time he'd be missing and not a word to herself or any of us about when he'd be back. He worked for the government, very hush-hush stuff. Didn't even tell the mistress what he was up to, and I think she resented it."

"What did Mrs Updike do when her husband was absent?"

"The first year I was with them she used to give small dinner parties. Then one day Mr Updike came home right in the middle of one. He looked a bit the worse for wear. His clothes were torn and he was covered with mud. Smelled like he'd fallen into a brewery. Anyway, he wasn't best pleased that the missus was entertaining while he was off doing who knows what. They had a proper barney about it. She stopped giving parties after that."

"When did they stop living together?" I asked.

He pondered for a moment before replying.

"It was not long after they bought the place in Italy. That was, what, about three years ago. The mistress found a villa outside Rome. Lovely it was, high in the hills with such a view... Anyway, she loved that place. Took to the country like a duck takes to water. The people, the food. After that she just stayed put. Mr Updike, his visits to her became fewer and fewer, and then they just stopped altogether. There was no quarrel, at least not that I saw. More like they just drifted away from each other. Then again, even servants don't know what goes on between a man and his wife, not even when they live under the same roof."

I picked up my pipe, thought the better of it, and set it down on the mantel. "Was there animosity between them?" I said.

"On her part, yes, there was, Mr Holmes. Women hold grudges, don't they? I didn't really know how much she hated him until she came swanning in the other day, and the man already in the ground. Couldn't be bothered to come back for the funeral, nor even to see him when he was unwell. Wicked woman!"

"Quite. I suppose you do not know anything about Mr Updike's will?"

"I do, in fact, Mr Holmes. I was with him when he signed it a few years back. Everything goes to the mistress with a small amount to myself and to Mr Slattery, that's Mr Updike's business partner. Oh, and he left a thousand pounds to charity, divided evenly between Doctor Barnardo's and the Ragged Schools. Loved children. Broke his heart that they were never blessed."

"The will has not been changed since then?"

"No, Mr Holmes. Mr Updike would have told me. Besides, the mistress made mention of it a few days ago and it was clear it was the same will I saw him sign."

"What did she say?"

"That she was giving ten pounds to each of the servants by way of a thank you for our service to the master. Then she called me into the study and said that Mr Updike had left me a hundred pounds in his will, which is what I knew he had left me. She said she would have given me a little more in honour of my long service, else. I will say she was generous enough.

Whatever quarrel she had with the master, she didn't hold it against the servants. Gave me time off, too. She knew how upset I was about the master's passing."

This last was a grudging acknowledgement.

"I suppose you have no theories of your own about what happened to Mr Updike, Mr Townsend?"

"I wish I did. I've thought on it long and hard. Mr Updike was a strong man. I mean robust. But he also had a remarkable mind. I would say you remind me of him, Mr Holmes."

He bit his lip and I could see there was something else to come. I waited.

After a moment, the man said, "I know something was worrying him. He wasn't the sort of man to worry as a rule. Even when his marriage fell apart, he never once got cross or made any complaint. But in those last few weeks before… before he was found, he was fretting about something."

"You have no idea what it was?"

"I asked him, Mr Holmes. One day as I was helping him dress, I observed that he seemed troubled. He said, 'If you knew the things I know, Townsend, you'd never get out of bed.' I was shocked and when he saw my face, he chuckled. 'There now,' he said, 'you need have no worries when men like Mr Mycroft Holmes and, dare I say, myself are toiling day and night for the protection of the realm.'"

"But he did not seem to be worried about anything specific?"

"He did say something odd one day. Mr Updike often liked to relax by building houses of cards. He had a knack for it; he had a good eye and the steadiest hands I've ever seen. One day he was placing a card on the sixth level as I came into the room. I stood still, so as not to disturb the game. He set the card in place and chuckled. Then he said, 'Watch this,

Townsend,' and he pulled out a card in the middle. The entire house collapsed.

"'You see,' he said, 'if you remove exactly the right card, the entire structure collapses.' I was confused and probably looked it. Mr Updike said, 'As with cards, so with governments. If you remove the right card, you can bring an entire nation to its knees.'"

"Thank you for your candour, Mr Townsend," I said as the man rose to leave. "You may be assured I shall continue to work on this case and do whatever is in my small powers to bring the culprit to justice."

"Thank you, Mr Holmes," he said. "That is all I ask."

"In the meantime, I would be obliged if you would keep your eyes and ears open. If you hear anything else about your master's last weeks, or his finances, or his wife, please contact me at once."

"You have my word," he said. He shook my hand, and left.

11

B invited Watson and me to dinner. I was surprised to find my brother was also a guest.

"Your wife wanted to celebrate the anniversary of your birth, brother dear," Mycroft said, shaking my hand. "I allowed her to persuade me to attend."

"Less for my sake than for Mme Chabon's culinary skills, I suspect," I said.

He patted his enormous abdomen with satisfaction and said, "It may have been a factor."

Good company, an excellent meal, and several extravagant gifts made for a perfectly delightful evening, marred only slightly by my persistent discomfort and by the case that continues to gnaw at me.

I told Mycroft of my conversation with Townsend. "Remove the right card?" he echoed. "That is odd."

"Presumably the Prime Minister," Watson said.

"Perhaps." Mycroft did not seem convinced. "Whatever he meant, it seems the risk to the government has not been removed."

"Not the Prime Minister," B said, "At least, not if the house of cards metaphor was accurate."

"Why not?" Watson asked.

"Because the Prime Minister is top of the government. Cards on top of a pyramid are not as vulnerable as the ones on the bottom."

Mycroft's eyes met mine and I read the same alarm there as I felt in my own heart.

Monday, 9th January

I spent the last few days in Wimpole Street and did not return to Baker Street until this morning. Mycroft has undertaken to examine any potential vulnerabilities in the government, and I have been pouring over Sir Christopher Carandini's notes. Thus far, nothing presents itself as far as finding the Sorcerer. The cases he documents are too diverse and too lacking in specifics. The anecdotal evidence is certainly suspicious, but there really is nothing to link them.

Lunch was an adequate if less than elegant meal than I have enjoyed these past few days. I ate in silence, playing the details of the two cases over in my mind. I dislike having to divide my focus, but it cannot be avoided at present.

I feel I have overlooked something, something of importance. It is exceedingly frustrating that I cannot remember it.

Watson's voice cut through my thoughts with a sudden, "I wonder…"

He broke off without finishing the sentence.

"You wonder?"

"Hm? Oh, I was thinking about the Sorcerer and our difficulties in finding him. I forgot to mention that I went to see Mme Bronski yesterday. I hoped if I told her we had learned his name, Angel Frankall, it might persuade her to share more information about him."

"And did it?"

"No. She would add nothing to what she has already told us. She is frightened, Holmes, and that troubles me.

"In any case, it got me thinking about other people who might be able to help and I wondered if our old friend Rabbi Steinmetz might know something. He seems wee versed in many esoteric subjects."

"It is certainly worth asking. Will you accompany me, Watson, or do you have other plans?"

"I am at your disposal, Holmes, but I was about to suggest that I go alone. You really are looking quite peaked. I do not like that cough you are developing. A day or two in bed would do you a world of good."

"I have hardly left bed the last few days."

His look was cryptic. "I meant rest… Well, I suppose a little fresh air and exercise cannot hurt, as long as you promise not to overdo things."

"You have my word. Let us be off as soon as you have finished your coffee."

The rabbi was delighted to see us. "Come in, my dear Mr Holmes. Doctor, how delightful it is to see you again. I was just saying to Miriam last night that it has been too long since we last saw our dear Mr Holmes and Doctor Watson. Sit, sit."

We sat in the rabbi's living room, a small space crammed with books. They jutted from the ceiling-to-floor bookcases, made piles around the floor and on the table, and almost obscured the windows. The old man studied my face intently. "You have been unwell, Mr Holmes. Forgive me, but you do not seem to have your usual robust energy."

"I had a small accident," I replied. "Recovery is taking longer than I should like."

"Because you will not rest or listen to your doctor," Watson said. "He really is a dreadful patient, Rabbi."

Rabbi Steinmetz chuckled. "There is no one as deaf as the man who will not listen."

His wife Miriam served us tea flavoured with black cherries. "How have you been, Rabbi?" Watson asked as we drank. "You look well."

"We are all well, praise be. You heard our friend Glaser's wonderful news?"

"No," Watson said, "We have not spoken to him for some time."

"He is to be a father. Such a blessing on his house. He is so excited he doesn't know what to do with himself. They're not married five minutes and Rivka is pregnant already. Such *simcha* – joy, that is.

"What of Constable Stevens?" Watson said. "Is he still here?"

"Alas, no. Our young friend has been recalled to Scotland Yard."

"A sad loss to this community," I said. "He and Glaser worked so well together. I know that Inspector Lestrade, indeed, most of the senior men at the Yard, have great expectations of that young man. I just hope they are giving him tasks that are worthy of his talents."

"He learned from the best," the rabbi said, smiling at me. "And he is an excellent student."

I could deny neither of these appraisals. "Yes, indeed," I said.

"How is our friend Lady Beatrice? Have you heard from her?" He said it with a certain glint of amusement, which I chose to ignore. No one outside my most intimate friends knows of our secret marriage. I sure the rabbi suspects, however.

"She is well. I shall pass on your regards.

"I am working on a most peculiar case, Rabbi," I continued. "I realise this is not exactly your area of expertise, but I wondered if you had ever heard of a man who calls himself Angel Frankall? He is also known as the Sorcerer."

116

"*Puh-puh!*" the rabbi said, shaking his head. "That is not a name I care to hear, Mr Holmes. Yes, I have heard of him, terrible things. I would caution you most earnestly to have nothing to do with him. Evil follows that man. Oy, it pains me to say such a thing about a fellow human being, but what can I do? He is wholly evil."

"That is very strong. Can you be more specific?"

The rabbi's wife came into the room and her husband said, "Miriam, would you be so kind as to send word to young Glaser that Mr Holmes is here? He would never forgive us if we let our friends leave without having a chance to wish them the compliments of the season."

Mrs Steinmetz needed no other hint. She nodded and left us alone.

"Forgive me, Mr Holmes," the rabbi said, "But this business would alarm her. Besides, Glaser can tell you more than I about this fellow. All I know are stories, appalling stories."

"What can you tell us, Rabbi?"

After a brief silence he said, "I dislike spreading gossip, but in this instance I think I am justified as I believe what I am about to tell you is the truth. Also, I am sure you are not asking out of idle curiosity."

"No, indeed. I suspect there may be lives at stake. You may be assured I will treat your information with the greatest respect and as much confidence as I can."

"Well, then," he said, "I will tell you what I know and you must decide how much weight to give it. I should preface my comments by saying at least part of this story comes to me second-hand, though the source is completely trustworthy and I have no doubt as to its veracity."

"I understand completely, Rabbi. Thank you. Please…"

"Very well. We used to have a member of our congregation who was fascinated by the so-called occult arts. I fear such things always have a draw upon a certain type of person. Chaim Horowitz was passionate about learning. He took such notes, beautiful. Everything he learned, he wrote down. What a mind he had. He was an outstanding Talmudic scholar and had a particular interest in the Kabbalah."

"Kabbalah?" I asked.

"It's a form of Jewish mysticism, isn't it?" Watson said, surprising me once more.

"You are correct, Doctor," the rabbi said, "That is exactly right. It is to Judaism what Gnosticism is to Christianity: an alternative, unorthodox viewpoint. Many of its practitioners see it as a form of mysticism, and it was this interest that ultimately led Horowitz to the Sorcerer. I cannot tell you how he learned of the man, only that he became convinced that the fellow possessed a secret power.

"From that time on, he was lost. He stopped attending services and studying the Torah. His entire focus was on the black arts as practised by this evil man. I began to hear whispers from members of the community about Chaim's activities.

"At length, I decided to pay him a visit to see if I could assist him in any way. He was a good man, Mr Holmes. He was kind and charitable, and his heart was as good as his brain. You can imagine how horrified I was to see what a terrible change had befallen him.

"He seemed full of rage and hate. He accused me of interference and banished me from his home. The next day, he disappeared. His wife, who had suffered this change in her beloved husband's temperament with admirable patience, was in anguish."

"What happened to him?" I asked.

"I do not know. He left his home that very day and we have not heard from him since. This was five years ago. It is a grievous thing for his family not to know what has befallen a loved one. If a man is dead, you can grieve, but when you have nothing but questions... It is a great burden. Perhaps I am unfair in condemning this fellow, this Sorcerer, but Horowitz was perfectly content and respectable until he came along."

"There is something you're not telling us, Rabbi," I said. "What is it?"

He sighed and took off his glasses, rubbed his eyes, and put the spectacles back on his nose. "I went to see him," he said.

"You went to see Horowitz?" Watson said.

"Not Horowitz. I went to see this fellow called the Sorcerer."

12

"What?" Watson and I cried together.

"Good heavens," Watson said, "that was a dangerous thing to do."

The old man took off his glasses and wiped them. "Perhaps," he said, "but I felt I had a responsibility to Chaim and his family. This man was the last person to see him, as far as we knew. I thought he might be able to help."

He gave me a look, self-mocking, distressed. I was alarmed by his air of disquiet.

"Do you know where I can find him, Rabbi?" I asked.

"I have only his old address. I will give it to you, certainly, but he moved shortly after my visit and I do not know where he went. Perhaps David can tell you more."

"Thank you. Forgive my interruption. Pray continue."

"I was shown into a library," the rabbi said. "You have never seen such luxury: the carpets, the furnishings. Everything was elegant and expensive. Civilized, you understand? Even the Queen does not live so well.

"While I waited, I examined the bookshelves. Plato, Spinoza, the Talmud; all the greatest minds in the world were there. Many of the titles were ancient Hebrew texts; others were in languages I could not even begin to guess, although I consider myself something of a scholar.

"I was so engrossed in examining the volumes that I did not hear him enter. He walked like a cat. Silent, stealthy. He is very tall and thin, with a face many would describe as sensual, even handsome. His lips are full and his eyes dark and brooding. The man was at pains to present himself as a gentleman. On the surface, everything was as you might expect." The rabbi dabbed his forehead with a handkerchief.

"And yet?"

"And yet I have never felt such evil. It oozed from him like a poison. He was loathsome, Mr Holmes, utterly loathsome. I give you my word, this is a man who has shed blood and found pleasure in doing so. A man who sees all human spirits as toys for his amusement. We have no concept of Satan in Judaism, but this fellow could make me believe he exists and that he walks among us as an English gentleman."

If any other man spoke to me in this manner, I should scoff. Yet the rabbi is one of the clearest thinkers and the most gentle of men I have ever met. To hear him describe Frankall in these terms was chilling.

"What happened?" Watson said. He was pale.

The rabbi said, "Nothing. We had a perfectly civilized conversation. There, that must disappoint you, but so it was. Perhaps you will think me a hysteric for my reaction."

"Not in the slightest," I said. "I have encountered evil. I believe in its existence, just as I believe in goodness."

"You are wise, Mr Holmes," he replied. "Frankall offered me coffee. I was glad to have the excuse of *kashrut* to refuse him. I should be most reluctant to eat or drink anything offered by that man. Incidentally, Miriam does not know I went to see him and I would prefer to keep it that way."

"I understand. You may trust to our discretion."

"I asked Mr Frankall about Horowitz. He replied that he not seen my friend in several weeks. Chaim had borrowed a rare book. It was of considerable worth, and had not been returned. Frankall claimed to have no idea that Horowitz had moved out of his family home."

"But you did not believe him."

The rabbi took a breath and said, "He struck me as a well-practiced liar. I should be loath to believe anything he said. I knew I would get no truthful answers from him so I left."

There was a knock at the door and he said, "Ah, that will be Glaser. I am sure he will have even more to tell you, Mr Holmes."

The tension in the room dissipated at Glaser's arrival. The policeman was obviously delighted to see us again.

"My dear Mr Holmes, Doctor," he said, shaking our hands vigorously. "What a wonderful surprise. How good it is to see you again. You both look... I trust you are not unwell, Mr Holmes?"

"I fell down a flight of stairs," I replied, "but there is no permanent damage. I understand congratulations are in order, Glaser," I said. "*Mazel tov!*"

"Thank you," he said, beaming. "I am so delighted, I cannot tell you. And Rivka is delighted, too. The only one who grumbles is my old friend Solberg."

"I thought you and he were the closest of friends," Watson said, ignoring my impatience at these social niceties. "What happened?"

"Oh, I exaggerate," Glaser said, chuckling. "Daniel is just having a little difficulty coming to terms with being a grandpapa. He is too young, he says. He doesn't mean it, of course. It's just a little play for our amusement. He is delighted, really."

Miriam brought in more tea and a cup for Glaser. "Rivka is well?" she asked. More domestic inanities.

"She is blooming like a summer rose," he replied. "And twice as beautiful."

"Ah, a man who loves his wife, now that is a blessing." She patted his shoulder then, with a dry look aimed at the rabbi said, "Men's talk, I know, I know, I'm leaving…"

"You need my help, Mr Holmes?" Glaser said, as soon as the door closed.

I reviewed the facts of the case from the beginning. I often find it helpful to relate the details to another person; the recapitulation helps clarify my thoughts.

Glaser and the rabbi sat in silence as I spoke, their expressions becoming increasingly anxious.

"Oh dear," the rabbi said, when I concluded. "That poor man and his family. We have heard of this Sorcerer fellow before, have we not, *Dav-eed*? I was just telling our friends about poor Chaim Horowitz."

"Horowitz, yes. That was a bad case. I looked into his disappearance, you know."

"What did you discover?" I said.

"A lot of hints, conjectures, and false leads. No one is willing to talk about this man, this Sorcerer. Just the name alone makes him alarming. I have been thinking about this: If a man gets a reputation for a certain thing, people will expect it whether the reputation is justified or not. If you believe a man is a liar you will doubt every word that falls from his mouth, even when he tells you the truth."

"And if you believe a man has supernatural talent, you will attribute magic to even the most banal events," I added.

"That is true," Watson said. "I have seen it with other members of my profession. A doctor gets the reputation of saving most of his patients, and he will have lines of sick people demanding to see him. On the other hand, if he has been unfortunate enough to have lost several patients over a short period of time, even if it had nothing whatever to do with

123

his talent or diligence, people will shun him, no matter how good he may be." He jerked his head towards me, "And if people believe you're the greatest consulting detective in the world..."

"Yes?" I said.

He smiled. "Well, you're the exception who proves the rule, Holmes. You made your reputation honestly, and you deserve every ounce of acclaim that comes your way."

This was generous, more than generous.

"Thank you, Watson," I said with some feeling. I was in danger of becoming maudlin, a sure sign that I was unwell. I brought the subject back to the disappearance of Horowitz.

"Tell me more about your investigation, Glaser."

"I am afraid it was fruitless." He reviewed the events, expanding on what the rabbi had already told us.

"The problem with Horowitz was he had too many brains. He was arrogant, too, thinking he knew far better than any other man about, well, anything, really.

"He was an outstanding scholar, not only in the Talmud, but he was fluent in several languages. In addition to half a dozen or so European tongues, he could read Russian, Arabic, and Aramaic.

"I believe it was this talent that made him interesting to Frankall. I went to see him," Glaser said. "Frankall."

"You knew where to find him?"

"Horowitz's wife knew. She's no fool, is Esther. She found out somehow."

"Could I meet her? Perhaps she may be able to further my investigation."

"I can take you to her, if you feel up to the walk," Glaser said. "I am sure she will be glad to tell you everything she knows. Even now, she is anxious to learn what became of her husband."

"Splendid," I said, and winced at the sudden sharp pain. "But I interrupted you. Pray, continue."

"I questioned Frankall about Horowitz. Although he downplayed his intimacy with our old friend, there was no doubt they were well acquainted. Eventually, I got him to admit that Horowitz had translated documents for him. Frankall tried to pass it off as a mere business matter, but I felt in my bones that he was lying. Of course, I had no proof of anything and he knew it.

"I questioned Frankall's neighbours, but few would talk to me. They were terrified of him and spoke of him in whispers, as if they feared he could hear them through the walls.

"One fellow told me when Frankall first moved into the house, he threw a party that went on until late in the night. A neighbour, a knight of the realm, in fact, went to Frankall and complained about the noise. The man fell down dead the following day."

"Coincidence."

"That is what I said, but apparently the incident was not isolated. Two other men died within hours of a conflict with Frankall."

"What were the medical findings?" Watson said. "Were the bodies examined for foul play?"

"Nothing untoward was found. Frankall has no police record. As far as I can tell, he's never even been questioned before, at least, not under that name."

Glaser fell silent and I sensed there was something else he was trying to put into words. After some moments, it came.

"Frankall defies description, at least for a simple man like me. On the one hand, he conveys a veneer of civility, but on the other, he exudes utter malice. No doubt you think me a fool."

"By no means," I said. "I, too, have met many of the most evil men in England and I recognise the sort of animus you describe. One of the worst was a blackmailer, a gentleman as far as the world was concerned, and yet he made my flesh crawl. You remember, Watson"?

"Milverton," Watson said, shuddering. "Impossible to forget the bounder."

"But you never discovered anything else about Horowitz's disappearance?" I said.

"Nothing. The trail ran cold and he simply vanished. The case still bothers me. His unfortunate wife is left to raise their three children alone and cannot even remarry."

"This is what comes of meddling in the so-called dark arts," I said.

"You never felt compelled to explore the esoteric, the philosophical, Mr Holmes?" the rabbi asked.

"Someone once said the proper study of Mankind is Man," I replied. "That is my first, best interest."

"Alexander Pope," the rabbi said. "'Know then thyself, presume not God to scan, the proper study of Mankind is Man.' It sounds wise enough, so far as it goes."

"You do not agree, Rabbi?" Watson said.

"Puh-puh," the rabbi said. "If I did not presume to study the Holy One, blessed be He, I'd be out of business." He winked. "I'd have to get a real job."

Hands shaken, farewells exchanged, we left with Glaser. He led us through the rabbit's warren of lanes and streets behind Hatton Garden. In deference to my health, he turned his usual gallop into a stroll.

At length we arrived at a squalid building. The dark, forbidding hallway reeked of porter and vomit and human excrement. Watson held a handkerchief to his mouth. I would have thought a physician would be used to the more unpleasant odours human beings manufacture.

We climbed the slippery and fetid stairs to the third floor. By the time we reached the landing, I was bathed in perspiration. I leaned on the rail and gasped for breath. When I recovered, Glaser led us down a dingy hallway. He knocked on the door. An emaciated woman answered.

"*Shalom*, Mrs Horowitz," Glaser said. "I apologise for surprising you like this, but I have brought Mr Sherlock Holmes to meet you. May we come in?"

"Mr Holmes?" she said. "Indeed, I am happy to make your acquaintance. Please, come. Sit down."

Despite the squalor of the building, the room was spotless. Threadbare, but spotless.

We sat on an uncomfortable sofa and the flustered woman tried to think of some form of hospitality to show us. "I don't have any tea…" she began, anxiously.

"We just had tea with Rabbi Steinmetz," Glaser said. "Please, sit down. How are you?"

"Oh, I get by," she said, belying her pale and gaunt appearance. At the table, two children aged about eight and nine were busy reading. A third, a girl aged about twelve, was practicing scales on a battered piano. A relic of better times, no doubt.

"I wanted Mr Holmes to hear about Chaim," Glaser said. "He might be able to help."

"After all this time?" she said. "Is that even possible?"

"If any man can find him, it is Mr Sherlock Holmes," Glaser said.

The woman still looked puzzled, as well she may. She might be in desperate straits, but she was not about to take me on face value. "I still do not understand," she said. "Why now? What have you heard about Chaim?"

"I came by your husband's case through another I am working on," I explained. "They seem to lead to the same place."

"The Sorcerer?" she said in a whisper. She glanced at her children but they seemed absorbed in their work.

"Quite so," I said, quietly. "It is possible that solving one puzzle may solve others. It would relieve your mind, I'm sure, to know what happened to your husband."

"It would be a relief... I think it would. I suppose it depends on what you discover."

"But you would want to know? That is, if I should learn that he is dead, or has set up another family somewhere... Forgive me, but I cannot presume to anticipate the outcome."

"I want to know the truth, no matter what it is." Her unblinking eyes met mine and I saw a remarkable strength.

"Excellent," I said. "Now, what can you tell me about your husband and his involvement with this creature called the Sorcerer?"

She told me the same story that I had heard from Glaser and the rabbi. Her husband was an intelligent man, a man of hubris, who had been utterly beguiled by the promises made by this fellow, Frankall.

"At first he was sceptical," the woman said. "He heard of this fellow from someone or other and was interested in seeing what truth there may be in the tales. He said he was expecting to be utterly disappointed. He left in high spirits. In many ways, that was the last time I saw my husband."

"The last time?" Watson said.

"The man who came home that evening was a different fellow entirely. He was quiet, secretive. He would tell me nothing of what he had seen; only that it had surprised him greatly. 'The universe has opened up for me, Esther," he said. 'I have seen things I would never have thought possible.' Not another word would he speak. The next night he went back to this Sorcerer, and the night after. Soon, he was neglecting his work, failing to come home. Long days passed and when he did return he was merely a shell of a man. Bills started to pile up; Chaim had no money to give me, he said, though he, himself, seemed to be eating very well."

She stopped and frowned. It seemed to me she was fighting back her understandable anger towards her husband.

After a moment, she recovered and continued, "I asked Chaim to tell me more about this Sorcerer, but he was as tight-mouthed as you please. I did pick up a few things, however…

"He had begun to talk in his sleep and, by the sounds of it, was haunted by terrible nightmares. He often woke up screaming. Once, he talked about being buried alive; another time a malevolent spirit was holding him prisoner. Terrible things, but not helpful, I'm sure."

"We cannot say what might be helpful at this stage, Mrs Horowitz. Anything you can tell me may be of great use. Who can say where it may lead us?"

"Sometimes he came home and his clothes were filthy. He was always such a neat and tidy man, but during the last week… There was, too, a pungent odour that clung to him, as if he had bathed in a foul-smelling tobacco. It made him cough and wheeze, but he refused to see a doctor.

"The last time I saw him we had a dreadful quarrel. He insisted on going back to his terrible new friend. 'The Master is awaiting me,' he said. The Master. As though my brilliant

Chaim was a servant who had to do this man's bidding. I tried to stop him but he struck me and screamed, 'I cannot stop now! You do not understand. I cannot stop!'"

At this, the woman's stoicism broke and she began to weep. "Perhaps if I'd been more understanding he would not have left," she sobbed.

"He was under the influence of an extremely powerful mind," I replied. "There is nothing you could have done that would have made him stay."

Later, as we walked through the serpentine streets back towards Hatton Garden, I asked Glaser what conclusion he had drawn from Mrs Horowitz's tale.

"I confess I am bewildered by it, Mr Holmes," he said. "The entire affair is upsetting to everyone who knew Chaim. It may sound harsh, but I hope he is dead. I would hate to think he is alive and well and deliberately leaving his family in such straits. The community helps that family as much as possible, and she cleans for a couple of families. It's a waste, because she has an exceptional mind. Not even Chaim was her equal."

Glaser left us with an invitation to join him and Rivkah for dinner after the holidays. Watson and I took a cab back to Baker Street. The steady rain had become sleet and all of London seemed as disconsolate as I felt.

"How much money did you give her?" I asked Watson.

"Not much, just a couple of guineas. Well, it is the season of goodwill."

"They do not celebrate the holiday, you know."

"No, but they do eat. Do you think he's alive, Holmes?"

"Horowitz? It's possible, but I think it unlikely."

As soon as we reached Baker Street I retired to my bed. I cannot remember when I last felt so wretched.

13

Tuesday, 10th January

I have developed pneumonia. Watson insists I stay in bed and, for once, I am in no mood to argue with him. Neither was I in the mood to listen to his sermons on the importance of rest and fluids. I sent him to Belgravia.

"Be careful and circumspect, Watson," I cautioned. "See what the neighbours can tell you about the man."

"The Sorcerer is long gone from there, Holmes. Surely there is no risk."

"He may yet have cronies in the district. I implore you, be exceedingly cautious."

"You can count on me," he said.

I fell asleep and it seemed only a matter of minutes passed before he was waking me up with a cup of tea.

"Watson? You are back already?"

"Already? I have been gone two hours. How do you feel?"

"Tired and uncomfortable."

"Well, you do insist on running around rather than letting your body heal. I am not surprised you developed pneumonia. You absolutely must take it easy for a time. I stopped by Whitehall to let your brother know about your condition. He says you must not worry about the Updike case and William Melville will look into it for now."

"Melville. Hmph,"

"Your brother seems to think highly of the man, Holmes, and he has accomplished extraordinary things. Without him, the Jubilee and the Walsall Plots could have had disastrous consequences. He's doing fine work with the Special Branch."

I sipped my tea and asked about his visit to Belgravia.

"His neighbours were most reluctant to speak of him. Even though he has not lived there for years, they are still in terror of him. The family who live at his old address had no idea where he's gone. 'He was not well liked, as far as I can tell, sir,' the current mistress of the house said. 'I doubt anyone could tell you where he went. Seems I heard that he went abroad, but I couldn't tell you who said it or if it was just speculation on their part.'"

"Damnation!" I moaned.

"I spoke to the tradesmen in the area. They knew nothing of the man himself, but said all the bills and so forth were handled by a man called Timms. He seems to be an unsavoury sort. 'Not a gentleman,' was how the local publican put it."

"You took pains, Watson. It is unfortunate you did not have better luck. Cheer up, my good fellow. It is not your fault. Not this time."

Someone knows who this creature is and where to find him. I have an idea how to lure him into the spotlight but it is dangerous. I must be certain before I ask B to take such a risk.

Saturday, 14th January

This morning, I received a letter from Sir Christopher Carandini. He wrote,

Dear Mr Holmes,

No doubt there are many others who are victims of this Sorcerer, however, I was able to find addresses for only a few. Over the years, files have been lost or mislaid. I fear my memory is not what it once was.

I believe all these people have been victims of that monster, though, of course, I cannot

guarantee that any of them will speak with you. I wish you every success.

Your servant,

C. L. Carandini

Attached to the letter was a list of five names and addresses, all in London. I gave it to Watson and sent him to meet with as many of these alleged victims as he could. As soon as he was gone, I lit my pipe. I coughed savagely, but at least I did not have to endure my friend's tutting.

When Watson returned a few hours later, I was sitting up drinking tea. "Did you have any difficulty?" I asked.

"Of the five names Sir Christopher gave us, two have changed address. One flatly refuses to acknowledge that the Sorcerer had anything to do with the death of his wife. A fourth was too frightened to speak."

"And the fifth?"

"Will join us at six o'clock this evening so you may question him yourself."

Promptly on the hour there was a knock on my door and Phineas Carton entered. His face was the burnished bronze of a man who has spent many years in the tropics. He wore the uniform of an army major, but even in civilian garb I would never have taken him for anything but a military officer. His bearing was impeccable. Though scarcely out of his thirties, his hair was threaded with silver. His features, unmistakably those of an English gentleman, suggested a man who had known great sorrow. I vow it took all of Watson's control not to snap to attention and salute, so commanding a figure the man made.

"Thank you for coming to see me, Major," I said.

"It is a pleasure to meet you, Mr Holmes," he replied, shaking my hand. "I am aware of your reputation, and I should be glad to help you in any way I can. The strange circumstances of my parents' deaths have disturbed me for many years."

"As the good doctor has told me. I should like to hear the details from your own lips. Please, make yourself comfortable and tell me the facts."

"I should begin by telling you that at the time these events occurred I was stationed in India. I can provide you nothing more than second-hand information.

"My dear father was a good man, well-liked, and always cheerful. It was often said that he had a talent for happiness, and that is true. It was, therefore, a profound shock when he died suddenly and, I was told, by his own hand."

"Indeed? What were you told about his death? Pray be as specific as possible."

"I received a letter from my poor mother. It was almost incoherent and stained with tears. She said my father had suddenly flung himself through his bedroom window and been impaled on the railings beneath. She was utterly baffled and horrified, as was I.

"Three weeks later, my beloved mother also died." He paused and took a breath. Watson poured a glass of brandy and handed it to him. The major drank a mouthful before continuing.

"Forgive me. Even after all these years, the memory is distressing."

"Of course," Watson said.

"Prior to his death, your father was in good health?" I said.

"Yes, indeed," the major said. "He and my godfather Peter Mountjoy had been planning a walking holiday in Scotland. They were to leave just a few days after… after Father died. Peter was devastated. He and my father had been friends for thirty years or more."

"And no one was in the bedroom with your father immediately before he died?"

"No one. Mother was finishing breakfast and the servants were busy with their chores."

"The servants were people of good character?"

"Impeccable. They had all been with us for many years. Besides, my father's bedroom door was locked from the inside."

"Am I to take it the window was closed?"

"Yes, he did not even open it. The police at the time said he must have hurled himself with great force in order to break through the glass and frame. Even then, he might have survived, but he landed upon the railings below…"

He paused and took another sip from his glass.

"What verdict from the coroner?"

"Suicide while the balance of his mind was disturbed." He leaned forward and said, "It is ridiculous, Mr Holmes. My father was cheerful, in good health, and had no worries. There was no reason he should take his own life."

"How long ago was this?"

"Eight years ago. April 24th, 1891."

"A black day," I said.

Watson said. "Yes, for all of us."

That was the day I faced Professor James Moriarty on the Reichenbach Falls.

"Tell us about your mother's death," I said.

The Major closed his eyes for a moment and I could see he was composing himself. The loss of one parent in mysterious circumstances is troubling enough; to lose both must be devastating.

"Mother went to meet Peter at the solicitor's office. They meant to challenge the will, but she never arrived.

"Her body washed up on the banks of the Thames five days later. An open verdict was returned. The officials believed she committed suicide because she was despondent about my father's death. It is a ludicrous notion. Why would she leave the house to go to the solicitor and decide en route to take her own life? It is preposterous."

"Indeed," I said. "Why did she intend to contest the will?"

"My father left me the house and an allowance of one thousand pounds a year."

"That seems generous," Watson said.

"My father was exceedingly wealthy. His annual income was in excess of forty-thousand pounds. In addition to our home in Belgravia, he owned a factory in Yorkshire and a cottage on the Isle of Wight." Carton's anger was unmistakable although he controlled it well.

"I was his only child," he continued. "My father told me often that I would inherit his entire estate, except for one or two smaller bequests to my godfather. That he should have reduced my inheritance so savagely without discussing it with me... He would not have done such a thing. Moreover, he left no provision for my mother. My beloved mother whom he adored."

"How extraordinary," Watson said.

"There had been no quarrel between you?"

"Not at all. We were on the best of terms."

"When had the will been changed?"

"A month before my father's death."

"That is curious. To whom did your father bequeath the remainder of his estate?"

"Everything else was left to a charitable institution that was unknown to me or my mother. It was called Brother Costello's Church of Spiritual Enlightenment."

"I have never heard of it. Watson?"

"No, nor I."

"Did you investigate it?" I asked the bewildered soldier.

"Not personally. I was, as I said, in India, a lowly captain. My colonel was sympathetic but we were in the middle of an uprising and he could not spare me. By the time I returned to England almost three months had passed. However, my godfather Peter undertook the investigation on my behalf." He hesitated.

"What is it, Major?" I asked. "You are among friends."

"Forgive me. I was just thinking that Peter actually planned to consult with you on the case, but that was not possible."

"No."

No, he could not, for I was even then making my way across the Alps towards Tibet and obscurity.

We fell silent, each of us shackled to the darkness by our thoughts. I roused myself and said, "I assume you contested the will yourself? What was the outcome?"

"Peter engaged a solicitor for me, but the judge found no reason to set aside my father's wishes. He seemed disinclined to hold against a church, no matter how obscure it may be. My father was in sound mind when the will was written."

"I see. Would your godfather know any more of the events of that time?"

"I sent him a note after Doctor Watson's visit. He would have accompanied me here but he had another engagement this evening that he could not break. He shall call upon you tomorrow, however."

"Thank you, Major Carton. I should like to question the staff who were present at your father's death."

"I am afraid I do not know where to find them, Mr Holmes. After my mother's death, and since I expected to be abroad for a long time, I shut up the house and dismissed the servants. Peter made the arrangements, so he may be able to tell you where to find them."

"Very well. Are you planning on staying in London for the moment?"

"Yes, I have been assigned to Aldershot but I do not take up my post for six weeks."

"Excellent. Be assured, if I can find any information about these peculiar events, I shall let you know."

He rose to leave and said, "Mr Holmes, do you believe either or both of my parents were murdered?"

"Would it shock you to learn that was the case? I do not say it is; only that I suspect it may be."

"Shock me? I would be shocked, yes, but I must admit it would be a relief to know they had not been in despair."

Sunday, 15th January

This morning about eleven o'clock Peter Mountjoy called upon us.

"Mr Sherlock Holmes?" said the man, looking first at Watson and then at me.

"Your servant, sir," I replied and shook his hand. "This is my friend and colleague, Doctor Watson."

"Of course," he said. "Your names are familiar to me."

"Ah," Watson said, "Do you read my stories?"

"Uh, no," he replied, "but I had a friend who served with the late James Barclay. He mentioned the work you did, Mr Holmes, in solving the mystery of the major's death."

Watson's chagrin was a delight to behold. I said nothing, of course.

"Ah, the 'Crooked Man' case," he said, in the misty tones he uses when his stories are mentioned.

"Uh, quite," I said. "Won't you sit down, Mr Mountjoy? It is very good of you to call upon us. I believe your godson told you we are looking into a case that may be connected with the deaths of his parents."

"If I can do anything to help you prove dear Lionel and Margaret did not take their own lives, you can count on me completely. What happened to them was appalling. First, Lionel's horrifying plunge onto the railings, then the peculiar drowning of his wife, and to cap it all, his son disinherited of his fortune. Outrageous."

"Thank you, Mr Mountjoy. Perhaps you would tell us as much as you can about those events and the days that led up to them?"

"There is not a lot to say," he replied. "It was all so ordinary, you see.

"Lionel and I had dinner on the Sunday and made plans for our holiday. We had arranged to go on a hiking tour of Scotland, and perhaps do a little climbing, too. It was something we often enjoyed. He was fit as a fiddle and in excellent spirits. Young Phineas was rising up the ranks of the Mallows and seemed on the path to greatness. In short, there was nothing troubling him, nothing to make me think his mind was disturbed."

"And yet two days later he flung himself through a window of his Chelsea home."

"He did. At least, that's what they tell me. But upon my word, Mr Holmes, Lionel simply would not do such a thing. He was in excellent spirits, good health, sound in body and mind. I vow someone must have pushed him."

"But weren't the door and the windows locked?" Watson said.

"Yes, that's true enough. But there is an error somewhere, there must be. I am a scientist, a chemist. I know that elements have specific properties. An acid will not suddenly behave like an alkali. People have properties, too. I've known Lionel Carton since I was a boy; not even his wife knew him better than I. The theory as it stands is impossible, therefore some element or other is incorrect. It would mean a great deal to me, Mr Holmes, if you would prove my friend did not take his own life. No, I am convinced he was murdered and likely Margaret, too. Someone wanted his fortune." He sank back in his seat, exhausted by this outburst.

"There was no note, I suppose?" Watson said.

I made a small pfft sound. "We would hardly be debating the likelihood of murder if there had been a note, Watson."

I wanted my pipe and the hunger for tobacco was making me cranky. Watson seemed unperturbed by my rebuke however. I continued to question our guest.

"Is there anything about the scene that you can tell me? Anything that seemed odd or out of place?"

"Other than the extraordinary method my friend apparently employed to end his life?" Mountjoy sank back into silence and remained that way for several minutes. I waited.

"There is only one thing that comes to mind," he said. "A letter had arrived in the post and the butler, Lang, had given it to Lionel just moments before the… incident. That was what Lang said, anyway."

"And what were the contents of the letter?"

"That is the thing. No one knows. It vanished. We all looked, but there was nothing in the room nor on the body. We do not know where the letter came from, or who sent it."

"And when the body landed…" I decided not to be graphic. "When he was discovered, who arrived first on the scene?"

"There was a small crowd. No London street is ever completely deserted, as you know, Mr Holmes. There were the usual gawkers. A man tried to give medical aid but nothing could be done. Margaret and the staff heard the crash and came rushing out of the house. One of the railings on which my friend landed punctured his lung and he died almost immediately."

"He did not speak?"

"He was beyond speech, I believe." Mountjoy stopped suddenly and seemed on the point of tears.

"Forgive me," he said, when he had regained his control. "Even after so many years, I still feel the loss most grievously. It is a bitter thing to lose a friend, particularly one who is closer than a brother. And to lose him in such a dreadful manner…"

"Yes," I said, awkwardly, "I am sure the sense of loss is immeasurable." I avoided meeting Watson's eyes.

"What can you tell us about Carton's will? I understand the contents were unexpected?"

"Ah, the will. Yes, you could call it unexpected. I call it damned peculiar.

"Lionel made a will in '89. There was that terrible influenza outbreak, if you recall, and my friend was stricken with it. He was lucky to survive. The experience made him think for the first time about his own mortality. Once he recovered, he had a will drawn up. I was his executor."

"There was nothing unusual about the bequests?"

"No, indeed, it was precisely as one would expect. He left his property and fortune to his son, and made ample provision for his wife. He left me a large sum, some artwork, and the contents of his cellar. We shared a fondness for wine."

"But this was not the will that was read after his death?"

"No, it was not. He left the house in Belgravia and secured a thousand pounds upon my godson Phineas, and nothing more. Margaret was not even mentioned. Everything else went to some church none of us had ever heard of."

"Brother Costello's Church of Spiritual Enlightenment."

"That's the one. It was damned peculiar. I beg your pardon."

"Your epithet is perfectly understandable," I replied. "I understand Mrs Carton intended to contest the will."

"Yes, she did. She gave instructions to the solicitor and was to meet with him a week later to see how things were proceeding. I was to join her at the office." Mountjoy leaned forward, his hands clasped before him, almost as if he were in prayer.

"You did not accompany her?" I said.

"I had business in the city that day and it was not convenient. Not convenient. I should be horse-whipped. Had I collected her as a gentleman ought, she might still be alive."

"I am sure her death is not your fault," Watson said.

"Please, continue," I said.

Mountjoy composed himself and said, "I arrived at the scheduled time but Margaret never arrived. It was most unlike her not to be punctual. After waiting for half an hour, I went to her home in Belgravia. I assumed she was unwell or there had been a crisis of some sort. However, the maid told me she had left in a cab an hour earlier. Five days later her body was pulled from the Thames. I was asked to identify her." He shuddered. "It was one of the most horrifying sights... the only small comfort I can find in the event is that it was I, and not her son, who undertook that loathsome task. Best Phineas remember her as she was."

"What were the coroner's findings?"

"Suicide. They said the cause of death was drowning."

"Yes, they could not be bothered to look too deeply into the matter."

"I would have consulted you, Mr Holmes," Mountjoy said, "but you were abroad at the time, I believe."

"Yes, I wish I had been in London and could have handled the case, Mr Mountjoy. You may be sure I shall look into it now."

"That is a comfort," Mountjoy said, "not only for my sake but for my godson's. I will be frank with you, gentlemen. I have never hated anyone in my life before. I was raised to believe it is wrong to hate, and yet I cannot help myself. I want exquisite vengeance upon the man who caused such misery for the people I love. I want him to suffer agonies. I do not even need to see it. It would be enough to know he lived in anguish. It is wrong of me, I know."

"Understandable," I said.

"Human nature," Watson added. "No one can blame you for feeling as you do."

"Thank you. You are very kind, both of you. Mr Holmes, tell me frankly, do you think my friends were murdered?"

"I do," I replied. "Someone wanted Carton's fortune. It is fortunate young Phineas Carton was in India or likely he would have faced the assassin, too."

"Good God," Mountjoy cried, "I had not thought of that."

"What did Mrs Carton's solicitor say about the revised will?"

"He knew nothing of it. It had been drawn up by a fellow called Gradgrind. Thomas Gradgrind. I remember because I thought how well-suited a name it was for the fellow."

"Well, I think we must call upon this man and see what he can tell us. What was the outcome of the court case?"

"The judge found there were no sufficient grounds to contest the will. Lionel was in sound mind and the document had been legally drawn up and signed. Once he saw the beneficiary was a church and not an individual, his mind was made up. He even suggested Lionel had been 'touched by God' – those were his very words – and it was greed that made the family contest it. Utterly preposterous."

"Quite. One last question, if you would, Mr Mountjoy, do you know what happened to your friend's staff? I would particularly like to speak to the valet who delivered that mysterious letter."

"I cannot recall at present, Mr Holmes, but I am sure I have the information in my records. I shall let you know as soon as possible. Yes, by Jove. Whatever you need to help young Phineas, you can count on me."

Monday, 16th January

Plagued by an endless cough, pain, and the frustration of my current cases, I could not rest. My mind ran the hurdles, sprinting from one obstacle to the next, leaping over some, and being knocked down by others.

I slept in brief, wretched snatches, like stones skipping over the ocean.

Something kept dragging me back to Ireland. Something I forgot or overlooked. In my mind I revisited the case, the villain who had managed to escape, the sneering hatred of McKenna. How could anyone hate so much? A whole lifetime spent in malice. Well, he would hang tomorrow and that would be that. He would carry his searing hatred to the grave.

A black slumber was followed by a miserable dawn. Around six o'clock, I fell into a deep sleep. I dreamed of Kells. The noose hung from the newly erected gallows outside the courthouse, and McKenna, more than half-corpse, ascended the steps. The rope around his neck, he screamed, as he had that day I unmasked him, *My curse is all you'll get from me. I'll see you suffer yet.*

I woke to an unsympathetic morning. Cold, trembling, I sat up on the side of the bed.

By this time tomorrow, McKenna would be in a pine box and all his hate and his thirst for vengeance as dead as himself. Exquisite vengeance, Mountjoy called it.

What was it he said? *I want exquisite vengeance… I do not even need to see it. It would be enough to know he lived in anguish.*

I ran into Watson's room and shook him awake.

"Good God, Holmes," he cried, "you look like the wrath of God."

"Hurry, my dear fellow. There is not an instant to lose. Hurry!"

Within half an hour, our cab careered through the early morning traffic.

"I am sure there is no cause for alarm, Holmes," Watson said. "Surely the danger to the Hardwickes has passed. In any case, I could have gone alone. It is much too soon for you to be out and about."

"But can we be sure the danger has passed? McKenna is due to hang tomorrow. If he still burns for vengeance, it is possible the Sorcerer will act now, at the last minute. I want to caution them to be on the highest alert."

We arrived. The door opened and I was startled to find myself faced with a police constable. I felt my entire world shrink into that moment.

"The boy?" I cried.

"No, Mr Holmes," Inspector Bradstreet said, joining us. "Mrs Hardwicke."

14

"Dear God, what happened?" I cried.

We were shown into the drawing room where a ruin of a man, Edgar Hardwicke, tried to rise from his seat to greet us. He seemed a full twenty years older than the last time I had seen him.

"She took her own life," he said. "Hanged. Oh God!" Hardwicke spoke as if English had become a foreign language, indeed, as if all speech were beyond his power. He collapsed suddenly and would have landed hard on the ground if I had not caught him.

Watson and I helped him to lie down on the settee. His colour was ghastly and he scarcely seemed to be breathing.

"Fetch me blankets and brandy," Watson ordered the policeman. He hurried to obey.

"What can I do?" I asked.

"Get that pillow and put it beneath his feet. I'll lay him flat. What a nuisance I did not bring my medical bag with me."

As my friend tended the widower, I spoke with Bradstreet.

"I should have come sooner," I said. "What happened, Inspector?"

"I arrived only a few minutes ago. I have seen the body and was just about to question the husband. You seem to know more about this matter than I."

Leaving Hardwicke in my friend's excellent care, Bradstreet and I went up to the bedroom of the doomed woman. Along the way, I briefly related the events of recent months that had brought Hardwicke to consult with me, his son's kidnapping, and my search for the Sorcerer.

"Thank you, Mr Holmes," Bradstreet said. "I daresay it would have taken me hours to piece all that together from the husband. According to the maid, the victim was in excellent

147

spirits this morning. She ate breakfast with her husband, and then came upstairs to get dressed. After a time, when she did not return, he went to investigate and found her. She's in here."

The body of Anna Hardwicke lay upon her bed. Her neck bore signs of the noose she had fashioned with a cord from the curtains. Her face bore that dark, almost black colouring of the asphyxia victim and her eyes were bloody from petechial haemorrhaging.

"With your permission, Inspector?" I said.

"Please."

He stood in the doorway and watched while I began my analysis.

"Yes," I said, examining the victim's neck. "There is no doubt this was self-administered. You can always tell by the angle of the ligature. She fashioned a noose out of that curtain cord. No less lethal than hemp."

I scanned the ceiling and the fixtures. The brass hook between the windows caught my eye. It had no real function; it was purely decorative. Presumably, a woman would hang a hat or a shawl upon it. Or, in Mrs Hardwicke's case, use it to hang herself.

"This hook is coming loose from the wall," I said. "This is where she attached the cord."

"You are quite correct, Mr Holmes. Her husband tried to free her, but could not do so. Life was already extinguished in any case. She was still hanging there when the first officer arrived a few moments later. He kept the scene intact and secured the room."

"Good. You are doing a much better job of training your constables these days, Inspector. I congratulate you."

Watson joined us a few moments later. I was still examining the body.

"She has a small cut on her right index finger," I observed. "Small but deep. Her mouth smells of sage. Everything else is unremarkable. Watson, do you concur?"

My friend conducted his own brief, but thorough examination. "Yes, indeed, Holmes," he said. "It would have taken her several minutes to die. She made a poor fist of the noose so it took her several minutes to strangle to death. If she had positioned the knot in order to snap the neck, death would have been instantaneous. I didn't notice the sage. Is it significant?"

I was already surveying the room. "She was in a state of panic," I said. "See where she pulled the curtain rope, fraying the fabric as she did so. There is violence in that action."

"Why hanging?" Watson said. "In my experience, women tend to take drugs. Some cut their wrists. Hanging, well, there are exceptions, of course, but it tends to be a man's method."

"Speed, Watson," I said, "She chose the quickest method. She was insane with terror."

Suicides can act impulsively, of course. Who can tell the thoughts of a man who steps off the roof of a building. Does he regret his decision the instant he begins to plummet to his death?

Mrs Hardwicke's death was impulsive. She forged her demise with items at hand. She cut her finger and did not even take time to apply a plaster. A droplet of blood congealed on her right index finger. A smear of blood stained the deadly cord.

The bedchamber was small and comfortable. The fire in the hearth gave welcome heat. It was bitterly cold outside. I examined the carpet, the dresser, and every part of the room.

The process took some time. I came last to the hearth, and here I knelt and raked through the ashes with the poker. I found the singed remnants of heavy blue paper and something else. A piece of coloured card.

"Ha!" I cried. "Bradstreet, ask your constable to summon the butler, if you please."

As we waited, the inspector said, "Did I miss anything?"

"I doubt your powers of observation have diminished."

His look was sceptical. "And my powers of deduction?"

"Ah, that is another matter."

"Tell me. It seems to me that the victim acted of her own volition. You seem to have drawn another conclusion."

"You suppose correctly, Inspector. I believe this is a case of cold, calculating murder."

"The maid says no one else came into the house," he persisted.

"You saw the blood on the woman's finger?"

"Yes, I made note of it."

"And what conclusion did you draw?"

"That she pricked her finger on something a few moments before she died."

"On what?"

"Excuse me?"

"You noted the blood on her finger. You surmise, quite correctly, that Mrs Hardwicke pricked her finger just moments before she died. But, observe: There is nothing sharp on her bedside table. It contains nothing but a Bible, a glass and pitcher of water, and a rabbit's foot, none of which have sharp edges. The victim's nail scissors and the edges of the furniture are clean. There is no blood on anything but her finger and the cord."

"It isn't much of an injury, Holmes," Watson said, examining the wound. "Hardly more than a pinprick. It did not bleed very much."

"But it did bleed. Between the time of the injury and her death, there could not have been more than a few minutes. She made no attempt to stem the bleeding."

We were interrupted by the arrival of the butler. A stately old gentleman by the name of Soames. His eyes were red-rimmed from tears. A measure of devotion; it takes a great deal to unsettle the English butler.

"When did you last speak to your mistress, Soames?" I said.

"A little over an hour ago, Mr Holmes."

"That is when you brought her a letter?"

"How in the world...?" he exclaimed. Then, recovering himself, "Yes, indeed, sir."

"Describe it, if you would."

"It was a pale blue envelope. Sealed."

This was not helpful. "Can you remember anything else? Any detail, no matter how small, may prove to be key. Did you notice the facing? Can you remember from which district it had been posted?"

"No..." His face brightened. "Now I think on it, there was no postal stamp; no address either. It simply had the mistress's name written in a florid hand. The ink was dark blue."

"Did you see the person who delivered it?"

"No, Mr Holmes, I found it on the mat this morning."

"Can you remember anything else? Did the envelope contain anything other than a letter? Something sharp, perhaps?"

His brow furrowed up to the scalp of his bald pate. "Why, however did you know that? I remember when I put it on the tray to deliver to the mistress, I noticed it seemed to contain something hard, like thorns or shavings of wood. Oh, and it felt like it contained a card rather than a letter. I do not think it could have been bad news, Mr Holmes. I heard the mistress laughing just a few moments later."

"Laughing?"

"Yes… Though, you know, there was something…" he laboured to find the word, "something rather hysterical about it. All the same, I thought nothing of it at the time. I was just pleased to hear Mrs Hardwicke in such good spirits, for so it seemed."

"What did your mistress have for breakfast, Soames?"

"Just a cup of tea. She does not usually eat until the master and the children have left."

"She consumed nothing containing sage?"

"Sage? No, indeed, sir."

"Excellent. Thank you, Soames, you have been enormously helpful."

As soon as the man left, I drew my pocket-knife and carefully scraped the surface of the dead woman's tongue. I saved the greenish coating in a small envelope. Next, I excised the tissue around the index finger.

Bradstreet cried, "What on earth—?"

"Have no fear, Inspector," I said. "I have left a sufficient amount of tissue for your surgeon to examine, if he has a mind. You will forgive me if I have more faith in my own chemistry, however."

"You expect poison?" the policeman said.

"I do not expect anything. One should never conduct an investigation with a preconceived notion. It makes for bad science and bad detection. I shall see what the microscope reveals."

"I am sorry, Mr Holmes, I fancy I am no stupider than any other man, but I still do not follow…"

"Consider, Bradstreet," I replied, "A woman – a superstitious woman – is sent a letter that contains a sharp object. She opens the envelope and pricks her thumb. What is the usual reaction in such a situation?"

Watson said, "She put her thumb in her mouth and sucked the wound."

"Precisely. That is what we all do, is it not? It is instinctive.

"All we know of this letter is that it was hand delivered. The lady laughs in what the butler describes as a hysterical manner when she reads it. She throws the letter into the fire."

"And whatever that sharp object was," Watson continued, "it was coated in some sort of drug. She sucked on it and it immediately entered her bloodstream."

"Precisely. The sublingual mucosa allows for rapid absorption. It is how nitroglycerin is administered, for instance."

"Nitroglycerin?" Bradstreet looked confused.

"Not the explosive, Inspector," Watson explained, "the medication that is used to treat heart complaints. We have been using it successfully for over a decade."

"Could not the poison, if there is poison, have entered her bloodstream from the cut?"

"Only if there were an extremely potent toxin, and in sufficient quantity," I replied. "However, as you observed, the wound was slight and only scratched the epidermis. Furthermore, if you examine the victim's mouth, you will see the tongue and palate are blistered and discoloured, suggesting a fast-acting poison."

"You said she was superstitious. How do you know...? Oh, the rabbit's foot."

"Precisely. Although it is only fair to point out that Doctor Watson and I have the advantage of having met the lady several weeks ago."

"You have a theory, Mr Holmes. I would like to hear it."

"Very well. I may be incorrect in one or two particulars, but this is what I suspect:

"Mrs Hardwicke scratched her finger on a sharp item in that envelope, perhaps a thorn as Soames suggests. Whatever it was, the fire has consumed it. However, from her symptoms and her behaviour immediately prior to her death, I suspect the item was laced with a potent hallucinogen. I have heard the Mazatec Indians in Mexico use a derivative of salvia for its hallucinogenic properties. Salvia is related to sage.

"The victim stabs her finger, places her finger in her mouth, sucks the wound, and the drug enters her bloodstream within seconds.

"If my supposition is correct, the drug forced her into a horror of her own mind. A horror so dreadful that immediately upon ingesting the drug, she took her own life. This is not suicide. It is murder. And here is the proof."

I showed him the scrap of coloured card I had rescued from the fire.

"I do not understand," Bradstreet said. "What is it?"

"Watson?" I said.

He stared at the card and blanched.

"It is the remnants of a tarot card. The Death card."

15

Tuesday, 17th January

For the rest of the day and well into the night, I studied slides, reviewed my books, and made notes. When Watson arose this morning, he frowned at my state and the state of our room.

"Oh, really, Holmes," he scolded. "How can any man think clearly when he has been up all night? And when you're supposed to be convalescing, too."

"I could not sleep," I said.

"Can you at least move these books? Mrs Hudson shall have nowhere to set down the breakfast things."

"Pah, breakfast," I muttered.

"Those of us who are not possessed of Herculean strength need to eat," Watson said. He really was in a most irritating mood. Mrs Hudson added to my woes a few moments later. She stood at the door with her laden tray and tutted at the small amount of clutter I had accumulated during the night.

"Really, Mr Holmes," she protested, "This is too much. How are civilised people meant to eat surrounded by such paraphernalia?"

"All essential, I assure you," I replied. "Oh do, please, be careful not to close the books. It took me all night to find those exact references."

Despite my protests, I was forced to stop working and join Watson at the table for a meal. I managed toast and a little herring, washed down with a cup of coffee.

"There, now," I said, "I must get back to work."

For all my efforts, however, I could determine little beyond confirming that there was a substance in the dead woman's mouth and it may be related to the salvia plant. I tried burning the scrapings and inhaling the vapour, but all I got for my trouble was an exacerbated cough and a headache.

By the time I finished my experiments and raised my head, I was surprised to find it was growing dark outside.

Watson was sitting by the fire, reading a book.

"You'll forgive me for saying so, old fellow," he said, "But you look wretched."

"Thank you," I said. Truthfully, I felt quite wretched. Too many hours hunched over the microscope and books made my back ache and my eyes burn. Though I was loath to admit it, I felt exceedingly weary.

Watson poured me a cup of coffee. "It should still be warm," he said.

It was. Barely. Nonetheless, I drank it almost in one gulp, and then poured another.

"Have a chocolate biscuit, Holmes," Watson said, offering me a tin. "You missed luncheon, but this should tide you over until dinner."

"You are worse than a mother," I protested, though I took the biscuit and ate it, then ate three more. "Or a wife. Speaking of such creatures, has there been any word from B?"

"Not since Thursday. She came to see you, but you were asleep and she did not want to wake you." He turned a page. "I suggested she might come to dinner tomorrow night."

With this happy news, I ate enough supper to satisfy my friend, and went to bed.

Wednesday, 18th January

I slept late. When I awoke, I wrote a report of my findings – lack of findings, I should say – and dispatched it to Bradstreet. No sooner had I sent it than I received a telegram from Ireland saying an unrepentant McKenna was hanged yesterday morning. I also received a letter from Peter Mountjoy. He has arranged for Lionel Carton's valet, a man with the appropriate name of Butler, to call upon me this evening.

This afternoon saw the arrival of two visitors. Not long after luncheon, my brother stopped in to inquire after my health.

"You are certainly looking peaked, Sherlock," he said. "And that cough is quite dreadful."

"It is not very pleasant," I agreed.

"Your brother would mend soon enough if he would take better care of himself, Mr Holmes," Watson said.

"I do not doubt it," Mycroft replied. "I cannot stay long, I'm afraid. I have a meeting in…" he glanced at his pocket watch, "twenty minutes. Still, I would be a poor brother if I did not, at least, pay you a quick visit when I was going by your door."

"How does William Melville get on with the Updike case?"

Mycroft rubbed his hands together before the fire. "Not very well, I fear," he said. "He has learned that Mrs Updike made no changes to the man's will. Not that she needed to; she inherited almost everything. Nor is there any evidence that she has given a sum to any other party in payment for her husband's murder."

"Then if the answer is not domestic or gain, it must be personal malice or politics."

"Precisely." He turned to face me, completely blocking the fire with his bulk. "And it is the latter which alarms me."

"But surely if there was a plot against the government it would have manifested itself before now? It is months since

Updike was found on the moor." Watson's point was well made.

"Politics can be a long game, Doctor," Mycroft replied. "I confess my initial thought is that his killers meant to infiltrate the anti-anarchy conference. However, that does not seem to have been the case."

"That may have been their original intent, but they were obstructed by Updike himself," I replied. "I do not believe he told his tormentors what they wanted to know. Despite whatever torture they subjected him to, whatever drugs they injected into his bloodstream, he kept his secrets."

"Yes..." Mycroft said, but was shaking his head in denial of the word.

"You do not agree, Mr Holmes?" Watson said.

"As I said, politics is a long game. I cannot be sure that these people have not obtained their information from some other source." He rose slowly. "I must be off, I am afraid. It will not do to keep the minister waiting."

"I will continue to look into Updike's case, Mycroft," I said. "Even if it transpires there is no risk to Queen and Country, the poor fellow deserves justice."

"Yes. When you are quite well, Sherlock. Melville is a good man. Thorough. He does not possess your gifts, of course, but he is methodical and takes pains. I shall let you know if he turns up anything of interest. Doctor, I trust you will look after my young brother?"

"Of course," Watson replied.

Mycroft had not been gone half an hour when another visitor arrived. Peter Huggins looked deeply distressed. For several minutes he sat in the chair before me without saying a word. Watson put a coffee cup in his hands and he drank without seeming to be aware that he did so.

"We are all shocked, deeply shocked, at Anna Hardwicke's death, Mr Holmes," he said. "Poor Edgar is beside himself. And those children… Oh, God, those poor children. I cannot understand it. I thought, we all thought the danger was passed. Forgive me. You are unwell. I should not be disturbing you…"

"Please do not apologise, Mr Huggins. I share your outrage and I shall do everything in my power to bring this killer to justice."

"You believe it was murder, then, and not suicide?"

"Most certainly. McKenna hired someone, first to terrorise the family, then to kidnap the boy, and, finally, to compel Mrs Hardwicke to take her own life."

"What can I do, Mr Holmes? How can I help?"

"We are looking for a man who is known as the Sorcerer. The only name I have for him is Angel Frankall, but that is almost certainly an alias. I suspect this man has caused other deaths. Unfortunately, he is such a figure of terror, no one will speak of him. There is one man, however, a Major Carton, whose father died in similar circumstances as Mrs Hardwicke. In this instance, the murder was one of gain. The dead man's estate was bequeathed to a church, 'Brother Costello's Church of Spiritual Enlightenment'. There was a solicitor involved; or, I should say, someone who claimed to be a solicitor. I should like to talk to this man, if I can find him."

"Who is he, Mr Holmes? Perhaps I can assist in the search."

"I would be much obliged for your help, Mr Huggins. The man's name is Thomas Gradgrind and the case was in April '91."

Huggins noted the name and the date. "I shall track him down, Mr Holmes. You can count on me." He rose to leave.

159

"I should not detain you when you are unwell. I hope you are taking care of yourself."

"I am being taken care of, at least," I said, smiling at Watson.

"He is a terrible patient," Watson added, "but I do my best."

He shook our hands and turned to leave. "Ah, Mr Huggins," I said, "one word of caution: this man Gradgrind very likely does not exist. The name is almost certainly an alias. However, if I am wrong and you do find him, please do not confront him yourself. If he is in league with this Sorcerer character he is an exceedingly dangerous individual."

"I understand. I shall do nothing without your approval. I shall be in touch. Good day to you, gentlemen."

After he left I went back to bed for a few hours, more to have the quiet to think, than to sleep. When Watson stuck his head around the door to check on me a short time later, I gave a convincing display of a sleeping man. Or so I thought.

"Do stop fretting and rest, Holmes," he said. "I shall wake you at five."

At that point I did fall asleep, but my mind continued to work and my sleep was disturbed and restless.

I dragged myself out of bed at five o'clock when Watson woke me. By the time Mr Aloysius Butler arrived to answer my questions about Carton, I was quite alert. The fellow added nothing to what we had already learned. Yes, Mr Carton was in good spirits. Yes, he was healthy, etc. The only significant detail was his confirmation that Carton had received an unstamped letter on the morning of his death. Butler thought there may have been twigs in the envelope. He did not know what became of it after his employer's death.

B arrived this evening, lively and full of cheer. She entertained us with an account of her dinner last week with the ironically named Mrs Vertue.

"I have heard that she is quite scandalous," Watson said, greatly amused. "Does your godmother know you keep such company?"

"I see no reason to mention it to her," B said, smiling back at my friend. "After all, I do not ask who her friends are."

I chuckled. "How true," I said.

"Mrs Vertue has buried, how many, three husbands?" Watson asked. "It is said she smokes cigars and attends the Moulin Rouge and other questionable establishments."

"All true," B said. "Emerald has what they call 'a past'. The stories do not do her justice, however. She was fond of all her husbands and I believe she misses each of them. She likes to say that the first made her respectable, the second made her a countess, and the third made her rich. She is delightful company and exceedingly philanthropic. More to the point, she makes me laugh. My visit was not entirely social, however. I had a particular reason for wanting to see her. For all Emerald's shocking behaviour, she is well liked and she knows everyone. She also has one peculiar trait that only her closest friends know about: she enjoys séances."

"Ah," I said. "Now we come to it. Does she know the man we are seeking?"

"No, and she most certainly would have told me if she did. She knows no fear. I intimated to her that I needed to find someone in particular, someone who was quite secretive. Emerald understands secrets. In any case, she is perfectly willing to help. She has offered to take me to one of her séances. We have a plan to draw the fellow out."

"A similar thought had crossed my mind," I said. "But I would be most reluctant to involve you in such a dangerous case."

"I am aware that this man is deadly, Sherlock. That is why we need to find him. I promise to do nothing without your consent, but will you at least consider it?"

Reluctantly, I said, "Yes. I shall."

Thursday, 19th January

Bradstreet stopped by this morning. "Our analysts say their findings are congruent with yours, Mr Holmes. In broad terms. They said I must tell you that. 'Only in the broadest terms.' It seems there is not enough of the chemical to be able to make any definite identification. I take it you believe the same man – and, perhaps, the same chemical – may be responsible for some of those other deaths you mentioned?"

I reviewed the details of the cases and showed the inspector the file that Sir Christopher had given me. Bradstreet is a very precise policeman and he has a talent for grasping nuance that many of his colleagues lack. This occasion was no different. He followed my reasoning along every step.

"I should like to meet this Sorcerer, Mr Holmes. There are a great many questions I should like to ask him."

"As would I, Inspector, but we have no location for him, nor can we even be sure of his name."

"I shall circulate the information we do have. A lot of these mystics end up in the nick at some time or other. One of my colleagues may know something."

"It's certainly worth trying, Inspector. You might also want to get a description from Glaser in Holborn. He has met this man, although it was a few years ago."

"You say saw him yourself, Mr Holmes?"

"In Ireland, yes. He was well muffled up, however, and he sprayed something into my face, so I only caught the briefest glimpse. Watson did not get a good look, either."

Saturday, 4th February

Peter Huggins called to see me just after breakfast. He has conducted an extensive search, but he is forced to conclude that Thomas Gradgrind, that elusive solicitor, does not exist.

"I feel a failure, Mr Holmes," he said. "I have let you down." I assured him I had expected nothing less. This was, apparently, a blunder and I was obliged to apologise.

People are so ridiculously sensitive.

This afternoon I had an unexpected visitor and all my theories have fallen to the wayside, leaving only one.

It was around two o'clock and I had just finished reading the newspapers when Mrs Hudson ushered Mr Townsend into my room.

"I hope you will forgive me for intruding, Mr Holmes," he said, "but there is something I wanted to give you. Mrs Updike has decided to sell the house and all the servants have been dismissed. In recognition of my service to her late husband, she said I could have anything I liked to remember him. I chose his chess set. He was a grand master and he taught me to play. Anyway, I asked the mistress if I could have one more thing.

"As I told you, Mr Updike liked to build houses of cards to help him relax. Recently, he used this deck. It is unlike anything I have ever seen before. I thought you might like to have it, and the mistress had no objection."

He handed me a small drawstring bag of black silk and I opened it curiously. A pack of cards fell into my hand.

Tarot cards.

16

"Watson," I cried, "This is the same deck, is it not?"

"Yes, indeed, Holmes," he said, shifting through it. "See, here is the Death card. It is an exact match."

Townsend stared at me with curiosity.

"Is this helpful, Mr Holmes?"

"It is perhaps the most important clue in the entire case. Well done, Mr Townsend. Well done, indeed."

His eyes glittered with unshed tears. "I am very glad to have been of help, Mr Holmes, though I cannot imagine how."

"These cards link to another case I have been handling. That is, I thought it was another case. Thanks to you, I can now see same man is behind both mysteries. Tell me, did Mr Updike have this deck long?"

"No, Mr Holmes. He brought them home about a month or so before... before he was found on the moor. He threw out his other cards – they were just a standard deck and getting old – and he used these, instead. They seemed to amuse him. I asked him where they had come from and he said they were a gift from the most dangerous man he had ever met. Those were his very words, 'The most dangerous man I have ever met.' I replied that if the man was so dangerous I wondered Mr Updike would accept a gift from him."

"And what reply did he make?"

"He laughed and said the best way to deal with any danger was to understand it. That is all he would say, Mr Holmes. It seemed such a trifling matter. Mr Updike did not seem alarmed in any way. If he had, I should have mentioned it sooner."

"I understand. Thank you, Townsend, you have been of inestimable service."

"Please let me know if there is anything else I can do, Mr Holmes."

Watson walked him to the door and said, "What shall you do for work now that Mrs Updike has discharged you?"

"I have excellent references. I shall find something, I am sure."

"If we can be of any assistance, please let us know."

After the faithful Townsend left, Watson and I called upon B. I told her what we had learned, and concluded, "This is no longer a matter of domestic malice; we now know the Sorcerer was behind Updike's confinement and torture. We must find him as soon as possible. You said you had a plan. What is it?"

"I told you about my friend Mrs Vertue and her familiarity with these mediums," B began. "Emerald will arrange for me to attend the séances with her. We will let it be known that I am trying to contact my father. I shall say I have been having dreams about Papa and believe that there is something he is trying to tell me. There is no real risk until I am actually granted an audience with this Sorcerer person, and then he must arrange a place for us to meet. Once we know that I can step aside and you can take over. It is a splendid plan, is it not, Sherlock?"

I hesitated. "Any number of people attend séances every week. I doubt many of them get to meet the Sorcerer. Do you mean to simply ask about him?"

"Not at all," B said. "I shall claim that my father spoke to me in a dream, but I will refuse to relate the details. I will say that only a true mystic will be able to explain the dream to me. Then, I will say I am willing to pay a great sum to the man who can reveal the truth. Eventually, someone must inform our Sorcerer friend."

I clapped my hands. "Why, it is positively Shakespearean," I said.

"Rather older than that," Watson replied. "If memory serves, the Pharaoh made a similar demand of Joseph, the fellow with the coat of many colours."

"It is a good plan," I admitted, "Alluring, and offers an excellent chance of success. All the same, I do not like exposing you to such risk."

"The risk is minimal, Sherlock."

I considered all the factors then said, "Very well, we shall follow your stratagem, but I have one condition."

"What is that?" She hugged my arm and I was temporarily distracted.

I managed to find my thought and my voice and said, "You cannot go alone. Mrs Vertue is, I am sure, an amusing companion, but you must have security. I shall see if Lestrade will let Stevens help. You can pass him off as a poor relation."

"That is a perfectly sound idea," she replied. "So long as Stevens does not object, then neither do I."

She was on sparkling form. Despite my fears, I found myself smiling.

Later this evening, I went to Whitehall to update Mycroft.

"You may go straight up, Mr Holmes," Gillespie said. "He's just catching up on his paperwork. I expect he'll be glad to take a break about now. I'll bring up a pot of coffee."

"You seem much improved, brother dear," Mycroft said. "I am very pleased to see you. Ah, you have news, I see. About Updike?"

"Yes, Updike. Mycroft, you recall that other case I was working, the friend of Peter Huggins' who was being threatened by someone called the Sorcerer?"

"Yes. I saw the obituary for that poor woman. Nasty business."

"The two cases are linked. The man who killed Anna Hardwicke and Lionel Carton and who knows how many others also kidnapped and tortured Augustus Updike."

It takes a great deal to surprise Mycroft. I had, at least, the satisfaction of seeing the look of utter astonishment on his face.

"Good heavens," he gasped. "Are you quite sure?"

"Positive." I showed him the cards Townsend had brought to me. "These are identical to those used to terrify the Hardwickes. Townsend tells me this deck was given to Updike about a month before his journey to the moor. What is more, Updike said the cards were a gift from the most dangerous man he had ever known."

"Why didn't the man tell you this in the first place? It might have saved you weeks."

"I cannot blame Townsend. The matter slipped his mind, probably because Updike himself seemed so unconcerned. Besides, when I questioned him, he was greatly preoccupied with his employer's health."

"Well, that's fair enough, I suppose. Updike met any number of dangerous people over the years. He probably felt he was equal to this villain."

"Undoubtedly so, since he apparently accompanied this man to Devonshire."

"So Updike's kidnapper is responsible for other deaths; a man without a conscience. Who knows what havoc he might wreak? I need hardly impress upon you the importance of finding him."

167

There was a knock at the door and Gillespie came in carrying a tray of coffee and sandwiches. "Just a little something to tide you over, gentlemen," he said.

I drank the coffee and Mycroft ate the sandwiches. For several minutes we were silent, thinking.

"You said Updike was involved with the conference in Rome?"

"Yes, he was supposed to be my main adviser on that topic. I misspoke. He *was* my main adviser. He gave me dozens of well-researched papers on the politics of each country and recommendations for dealing with them. I had intended him to accompany our officials to the conference and make recommendations."

"And then he was to return to the Continent?"

"No, I planned to transfer him back to England."

"Mycroft?"

My brother finished his cheese sandwich before saying, in frustration, "I cannot live forever, Sherlock. That business with my leg during the summer really alarmed me. I need a successor, someone who can take over when I must stop."

"And Updike was to be that man?"

"Yes. He was the perfect candidate. Above reproach, an exceptional mind, and possessed of a fine grasp of the political landscape throughout Europe. He was exceedingly well versed on foreign matters, and needed only an equal grasp of the domestic. He'd have accomplished that in a matter of months."

"I thought you depended upon Quackenbush for domestic issues?"

He finished the sandwich and bit into a biscuit which showered him with crumbs. He idly flicked them off his coat.

"Quackenbush is a good man in his way. I can trust him with the mail and other such minutia, but he lacks imagination. He cannot see British affairs in a global context. A man in my position has to consider the whole world's stage, not just our corner of it."

I studied him. The lines of care etched deeply into his face, the fatigue that smudged his eyes.

"Mycroft... Are you ill?"

He brushed the crumbs from his coat before replying, "No. No, Sherlock there is no need to worry. I am in reasonably good health. But I am tired. I had hoped that if I began preparing Updike now, in about five years he could take over the reins completely. In the meantime, I could slow down a little. Well, 'man proposes, God disposes,' is that not what they say? In any case, our priority right now is finding this Sorcerer who has taken the life of an excellent man. How shall you proceed, Sherlock? Do you have a plan?"

"I have a plan, but it is dangerous."

"I need hardly tell you what is at stake."

"No, indeed. If the risk were mine alone I should take it without demur. However, it is not my risk, but B's."

Mycroft said, "That is the second time you have surprised me today, Sherlock. I am not sanguine about letting your wife, capable though she may be, get involved. You saw what this brute did to Updike. From what you tell me, the fellow has no qualms about murdering women."

"Do you think I don't know that?"

"Why let her do it at all? What is the plan? Perhaps we can find an alternative."

"The plan is B's own. She has a friend, Mrs Vertue—"

"I know Mrs Vertue."

"—who likes to attend séances. She has offered to let B accompany her. They will make it known that B will pay handsomely if any medium can help her contact her late father."

Mycroft licked his finger and dabbed up the last of the crumbs from the plate. "Why do you not do this yourself, Sherlock?"

"It is possible the Sorcerer may attend one of these séances. He knows what I look like. I doubt I could fool him for more than a few moments, even in disguise. The man studies people for a living. I must assume his gifts are almost equal to my own.

"B is known to be a wealthy woman. It is common knowledge that she lost her father a few years ago. Watson tells me it is women who are most likely to attend these séances... I do not like it, Mycroft, but as you say, finding this man is vital, even though it is so very dangerous."

17

Monday, 6ᵗʰ February

It has taken a little longer than I had expected, but our plans are now in place.

B insists she is up to the task. She was cross only at my use of the word, 'let'.

"There is no 'letting' me do this, Sherlock," she said with asperity. "Our contract makes it clear that I may act in whatever manner I choose."

"We made that contract when we were little more than strangers," I said. "However, I cannot refute your argument. Perhaps I used the wrong word. I am constrained to point out, however, that I would not phrase it any differently, nor have any fewer qualms if it were Watson who took this risk rather than you."

"Well… in that case I accept your apology."

"I did not apologise."

"You meant to."

We laughed like children and it was some time before we got our foolishness under control. For my part, I believe it had as much to do with anxiety as amusement.

Tuesday, 7ᵗʰ February

Mrs Vertue likes to shock. Every aspect of her being has been carefully manufactured, from the top of her artificially blonde head to the stainless fingers with which she smokes thin cheroots.

Her desire for attention would be irritating were she not so engaging. She has, besides, a vulnerability that is revealed only in glimpses. It is in the simple Claddagh ring she wears on her right middle finger, in the softness of her features when

171

she speaks of her home in County Clare, and in the genuine affection she has for my wife.

She greeted us in her drawing room wearing a dark green satin gown and an extravagant emerald necklace. A rather elaborate ensemble for a mid-afternoon visit, but B tells me Mrs Vertue dresses like this all the time.

B made the introductions. Her friend shook my hand in a forthright way and coolly appraised us. Watson was obviously beguiled and gazed at her in a rather idiotic manner.

"Thank you, for your assistance, Mrs Vertue," I began, "We are extremely grateful."

"Oh, tut," she said, with a dismissive wave of her hand, "What's life without a little excitement, eh? Amn't I delighted to help the great Sherlock Holmes?"

She linked her arm through Watson's and led him to the sofa. She sat beside him, rather more closely than was strictly necessary, and said, "Tell me, handsome, how is it that in all these stories of yours you've never mentioned what a fine-looking man you are?"

I guffawed and the woman laughed, too.

"Em, please stop teasing John," B said.

"Who's teasing?" the woman replied. "I know a woman's man when I see one."

B flopped down on the armchair and said, "You wouldn't want me to tell him your real name would you? Em." The last syllable fell with an emphasis. B smiled dangerously at her friend.

Mrs Vertue chortled and released Watson from her grasp. She moved down the sofa by several inches and sat with an expression that was supposed to be demure. I contained my amusement with considerable difficulty.

"I am sure the good doctor knows I am just having a little fun," she said. "But I know you are here on serious business so I shall behave. That is, I'll try."

I began by saying, "You should know, Mrs Vertue, that I have some reservations about involving you and Beatrice in this matter. The man we are seeking has killed several times in the past. He will not hesitate to kill again. Your charms and your sex will not protect you."

"Well, that's disappointing," she said, winking. "And it's Emerald, love. My friends call me Emerald, or Em." She said this while making a face at B. It was pleasing to see the easy friendship between the two women. Not for the first time I was struck by my wife's ability to fit in to any society. She can converse as easily with street urchins as with the Queen. It is an extraordinary gift.

"We thought we would begin with Mrs Croyer," Mrs Vertue said. "You are probably familiar with her, Doctor?"

"I have never met her, but I am familiar with her reputation. She is popular with the gullible set," he added to me. "Serious inquirers avoid her."

"Which makes her perfect for our purposes," B said.

"'Tis my understanding you'll be wanting someone greedy and unscrupulous," Mrs Vertue added. "Mrs Croyer fits the bill on both counts. She'll try to wheedle as much information out of B as she can. She'll say she wants at least a couple of sessions for the séance to work."

"Emerald has told me what to expect," B added. "Em, perhaps you could show Sherlock and John the room where the séance will take place."

"Very well."

The woman rose and sashayed into a small parlour in the front of the house that could comfortably seat a dozen people.

The room contained no furniture other than a round table and a dozen chairs.

"As you see, there is nowhere anyone can hide," Emerald said. "You have to keep an eye on these little devils. You wouldn't believe the mischief I've seen."

"Do you think you can persuade this spiritualist to come to your home, Mrs... ah, Emerald?" Watson said. "Most of them prefer to control the environment and so have their clients come to their own homes."

"I don't mind going out to them," she replied. "Half the fun is seeing how they try to fool you. But I know this is a serious matter and I would never put my friend at risk. It's safer here where we can keep an eye on things."

"I really wish everyone would stop treating me like priceless crystal," B said. "You are no less at risk than I, Emerald. But I do agree that having Mrs Croyer come here is a wise idea."

"Have you been able to confirm a date yet?" I asked.

"It cannot be any earlier than Saturday the twenty-fifth, I'm afraid," Emerald said. "For all Mrs Croyer is an obvious fraud, she is popular and her schedule is full. If I had been a stranger or not so well off, we probably would not have seen her until April."

"I dislike having to wait so long," I said, "But I would not presume to tell you your business. What can you tell me about your other guests?"

She listed them, counting on her fingers. "There's Beatrice and me, of course. Then B's friend Stevens if she can get him. Also Mr and Mrs Davenport."

"Ah, that is good," I said. "I am glad you shall have so many trustworthy people around you, B. The Davenports are dependable and I know they are devoted to you."

"Of course they are," Emerald said. "Haven't they known her since she was a wee lass? Have you spoken to them, Trixie? Will they come?"

"Don't call me Trixie," B said, in a tired voice that suggested she had said this many times before. "Yes, I saw them yesterday. They are eager to participate. Sherlock, have you spoken to Stevens?"

"I have, and he is willing to help. However, Lestrade is on holiday until tomorrow, and we need his approval. I am sure he will agree."

"So that makes five," Watson said. "Beatrice and Emerald; Stevens and the Davenports. Then there's Mrs Croyer. Six. Anyone else?"

"Mrs Croyer has an assistant called Ryan. He will attend, too," added Mrs Vertue. "I may have one or two of her old familiars here, too, just so she will not be suspicious. There will certainly be no more than ten."

B said, "As you see, Sherlock, I am in excellent company. Safe as houses."

I did not say that I have seen houses crumble.

18

Wednesday, 8ᵗʰ February

I encountered Bradstreet as I stepped out onto Baker Street this morning.

"I was just on my way to see you, Mr Holmes," he said. "I wanted to know if you had any new information for me."

As we made our way to Scotland Yard in his car, I brought him up to date on the recent developments and my plan – or, rather, B's plan – to lure out the Sorcerer.

"That is a devilishly dangerous thing to ask a woman to do," he said.

"I know, Bradstreet, I know. She will have as much protection as I can give her. All she has to do is attend and play the part of the grieving daughter. She has more wit than most men, and I trust her. I mean to ask Lestrade if he will allow Stevens to accompany her. I have a lot of faith in that young man."

"If you can persuade Lestrade to release him. Quite the golden-haired lad, is young Stevens. Bright, tenacious, and hard-working. You mark my words, Mr Holmes, we shall all be working for him in ten years or so."

"I would not doubt it," I replied. "He struck me right from the beginning as a man with great potential. I wish he had not entered the police force. I fear all your rules and regulations will stifle him."

"The force is changing, Mr Holmes. We need men like Stevens to bring us into the next century."

I found Lestrade in no happy mood. The cup of cold coffee and the fact that he had forgotten to take his hat off suggested his morning had not been a pleasant one. We sat in his cramped office and he heard my request in silence.

"Of course you do not want the young lady to come to harm, Mr Holmes," he replied, "but Constable Stevens has work of his own, you know."

"I understand that, Lestrade. I would not ask, only... this is Lady Beatrice. The Queen's goddaughter. I should hate to see her to come to harm, especially if we could prevent it. Questions would be asked."

"I do not keep young constables sitting around waiting for Sherlock Holmes, you know," he said. "Why does it have to be Stevens? Maybe I could give you one of the new recruits. If it comes to that, why do you not escort the lady yourself?"

"This fellow, Frankall, has seen Watson and me. Her Ladyship knows Stevens, she trusts him and he is devoted to her. I do not make the request lightly, Lestrade."

He played with the papers on his desk, not wanting to concede too quickly. Then he sighed and said, "For how long?"

"A couple of weeks should suffice. Certainly no more than a month."

"A month! Oh, come, Mr Holmes, it is one thing to let you have the man for couple of hours, but weeks?"

"The Queen's goddaughter," I repeated. "I need you to trust me, Lestrade. This case has serious implications for a lot of important people."

"It is Bradstreet's case, is it not?"

"There are several cases linked together here; Bradstreet has one strand, but there are many others. If we bring this off successfully, there will be credit enough to go around, and you have my word that you shall receive your share." I leaned forward and said, softly, "This could be a matter of international importance, Lestrade."

His tired eyes met mine and read my urgency. He called out the door, "Stevens, Mr Holmes has need of you."

After I left Scotland Yard, I went to Camden Town to visit old Gillespie's daughter.

Alice Prentiss shook my hand and brought me into her small study. "How good it is to see you, Mr Holmes. Bessie, please bring us some coffee."

Bessie bobbed in an adequate curtsey and hurried away.

"She is such a delightful girl," my hostess said, "Always cheerful and hardworking. I thank God every day that Doctor Watson brought her to us. We were in such despair last summer and Bessie helped restore our tranquillity, as did you, dear Mr Holmes. But I am sure it is not my domestic matters that have brought you here today."

"I wondered if you might be interested in a little intrigue. Nothing dangerous, just keeping watch on a neighbour and possibly passing on an occasional message. I will compensate you for your trouble."

"I am sure I need no compensation to help you, Mr Holmes. Tell me what you need."

Saturday, 18ᵗʰ February

An excited telephone call from B asking if I've heard that Émile Loubet has been named the new French president. I cannot remember when I last heard her so elated.

"After all our worries last year about Dreyfus and the trouble that ensued as a result, it is a relief to know there is a good and sympathetic man now ruling France," she said. "I wrote to Zola as soon as I heard. He must be delighted."

"I have no doubt," I said. "Although from my brief acquaintance with the man, I should not be surprised if he found some other reason for quarrel."

"Oh, that is hardly fair. He is just passionate about justice, as are you."

I took a deep breath and released it slowly. "You offered him assistance," I said.

"Of course."

"B, you cannot... That is to say, we have other priorities at present. I understand your concern, but we must focus on finding the Sorcerer. Mycroft is keeping close watch on the Dreyfus affair. I promised we would keep out of it."

"You promised for me?" I did not like the ice in her voice.

"No, I promised for myself. However, I have no doubt Mycroft inferred my vow covered you, too. B, I do not wish to quarrel with you over this. Return to France, march in the streets if you must, just wait until we resolve this matter with the Sorcerer."

A long pause. The telephone line crackled and I wondered if we had been disconnected. Then B's voice came back and she said, "I understand, and I shall do as you wish. I doubt there is much I could do for Dreyfus at present, in any case. I must go. I shall see you tomorrow."

Saturday, 25th February

My wife would brook no suggestions as she prepared herself for this evening's events. "I know what I am doing, Sherlock," she said, a bit sharply. I was dispatched to entertain Watson and Stevens in the living room below. It still feels strange to play host in her home. She scolds me for calling the Wimpole Street house 'hers', and yet I observe she calls 221B Baker Street mine. These are the delicate negotiations that make possible a marriage such as ours.

179

Stevens seems to have matured by five years and grown a foot since he became a policeman. He seems awed by the faith Lestrade has in him.

"Lestrade has any number of failings," I said, "but he is not a fool. He is clever enough to recognise your talent, in any case."

"He has been very good to me." Stevens hesitated and then added, "I must admit, though, I miss Inspector Glaser and my friends in Hatton Garden. I learned ever so much there. The inspector is one of the finest men I have ever met – present company excepted, of course."

"I think you are less stretched in your current role," Watson said.

"Lestrade is a good man, to be sure," I said, "but not an imaginative one. Perhaps you have started to realise the limitations of being a policeman?"

Stevens shuffled a little, caught between the truth and loyalty. "There is plenty of the mundane in the job, that is true, but I am only a junior officer. I hope to become a detective."

"Even as a detective, you will have to take the cases that fall to you. Trivialities."

"Come, Holmes," Watson said, "even trivial cases, as you call them, demand resolution and justice."

"No, I understand what Mr Holmes is saying, Doctor. I confess, I did not think of such things before. Being a policeman is what I longed to do, but there is a great deal of harshness in how the men are treated. Other men, I mean. One thing I will say for Inspector Lestrade, he is a gentleman."

"The suicide rate among policemen is alarming," Watson said. "Holmes, I do wish you'd stop pacing. There really is nothing to worry about, you know. Ah, here is Beatrice."

I turned at her footstep. While I floundered in silence, Watson stepped forward and kissed her cheek. He said, "How splendid you look, Beatrice."

"Very elegant indeed, your ladyship," Stevens said.

"You must remember to call me 'cousin Beatrice' this evening, Stevens, and I shall call you Maurice. Sherlock? Will I do?"

"You are magnificent," I said.

She wore dark red silk. A perfect colour against the cream of her skin and the sparks of copper in her dark hair. A diamond tiara decorated her coiffure, and a diamond and ruby necklace hung around her neck. Sometimes I forget my wife is one of the wealthiest and most beautiful women in the country.

No. I confess it here: I do not forget the latter.

"My mother's jewels," she said. "I do not wear them very often, just for special occasions. They seemed just the thing to dazzle a greedy 'medium'. Do you not agree?"

"I do, absolutely. They also serve as a nice contrast between your wealth and Stevens' want."

Stevens was wearing an old suit of obviously inferior quality. The studs in his cuffs were brass and his shoes were considerably past their prime. He released an elaborate sigh. "'Twas ever thus," he said.

B and Watson laughed, yet the tension did not lift from my spine.

"Time for a glass of sherry before we go," B said. "Sherlock, John, you will stay here until we return?"

"As we agreed," I said, filling her glass. "You are ready? You know what to expect?"

"Yes, my dear Sherlock. I really do not anticipate any difficulty, but I am prepared for whatever the evening brings.

Stevens – Maurice, I should say – will look after me, and I have Emerald and the Davenports at hand, too. I am surrounded by friends."

"Not to worry, Mr Holmes," Stevens said. "I shall take good care of her ladyship."

"I have not the slightest doubt of that. I just hope you will both be careful and take no unnecessary risks."

"You have my word. We know our parts and shall carry them off to the best of our ability."

I found myself exceedingly restless after they left. Sitting idle is not a thing I do well, not in the middle of a case, at least.

Watson said, "This first outing is nothing more than tempting Mrs Croyer with your wife's riches. Beatrice is perfectly safe."

He swirled the sherry in his glass and said, softly, "What is it that really worries you, old fellow?"

"This whole business of séances and delving into the supernatural is anathema to any rational mind," I said. "I cannot understand anyone who can be duped by such obvious trickery."

For a moment he said nothing. When he did reply, his voice was even. "The trickery is not always obvious. I know you will not agree, but I believe one or two of these mediums have an uncanny gift. Mme Bronski, for instance. Besides, I think you're rather missing the point."

I stared at him, dumbfounded. "I am? *I* am missing the point?"

"Grief, Holmes. I do not think you comprehend what a terrible power it has. When people lose someone they love, they try to fill the void any way they can. Many choose religion. They hope in the life to come and the mercy of God. But others long to hear that familiar voice… Perhaps in some part of our mind we know or suspect trickery, but the longing to believe that we are making true contact with a lost loved one is potent."

We fell silent again. The room was softly lit and the fire burned brightly in the hearth. It seemed the ideal setting for ghost stories. I roused myself and said, "What did she tell you? Mme Bronski, I mean?"

"She told me... She told me to get on with my life. She said Mary was at peace and I should not disturb her rest."

"Did she speak of me?"

"She said she could not reach you and there were mysteries that surrounded you that she could not penetrate."

"A typical response from a fraudster."

"On the contrary, Holmes, a fraudster would have made up some glib lie."

Again, silence.

I was too distracted to engage in any discussion. There was, vexingly, nothing to do but wait. And so, in silence, we waited.

By ten o'clock, I had convinced myself that something dreadful had happened. By eleven, I was ready to go to Belgravia and see for myself. I had just decided to set out when I was forestalled by the sound of a carriage. Moments later, my wife and Stevens arrived in a thoroughly disgusting state of high spirits.

There was an age, admittedly probably no more than a few minutes, where coats were removed, brandy poured, and the servants dismissed, before the two would sit and speak of their adventures.

"Oh, what a splendid night I've had, Sherlock," B exclaimed. Truly, the woman has no regard at all for my feelings. "I have never met a more charming or ridiculous charlatan in my life."

"Lady Beatrice was on splendid form, Mr Holmes," Stevens gushed. "Oh, when Mrs Croyer made those bird sounds—"

"Oh, oh," B cried, weeping with laughter. "And when she said her spirit guide was a former American president—"

"And you asked why he didn't have better things to do than help Mrs Davenport find her missing cockatoo. And then – Oh, Mr Holmes, it was magnificent! – then Lady Beatrice said, 'How the mighty have fallen.' I declare it was all I could do not to howl with laughter."

"You managed to control yourselves, I hope," I said, coldly.

"Of course," Stevens said. He tried to contain his mirth but it would bubble out of him. Though I wanted to be cross, I must confess it was impossible not to be amused, and I found myself smiling.

"Well," I said when they had calmed down, "perhaps now you are ready to give me a full accounting of the evening?"

"Certainly," B said. "Although to be honest, there is precious little to tell, at least so far as the case is concerned. Still, we shall tell you all.

"We arrived promptly at Emerald's home. Mrs Croyer, our erstwhile mystic, had already arrived. Emerald said to her, with a straight face, that it must be a change to perform a séance in a home such as hers, rather than Mrs Croyer's own flat in Hackney. At this, Mrs Croyer replied that 'the spirits are not as beguiled by the trappings of wealth as we are on this mortal plane.'"

B tried, unsuccessfully, to swallow back her mirth. "The entire evening was full of this sort of nonsense," she said. "I cannot think when I was last so diverted."

"She played all the tricks Doctor Watson told us to expect," Stevens continued. "The knocking on the table, the eerie music from beyond, revelations about various people who were present."

"Oh, yes," B exclaimed. "Mrs Croyer asserted that Stevens and Emerald should soon announce their engagement." At that, she was quite overcome with laughter and completely beyond speech for several minutes. Watson and I joined in. It was impossible to resist.

"These people keep their predictions pretty generic when they first meet a client," Watson added. "If the individual is well-known, they might make some comment that is common knowledge. They couch their statements in the form of a question, in order to elicit information from the person. 'You are troubled by a scandal, Lady Windermere... Is your husband very troubled by it?' That sort of thing."

"Mrs Croyer began by telling me I had suffered a bereavement."

"Indeed?" I replied. "With such perspicacity she ought to have been a detective."

"Oh, you would have been entertained, my dear Sherlock," B said.

"What answer did you make to this astonishing observation?"

"I replied that I had suffered a loss and was greatly troubled. I could say no more because I was consumed by tears."

"Her ladyship would make a capital actress, Mr Holmes," Stevens said. "Indeed, she almost had me convinced."

"I found tears were a good way of avoiding questions. The unfortunate Mrs Croyer and her lackey Mr Ryan were utterly confounded. All I would say was that my father had appeared to me in a dream and had asked me a question. I needed to know how to answer it. I refused to tell them what the question was, however. I said that I would pay handsomely to anyone who could tell me both question and answer."

"And what reply did you receive?"

"Mrs Croyer said she would need to commune with the spirits. Stevens and I are to return next week, although it must be to her flat in Hackney this time. In the interim, I suppose they will learn whatever they can about me."

Stevens rose. "And I must do my part now. I shall walk to my new flat in Camden Town and become your feckless cousin, Lady Beatrice."

"You make a charming relative and an excellent companion, Stevens," B said. "I am in your debt. You will be careful?"

"Of course. Mr Holmes has taken care of all the arrangements: the flat, a way of getting messages out. It's all in hand. I shall call upon you in a few days."

Watson rose, too. "I should leave, too."

"Wait a few moments, Watson," I said. "Let us see if Stevens is followed. If he is, you can leave as soon as his shadow is gone."

I watched from the corner of the window as Stevens, hunched over against the rain, the embodiment of misery and self-pity, slouched down the sodden street. A few moments later, a man followed behind.

"You see," I said, chuckling, "the predictability of the scoundrel. I think you may safely leave now, Watson."

"Please take the carriage, John. It is a miserable night. Alas, poor Stevens will be soaked."

"Thank you," he said. "That is kind. Good night, Beatrice, Holmes."

Saturday, 4th March

This evening, B and Stevens repeated the exercise. Now that Mrs Croyer smells money, she is anxious there should be no delays in pursuing this most promising new client.

This time, B and Stevens arrived back at Wimpole Street shortly after ten o'clock.

"Well?" I said, as soon as we were comfortably gathered in the music room. "Your mood suggests adventures. Tell me."

"They began by suggesting that my financial state was in peril," B said. "My father wished to warn me not to trust charlatans."

"Ha!"

"Indeed. I scoffed and said they obviously knew nothing, were wasting my time, and I would denounce the entire Spiritism movement as a fraud."

"You should have seen the way B delivered this line, Mr Holmes," Stevens said. "The Queen, herself, could not have commanded greater disdain nor shown more contempt."

"I made to rise, scolding Emerald for being too naïve and gullible. Suggesting she might, in fact, have some nefarious motive of her own in bringing me to such people."

"The way she said 'people'," Stevens interjected. "Had she called them crooks and swindlers it could not have sounded more scornful."

"Mrs Croyer apologised and claimed the spirits sometimes confused one client with another. There was some nonsense about – what did she call it? – the 'astral plane.'"

I chuckled.

"I said if the spirits truly existed, they would want me to meet with a true medium. Someone whose gift was beyond question.

"At this, there was a long silence then Mrs Croyer said, 'You may, perhaps, benefit from meeting the highest practitioner in the land.'

"'Who is this person?' I demanded.

"'His name... his name does not matter,' she said. And then, oh, Sherlock..."

"Go on," I urged. "And then?"

"And then she said, 'In our circle he is known only as the Sorcerer.'"

I clapped my hands. "Excellent!"

B said, "I told her I want to meet him, and soon. I said that time was of the essence."

"And? What did she say?"

"She said she would send word to this fellow and someone would contact me. She said I must be patient."

"And so we wait," Watson said.

"Hmm."

"Sherlock? You do not seem pleased. This is what we wanted, is it not?"

"Yes... I am just concerned that Frankall may do some investigating of his own. You must be very careful from now on, and there can be no meetings between us. The telephone and letters must suffice. It is likely Frankall will have you watched."

"You do not think B might be in any danger, Holmes?" Watson said.

"This is a fellow who planned to murder a small boy. Who compelled that boy's mother to hang herself. Do you really think he would have qualms about attacking another woman, even if she is the Queen's goddaughter?"

"Perhaps we might find one of Stevens' colleagues to pose as Beatrice's manservant?"

"Excuse me," B said. "Not that I do not find your concerns perfectly charming, but I will not change my life one jot. I will continue to do exactly as I have always done. No, I will brook no arguments. If this fellow, Frankall, is as intelligent and resourceful as you believe, Sherlock, then any change is likely to draw his attention. No, I must go on as I have always done."

19

Saturday, 18th March

Lestrade stopped by this evening to ask some unsubtle questions about the case.

"There is nothing to report. I shall tell you as soon as there is any news."

"Well, I appreciate that, Mr Holmes. We old friends must help one another, eh? I do hope you and Stevens are being careful."

"I have nothing to fear when I have the valiant Dr Watson at my side," I said, "nor is there any risk to Stevens. It is Lady Beatrice who is in peril. I am grateful to you for letting Stevens assist her. He has a flair for undercover work. His version of a disgruntled poor relation would do justice to Drury Lane."

Last night, Glaser called in. He looked tired and did not stay long. Like Lestrade, he was curious about the case.

"We have something of a personal interest in the matter, as I am sure you can appreciate, Mr Holmes," he said. "We want to know what became of poor Horowitz. If I can be of any help, I hope you will let me know at once."

We are surrounded on all sides by good friends and noble intentions. Yet no movement has there been on the part of this Sorcerer.

Tuesday, 28th March

I received a telephone call from B this evening. "I cannot talk for long," she said. "I just received an invitation to a special meeting on Saturday week with the man they call the Sorcerer. There are conditions attached."

"What sort of conditions?"

"I must go alone. I am to tell no one of the meeting. And I must bring two hundred guineas."

"I do not like the idea of you going alone."

"Nor do I, but those were the conditions."

"Decline."

"What? Sherlock, this is exactly what we have been waiting for."

"It is too dangerous. Tell them you will bring one hundred guineas and pay an additional three hundred if the Sorcerer is successful. Insist on bringing your cousin, Maurice Stevens. Say that no lady would travel alone in the evening. He should have no quarrel with that."

"What if he declines?"

"He is greedy. He will agree to your terms if he thinks he can get his hands on your fortune. We must try to keep some measure of control over the game."

There was a long silence followed by a heavy sigh. "Very well," she said. "I will do it your way, Sherlock. All the same, I wish this matter was over. I miss you. And there is a concert tomorrow evening I should have liked to attend."

"I know," I said, "But it cannot be helped."

Saturday, 1st April

A telephone call this evening from B. The Sorcerer has agreed to her counter-offer. She has been given an address in Highgate, near the cemetery.

Saturday, 8th April

A few moments before seven o'clock, a stately retainer wearing spectacles, an enormous moustache, and a top hat drew up in a Brougham outside a certain house in Wimpole Street.

191

Precisely on the hour, the door opened. A lady and a shabbily-dressed young man climbed into the back of the carriage. The old retainer wheezed rheumatically.

"You really ought to do something about that cough, William," the lady said. "What does the doctor say?"

"He says I am fit to work, my lady," said the old man with a wink.

A few minutes later, the carriage sped through the streets of London. We turned left onto Great Portland Street and made our way north. At least the wooden blocks on the road made for a fairly quiet journey. Once we got closer to Highgate, the surface changed to cobbles, and shortly thereafter to asphalt. A blind man could find his way around the city just by the materials used to cover the roads. I suppose we shall eventually settle upon some uniform material for the entire city. Better for the horses, of course, and certainly more pragmatic for the general public. Less helpful, though, for the consulting detective who relies on such quirks to determine where a client or villain has been.

Forty-five minutes later, we arrived at a large gothic-style mansion not far from Swain's Lane.

"You'll need to leave the carriage here, m'lady," the gatekeeper said.

"And walk? In this weather?" said the lady with regal hauteur. "Certainly not. My man shall drive me to the front door or I shall leave this instant. Walk!" She spat the last word as if it were the most outrageous epithet she had ever heard. With some effort, I composed my face and swallowed back a guffaw.

The fellow, thoroughly demoralised, relented at once. "I beg your pardon, m'lady," he said. "This way."

There was more consternation when we arrived. A tall, slender man with saturnine features swept down the steps and opened the carriage door.

"Be ready for me, William," she said.

I coughed my assent.

She frowned. "I do hope you shall not keep coughing all the way back to Wimpole Street." Behind her back, Stevens gave her a mocking look. It was so utterly convincing, I had to stay an impulse to punch his nose.

"The fellow can't stay out here for an hour, Cousin Beatrice," Stevens said. "He'll catch his death."

"Oh very well. I suppose he can stay in the servants' hall until we're ready." It wasn't a question, but rather a presumption. The air of someone who is so used to getting her own way, she cannot comprehend refusal. She was, in that moment, every inch the Queen's goddaughter. It was delicious.

"I do not usually let strangers into my home," Frankall began.

I coughed.

B pursed her perfect lips.

"But I suppose in this instance I can make an exception," he conceded. "My man will show you the way."

I bowed and followed the surly gatekeeper to the servants' domain. B and Stevens swept up the steps of the main entrance.

"Sit there and don't move," the servant commanded me.

The kitchen was warm and smelled of roast beef.

The maids gave me a curious look and giggled. Cook, harried, busied herself with stirring, supervising, and commanding.

"Can I lend a hand, ma'am?" I said.

She gave me a doubtful look. "I don't know… I suppose you could whisk the egg whites."

"Happy to, ma'am," I bowed slightly, and took the bowl.

"Yes," she said, "Just like that. You're more useful than most men." She shot the gatekeeper a belligerent look. No love lost there.

"My late wife was a cook," I said. "God rest her. It's a hard job."

"Indeed it is," she said. "When did you lose her?"

"Oh, 'tis five year now," I said, "but still I miss her."

We continued to exchange pleasantries and I learned more than I really cared to about her history. My ears pricked when she talked about Frankall.

"Not been here too long," she said, "Only two years. Still, he pays well and I have a free hand with the meals. No mistress to answer to."

"Not sure I'd care for it," I said, softly. "A man like that. The dark arts…"

She glanced around and, satisfied her staff were too occupied to eavesdrop, whispered, "He's a strange duck, and no mistake. All sorts of people coming and going at all hours. People of substance, too. Judges and Lords. Nothing to do with me, of course. I keeps me head down."

"You are wise," I said.

"That will do very nicely," she said, looking at the stiff peaks of egg. "I'll finish making the meringue."

One of the young maids was trying to reach a pot on the top of the shelf. I took it down and handed it to her.

"I told you to sit down," said gatekeeper, giving me what he thought was a terrifying look.

"Let the poor man alone," said cook. "I thought you had work to do."

She said it pointedly. No man with any sense would ever argue with a cook in her own kitchen. The fellow got up and headed to the door. There he paused and said, "You mind you watch him."

"Don't you fret about Timms," she said. "Sit there and have some soup."

"I'd like to use the facilities first, if I may," I said delicately.

"We have indoor plumbing," she said. "No convenience spared in this house." She chuckled at her own joke.

"Oh, that's a good one," I said. "I'll have to remember that."

"It's down the hall. Last door on the right."

Down the hall I went, but I did not avail myself of the convenience. Instead, I hurried up the stairs and took in the layout of the building. There was no time for a proper search now, but this would serve me well when I returned.

I counted five bedrooms, a library, and two formal reception rooms. There was a staircase leading down into the basement, too, but I had no time to explore it.

I hurried back to the bathroom and made a point of limping back into the kitchen.

"Thought you'd fallen in," cook said. "You shouldn't be walking around, you poor old thing. Sit down there."

She served me a bowl of soup and some thick crusty bread. "It's a shame you have to sit out in the cold and wet, a man of your age," she said. "Mr—?"

"William Williams, at your service," I replied, shaking her hand. "They call me Billy-Bill."

"Well, now, I'm pleased to meet you, Mr Williams. I'm Gertrude Pike."

We shook hands. I said, "This is the best soup I've had since my missus passed on, Mrs Pike. As thick and rich as you please."

The minutes passed. I ate the soup and listened to the conversation. I gathered when there was an 'event' – séance – the master dined late, not until ten o'clock at night. His clients were not invited to dine with him, though sometimes he served cocktails and hors d'oeuvres to special guests.

"What's with him? That Timms fellow?" I asked the cook.

"Him, he's a piece of work and no mistake," she said. "Best you steer clear of him. He and the master go way back. They met in Mexico, I think. He's got eyes in the back of his head. When the master goes away, Timms takes over and likes to act like he's the king of the place, with his ordering and his bullying."

"I hope the master doesn't go away too often, then," I said.

"Several times a year," Mrs Pike replied. "And he's due to go again soon. Some business in Europe he has to take care of. It'll be a long couple of weeks."

Before she could say more, Timms returned. "Well," he said, "I hope he's been behaving himself." He nodded at me.

"Mr Williams has been a perfect gentleman," she replied. Then, with a sniff, "Which is more than I can say for some."

"That woman, Lady Beatrice, is getting ready to leave," Timms said. "Better get your backside out into the rain, old man."

"Language, Mr Timms," Mrs Pike protested. She handed me some bread and cheese. "Just in case you don't get a proper supper."

"You're a lady and no mistake," I said, and kissed her hand.

For the first half of our journey, neither Beatrice nor Stevens spoke at all. There was none of the hilarity that followed their previous séances.

"Well?" I said as we turned back onto the Great Portland Street. "Aren't you going to tell me what happened?"

"I saw my father."

"What did you say?"

My rational, self-contained wife seemed shaken to the core. "I know it must have been an illusion, but I saw him as clearly as I see you. Clearer, in fact, for you are quite in shadow."

She said nothing more for the rest of the journey. We arrived at Wimpole Street. I left the carriage and helped her to the door, then whispered, "I shall return by the rear entrance after I've taken care of the horses."

Half an hour later, I entered the house through the back door. B and Stevens were in the study drinking brandy. B was pale and, though calm, I could see she was shaken to the core. Stevens, too, seemed bewildered.

"You are distressed," I said to B.

"Yes." She poured me a glass of brandy and handed it to me. "Foolish, is it not? It is almost five years since I lost my father. I am over my grief, though I still miss him, of course. Seeing him tonight was a shock. All the things Doctor Watson mentioned: knocks on the table, levitating objects, and so forth, all these things I was prepared for. But that…"

"Can you tell me what happened? It would help if you could be as precise as possible."

"We were shown into a sitting room at the back of the house. The curtains were drawn but I was surprised to find it well lit. I had expected near darkness."

"Was the gas lit or did he use lanterns?"

"Candles. He made some idiotic comment about the energy of the flame being compatible with the spirit world. But there were plenty of candles and I could see quite well.

"He had us sit at a small card table. There were just the three of us in the room, Stevens and Frankall and me. There was no trance, no speaking in voices. Frankall asked me who I wanted to contact. I said my father. He asked if I had a particular question to ask and I replied that I wanted to know the meaning of my dream.

"Frankall said he could not promise any result, but he would do all he could. He told me to close my eyes and concentrate on my breathing. He said I should picture my father in my mind, to focus on my memories of him and remember his face. He stressed that point.

"We three held hands. I assumed he would use his knees to knock on the table, but as I said, there was no knocking.

"I started to feel strange... I was on the point of asking for a glass of water, and then I saw him. My father."

Her hands shook, and she set the brandy snifter on the table before she spilled its contents. B unsettled. Were Mycroft to take up gymnastics I could not be more astounded.

"What do you mean, you started to feel strange?" I said.

For a moment, she struggled to put express experience in words. "I felt as if my head was full of clouds. There was an intensity of feeling, and yet I felt removed from it... I am sorry, I am not explaining it very well. Then I opened my eyes, and my father was right there in front of me. I think I cried out his name."

"Stevens, did you see the image, too?"

"No, I didn't see the late Professor Jacoby, but there was such a strange atmosphere. Cloying. It was hard to think straight."

"Did you smell anything?"

"Yes, a spicy sort of smell," B said. "But the fire was lit. I assumed it was the wood."

"I smelled it, too," Stevens said. "Spicy, like her ladyship says."

"I suspect it was an opiate, or something of the sort," I said.

They stared at me. "Oh," B said. "Of course! And it explains the time, too."

"The time?"

"I thought I had only been with Frankall for a half an hour or so. I was astonished to see how late it was when I saw the clock."

"How much time did you lose?"

"At least an hour. Yes, exposure to a drug is the only reasonable explanation."

"Well," said Stevens, "Unless you believe in the supernatural."

"The simplest explanation is always the best, unless it proves impossible," I said.

"I agree." B took several long breaths. Her hands stopped shaking.

I said, "I need to look into your eyes."

"Why, Sherlock," she said, "We have company."

She and Stevens laughed. It was a relief to see them cast off their air of doom. I had B sit under the lamp as I conducted my examination. "Your pupils are constricted," I said. "A sure sign that you were subjected to an opiate of some sort."

Stevens showed the same signs.

"What I don't understand," the policeman said, "Is how Frankall himself wasn't affected. He breathed the same air we did."

199

"But he placed us near the fire, if you remember," B said. "He sat near the window, and it was open. I noticed because I was expecting some sort of chicanery. He may have experienced a slight effect of the drug, but he was expecting it."

"Yes, I encountered a similar case a couple of years ago in Cornwall," I said. "A family rendered insane or killed outright by exposure to *radix pedis diaboli,* or the 'devil's foot root'. The mechanism here is similar."

"I should leave," Stevens said, standing. "Head off to Mornington Crescent, just in case they're watching."

"I think that is wise," I said. "I suspect you will be contacted in a day or so. On no account forget your instructions: As soon as you hear from them, leave that plant on the windowsill. My old friend Mrs Prentiss will keep watch and send word to me. If you need to send me a direct message, she will be in the park every day at two o'clock. You can give her your report then, but be careful. You must assume they are watching your every move from this moment on."

"I understand, Mr Holmes. I shall be on my guard."

B and I were silent for a time after he left, lost in our own thoughts. She roused and said, "It was the most unsettling experience, Sherlock. I have always been able to rely upon my own wits. To suddenly see my father... the rational part of my brain told me this was impossible, and yet, there he was."

"The effects of hallucinogens are disquieting enough if you are expecting them. To be exposed to such things without your knowledge or consent is unconscionable."

"But how could Frankall know what I would see?"

"He prepared you for it. You said he told you to concentrate on your father, picture him. The drug merely enhanced the effect. I suspect he used a similar method to compel those unfortunate people to kill themselves."

"But surely no one, no matter how much of that filthy stuff they may have inhaled, would end their own lives?"

"Watson made the same argument. But I do not think it is the drug alone. I believe he prepares the minds of his victims and preys upon their fears."

"How so?"

"Well, in the case of Updike, we know that he had a terror of snakes. I suspect the burns on his feet and ankles when we found him were meant to suggest snakebites to his drugged mind. Mrs Hardwicke was terrified of the tarot and believed that if she ever saw the Death card, she would die. McKenna knew this and told our Sorcerer friend."

"That is appalling. But to hang herself merely because she saw that card…?"

"Not only because of the card, although that served as the impetus. The drug prepared her mind to make her deeply suggestible. I suspect something of the sort also occurred with Lionel Carton.

"Think how unsettled you were to see your father. That is the power of Frankall's drug. Imagine all your horrors magnified by that poison. Of course, some people probably proved more resistant, or perhaps Frankall was unable to determine their secret fear. Those are the people who had 'accidents', as Sir Christopher believed."

"I am amazed that old gentleman wove so many threads together," B said. "It is one thing to note the oddity of a man flinging himself through a window. It is another matter entirely to see a random street accident as anything more than, well, an accident."

"I agree. I tried asking Sir Christopher about it, but his age tells against him and his memory is vague and sometimes plays tricks on him. I cannot imagine a more dreadful fate than to become unable to trust my own mind."

"What is your next step?"

"We need only wait. Once Frankall acts, we can have him arrested."

"I hope we do not have to wait for long," B said.

"As do I. We must be patient. I was precipitous in my dealings with the late Professor Moriarty. Had I allowed my agents to act, perhaps events would not have unfolded as they did."

B studied my face for a moment before replying. She has a most unsettling way of looking at me.

"Events with the professor still turned out for the best, didn't they? You ended his organisation. You stopped him, literally, in his tracks."

"But at what cost?"

I still wake up at night reliving the cold terror of that encounter at Reichenbach. The struggle with the fierce and murderous man under the torrent of the falls. Then suddenly breaking free and seeing him plunge to his death. Even now, years later, it is the stuff of my nightmares. It was eight years ago and yet the wounds still burn.

How much of this B saw in my face, I cannot say. Enough, I think, for she seemed troubled and squeezed my hand.

"We should not dwell on such dark things," she said. "What do you think will happen next?"

"Someone will search the flat I arranged for Stevens to use. They will find an unhappy pile of bills and demands for payment, as well as a rather churlish letter from his cousin Beatrice denying him a loan. They will draw the inevitable conclusion that Mr Stevens is not on good terms with said cousin.

"In the meantime, you can be sure Frankall has looked you up in the *Who's Who*. The Queen's goddaughter: that must be delicious to him. Your fortune will prove irresistible.

"Frankall will contact Stevens and make him an offer: He will arrange the death of the wealthy Lady Beatrice and arrange for Stevens to inherit everything. In return, Stevens will give the Sorcerer some percentage of his windfall. It is a tidy little scheme. They will make your death look like an accident or suicide, but even if anyone suspects foul play, there is no reason why suspicion should fall on Frankall. Where is his motive? Stevens has a motive but Frankall will arrange for him to have a cast-iron alibi. Yes, very neat."

"Neat. And chilling," B said.

"Not to worry, Beatrice," I said. "It will all soon be over."

20
FROM THE DIARY OF DR JOHN H
WATSON

Friday, 14th April

I have seen nothing of Holmes all week and have taken advantage of his absence to catch up on my reading and writing. He does rather demand one's attention when he is home. I do not mind as a rule, but a writer needs peace and several undisturbed hours if he is to do justice to his work. I assumed my friend was working on a case or staying with Beatrice, and so I was greatly disturbed when the commissionaire brought me a letter from Stevens. I copy it here in its entirety:

Dear Mr Holmes and Dr Watson,

Despite all our plans and calculations, I still have had no word from Frankall. No one has been to the flat; I have not been watched or followed. I'm not sure if I should stay here and, if so, for how long. I'd be obliged if you could send word. I'll stay put until I hear from you.

Your servant,

Maurice Stevens.

I wrote a note to Stevens telling him to stay where he was for the moment, and I would have Holmes get in touch with him. Letter dispatched, I telephoned Beatrice.

"No," she said, "he is not here. I have not seen him since Sunday. He left in the middle of the night. Are you saying he never returned to Baker Street?"

I tried to make light of it, but she is too clever. She said, "Sherlock meant to see Inspector Bradstreet on Monday. You might see if he has any information. You might also want to see if the Irregulars know anything."

We agreed that we would telephone if either of us had any news. I alerted Mrs Hudson and told her my plans. "If you hear from him, Mrs Hudson, please let me know at once."

"I shall, Doctor. Oh dear, I do hope he is safe. I do not think I can go through all that again."

The Irregulars, rough and full of bravado as they are, seemed genuinely concerned about my friend's disappearance.

"I shall pay the usual rates for any information, Kevin," I said.

"Usual rates?" he spat on the ground. "Naw, Doc, no need to pay us."

I insisted and, in a gentlemanly fashion, he accepted the coins I pressed upon him.

When I arrived at Scotland Yard, I learned that Bradstreet was out on a case. I met with Lestrade and told him what I knew.

"Are you saying no one has seen Mr Holmes since Sunday night, Doctor?" he said.

"Not so far as I can ascertain, Inspector," I said. "He does sometimes go away for several days at a time, but never in the middle of a case. Certainly not so close to its resolution."

"I shall alert my men to be on the lookout for him. He's probably picked up the scent of some villain and forgot to mention it to you." He said this in a jovial manner, but I could see the worry on his sharp little face. He patted my shoulder. "Have no fear. We'll find him."

"You might start at the Sorcerer's home in Highgate." I gave him the address.

"We'll look into it, Doctor."

After I left the Yard, I vacillated for some minutes then I took a cab to Holborn.

"I haven't heard from him, Doctor," Glaser said. "But I'll spread the word that you are looking for him. I'll ask the rabbi to say a prayer for his safe return, if you do not think Mr Holmes would mind."

"I think that is an excellent idea. Thank you."

I was tempted to head off to Highgate on my own, but it was probably preferable to let the police handle the matter. Instead, I hurried to Whitehall.

Old Gillespie, that splendid aide-de-camp, met me with great warmth. "Always such a pleasure to see you, Doctor Watson," he said, shaking my hand. "You are on your own today?"

"Mr Holmes is missing," I blurted, forgetting the gentle speech I had rehearsed. "I wonder if I may speak to his brother. He may be able to shed some light on the matter."

"Missing?" Gillespie's anxiety racked my own up several levels. I felt quite ill as my apprehension grew.

A few minutes later, I was shown into Mr Mycroft Holmes's office. The portly gentleman rose from his desk and shook my hand.

"My colleague, Mr Quackenbush," he said, introducing me to a slight man with a prematurely hunched back.

The fellow mumbled a greeting and said, "I shall continue to review the Bloemfontein agenda, Mr Holmes," then he scurried away.

"Come, sit with me," Mycroft said as soon as the door closed. "What is my brother up to?"

He heard me in silence and, when I was done, was quite pale. He mopped his brow with a white handkerchief and said, "What happened at this séance, do you know?"

"Your brother telephoned me on Saturday night after he brought Beatrice home to Wimpole Street. He said everything had gone as planned and he expected to bring the case to a successful conclusion in a matter of days. When he failed to return to Baker Street, I assumed he was still there with her."

"When did she last see him?"

"Late Sunday night. No one has seen or heard from him since." I sipped the glass of water Gillespie poured for me. "I had hoped that perhaps you had sent him on some urgent mission abroad." Even as I said it, I could hear how ridiculous it sounded.

Mycroft did not sneer or laugh, however. He seemed as distressed as I, myself, felt.

"Damnation," he exclaimed, "I always knew this business of his would bring him to grief. Did you come straight here, or have you taken steps on your own to find him?"

I related the events of the morning and he heard me without interruption.

"Well done, Doctor," he said, "You have been very thorough."

Mycroft said, "Gillespie, send word to our friends in the ports here and abroad to be on the lookout for him."

"You surely do not think he has left the country?" I exclaimed.

"Best be on the safe side," Mycroft replied. "And send word to all our agents and offices."

Gillespie hurried out and Mycroft rose. "I shall start some investigations of my own, Doctor," he said, shaking my hand. "I will not insult your intelligence by saying not to worry. I do make you this promise, however: We shall find him. If we have to lift every rock in the kingdom, by God, we shall find him."

Every step of my return to Baker Street was a prayer that my old friend would be waiting for me, amused by my anxiety. Offering a fleeting and perfectly rational explanation for his absence.

He was not waiting for me.

Mrs Hudson came to the door as soon as she heard my key in the lock. "Oh," she said, "I was so hoping it was Mr Holmes."

"I have the entire police and military looking for him, Mrs Hudson," I said, much more positively than I felt. I repeated Mycroft Holmes's words: "We will find him."

It was almost five o'clock and the weary sun was setting over Baker Street. Soon it would be dark. Dear God, where was he?

For the next hour, I dithered between going out and searching the streets, or staying in Baker Street in hopes of getting some news. I finally decided on the former. I had just put on my hat when the doorbell rang. I leaped down the stairs and opened the door before Mrs Hudson had even come into the hall. To my immense surprise, there stood Mycroft Holmes.

"Come in," I said.

Mrs Hudson, wiping her hands on her apron, said, "Oh Mr Holmes, we are that worried about your brother. Have you any news, sir?"

"Not yet," he said. "But it is just like Sherlock to chase off after some merry puzzle and forget the people who are worried about him."

"Then you think he is safe?" she said. She dabbed her eyes with the corner of her apron.

"Certainly I do," he said, and with such conviction, even I was almost fooled.

"Do you think you could bring us some coffee, Mrs Hudson?" I said.

"Of course. Will you stay to supper, Mr Holmes? I have a nice leg of lamb in the oven."

He smacked his lips and said, "I can never refuse your meals, Mrs Hudson. That would be delightful."

In the sitting room, Mycroft's demeanour changed and his anxiety was quite apparent. "I have done everything I can, Doctor," he said. "I fear there is not much else we can do but wait. Finding my brother is a matter of the highest urgency not just for those of us who care about him, but for the nation."

"Did someone check this Frankall fellow? I was on the point of heading out to Highgate when you arrived." I realised, belatedly, that I was still wearing my hat. I removed it and tossed it onto the bookcase.

"I spoke with Lestrade and with Bradstreet," Mycroft replied. "They have been to the house but say no one answered their knock."

"Well, what were they expecting?" I cried. "Did they really think a villain like Frankall would just open the door and hand over your brother?"

"Hush, Doctor, calm yourself. The house is boarded up; no one is there. It appears the occupants left some days ago." He raised a hand before I could protest further. "My agents are already tracking their whereabouts. If they have Sherlock, I assure you, we will know it."

"If?" I exclaimed. "There can be no doubt, surely?"

His pale eyes met mine. *"Post hoc, ergo propter hoc,* Doctor. Because Sherlock's most recent case was this Sorcerer business, it is natural to assume there is a link between that and his disappearance, but it does not necessarily follow, you know. Given the number of puzzles my brother has solved and the peculiar nature of them, we cannot ignore the possibility that his disappearance is related to one of those. In addition, we cannot rule out the possibility that Sherlock left of his own volition."

He was about to elaborate when there was a ring at the doorbell. I was instantly on my feet, but several pairs of footsteps came running up the stairs and burst in the door before I had taken more than four steps.

Three urchins fell into the room. Two I recognised: Billy and young Kevin. The third took me a moment or two longer.

"Beatrice!" I exclaimed.

She raised a finger to her lips and winked. "Wotcher, guvnor," she said, in a perfect Whitechapel accent.

Mrs Hudson came into the room a moment later. "Some of Mr Holmes's lads," she announced unnecessarily. "Sit down, boys," she commanded. "Try not to touch anything."

"How's about a cup of tea, Mrs H?" Billy said.

"Yeah," said Kevin.

"Yeah," said Beatrice.

Mycroft burst out laughing.

Mrs Hudson, not comprehending the joke, said, "Well, if you have news about Mr Holmes, I suppose I could spare a pot of tea."

"Now, Beatrice," Mycroft said, after the landlady left. "What is this extraordinary behaviour? I can only assume it is in relation to my brother's disappearance."

"It is," she replied in her normal voice. The contrast between the woman's polished vowels and a boy's filthy clothes was utterly disconcerting. "After you telephoned, John, I decided to find out more for myself. I changed, as you see, then I went to Highgate to see what I could learn. I did not want to be recognised, and so I, ah, transformed myself."

Mycroft chuckled. "Ha! Well done. What did you learn?"

"One of their neighbours said they all took off in the early hours of Tuesday morning. There were four carriages and made quite a clatter as they sped off through the village."

"Me and Kevin had the same thought as her ladyship," Billy said. "Mr H, he told us about this Sorcerer fellow and said we should keep our ears to the ground. He told us where this bludger was keeping hisself and said to keep clear of the place, but let 'im know if we heard ought.

"Any road, we 'opped over the wall of the house to take a closer look. There were sheets over all the furniture and such. We found an unlocked winder and let ourselves in, like."

"The place is empty," Beatrice said.

"What, you took a look, too?" I asked.

"Of course I did. Took me a minute to climb over the wall – I am rather of practice – but I managed well enough."

"She did," Kevin said, with unadulterated admiration. "Think she'd been born on the streets, you would. No offense, Miss."

"I thank you for the compliment, Kevin," Beatrice said. "Anyway, over the wall I went and got in by the same window. It let into the kitchen. We searched from basement to rafters but there wasn't even a rat left behind."

She paused and I could see she was struggling to say what was next. My heart skipped a beat, then two. She took a long breath then said, "There was something there, though. Blood."

Before Mycroft or I could react, the door opened and Mrs Hudson arrived bearing a tray. She sat it down on the table and made to say something. The look on our faces must have shocked her, for she raised up her hands like she was warding off a danger, and she backed out of the room.

Mycroft said, "How much blood and where was it?"

I saw that B was pale beneath the layer of dirt on her face. She took several deep breaths before saying. "There was a fair amount, splattered around the north wall of the basement, and on the floor. It is fresh. The smell of copper is still in the air."

"What else?" Mycroft said.

She swallowed hard. "Manacles on the walls. Chains. Whips... Mycroft, it is a torture chamber."

21

For the first time since I met him, Mycroft Holmes had no appetite. In fact, none of the adults had much interest in food. The boys, resilient as boys are, made quick work of the lamb and the roast potatoes.

Mycroft went downstairs to use the telephone and returned a few minutes later. "Bradstreet will be here, shortly. He's going to bring Stevens with him. Ah, Beatrice…"

"I shall hide in Sherlock's bedroom when they are here. No point sullying my reputation any further." She said it with a smile, but we were none of us in a mood for mirth.

A torture chamber. My gorge rose at the thought. Dear God, if Holmes were subjected to some sort of barbarism… I was reminded of the unfortunate Augustus Updike and the horrors he had endured. Hideous thoughts filled my mind and refused to leave. For the sake of my friend's wife and brother, I resolved to be as stoic as I could.

Less than an hour later, Bradstreet and Stevens arrived.

Billy told a modified version of the tale we had heard from Beatrice. A neighbour saw the company leave in the early hours of Tuesday morning. Billy was so worried he hopped over the wall.

"No harm done," Mycroft said. "The lad was using his ingenuity."

"There would be an outcry if the official police were to use such tactics, as well you know, Mr Holmes," Bradstreet said. "Still, we won't quibble. Carry on with your tale, lad."

Billy continued with the story and said it was he who discovered the torture chamber in the basement. He described the instruments of pain in as flat a voice as I have ever heard.

"We just came from the house, but found it locked up. I shall go back and take another look," Bradstreet said. "Stevens, you're with me."

"Yes, Inspector," Stevens said. "If you hear anything further, you will let us know?"

"Certainly we will," I replied. "And I trust you, too, will keep us informed."

As the inspector put on his coat, Stevens said, softly, "And Lady Beatrice, she knows what has been happening?"

"She does," I said. He nodded, and followed Bradstreet out into the night.

Beatrice joined us in the sitting room as soon as they left. She stood at the window and watched the policemen get into their car and drive off into the night.

"I share your brother's general mistrust of the regular police force," she said, turning to Mycroft Holmes, "Although Bradstreet and Stevens are very capable men. But I must do something."

"You cannot go running off on your own," I objected. "You've seen the sort of men we are up against. Besides, Holmes would want me to protect you."

The slightly mocking look she bestowed upon me reminded me uncannily of my missing friend and I knew there would be no restraining her. She would find Holmes, no matter what the risk or the cost.

"What did the policeman mean by the grounds?" Kevin asked suddenly.

"Excuse me?" I said.

"He said they'd search the house and the grounds. But if Mr H were in the grounds he'd have called to us."

Gently, Beatrice said, "They're looking for a grave."

214

The boys paled. For a moment, I thought Kevin would cry. Billy put his arm around the younger lad's shoulders and the two slumped into an unhappy silence.

I poured a stiff measure of whisky for us adults. Beatrice took the glass, but did not drink. Turning to her brother-in-law, she said, "Mycroft, I assume you have alerted all your contacts? When do you expect a response?"

"Any time," he replied. "Gillespie is at the office; he will telephone if he hears anything."

"We'll help, too," Billy said. "I've sent the lads all over the city. I reckon we'll hear word before you do."

For the next half hour, silence reigned. Only the sound of the carriages hurrying through Baker Street broke the stillness. None of them stopped, however.

We all jumped at a knock at the door below. Young footsteps tore up the stairs and Little Joey exploded into the room.

"Well," Billy said, rising and facing the boy like a general.

"They took a cab to Victoria Station. The cabby, old Will from 'ackney, he 'elped 'em with their bags and suchlike. They took the express train to Dover and Will said he heard 'em talk of France."

"When?" Beatrice demanded, too agitated to remember to use her Cockney accent. The boy stared at her in astonishment.

"Early Tuesday mornin'… Miss."

"Well done, lad," Mycroft cried.

"How many?" Beatrice said.

"Boxes?" Joey asked.

"People. How many people?"

"Oh." He counted on his fingers. "Four. There were that bludger. Creepy, he were, says Will, and some nobbler 'e didn't like the look of. There were some dark, bearded gent what never spoke, and a feller who were elephant's trunk."

"Drunk?" Mycroft and B said it together. I think I may have said it, too.

"'e 'ad to be 'eld up and carried onto the train."

"What was his appearance?" Mycroft demanded.

Little Joey bit his lip. "I'm sorry, sir, I didn't think to ask."

"Aw… Joe," Billy said. He sounded so disappointed. The little lad looked on the verge of tears.

"But I did tell old Will to come by Baker Street when 'e's finished his work," Little Joey added. "I thought you might 'ave more questions for him, like."

"Splendid! Well done, well done, indeed," Mycroft said. "I begin to see why my brother has such faith in you lads."

"Sit down, Joey, and see if there's any food left," I said.

He needed no urging. As the lads ate, we adults discussed our best way of proceeding.

"At least he is still alive," I said, "or was on Tuesday. That is something."

"Assuming the apparently drunken man was he," Beatrice pointed out. "But I admit it is encouraging. I just do not understand why they have kept him alive."

"Quite." Mycroft rubbed his chin and fell silent for several minutes.

Our reverie was interrupted by the sound of the telephone ringing in the hall below. Beatrice was out the room and down the stairs before Mycroft or I had done more than risen from our seats. We hurried after her. She was listening closely, and then said, "Thank you. A moment, if you please, Mr Gillespie. Mr Holmes is here."

She handed the receiver to my friend's brother and an unrevealing conversation ensued. All we heard from Mycroft was, "Yes... Very good... I understand... That would be splendid..." He hung up the receiver and said, "Come, I shall tell you upstairs."

Back in the sitting room, Mycroft said, "It is confirmed. They have left the country and were last seen headed to Paris. Gillespie has sent word to our agents to keep watch for them. It seems this Frankall fellow is known in France and they would like to talk to him in any case."

"That's all well and good," I protested, "I am sure they are every bit as efficient as our own police force, but we cannot sit idle."

"No we cannot," Beatrice said. "We must go to France."

Before she could say anything further there was a knock at the door, and moments later, an elderly man with ruddy cheeks and watery blue eyes joined us.

"You'd be the cabby, Will from Hackney?" I said. I indicated the sofa. The little living room was becoming quite cramped with so many people.

"The boy," he wheezed, nodding towards young Joe, "Asked me to stop by and tell you gentlemen about the people I took to Victoria on Thursday morning."

"It is good of you to take the time," I said. "I assure you, we shall make it worth your while. Now, please, tell us in the all you remember about the people and their conversation."

"Well, sir," he said. "I bin wracking my head since the boy talked with me. I wanted to be precise. They do say Mr Sherlock Holmes is the smartest man in London."

Mycroft snorted.

"Anyway," the man continued, "I were making my way down Highgate. I'd just dropped a young man off at the end of Swain's Lane and was headed back to Highgate Road. That's where I have my base, you understand. It were a long night and I was about done in. Then some geezer comes out of this ruddy great house – begging your pardon, gents – down by the cemetery, and asked if I'd like a fare. They'd hired some vans to take their trunks and boxes and Lord knows what else to the station, but they was a bit cramped. I said they'd fit four in my cab easy as you please, and they was well chuffed with that.

"So in they get, this lanky gentleman I didn't like the look of, and a bearded chap. There were another fellow with reddish hair and a pretty sour face. The fourth I did not see so well. He seemed to be sleeping. 'e 'ad a cloak wrapped around him and I must say he smelled of whisky something fierce." Despite the disapproving tone, he smacked his lips and cast a longing eye at my glass.

"Go on," Mycroft said.

"So in they gets and off we sets to Victoria. They had a first class compartment and I helped 'em get the sleeping gentleman on board. As I helped him onto the seat, I noticed he were bleeding. There were a fair bit of blood, but I couldn't rightly say where it were coming from. I think, perhaps, his back."

Beatrice stifled a cry and went back to the window. She stood there and remained silent.

The cabby gave her a puzzled look and said, "They 'ad the van drivers and the lads in the other vans 'elp them with their trunks and cases and the like."

"Did you see an address? A label? Anything to indicate where they were going?"

The fellow pondered for several moments. Then he said, "They talked about the cold mountain air and the need for warm clothing."

"The vans," B said, without turning around. "Do you know the name of the company?"

The fellow seemed more bewildered than ever at the unexpected voice. "I saw their name on the side of the van, something peculiar it were. Let me think… Something to do with Christmas."

"Christmas?" We all stared at one another. Even Beatrice turned back from the window to stare at the man.

"Yule? Noel? Tree?" We each offered up suggestions. The fellow waved away all our offerings. Then he clicked his fingers.

"Winters! That was it. Winters' Vans."

"I know them," Beatrice said. "They have an office in Marylebone Street."

"Yes, that's right," I said. "I've heard of them."

"You've done very well," Mycroft said, rising and drawing five guineas from his pocket. The old man stared at the treasure in astonishment.

As he turned to shuffle away, Beatrice said, "Did he say anything? The injured man."

He had his hand on the door handle. He seemed frozen on the spot. Then he said, "Aye, now you mention it. Not sure I 'eard it right, but 'e said it a few times, like 'e wanted me to remember."

"Well?"

"Well, it sounded like 'e said 'rike and back.'"

We all of us said it together in horror:

Reichenbach.

22

"It may mean nothing," Mycroft said.

We were alone, now, just the three of us. At that hour even Baker Street was nearly silent, except for the occasional rumble of a passing carriage.

Mycroft was as weary as I have ever seen a man. Beatrice, too, seemed exhausted, and yet I knew she would not sleep. Her anxiety and fear injected her with fresh visions of horrifying possibilities every moment. I offered her a sedative but she dismissed the notion without consideration.

"My husband is who knows where, suffering who knows what torments," she said. "I will rest when we find him."

Over the next two or three hours we formed a plan. Beatrice and I would take the dawn boat-train to France. Mycroft would follow up with the van company and try to get an address for Frankall on the continent.

"I have a limited number of operatives in Europe," he said, "At least in comparison with what I have here in England. However, I know some people who might be able to help. I need hardly say that all our resources are at your disposal."

We decided to try to get some sleep. Mycroft took a cab back to his own home. Beatrice agreed to lie down for a while in her husband's room, to try to rest even if she could not sleep. She sent word to her home to have a bag packed for travel the next morning. She and I would take the train from Victoria at ten o'clock and would reach Paris at 6.50pm.

Saturday, 15ᵗʰ April

Trains have improved greatly in recent years, and we were as comfortable as we could reasonably expect. Our Pullman seats were spacious; the April air was crisp and the light sparkling; and the boat sliced through the water efficiently. Were it not for the fear and trepidation that tortured us, we would have enjoyed a pleasant journey.

In less than two hours, we stood on French soil.

The next leg of our journey on the Nord line took rather longer, and Beatrice finally slept. It was an uneasy sleep and she jerked awake several times. I hushed her back to sleep and she dozed for another short while.

We alit in Paris at the Gare du Nord. A small bird of a man with a large nose and piercing eyes, greeted us. "Doctor Watson? Lady Beatrice?" he said. "I am René Moody. I was asked by M Mycroft Holmes to meet you."

"Has there been any news from London?" I asked.

He raised a cautionary finger to his lips and said, "Not much. A little. We shall discuss, but not in so public a place."

I took the hint. Moody led us to a private carriage which sped us through the Parisian traffic at a terrifying speed. We soon arrived at M Moody's apartment near the Seine.

Over coffee and brioche, he said, "I know you are fatigued and must rest, but there are two matters I must first discuss with you.

"M Sherlock Holmes arrived in France on Tuesday evening. He was accompanied by three men."

Beatrice and I both spoke at once: "Was he injured? Did he leave any messages?"

Moody shook his head. He sipped his coffee and said, reluctantly, "He was injured but he managed to break free of his captors. Yes, I believe 'captors' is the word."

"Then he is safe? Where is he?"

"Hush, Madame, I fear his attempt to escape was not successful."

"I do not understand."

Moody shook his head, "This happened at the border. M Holmes broke free and ran to the *douanier*, what you would call a border official. M Holmes identified himself, pleaded for help, and demanded his captors be arrested."

"Yes?" I said. I did not like the misery in Moody's voice or the embarrassment on his face.

"The *douanier* did not believe him. The men with M Holmes claimed he was a dangerous mental patient whom they were escorting to a sanatorium."

"And he believed them?" B gasped.

I do not know which of us was more aghast.

"It is to our shame," Moody said, "Our everlasting shame. Yes, the fool believed the lies of those evil men. One, a tall man, claimed to be a doctor. He seemed plausible."

"The Sorcerer himself," I said. "What happened?"

"Once their papers were reviewed and found in order, they were allowed to continue on their journey."

"Damn it all to hell!" Beatrice cried. She sprang to her feet and paced the room.

"I spoke with this fool myself, Madame," Moody said. "Imbecile! He has been suspended from duty. There will be an inquiry. You may be sure he will be severely punished."

Beatrice gesticulated with her hands, as if the words were wasps she might swat away. "What does that matter to me?" she said. "What of Sherlock?"

"At least we know where they are headed," Moody said. "M Mycroft Holmes sends news."

He handed me two telegrams. The first read, "They are on route to Meiringen, Switzerland." This was followed by one that read, "Ericson will meet you there."

"Meiringen," Beatrice said. "I am not familiar with that place."

"I am," I replied. "It is less than two miles from Reichenbach. It is where we stayed, Holmes and I, during… I mean, when…" I found myself unable to finish the sentence. My heart pounded as I remembered the dreadful Falls and my futile attempts to find Holmes after his encounter with Professor Moriarty. Surely returning to that fearful place could be no coincidence.

"John?" Beatrice said, squeezing my hand. "Are you all right? You are very pale."

"I am perfectly well," I said. "Just fatigued from the long journey."

I am not sure I convinced her, but she said no more.

Moody said, "I shall escort you to this place, Doctor, Lady. We leave first thing in the morning."

Sunday, 16th April

This morning we took the train from Paris headed east. M Moody made several attempts to entertain us by pointing out various important buildings and the magnificent scenery, but neither Beatrice nor I were interested. We fell into a silent reverie and this continued during the next long and weary hours.

I wondered how much Beatrice knew about the Sorcerer, about the extent of his malice. The truth is I know little about my friend's relationship with his wife. I have seen his affection for her grow, sometimes to his bewilderment, and have been happy to see his life so enriched by her. Despite their affection, settling down into a home together, having children and a normal life does not seem to be of interest to either of them.

She has helped us with cases, of course. Sometimes he has her take photographs of a murder scene and he spends hours examining them. She never seems unsettled, no matter how grotesque the sight before her. In these moments he speaks to her as if she were merely another assistant. Yet there is an ease between them that suggests a true intimacy. I am intrigued by it, I confess. Does he share sordid details of his cases with her? I know of old how he likes to ruminate. Beatrice, too, has an exceptional mind and frequently offers suggestions Holmes finds helpful.

At some point during all these ponderings, I fell asleep. When I awoke, it was dark. Beatrice was staring out the window with eyes that saw nothing. We were in the mountains and a waxing crescent moon hung low over snowy peaks. Moody was snoring gently.

"Where are we?" I asked.

"I do not know," she replied. "Not far from Switzerland, I think. All my great education and I know little of the geography of Europe. It is shameful."

"Nor do I," I said. "I am afraid it's not something that is given a great deal of attention. At least, it wasn't when I was a boy. Mind you, that was a long time ago."

She managed a smile. "Not so long ago as all that, John dear."

"We will find him," I said. "He knows this countryside. I suspect he knows it far better than Frankall. He was strong enough to break free from his captors once. He will do so again at the first opportunity. After all, he is Sherlock Holmes."

"I keep telling myself all that," she said. "I seem to swing from despair to hope and back again in the space of an instant."

"I know. I do, too."

Moody suddenly roused from his sleep, leaped up, and retrieved his bag. From this he produced some sandwiches which he handed to us. "Come, eat," he said.

"I have no appetite," Beatrice said.

"We do not know what lies ahead," Moody said. "You would not wish to faint from hunger at an inopportune moment."

She took the food. We ate in silence, and washed the meal down with a bottle of wine, also produced by the remarkable Frenchman.

After we dined, Moody cleared away the detritus of our meal. As he sat down again, he said, "You will pardon me, my friends, but something puzzles me: If this villain has captured M Holmes, why not simply kill him? Why take him captive? And why bring him to Switzerland?"

"I have the dubious advantage of having met Frankall," Beatrice said. "He strikes me as a man who has an appetite for power. Information is power. He craves to know every man's secrets and Sherlock Holmes knows more secrets than most. It may be of great value to Frankall to… extract them.

"Terror is his weapon. He used Updike's fear of snakes to drive him insane. He used Mrs Hardwicke's horror of the Death card to compel her to take her own life. Perhaps he thinks taking Sherlock to a place that haunts his dreams will loosen his tongue."

"I think you are right," I said. "More than once I have heard Holmes cry out in the night, and it was apparent he was dreaming of that awful experience at the Falls."

"He spoke one word to the cabby at the railway station: *Reichenbach*. It was uppermost in his thoughts," she said.

The train sped on through the mountains. Moody went back to sleep, but Beatrice and I remained wakeful.

After a time, I said, "Holmes thinks I am angry at him because he let me believe for years that he was dead."

"Are you?"

"I was at first. I believed he did not trust me enough with the truth, or, what may be worse, that he gave me not a moment's thought. We talked about it a couple of years ago, around the time when we were looking into the Rillington Manor murder. Holmes apologised and I forgave him. There are still moments when it rankles, but I vow I shall never be cross with him again, if only we find him alive and well."

I found I could say no more. Beatrice squeezed my hand. "He knows we are coming for him, John. He knows that Mycroft, and you, and I are looking for him. That will give him hope."

A short time later, Beatrice added, "What puzzles me is how Frankall knew Sherlock was investigating him. He could not know about our marriage; it is a closely guarded secret. When Sherlock drove me to the house in Highgate it was after dark and he was in disguise."

"Frankall saw us," I said. "When we were in Ireland looking into young Hardwicke's kidnapping."

"And you think he was keeping watch? It's possible, I suppose."

"Something else is troubling you, Beatrice. What is it?"

"That séance... I lost track of time. We arrived, sat at the table, and it felt like just a few moments had passed before we left. I was astonished to discover we had been there for an hour and a half."

I shook my head, not following her train of thought.

"Sherlock thinks we were exposed to an opiate. Is it possible that while I was in that state I revealed something of Sherlock's business to Frankall? Is this my fault?"

The tears that had remained in check all this time, now spilled. They streamed down her pale cheeks and splashed, unheeded, onto her tightly clenched hands.

"Hush," I said. "I do not believe that for a moment. I have been to séances. That odd thing about time contracting is not unusual. Besides, even if you were exposed to any sort of drug, it is not in your nature to betray Holmes, or anyone else, for that matter."

She nodded, but I could see she was unconvinced.

On the seat opposite, Moody snorted, coughed, and woke with a start. He released a stream of epithets in French, few of which I understood. Beatrice did, however, and laughter mingled with her tears.

Less than an hour later we passed the border, our papers were examined, and we travelled on to Basel, then Bern, and, finally, to Meiringen.

We stepped off the train and instantly my skin constricted in the cold. I pulled my hat down over my ears as I stared at the distant mountains. I had forgotten how terrifyingly beautiful they were. Moonlight sparkled on the ice and glittered the frost on the trees. Just beyond, I beheld the town, burnished gold against the deep blue night.

"Herr Doctor Watson, Lady Beatrice?" a man greeted us. "I am Olaf Ericson. Herr Mycroft Holmes asked me to take care of you while you are here in Meiringen."

"Thank you," I said. I shook his hand and made the introductions.

"I have rooms reserved for you in the Englischer Hof," he said. "It is not far."

"I remember," I said. "That is where Holmes and I stayed… last time."

"What a dreadful opinion you must have of us, Doctor," said he. "The only times you come here are during periods of great fear and danger. You must promise to return when there is nothing but pleasure and peace on your mind."

"If we find my friend alive and well, I shall gladly make you that promise for myself, at least," I replied.

We were soon at the hotel and checked into our rooms. We then joined Ericson in the manager's office. Although he was not dressed as a policeman, he bore an air of authority that commands instant obedience. As his assistance had been arranged by Mycroft Holmes, I assumed he was a government or police official. I tried later to ask him but was met with a silence as profound as a monastery.

He was far more revealing about our quarry.

"I have learned from the local officials that the men you seek arrived two days ago," he said. "There were four, one of whom matches Mr Holmes's description. The leader, the man you call Angel Frankall, was injured."

"That will be Holmes's doing," I said. "I suspect my friend struck the bounder."

"Where are they now?" Beatrice said.

"That is not so clear. I have asked the local officials to make inquiries. You must understand, there are remote areas here, and reaching some places takes much time, much effort. We shall find them, though. Of that you may be sure."

"You might send word to the hospitals and physicians in the area to be on the lookout," Beatrice said.

"Hospitals?"

"You said Frankall was injured. He may need medical attention."

"Ah, splendid. Yes, that is an excellent suggestion. I shall see to it."

"You should add pharmacies to the list, too," I said.

"I will inform to the *Schutzpolizei*. We have alerted the neighbouring towns to keep watch, in case our friends, as you would say, have moved on."

"They will not have moved on," Beatrice said. "Forgive me, but I believe they chose Meiringen for a specific reason. They will stay here."

"What would bring them here?" Ericson said.

"The Falls."

It was late and it was dark. We were suffocating in our anxiety, but there was nothing we could do at such a late hour. We retired to our rooms and waited for morning.

Monday, 17th April

Ericson met us at breakfast and shook his head at our appearance. It was evident, I suppose, that neither Beatrice nor I had slept. Moody seemed as unperturbed as ever.

"Anything?" Beatrice said, before we even sat. She did not even say good morning.

Our Swiss guide, all grace and compassion, seemed unhappy to have so little to report.

"It is early yet," he said. "But we will find these men and Herr Holmes, too. You must have faith, my lady."

I poured a cup of coffee and placed it in her hands. She hardly seemed to notice. Then she said, "I should like to see the Falls."

"That can be arranged, certainly," said the policeman.

"How soon?"

"Whenever you like; they not far. See…" He pointed out the window.

"So close," Beatrice said. "I had pictured them much further. How high are they?"

"The total drop of the actual Falls is a thousand feet, my lady. It is, in fact, a series of seven falls, with the upper being amongst the highest in the Alps. We are building a funicular railway, but it is not yet in operation."

"I assume there are several different approaches to it?"

"Yes, a number." He looked puzzled. Neither Moody nor I could enlighten him, however.

"I should like to take the most difficult path," Beatrice said. "No matter if it takes a little longer. Can we leave in thirty minutes?"

"We can, of course," Ericson replied, "But... the most difficult path?"

"They will take the easiest, most direct route," she said. "Most likely late in the evening or early in the morning.

"John, M Moody, please make sure we have enough supplies to last us for several days. Warm clothes, too. I am sure it will be very cold on the mountain."

"You mean to stay up there?" I gasped. "But for heaven's sake, why?"

"Because they will bring him there. They must."

"They may have already done so, *chère Madame*," Moody said.

"My... Holmes is hurt. He will exaggerate his injuries in order to make things as difficult as he can for his captors. Frankall, too, has sustained an injury. He needs to be able to control the situation, and this would be difficult if he were wounded. No, he will wait until he has recovered. After all, he does not know that we are looking for him."

"So your plan is to lie in wait and catch them there, on the Falls?" I said. "Well, it makes sense. But you cannot come."

"Forgive me, John, but you cannot stop me. I am going."

"It is exceedingly dangerous, Lady Beatrice," protested Ericson, his accent thickening in his agitation. "We gentlemen can attend to the matter. I shall bring the most experienced men. Truly, it is much too dangerous."

"You cannot deter me," she replied. "Now, I shall go and dress appropriately and meet you here in half an hour."

She hastened from the room and left us standing in some bewilderment.

"Well," I said, "There is nothing for it. If we do not assist, the lady will go on her own."

"On her own?" Ericson was aghast. "Doctor, I promised Herr Mycroft Holmes I would answer for the lady's safety. How am I to do that in the face of such folly? It is true the Falls are picturesque, but they are deadly. To stay there at night... it is madness."

"I do not disagree," I replied. "But you will not talk her out of it. If Beatrice stays there, then I shall, too."

"*Moi, aussi*," Moody said. His jutting chin left no room for doubt.

Ericson sighed and said, "As you wish. I shall meet you here in half an hour, as the lady requested. I shall bring the finest climbers I can find."

"Not too many, Ericson," I said. "We do not want to attract a lot of attention."

"A woman climbing the Falls will attract attention, no matter who accompanies her," he replied. "Your pardons, gentlemen."

As it transpired, it was not a woman who climbed the Falls that day, but a young man called 'Jack'. He wore stout climbing boots, heavy trousers, and a hat pulled low over his eyes. He carried a large knapsack and this seemed to be well supplied.

Moody and Ericson gasped when they saw our companion join us. "Gentlemen," Beatrice said, "Apologies for startling you with my appearance, but I think it wisest not to cause comment. Are we ready?"

Moody seemed vastly entertained by the lady's appearance. At one point he offered her his hand to climb up some steps, but she gave him an amused look. "You would not assist a young man, *monsieur*," she said. "And that is how you must treat me."

Ericson brought two well-armed policemen. Lang and Klein were, he said, the finest shots in all of Bern and excellent climbers. Neither of them seemed to notice anything amiss or, if they did, perhaps they put it down to English eccentricity.

The mountains stood in crisp contrast to the azure sky and I was reminded of that May morning eight years ago, almost to the day, when Holmes had his final encounter with Professor Moriarty. Although my friend survived, I still felt a chill of superstitious apprehension as the Falls loomed closer.

The torrent was no less vigorous this day. The agitated waters, swollen by the melting snows in the mountains above, cascaded down the coal black rock in a green river until they reached the immense chasm below in a spray of white foam.

We followed Ericson up the difficult path, and all our attention was on the climb. Still, the thunder of the water screamed in our ears and I was again transported to that time when I first beheld the Falls. I thought them fearful, then. Now, with so much at stake, they seemed utterly terrifying. I felt dizzy then at the din and the whirl; I felt no less so today.

There was little comfort in the fact that our approach was different from the one my companion and I had taken all those years ago. Something lingered in the smell of the rock, and the loam, and the pretty, white flowers. There was an echo of terror in the trees. This was a place where a fanciful man could become utterly lost.

We made our way through thick dark trees, so tall they all but obliterated the sky. The slippery rock beneath our feet vibrated from the tumult.

Although the climb was not particularly difficult, it was tiring and required some concentration. Beatrice was silent but kept pace easily. Only once did she stop and listen intently as if she had heard something.

"What is it?" I said. "Bea – I mean, Jack?"

"I thought I heard a cry," she said.

"Over this din? It doesn't seem likely."

"No. I suppose not."

She said no more, but as she continued the ascent, I saw her pause from time to time and listen.

At length, Ericson stopped and pointed, "There," he said. "You see, the platform over the Falls. Is not that where Mr Holmes encountered Professor Moriarty all those years ago?"

"Yes," I said, swallowing bile. "That's the spot."

"How do you wish to proceed?"

I examined the terrain, forcing myself to think like the old campaigner. "We need to be able to reach that platform quickly if Frankall shows. We cannot risk losing him."

"More to the point," Beatrice added, "We need to be able to rescue Sherlock. That is our priority."

"I remember Holmes telling me there is a ledge above the Falls that is several feet deep and covered in moss. A man could hide there and keep watch."

"They would not be able to reach Sherlock," Beatrice said. "Not quickly."

"No, but they could shoot anyone who tried to harm him."

Ericson nodded. He spoke in German to Lang. The man nodded, and hurried off through the trees.

"Carl knows these Falls better than anyone," Ericson said. "He knows the place you mean, and shall hide himself there."

"Good," Beatrice said. "Now, how many of us can get onto that platform and can we do so undetected?"

The policeman stared at her. I must say that while I have known Beatrice for a couple of years now and am familiar with her sometimes wayward behaviour, this seemed extreme.

"Lady Beatrice," Ericson said gently, "The area is not large. Two men, perhaps, could hide there, but there is no guarantee they would not be seen by someone with a telescope. Besides, even at this time of year there are visitors who must remark upon the presence of people who appear to be loitering. Moreover, there is the risk that the fellows would just turn and run; we would not have the means of cutting off their escape."

She frowned and her eyes scanned the view. Her attitude of close concentration and analysis reminded me irresistibly of Holmes.

"What about the path leading up to the platform? Is there somewhere along the way where we might conceal ourselves?"

Ericson again consulted in German with the second policeman, Klein. Apparently satisfied, he said, "There are trees that would provide some cover. Still, if anyone is watching, particularly if they have a telescope, they may spy our approach."

"We must risk it," Beatrice said.

Useless to remonstrate with her.

The ground was wet and muddy in places. The wind was high from the mountain and tasted of snow. For all that, Beatrice was undeterred. She would wait, alone if need be.

So we waited.

Moody, resourceful as ever, produced some bread, cheese, and fruit. We men ate heartily. The climb and the mountain air had sharpened our appetites. Beatrice, however, pecked at the meal and refused the flask the Frenchman offered. The day trickled on.

Despite the weather, the little Frenchman was in excellent spirits. His humour and indefatigable mood cheered us no end, and even Beatrice seemed uplifted by his optimism.

"Why so sad, *ma cher*?" he said. "Your friend is no ordinary man who may be destroyed by a monster. He is Sherlock Holmes. No man has more strength, or more guile than he."

"Thank you, dear M Moody," Beatrice said. "Your reminder gives me hope."

The sun crept across the mountain and eventually vanished. I felt that all the light in the world had been snuffed out, leaving us, a weary, frozen group of stalwarts, waiting for the end of time.

Ericson rose and said, "Well, my friends, I think it is dark enough now for us to make our way down to the trail. Please follow close behind Klein. It would be very dangerous to get lost here."

We took him at his word and formed a silent file behind the policeman, with Ericson bringing up the rear.

Although we did not have far to travel, the darkness slowed us down and made us exquisitely cautious. The half-moon made diamonds of the water, but I doubt any of us were in any mood to appreciate its beauty.

Almost an hour passed before we reached the path. From this spot, we could see the platform a short distance beyond.

We made camp in the trees and waited in silence. Ericson set the young policeman a little further along the path to keep watch.

After about an hour, Moody whispered, "You do not think we may have missed them?"

"I think it unlikely," Ericson replied. "By all accounts this Frankall fellow was limping badly. As you have seen, the path up to the Falls is not difficult, but it is steep and requires some stamina." He hesitated and then added, "I suppose he might have sent one of his men to do the job."

"He will not send anyone else," Beatrice said. "He has reason for bringing Sherlock here. As far as he is concerned, there is no need of haste." Even in the splintered moonlight, her anguish was clear. "He has been hurt by my… friend, and will want to exact his revenge."

"I do not understand why he brought M Holmes here at all," Moody whispered.

"For two reasons," Beatrice softly replied. "Firstly, he wanted information. He tried to get it from another man. Tortured him. The man managed to escape but later took his own life, unable to live with the horror of his experience. Frankall thinks he can get this information from Sherlock. That is my theory."

"What information?" Ericson said. He suddenly seemed like a policeman. An utterly formidable policeman.

Beatrice made a gesture that he should lower his voice. Given the din of the Falls, I doubt anyone could have heard us even if they were only a few feet away. Still, better to be safe.

"What information?" Ericson whispered.

"Something to do with the British government. I do not know. Frankall has undoubtedly promised someone that he would obtain this information by any means. Since he failed on his first attempt, he hopes to extract it from Sherlock."

"Frankall made promises?" I said.

"He is a mercenary," she pointed out. "A labourer for hire. His reputation rests on keeping his promises. I would imagine by now he is desperate. He will come to the Falls, and soon. He hopes to terrorise Sherlock into telling him what he wants to know."

"You said two reasons," Moody said.

Dropping her voice even lower, Beatrice continued, "Sherlock has become a nuisance to Frankall. More than that, he has wounded him. Nothing is more dangerous than a wounded animal. I suspect whatever information Frankall thinks Sherlock has, it is secondary to his thirst for revenge. He wants to see Sherlock suffer."

The night deepened. The moon rose high above the mountains and glittered on the water. Beneath us, the ground thundered from the ceaseless rush of the water.

Moody fell asleep with his head tucked into his arms and his shoulders hunched over.

For some time, Beatrice paced, and then, finally, settled down in a troubled silence upon the tarp.

Tuesday, 18th April

I must have fallen asleep. I started as a hand shook my shoulder. Beatrice, her hand on my mouth, whispered into my ear, "They are here."

The sky hinted at the coming dawn. Already a greenish luminous light glowed along the eastern horizon. It glowed on the face of Beatrice, terrible as Nemesis, as she stood at attention with a weapon in her hand.

The young policeman had returned. He whispered in Ericson's ear and gestured towards the path. Moody stood in lethal calm, a revolver at the ready. It took me a moment, but then I heard the catch of voices weaving through the din of the Falls. They were not making any attempt at circumspection. No doubt they thought themselves invincible.

A few moments later, the men emerged from the trees. I could not tell how many. The stealthy dawn played tricks with the shadows.

"You will lower your weapons, please, gentlemen," Ericson commanded.

I held my breath and peered through the darkness for Holmes. Then someone cried out and chaos followed. The path suddenly seemed overcrowded. As I ran through the trees to help my companions, I heard screams and the sound of running feet. Blows rained and bodies collided. Someone struck my face and I fell backwards.

I still clutched my weapon but dared not fire for fear of hitting an ally. Even the man who struck me, though only a few feet away, was a shadow.

Someone ran past me towards the platform with another quick on his heels. I did not see Beatrice.

Gunfire ricocheted through the mountains and the man who had struck me fell dead at my feet. I peered at his face but did not recognise him.

I looked up and was alarmed to discover the path was now empty. What had happened to the others? And where, dear God, was Holmes?

"The Falls!" Moody cried, rushing past me from who knows where. We ran up to path to the platform, slipping and falling on the treacherous stone. I beheld two men struggling on the platform and I felt a frisson of terror. The scene echoed that deadly battle of eight years ago when Holmes faced Professor Moriarty on that very spot.

Then, it was Holmes's knowledge of Baritsu, the Japanese method of defence, which saved him.

The sun suddenly sparked through the trees and transformed the deadly waters into a rainbow of colour. It would have been a thing of spectacular beauty had the life-and-death struggle not been so terrifying. My eyes were momentarily blinded by the light and I could not identify either of the combatants. As my sight improved, I beheld the smaller man strike an almighty blow. The other, stumbling backwards, reached out and grasped his foe by the coat. In the next instant both went tumbling over the falls into the raging chasm.

23

"Watson!" I felt rather than heard my name through the torrent. I saw Beatrice at the end of the platform kneeling over a prone figure. I ran, fell, slipped along the stone, and stumbled to their side.

She was cradling him in her arms. He raised a hand and I grasped it with immeasurable joy. His eyes skimmed mine then closed.

"Holmes!" I cried. "Oh thank God! We must get him off this mountain. He's in a bad way."

Between us, Moody and I clumsily carried Holmes down the path to where Ericson stood over the bodies of two men.

"Your friend? He is alive?" Ericson greeted us.

"Yes, but he is badly hurt," I replied.

He gave some rapid instructions in German to the policeman and then explained in English, "I have asked Klein to secure this area. He will send Lang to run on ahead and get help. This fellow," he prodded one of the bodies with his toe, "clings to life. No, Doctor, you see to Herr Holmes. Klein will be sure to keep our prisoner alive, never fear. Now, stay close to me and we shall bring Mr Holmes to safety."

We made the brutal journey back to the hotel in silence. Ericson, Moody, and I carried Holmes down the endless path. Beatrice kept pace. At the base of the cliff, a group of emergency workers joined us. They placed Holmes on a stretcher and carried him the rest of the way.

When we reached the *Englischer Hof,* I urged Beatrice to lie down, but she would have none of it. She ordered servants to build up the fire, to bring hot water and towels, to fetch whatever supplies I needed. When they did not understand her English or her rough German, Moody translated.

I have beheld Holmes injured, ill, bleeding, and suffering from the effects of his seven-and-a-half-percent solution of cocaine, but I have never seen him so close to death.

Beatrice helped me undress him and bind his wounds. He had suffered a number of beatings, and, from the rosary of bruises on his arms, it was evident he had been held by vicious hands while he was pummelled. His back bore three diagonal wounds from the right shoulder down to the left hip, and these still bled. More even than these wounds, were the punctures that scarred his forearms. So this is how they had controlled him: by injecting him with some filthy poison.

I held my outrage in check as I got to work. As a physician, I am accustomed to donning an outwardly optimistic demeanour, no matter how great my inner turmoil. I donned this façade now, as much for my own sake as for Beatrice's.

She and I did not speak except on the business of medicine. Not until the wounds were dressed and my friend wrapped up in warm blankets in a comfortable bed did I look at my nurse. Beatrice sank onto a chair by Holmes's side, silent and pale, and held his hand. I do not think she even noticed the stream of tears coursing down her cheeks.

Moody placed a mug of hot chocolate in her hands, and another in mine. "You will do *monsieur* far more good by keeping well," he said. "Please, drink."

We obeyed him. I became aware of my hunger. It felt like days since we had eaten a proper meal – not since Paris, really. More even than food, I felt the need for sleep.

Moody, in his prescient way, set up a makeshift bed on the sofa. "You shall be near M Holmes if he needs you, Doctor," he said. "You will aid him more if you are rested. As for you, Mme Holmes," he said, addressing Beatrice by her married name for the first time, "The bed is big enough if you should care to sleep beside your husband."

For all her weariness and distress, his words did not go unnoticed. She managed to smile. "I think I shall, M Moody," she replied. "I trust you shall take yourself to bed, too?"

"I shall, by your leave. Unless you have something for me to do?"

"Only to take your own advice and rest, my dear friend." She kissed his cheek and he smiled, fanned himself exaggeratedly with a little *ooh-la-la* noise, and then left the room.

Saturday, 29th April

After a wretched week, Holmes's physical wounds began to mend. Thank heaven for his remarkable constitution. However, he continued to cry out in his sleep. I feared the wounds to his mind would take much longer to heal.

Beatrice and I remained at his side, except when the redoubtable M Moody ordered us to sleep.

Our *cher ami* managed the hotel staff, mediated with officials, kept Mycroft up to date, and ensured that Beatrice and I ate, slept, and had everything we needed. He was endlessly energetic and cheerful. I confess I do not know how we would have managed without him.

Ericson called in to see us a few days ago. He has pieced together much of the Sorcerer's story.

The two men shot on the path were Timms, Frankall's disreputable servant, and Hoffmann, a Swiss of dubious character who had been working for Frankall since the man's arrival in the Canton.

Timms died instantly, thanks to a shot fired from the ledge above the falls by the eagle-eyed Lang. Ericson felled

Hoffmann, though the fellow's injuries were not life-threatening. Ericson persuaded him, who knows how, to confess his part in Frankall's activities.

The Swiss claimed he met the Sorcerer in France some years ago. When Frankall wrote to say he was coming to Meiringen and needed a 'discreet' chalet for his use, Hoffmann assumed some sort of nefarious activity. This bothered him not at all. The more deadly the plan, the greater the fee at the end of it.

Frankall arrived with his servants, a brute called Timms, and a Jew by the name of Horowitz. There was another man, too, but Hoffmann never learned his name. He blanched to learn the other was the renowned detective Sherlock Holmes.

Holmes caused Frankall endless frustration, Hoffmann said. From some scraps of conversation, he gathered that Holmes possessed information of immense value. Information that could destroy every great house in Europe. The man who could glean that information would be a king. A god. These were Frankall's ramblings. All that stood in his way was my friend's silence. Holmes was stubborn, however, and held his tongue no matter what 'inducements' were brought to bear.

Frankall meant to take Holmes to the Falls. Holmes had spoken of them with revulsion while he was under the effects of some drug, according to Timms. Hoffmann did not know anything else. He had not broken the law.

Ericson pointed out that he broken into the home of Herr Deiter while that good man conducted business in Stockholm, and there was the small matter of kidnapping…

"By the by," Ericson told us, "We identified the two men who went over the Falls. One was the fellow you called Frankall, and the other a Jew by the name of Horowitz."

After he left, I said to Beatrice, "There can be no question now that they had all of these plans in place before you ever met Frankall. This was not your fault."

"That is true, isn't it? Yes, it is a relief, but I am puzzled. How did Frankall know of Sherlock's interest in him?"

"He saw us in Ireland. Probably he recognised us."

"Perhaps." She did not seem convinced.

Friday, 5th May: Paris

Beatrice suggested Holmes would recover more quickly if we moved him from the shadow of the Falls. I confess I had some reservations about my friend's ability to withstand the journey, but he nodded his assent with as much vigour as his weakened condition would allow.

Moody clapped his hands with glee and said we should worry about nothing, he would arrange everything. And so he did. Our every possible need he anticipated and met. B said he had learned efficiency from the Swiss. With a smile and a wink he replied, *mais, non, chere Madame,* it was the Swiss who learned efficiency from him!

Ericson came to the train station to see us off. "Try not to think too badly of us, Herr Holmes," he said. Holmes shook his hand. I thought for a moment he would reply, but he said nothing.

Last night we arrived back in Paris and are again M Moody's guests. For the first time in weeks, all of us slept soundly.

As you requested, my dear Holmes, this is a full account of the days you were missing and the steps your friends took to find you. I hope you will find them sufficient to 'complete the narrative' of the Sorcerer case.

24
FROM THE DIARY OF MR SHERLOCK HOLMES

Tuesday, 9th May

I am sitting by the window enjoying the warm, pink Parisian air. Somewhere in the distance, a young girl is singing Shubert's *Ave Maria*. The purity of the music pierces me like the point of a sword. For the first time in weeks, I am alone. My condition has improved sufficiently that my friends deem me safe to leave for a short time.

Such a ridiculous production. "I can stay if you want, Holmes…" "I shall not be gone for long, Sherlock…" "I'm sure M Moody can keep you company…" As if an intelligent, self-sufficient man cannot be trusted to his own devices for an hour.

I am peevish. I understand their concern and were our situations reversed, I have no doubt I should be as anxious as they. Still, I am irked by their relentless solicitude.

Watson has gone to lie down. He is utterly exhausted. He is my friend and I have the greatest affection for the fellow, but at present I am sick of the sight of him. His endless patience, his calm, his refusal to react to my most insufferable behaviour make me feel a wretch. I vent my frustration on him, and so the cycle begins again.

B has gone out to lunch with some of her old friends. She, too, is gaunt with anxiety. I cannot bear to see her so concerned yet I am unable to do anything to alleviate her worries, and so I sit and fret and agitate myself.

I am profoundly grateful to M Moody. He, alone, is cheerful and seems indifferent to my health. He bounds into the room each morning with a sunny, "I hope you are well, monsieur!" He does not wait for a reply, and carries on as if everything were perfectly normal. Normality is such a relief.

He taught me to play backgammon. We sit at the board and he tells me about the world outside this room. He speaks intelligently about the sciences and music. His understanding of European politics is profound. Mycroft would enjoy a conversation with him, I think.

Last evening he brought me a gift. An elegant journal bound in ox-blood leather. The pages are a delicate cream and very fine.

"Sometimes it is easier for a man to share his thoughts with a page than with a companion," he said, as he handed it to me.

The thought was as wise as it was kind, much like M Moody himself. It was he, too, who persuaded B and Watson to give me some time alone.

"It is difficult for a Frenchman to admit it," he said, with a twinkle, "But even of love there can be too much. Let the man be. Give him some air. You will all be the better for it." And so – oh, bliss! – a few hours alone with my new journal and Schubert.

I want to begin by piecing together the events of the last weeks. Remembering is painful, but essential. Sharing these thoughts with my friends would wound them; better to write them down.

It is difficult to reconstruct the past few weeks. Between pain and drug-induced hallucinations, I cannot be sure what is real and what is not.

I remember leaving B's house in the early hours and starting the walk home to Baker Street. It was a crisp night, with frost crunching the ground underfoot and the stars coldly beautiful. I heard a sudden gallop of horse's hooves… That is my last clear thought for many days – indeed, weeks.

There are moments of lucidity. Hearing a voice speaking my name, the sound of laughter, the burn of the needle in my vein.

I remember waking in some underground room. For several minutes, I pretended unconsciousness and used the time to explore my surroundings. I was lying on a cold concrete floor. The back of my head throbbed and I could taste blood in my mouth.

Without moving or changing my breathing, I let my mind explore the room. It was small space, low-ceilinged, about twelve feet square. From the dullness of the sound, I did not think there were windows. There was one door and this was a sturdy beast of a thing.

"So you are awake, Mr Holmes," a smooth voice said. Then, "Pick him up."

I was hoisted to my feet by two pairs of ungentle arms.

"That is better, is it not?" Frankall said. "Men should speak to each other face to face."

He was precisely as Glaser and the rabbi described: tall, thin, with a sensual face. His eyes were dark and intense. I could understand why people considered him hypnotic.

"Well, sir," I said, calmly. "This is extraordinary behaviour. To snatch a gentleman from the street and hold him against his will. What do you mean by it?"

"It is useless to play the fool with me, Mr Sherlock Holmes," he replied. "Do you think I did not recognise you in Ireland?"

There was no point in denying it. "And I saw you in Kells," I said, "When you kidnapped Hardwicke's son. For shame, sir. No one but a cad would abuse a child."

He smirked. "I had no person animus towards the boy. I am a businessman, guided by pragmatism. I have no use for your outmoded ideas of morality."

I said, as cheerfully as I could, "I have my own ideas of morality. But a child? And women, too, you have destroyed. Not only those whose minds you ruined, but others whose husbands you have stolen. A Jewish woman in Hatton Garden grieves the loss of such a husband and struggles to raise their children without him."

One of the men holding me cried in anguish. Frankall froze him with a glance.

"So you recognised my little lapdog?" he said. "Well, well, are you not a clever fellow? Not clever enough, I fear."

"You would match your wits against mine? Better men than you have tried and failed."

"Indeed? Yet here we are. You are my prisoner, Mr Holmes; not vice versa."

"You really think my friends will not suspect where you have taken me? They will come looking."

"Let them look."

At that, I lunged at him and struck a powerful blow to his head before Timms overpowered me. He bludgeoned me with his fists while a tentative Horowitz held me down. Frankall, streaming blood from his nose and mouth, came at me with a whip. I believe he would have killed me in his fury, but Horowitz cried, "My Lord, surely he is more use to you alive?"

Frankall lowered the dripping weapon and said, "Good. That is well thought of, Horowitz."

They shackled me to the wall.

"You two can leave," Frankall told his underlings.

The two scurried from the room. Frankall said nothing for some minutes. I studied my surroundings more openly. We were in a subterranean room. Faintly in the distance I could smell bacon frying. So, Highgate, the basement of Frankall's home, morning.

My captor said, "It is a waste to destroy a brain like yours."

"You had no compunction about destroying Updike," I replied.

"My, my, you have been busy. Yes, it was a shame to unpick Updike's brain, but he would resist me. It is unsound – you must realise this, Mr Holmes – it is unsound reasoning not to submit when one has met a superior mind. That is the trouble with men like Augustus Updike and you, and, I dare say, your brother Mycroft: You all believe so resolutely in your own superiority. You forget how limited you are by your outmoded standards: Queen and Country and Honour. It is all nonsense, you know."

"There are things in the universe greater than the individual," I replied, "Even a superior individual. Without a sense of honour a man is no better than…"

"Than?"

"You."

He chuckled. "I am what a man should aspire to, Mr Holmes. I have studied all the ancient texts, the codices and the various philosophies. I even brought in Horowitz to teach me. His studies were far superior to mine and I had hopes that he would bring me enlightenment. Yet for all his learning, he is as lost and hopeless as any other man. Consider, the fool believes he is damned eternally if he eats a little bacon. Such beliefs are a shackle to the mind. Eventually, I realised that all philosophy and religion serve the same purpose: to keep a man in check. To force him to be a sheep."

I yawned.

"Do I bore you, Mr Holmes?"

"A little."

"I tell you these things because I believe you have a mind almost equal to my own. I have no desire to cause you pain, but neither will I shirk from it if you present me with no alternative. I want you to think, Mr Holmes. Tell me what I need to know and I will be generous. Refuse and... well, let us say refusal is not an option."

"And what is it you want to know?"

"Your brother Mycroft, Mr Holmes. I want you to tell me about your brother Mycroft."

"Who?"

The next hours, days, perhaps, were... unpleasant. Almost as bad as the brutality was Frankall's clinical detachment. He never raised his voice. Sometimes he wrote in his notebook when my resistance surprised him. I might be an animal subjected to experimentation for all his compassion.

He refused me food and drink. "Even Sherlock Holmes's strength is not bottomless. Let him thirst and hunger and he will submit."

I did not submit.

Eventually, he resorted to the needle.

Unlike the familiar sensations of my seven-percent solution of cocaine, this cocktail created horrifying images in the brain. I saw myself running through the moors with a blood-red moon lying low on the horizon. A hound bayed and snarled. Then the scene changed and I was there, on the mountain, with *him* at my throat. As if he had never died but continued to cling to me, his white and ghastly fingers clutching at me. The Falls spat in my face and I think I cried out.

All the while I heard Frankall's voice, soothing, hypnotic, promising me any number of pleasures and comforts if only I would answer his questions.

Mycroft, he said. Tell me about Mycroft. Tell me about your brother, Mr Holmes.

I remembered Mycroft. He seemed unreal, like a character in a story, and yet I clung to the memory. I remembered our long walks together when we were children. The way he sought to protect me. All the things he taught me.

"Use your brains, Sherlock," he said so often. He said it to me now.

I have survived on my wits all my life. I would not, now, surrender to fear and pain.

I remembered Tibet and the time I spent studying meditation with the monks. Dorjeh, my guide, challenged me to explore the confines of reality, to see beyond the obvious to what lies in another realm. These teachings sustained me over the long, bloody hours in that basement.

My mind would sustain me. It would see me through fear and pain. Cling to that.

Updike had once spoken of Mycroft being the Queen's linchpin. The card in the middle. Remove him and the house topples. Updike died protecting Mycroft, a man he hardly knew. How could I, his brother, be less faithful?

Someone suspected Mycroft's role, a role that is known only to a very few people. Watson and I were long acquainted before I even told him of my brother's existence. It was not until several years later that I revealed to him the truth of his extraordinary position.

But someone suspected Mycroft's role. Suspected only; they did not know for sure. What would they do with such information once they had it? I could not say, but I knew it must be catastrophic.

If I were to protect Mycroft, I must know who it was who threatened him.

More poison in my arm. More blackness and terror. Voices filling the void.

"This is not working…" Whose voice? Horowitz?

"He is resilient. We must increase the dosage."

"It will kill him."

Voices coming in and out of focus. Eventually, I gathered they were discussing taking me abroad.

"The risk, my lord…"

"…Worth it… England too dangerous… powerful friends… *He* means to destroy me…"

Well, if they were planning on taking me out of the country, that would afford me several chances to escape. Who was 'he'? Not me. Some other enemy.

My first opportunity came when they took me out of the house. Unfortunately, they had drugged me so heavily that despite my best efforts I could not rouse myself to full consciousness. An old cabbie helped me into his Hansom and I tried to speak. My words slurred however, and he drew the obvious if erroneous conclusion that I was intoxicated.

I was pinned between Timms and Horowitz at the railway station but I left a trail of blood behind me. I hoped someone would notice, but it appeared no one did. The great indifference or blindness of the general public worked against me. *Reichenbach,* I managed to say, over and over.

Blackness. When I awoke, we were on the boat. The sea air revived me somewhat, but I continued to play the part of the drugged man. When we landed at the port, I took my chance. I struck Frankall with all the force I could, sending him reeling, I heard the crack of bone as he fell. I fled. I shouted for a *douanier*, and a particularly stupid specimen stopped me.

"What is this, monsieur?" he asked.

I babbled my name and told him to contact my friends in Paris or in London. They would attest to my identity.

In the middle of this exchange, Horowitz and Timms caught up with me. Calmly, with all the craftiness of his sort, Timms said that I was a mental patient they were transporting to a sanatorium. I was dangerous, and had already injured the doctor in charge of my case. A bloody and bloody-minded Frankall arrived, limping badly. Seething. But he is smooth, that one, and easily convinced the foolish official that he was telling the truth.

"I am Sherlock Holmes!" I cried, but no one believed me.

Back on the train, and only the chance of drawing attention kept Frankall from doing me mischief. Again, I was dosed with the drug.

I have no recollection of the rest of the journey. Watson tells me we spent a few days in a chalet, but I have no memory of that, either.

It was not until we were headed towards the Falls that I began to rouse. The drug amplified my horror of that ghastly place. They half-dragged, half-carried me up the mountain. Darkness shrouded everything. The thunder of the Falls heralded death.

Despite everything, I refused to surrender to despair. I still had my wits. I had good friends and a brother. They were certainly looking for me by now. I could rely on them to move heaven and earth to find me. The cabbie in London would remember me; he would lead my friends to the station. I had told him where we were going; perhaps he would pass that word along. Would he remember 'Reichenbach'? I prayed so. The foolish *douanier* in France, too, would remember. Perhaps even now he had had second thoughts and was alerting officials along the line. A vain hope, I knew, but that was all I had to sustain me. No, not quite all. There was the satisfaction of seeing the injuries I had caused Frankall. He was almost as bloody and beaten as I. And I had one other asset: Horowitz.

It was he who brought me food and water in defiance of Frankall's orders. He did what he could to treat my wounds, too, and he whispered to me what he knew of the Sorcerer's plans. Only one thing he would not do: facilitate my escape. Giving me water and food was as much as he dared. To be fair to the fellow, even that much was a grave risk.

Frankall hired a man called Hoffmann as a guide. The fellow was, I gathered, a petty crook, and had no belly for violence. The sight of blood made him ill. A gun ensured his allegiance.

"It is not for long," Frankall snapped. "We will take him up the mountain. The sight of the place and the drug in his vein will open his mouth. We cannot afford to fail. Not now."

And once I opened my mouth, into the chasm I would go, I had no doubt.

We set out in the middle of the night. Frankall, still limping, muttered oaths. Even Timms, as contemptible a creature as I have ever met, cowed in the face of his master's fury. The men tied my hands behind my back and forced me up the steep incline of the mountain. When I dug in my heels and refused to walk, they dragged me over the cruel ground.

Then I saw it. So benign it looked in the silvery dawn, so terrifying: The platform where Professor Moriarty and I fought eight years ago. In my drugged and battered state, I believed I could hear the professor's voice cackling with laughter from the waters.

Then, just as all of my hopes tumbled into the abyss, they soared again: someone was commanding Frankall and the others to lower their weapons.

What happened next is a confusion. I remember Frankall shrieking in fury; a shot – or was it two? – roaring through the canyon; a melee of pounding fists and the spume of blood.

Frankall dragged me onto the platform, determined that if this must be his end, he would not die alone. Unlike my last encounter at the Falls, this time I had no strength, no guile to protect me. Then, from nowhere, Horowitz lunged at the fellow.

I hugged the rock, too spent to do anything but watch in horror as the two mirrored my battle eight years ago. This time, however, both men plunged to their deaths.

The rabbi once told me of a Jewish maxim: Who saves one life saves the world entire. I wonder if that was on Horowitz's mind as he sacrificed himself to save me. He would, I am convinced, deem it a means of atonement for whatever evil he had done in Frankall's name.

Saturday, 13th May

I continue to gain my strength. This evening, feeling much more myself, Beatrice and I dined alone in a small restaurant in the city. There is comfort in civility, in the chink of crystal and the glow of candlelight. Here, in this City of Light, one can be nearly persuaded that darkness does not exist.

Beatrice was pleased to see me do justice to my meal. We talked of music and art. A civilized evening shared by two civilized people.

Later we walked arm in arm along the banks of the Seine.

"You seem destined to come to my aid, my dear Beatrice," I said. "Not for the first time, I owe you my life."

"I cannot claim the sole credit," she replied. "Watson was stalwart. You have never seen a man so determined. Mycroft, too, helped in so many ways, as did Moody. When I think of the people who might have helped you and who failed, I am full of fury."

We sat on a bench and watched the lights perform a tarantella on the river.

"The Falls still haunt me," I said. "This gentle river is more to my taste. I think I shall never again take pleasure in fast-moving waters."

"No, indeed," she agreed. "I expected the Falls to be terrible from everything you and John told me, but their magnitude far surpassed my imaginings. Dear God, Sherlock. How on earth did you escape from the Professor?"

I had no answer to that. I have spent years trying to forget it. "I would not have survived this time had Horowitz not come to my aid."

"Did you write to his wife?"

"No. I thought it would be better to tell her such news in person. She should take comfort in knowing he found his honour at the end."

"I am here if you need to talk, my dear," Beatrice said.

I shook my head. "It is not the blackness of men's hearts nor the dread of nature's majesty that occupy my thoughts. I suspect there is more to this case than I first realised."

Beatrice smiled.

"What is it?" I said.

"You are thinking of the case. Now I know you are getting better."

25

Friday, 19th May

Home.

Gillespie met us at the station with a carriage. Mycroft sent him; he would trust my safety to no other.

Ah, the smell of London. A soft rain, as the Irish would call it, drizzled over the beloved streets. Paris is beautiful, but London is home.

Mrs Hudson greeted me with tears, embraces, and, most remarkable of all, silence. Try as I may, I could not persuade her to unclench her hold. Her head bobbed on my shoulder as she sobbed. It distressed me to see the good woman in such straits, but I never know what to say in these emotional moments. Fortunately, Watson took care of her. I hastened upstairs.

I was startled to find my brother waiting for me.

Mycroft, to my considerable astonishment, greeted me with an embrace. "I feared I would never see you again, my dear brother," he said. "I am very glad you have returned home safely."

For the next hour, we shared our stories. No longer fearful of my health, Watson and B spoke openly about their own adventures. I learned how B climbed up to the waterfall to wait for me; how she deduced Frankall's plans and set a trap to catch him.

"Remarkable," Mycroft said, in admiration.

"We would not have managed without M Moody," my wife replied. "He helped us in more ways than we can count."

"He is a highly intelligent and trustworthy man," I said. "Have you met him, Mycroft?"

257

Mycroft gave me a look I could not decipher, and then he laughed loudly. "Of course, I know him. Moody works for me. Did you not know?"

"What?" we cried.

In retrospect, it seemed obvious. I was annoyed with myself that I had not realised it.

"You must not be too hard on yourself, brother dear," Mycroft said. "Moody is extremely circumspect and would not have discussed his work openly. Besides, you were hardly yourself."

Mycroft asked about my experiences as a captive. He and the others listened in silence to my edited account of the events. Only when I concluded my narrative did he lean forward and squeeze my shoulder. My trials have made him remarkably effusive.

"I cannot imagine how you survived, Sherlock."

"I had Horowitz helping me. I knew all of you would be looking for me. When the night was particularly unpleasant, I remembered music. B's piano sustained me in immeasurable ways."

She turned her head but not before I saw her tears.

Mycroft said, "What was Frankall's interest in me, Sherlock? Do you know?"

"Horowitz told me Frankall was hired by someone else, someone with an interest in the British government."

"Did he know who it was?"

"No."

Mycroft's look was sceptical.

"He did not know, Mycroft. He would have told me if he had. He told me everything he could, everything he thought would help."

"Why?" Watson said. "Do not misunderstand me, I am very grateful to the man for all he did, but if he was so opposed to Frankall, why did he not simply turn him into the authorities?"

"Fear. Horowitz was in terror of the man. Initially, he thought Frankall shared his thirst for knowledge. By the time he realised he was a charlatan who only wanted to know enough to put a gloss on his lies, it was too late. I suspect Frankall thought that having Horowitz around, looking up to him, added to his prestige."

"Why did he not leave?" B said.

"Frankall introduced Horowitz to opiates and he soon became addicted. Frankall used the drug to compel his obedience. He also threatened Horowitz's family."

"Fascinating," Mycroft said in a bored voice, "but it does not advance our queries."

"No, it does not."

"The situation with the Boers is becoming alarming, Sherlock. We are planning a conference in Bloemfontein at the end of the month. I believe it will be our last chance to avoid war. If Frankall's ally has anything to do with that situation there may be a great many lives at stake."

Outside, the wind picked up and the rain slashed against the windowpane. The sound brought back hideous memories.

"I am sick of death," I cried.

There was an awkward silence then Watson said, "We all are, Holmes. But it's not all gloom, is it? You are home; you are safe you are with people who care about you."

I forced a smile. "That is true."

B put her hand on my shoulder and said, "It will take time, my dear. I am sure you will feel better just sleeping in your own bed tonight." Then, brightly, she added, "I hope I can persuade all of you to have dinner with me in Wimpole Street tomorrow?"

Mycroft patted his stomach and said, "Bella Chabon will prepare something special, eh? I can never resist your table, my dear sister. You may count on me."

"What about the Boers?" B said, teasing.

"They will not be deterred by my missing meals," Mycroft said.

"You can count on Watson and me, too," I replied. "It has been some time since you played the piano for me, B."

"I long for my music," Beatrice said. "Sherlock, is there anything special you should like me to play for you?"

"I feel a strange longing for Chopin," I replied.

"Chopin," Mycroft said, snorting. "Sentimental twaddle."

"Of course," B said, "I do not have to play at all…"

"Chopin will do," Mycroft said, quickly. "I am in a mood to be sentimental."

Saturday, 20ᵗʰ May

I slept better than I would have expected. There is a sense of security in being in one's own bed that lends comfort. Even the sound of the rain did not keep me awake.

I awoke around ten o'clock to a loud hammering on the front door. I staggered out of bed and stumbled into the sitting room, hunting for matches to light my pipe. The door to my room burst open and half a dozen of the Irregulars came tumbling in.

"Right, lads," Kevin said, giving me a positively imperious look. "'e's alive."

They turned to leave.

"Wait a moment," I cried. "What is this about? Kevin?"

"We saw all the blood in that basement, Mr H," he replied in a stony voice. "Didn't know if you was alive or dead. Would it 'ave killed yer to tell us you was all right, like?"

I fought back the grin that tugged at my lips.

"I am sorry, Kevin. All you boys did a splendid job. Lady Beatrice and Doctor Watson told me how much you helped. I am extremely grateful."

They stood staring at me. I found myself unbalanced by their mute accusation. "I should have sent word," I said. "I did not realise you would all be so worried."

Still no response.

"At the very least, I ought to pay you for your trouble."

I put my hands in my pockets and realised I was still wearing my dressing gown. Before I could look for my wallet, however, the little troop turned and marched from the room. Kevin lingered a moment at the door and said, "Stuff it, Mr H. You fink we just 'elp yer for the bangers 'n' mash, eh?"

Watson sat silently at the table throughout this exchange. Not until the front door closed and we heard the gaggle of lads hurry away did he burst out laughing.

"I do not know what they want," I said.

"Just to know you are all right," he said. "They're very fond of you, Holmes."

"And this is how they show it?"

"Certainly." He turned the page of his newspaper. "What did you expect, hugs and kisses?"

I decided not to worry about the boys. Instead, I enjoyed a leisurely breakfast (oh, kippers!), then I went to get a haircut, followed by a walk along the Strand with Watson. It felt a positive age since last I walked these beloved streets, not merely a few weeks.

Dinner this evening was all that is elegant and genteel. Mycroft waxed lyrical about Mme Chabon's cooking. The food was, indeed, splendid, but it was nothing to the delight that came after the meal. B indulged my every musical whim, playing piece after piece on the piano. Chopin and Liszt, Mozart and Bach.

I sat in utter joy, transfixed by beauty of the music and by my splendid wife. This place, an oasis of civility in a reckless world, was one I returned to in my mind many times over the past weeks. Sometimes it was the memory of B's playing that sustained me; sometimes it was recollecting the many conversations we had enjoyed here.

After two hours, she pleaded for a rest and we enjoyed an excellent claret. I sat back with my eyes closed and let the words of my brother, my wife, and my friend wash over me. What peace and joy in such simple pleasures.

I decided to stay the night in Wimpole Street but, although I was tired, it took a long time for me to fall asleep. B stayed awake with me as long as she could, but eventually she could resist her exhaustion no longer.

For hours I tried in vain to slow my mind and settle my thoughts. The fear and rage that sustained me over the past weeks continued to course through me.

Try as I may, I could not shake the black memories of my two encounters at the Falls. Though I made light of my struggle with Professor Moriarty when I first returned to Baker Street, the truth is that life-or-death battle continued to haunt me. Indeed, one of the reasons I renounced my former habit of taking opiates was fear that I might relive those experiences. Now I had indeed relived them, both in the real world and in the more terrifying one of my mind. I did not know if I could recover a second time.

I never told Watson, but one of the reasons I remained silent after my 'death' was because I wanted to forget. I used my time in Tibet to learn a number of mental disciplines. It was well that I did; they proved invaluable in aiding me through my recent torment. Even so, Frankall managed to penetrate my defences far more than I cared to admit. I have never seen myself as a sentimentalist or, indeed, anything but a clinician. I prided myself on my detachment, yet, compared with Frankall, I was as emotional as a new mother. I may not possess Watson's warmth, but I have always treated people as human beings. Not laboratory specimens.

While Frankall studied me, I studied him. And in doing so, I learned something about myself. Not only do I lack his frozen dispassion, but I would not have it at any price. Were I so thoroughly indifferent to the sufferings of others, I would have become a scientist or a mathematician. Deny it though I may, it is my desire for justice and my compassion for the needs of the vulnerable that spurs me.

I rose from the bed and sat in the meditative position the monks in Tibet taught me. I would not lose myself in the indulgences that could, I knew, destroy me. Nor would I deny the passion that burns within my heart. I am not an addict, nor am I an automaton.

I am Sherlock Holmes.

26

Sunday, 21st May

This morning I went to Hatton Garden. Horowitz sacrificed himself to save me. The least I could do was tell his wife in person.

I went first to the rabbi's house. He took one fleeting look at me and led me into his study. As his wife served me cherry-flavoured tea, the rabbi stoked more coal on the fire and gave me a blanket for my knees.

"I must look truly wretched, if you are so indulgent to me," I said.

"You look like a man who has suffered," the rabbi said. "But, praise God, your sufferings are over. You are home and surrounded by people who love you. You must be gentle with yourself, my dear friend. You are beloved. Remember that."

"Thank you. Rabbi, I have sad tidings for Mrs Horowitz. I thought you would like to be with me when I tell her."

"I would," he said. He called through the door, "Miriam, send one of the children to fetch Esther Horowitz. Mr Holmes has news for her."

"I thought I should go visit her."

"You are in no condition to climb those stairs. Sit. Drink your tea."

He sat back in his chair and studied me. "Sometimes, when we are in pain, it is hard to speak of it with the people who love us. Perhaps we fear to upset them. Perhaps we do not want them to think us weak or vulnerable. And yet talking of our fears can lend such comfort."

I set the cup down and said, "What is it you are trying to tell me, Rabbi?"

"I am an old man. If God spares me, I shall be older still. I have heard and seen horrors, dreadful things, yet the Holy

264

One, blessed be He, has chosen to sustain me. I suppose what I am saying, Mr Holmes, is I am a good listener. I hope you will talk to me if you feel a need to unburden yourself. You will find no judgement here, only a blessing."

It was an extraordinary thing to say and it moved me beyond words. I found myself unable to speak. The old man leaned forward and patted my shoulder. "When you are ready," he said. "Like the good Lord Himself, I am always open for business."

I managed a laugh. Not a hearty one, and not without tears, but a laugh nonetheless.

"That's better," the rabbi said. "It may be hard now to see it, but I believe the Talmud is right when it says '*gam zu l'tova*' – this, too, is for the good."

We sat and drank our tea. Although I had uttered not a single word about my experiences, I felt the burden ease and knew a peace of the spirit that had eluded me for many days.

Mrs Horowitz arrived a short time later. She came into the study and Mrs Steinmetz sat on the sofa beside her.

"You have news about Chaim, Mr Holmes?" she said.

"I am afraid the news is not good," I began, as gently as I might.

"… It is thanks to your husband that I survived, Mrs Horowitz," I concluded. "At the end, when Frankall would have thrown me into the abyss, Chaim Horowitz fought him and they fell together to their deaths. Whatever mistakes he may have made, I owe him my life."

"He found his honour in the end," the widow said, weeping. "I am grateful for that. Thank you for telling me, Mr Holmes. It is a comfort."

She rose to leave. I said, "If I can be of service to you or your children, Mrs Horowitz, I pray you will tell me."

For the first time since I met her, she smiled. "What you have told me is worth more than all the riches in the world, Mr Holmes. Thank you."

After she left, the rabbi and I talked for a long time and I stayed for dinner. Glaser stopped by around nine o'clock.

"Well," he said, "If you don't look like the devil. What have you been up to, Mr Holmes?"

"Seeing to the end of Frankall's reign of terror, and bringing news of Horowitz to his wife."

The rabbi said, "A sad tale, David, but Chaim found his honour in the end." He raised a hand and added, "We will not ask for more details just yet. Mr Holmes is tired."

I left a short while later. Glaser walked with me to Holborn. As he helped me into the cab he said, "You will not forget that you have friends here, Mr Holmes? Anything you need, even if it's just to talk, we are here."

Monday, 22ⁿᵈ May

I stayed up all night, smoking my pipe. My visit with the rabbi enabled me to move beyond my fear and focus, at last, on my work. No terrors, vague and indistinct, troubled my mind. I could concentrate on something that required patience, analysis, reason.

Watson joined me late this morning. "You're up early," he began, then amended, "Or you have not slept."

"I have been thinking."

"Well, that is good. It is, at least, big improvement over fretting. What have you been thinking about?"

"I must find out who hired Frankall."

"Yes, of course. So, how do we proceed?"

"I want to go back to the house in Highgate but, first, Scotland Yard."

My appearance at the Yard was greeted by an unnecessary amount of hand-shaking, back-patting, applause, and cheering.

Lestrade blew his nose and shook his head. "You have more lives than a litter of kittens," he said. "One of these days you won't be able to get out of a pickle and then where will we be?"

Stevens said, "How worried we were, Mr Holmes. Thank the good Lord you are safe." To my consternation, he embraced me tightly, before turning away in embarrassment.

Bradstreet, mercifully, contented himself with shaking my hand. "We were afraid we'd lost you, Mr Holmes," he said.

"I shared your apprehension, Inspector," I said, lightly, "but I managed to survive. I wanted to ask you a favour."

"Name it," he said. "I shall be happy to help you in any way I can."

"Frankall's house: Did you search it?"

"Only to look for you. I meant to return, but other matters pressed upon me."

"Might we go there now?"

"Certainly. Let me get my coat."

We rode out to the house together. Watson and Bradstreet maintained a cheery, if uninspired, conversation all the way. I sank into my thoughts, trying to gird myself to face this place again.

Bradstreet had the foresight to bring the keys, and he unlocked the gate to admit us. Even in the space of a few short weeks, the house had developed an air of desolation and neglect. To my troubled mind, it seemed that it had always felt so, only now the veneer of civility has been swept away.

The policeman unlocked the front door and we stepped into the hollow building. It felt to me as if the place were holding its breath, waiting for its inhabitants to return. They would never return.

I began my search on the ground floor. Bradstreet went down to the basement. He was gone a short while and when he returned he said, "There is no reason for you to go down there, Mr Holmes. It is just an empty room, full of spiders and shadows."

I did not reply, but continued to work my way through the house. For all its elaborate architecture, it was as prosaic as any other home. There were no secret rooms, no hidden compartments.

Horowitz's room was spartan, either because the master of the house had no desire to indulge a mere employee, or because his tastes ran to the austere. The only personal item was a prayer book.

The drawers lay empty, likewise the cupboard. The slight discolouration of one floorboard under the bed drew my eye. With the help of a penknife, the slat raised easily.

Yes! I drew out a fat journal, written in cramped Hebrew. I slipped it into my pocket and went downstairs.

The study was an elegant, opulent room whose overwrought furnishings matched the gothic architecture. I sat at the desk. I would have been able to unlock it in a moment even without Horowitz's whispered directions.

I found letters, a great many letters, and several vials of liquid. "By your leave, Bradstreet, I should like to examine these."

He hesitated, but only for a moment. "I really shouldn't, you know, Mr Holmes... You will let me know what you find?"

"Of course."

Finally, over the protests of my companions, I went to the basement.

I stood in the cold and the dark, remembering. Then, without a backward glance, I turned and re-joined my companions.

Bradstreet dropped us at Baker Street and returned to his duties. I set the journal and vials aside and turned my attention to the letters.

"I wonder if it would be better to have Scotland Yard examine those chemicals, Holmes," Watson said.

"Do you not trust me?"

"With my life, my good fellow, but those drugs I trust not at all."

"You misread me, my dear Watson. It is not with longing that I gaze upon those bottles, but loathing. I know the misery they cause."

"A drug is a drug and can exert an influence. I am uneasy with having them here."

"Well, then, I shall conduct my analysis now, and you may take them to Scotland Yard."

This seemed to satisfy him.

The analysis did not take very long. As soon as I completed the task, Watson swept the bottles into his medical bag as if he feared I might change my mind.

For the rest of the afternoon, I focused on the letters I found in Frankall's desk. Some were copies of invoices he had the effrontery to send his 'clients' for services rendered. Others were carefully worded pleas for assistance: "When it is in my means to repay you, you may be assured of my generosity..."

Watson returned and began to go through the documents I had not yet examined. A few moments later, B arrived. "May I help?" she said.

I indicated the stack of papers. She sat on the floor by the fire and began to go through them.

The golden afternoon turned into plum evening. I turned on the gaslight and B stretched and yawned. She moved her neck from side to side. "You told me once," she said, "That at least part of a policeman's success lay in taking pains. I did not realise you meant it literally."

I sat on the floor beside her and rubbed her neck.

"I think we have done enough for this evening," Watson said. "We can continue tomorrow. Mrs Hudson should be bringing up the dinner shortly."

"I can continue a little longer," B said.

"Then please sit in a chair," he said. "I cannot think it is good for you to sit on the floor."

"You would be surprised at how comfortable it is. I always used to study this way when I was a child. It's so much easier to spread one's books and papers around. However, to please you I shall sit at the table."

She had no sooner risen to do so than Mrs Hudson arrived with her small army of maids and commandeered the table for more prosaic use.

"That smells wonderful, Mrs Hudson," B said. "A proper meat pie."

"Nothing fancy," the landlady replied, "but tasty enough."

"I enjoy proper English food," B said. "My cook Mme Chabon is talented, but she does favour French cuisine. There are times when I crave a nice meat pie."

"Any time you want plain English cooking, or Scottish, you come here, Lady Beatrice, and I shall be delighted to oblige you."

"Then, if I may be so bold, perhaps you could do kedgeree for breakfast? Almost the only memory I have of my poor late mother was eating kedgeree with her on a rainy morning."

"I shall, and welcome," the old woman replied, glowing with pleasure.

I was obliged to leave the papers. Watson regaled us with tales of kedgerees great and small that he had dined upon. He expounded on the health benefits of the dish and then, oh, mercy, waxed lyrical on the inadvisability of adding sultanas. He concluded with a comparative analysis of the various Indian varieties and the Scottish. "It is odd, when you think about it," he said, "Given the dish was supposedly imported to these islands from India. Now that's a subject for a monograph, don't you agree, Holmes? Holmes?"

"I beg your pardon, Watson," I said. "I am afraid I stopped listening when you started discussing the 243 types of curry spices. I was thinking about the opera."

"*Rigoletto?*" B said.

"Yes. You said it is playing in Covent Garden next month?"

"With Nellie Melba. Yes."

"I shall see about getting us tickets. Watson, will you join us?"

"At the opera? Uh, thank you, Holmes, but I believe I shall be busy that evening."

"Doing what?"

"Testing kedgeree recipes."

Oh, it felt good to laugh.

After dinner, the table cleared, we returned to the papers. We had not been long at the task when B said, "Here is a letter from Brian McKenna. He says he is dying and would like to leave his entire estate to a worthy cause. Ah, this is interesting, 'Had my life unfolded as I planned, I might be married to the only woman I ever loved. Alas, she was stolen from me by an English lawyer by the name of Edgar Hardwicke, and a very comfortable life she has in Hampstead with her two children. I am sure she never thinks of a wretch like myself. I would like her family to have something to remember me by...' Well, that is as malevolent a letter as I have ever read."

"And it is perfectly clear what the fellow meant. Malevolent, indeed."

Watson picked up Horowitz's journal and said, "Irritating we cannot read this."

B took it and said, "This belonged to Horowitz? Ah yes, I see it has his name on the flyleaf."

"When did you learn to read Hebrew, Beatrice?" Watson said.

"Oh, I've been teaching myself the letters. I cannot read anything, really, but I can work out proper names. I think this is Yiddish, not Hebrew. I'm sure David Glaser would be happy to translate it for you."

"Yes. He has invited us to dinner, he and Rivkah, I should say. I shall bring him the journal in the morning and see if he can accommodate us on Wednesday. Are you free, B?"

"Wednesday suits me well. I shall be glad to see them again. They are such lovely people."

She tilted her head slightly. I took the hint and added, with amusement, "Does Wednesday suit you, Watson?"

"Who? Me?"

"Of course," B said. "I think the Glasers would be disappointed if we arrived without you, John. They are almost as fond of you as your friend Holmes and I."

"Well, it is good to have such friends," he said, with a chuckle. "I am at your disposal on Wednesday."

In thanks for – well, for a great many things – I played the violin. "Proper pieces, too," Watson said, with a wink at B.

"Yes," she replied, "we are particularly honoured."

"I always play 'proper pieces', as you call them," I protested. Too late, I realised they were teasing.

B retired early, whether because she was genuinely tired or because she sensed Watson and I needed to talk, I cannot say. Left alone, my friend and I sat together in that quiet companionship that has defined our relationship almost from the start.

"You should not stay up too late, Holmes," he said. "You did not sleep last night and you are still convalescing, you know."

"I know..." I was preparing to defend myself, but I remembered in time that his only concern was for my well-being. "Thank you, my dear Watson," I replied. "I have given you and my family sufficient cause for worry to last at least two lifetimes. I shall try to behave in a manner less likely to provoke your concern."

He chortled. "Ah, if wishing only made it so. You will try, Holmes, but you will forget soon enough." He leaned back in his chair and said, "I am glad you are taking B to the opera. It will do you both good. She hides her anxiety well, but she is still very worried about you."

"I know. I fear I am as bad a husband as I am a friend, or a brother."

"I cannot speak for Mycroft or B, but I would not have you other than who you are. Being your friend may sometimes be a challenge, but it is never less than an honour."

I did not trust myself to reply. After a moment, he added, "You know, I am sure, that I am ready to listen if you ever want to talk."

There was nothing I wanted less and yet I knew he was right. The last time I faced the Falls I chose to do so alone, and that decision has haunted me ever since.

For the next two hours, I told Watson everything. All the details I had kept hidden about my kidnapping and torment at the hands of Frankall. I withheld nothing. Not my fear, nor my pain, nor my rage.

"It was the helplessness that was worst," I said. "I am no stranger to pain and I can deal with it better than most men. But being constrained, being unable to control even my own thoughts, that was terror beyond imagining.

"Frankall, once he realised my horror of the Falls, used them to create foul and hideous nightmares. Again and again I saw myself plunging off that cliff with Moriarty's hands at my throat."

"Swine," Watson said. "A lesser man would not have survived, Holmes. Thank God for your remarkable constitution."

"I cannot claim all the credit, Watson. A great deal of thanks must go to Horowitz. Although he was too timid to fight Frankall or to help me escape, he did other things. He talked to me, for one thing. He reminded me that there is good in the world and encouraged me to cling to happy memories. It is thanks to him that I did not starve or go insane. At the last, he gave his life to save mine. I shall be forever in his debt."

Tuesday, 23rd May

This morning I walked to Holborn. I was anxious to have Horowitz's notes translated, but I also felt need for the exercise. Although B and Watson protested, I chose to go alone.

I met Glaser in Leather Lane. He had just completed his morning patrol of the area. He shook my hand and said, "Two visits in one week? Such an honour. You need my help, Mr Holmes?"

"Horowitz left a journal hidden in his room in Highgate." I handed the battered leather-bound notebook to him. "B says it is in Yiddish."

Glaser took it and skimmed through a few pages. "He had a brilliant mind, did Chaim. This looks like a record of his time with that Frankall fellow. He seems pretty effusive about the man, at least in these early pages."

"I have no doubt it started that way."

"Come, have coffee with me, won't you?"

We walked down the road to the little café at the end of Hatton Garden. The proprietor, Avram, greeted me with a handshake and a smile. "*Oy vey*, Mr Holmes," he said, "If you look like this, I'd hate to see the other man."

"The other man is dead," I replied.

He spat on the floor. "A plague upon his house. Sit, I shall bring you something special to put colour on your cheeks."

He must have been thinking literally, for he presented me with a bowl of borscht and a thick slab of bread. "I'll have coffee for you when you're done with that," he said. "Pie, too, if you're good." He winked.

"You're a big favourite with Avram," Glaser said. "He likes boasting to his customers that the great Sherlock Holmes is a special friend of his."

"Keeps the riff-raff away," Avram said from his counter. "I'll bet crime in Baker Street dropped by at least fifty percent when word got around that you had moved in."

"Closer to ninety," I said, chuckling.

"You must bring Doctor Watson here one of these days, Mr Holmes. I've been reading his stories and very good they are, too. My English reading is not so good, but with the help of a dictionary, I am managing."

"He'll be delighted to hear it. I'll make a point of introducing you. Which reminds me, Glaser, would you be able to receive three visitors tomorrow?"

"Rivkah and I would be delighted, Mr Holmes."

He thumbed through the notebook. "There's a lot to go through here; it will take time. Is there anything in particular you're looking for?"

"It's hard to say... Any references to illegal activity, politics, or my brother Mycroft."

Glaser's eyes sparked sapphire. "Your brother? How is he involved with this?"

Softly, I said, "I believe Frankall was hoping to learn something about my brother for personal gain. Mycroft works for the government. It would be helpful to anyone with a malevolent heart to have information about him."

"I will do my best." Glaser tapped Horowitz's journal with the end of his pencil. "I wonder... I am happy to help you, Mr Holmes, and I am honoured by your faith in me. However, I have to wonder if someone else might do a better job."

"I understood you were fluent in Yiddish."

"I am. I just wondered if Mrs Horowitz might be a better choice. She is fluent in several languages, including Yiddish. She knows her husband's style of writing. You could offer to pay her." The blue eyes met mine and I saw all the words he had not spoken written there.

"I may rely upon her discretion?"

"Absolutely. More than most, in fact, for she has every reason to hate Frankall."

"And to exonerate her husband."

"She is a woman of honour, Mr Holmes. She suffers no delusions about her husband's behaviour. I will gladly vouch for her. So will the rabbi. It was just a thought."

"And a good one." I pondered. "I would prefer the journal not be kept in her flat. I cannot risk losing it or having it stolen. But if she would be willing to work in a quiet environment…"

"Do you have somewhere in mind?"

"Yes, I do, but I need to make sure it is feasible. Will you approach Mrs Horowitz and see if she is willing? Assure her I shall make it worth her while."

27

Rather than return to Baker Street, I took a cab to Camden Town.

Alice Prentiss shook my hand. "How good it is to see you, Mr Holmes," she said. "We have been so anxious about you. Please sit down. You look a little under the weather, if you do not mind my saying so."

"I have been unwell, but I am mending. Mrs Prentiss, I need to ask you another favour."

"Anything at all, Mr Holmes. I am happy to help."

"I need a long journal translated from Yiddish. I have found a woman who can do the job, but her living conditions are far from ideal. I wondered if you would permit her to use your study during the day, when you are not using it yourself. I would pay you for the use of the room."

"Oh, is that all? Yes, of course she may. If she is a trustworthy person – and I assume she is if she is working for you, Mr Holmes – I have no objection. You need not pay me."

"There's a little more to it. The lady in question has children; two of them are the same ages as your sons. The third, a girl, is a little older. I wondered if they might join her after their school day. I do insist on paying you, though I should prefer to keep that a secret between us."

She hesitated, but only for a moment. "I have no objection to trying, Mr Holmes," she said. "And I cannot deny that an additional income would be most welcome. How long do you think the translation will take?"

"Several days; perhaps weeks."

"Well, let us try it for a few days and we shall see how we get along."

I arrived home to the news that Mrs Horowitz will be delighted to help and can start the task on Thursday. Glaser will hold onto the journal overnight and see if he can make a start.

Wednesday, 24th May

This evening, Beatrice, Watson, and I dined with the Glasers in their home off the Clerkenwell Road. There was an unnecessary amount of discussion about Rivkah's pregnancy, and how they are happily awaiting the big event, etc., etc.

"Poor Mr Holmes," Rivkah said, smiling. "I think we had better find some wickedness to discuss as an antidote to all this domestic news."

We dined well and then our hostess played the piano. She is not unskilled, but I doubt even Clara Schumann could bring more colour to music than B. I persuaded my wife to play and she accommodated with Chopin's mazurkas.

"Oh, I could listen to you play all day," Rivkah cried. "That was splendid."

"You play well," Beatrice said. "You have a real feeling for the music."

"Rivkah gives piano lessons to the children," Glaser said. "She's very popular."

"The mothers just want to get their boys and girls out of the way for an hour. I do not mind. Some of them show promise."

"There are few joys greater than seeing a child discovering music," B said, then fell silent. She was remembering a student of her own and it did not require any great deductive reasoning to see her sadness. Though we were in public, I squeezed her hand and she smiled at me.

"What do you hear from Stevens?" Glaser said.

"He is well. He has been helping Lestrade, but he misses his Hatton Garden friends. I do not think he is being used to his full potential."

B added, "He passed himself off as my discontented cousin when Sherlock was investigating Frankall. Undercover work seems to suit him."

"We miss him. Hardly a day passes without someone asking after him," Glaser said.

"What is his replacement like?" Watson asked.

Glaser bit into his cake. "Better than de Vine, but then, that's not much of a challenge. No match for Stevens, though."

Later, Glaser handed me Horowitz's notebook.

"I've taken a look, mostly at the end. Here's my translation of the last few pages. Poor fellow sounds utterly insane at times. He is often unable to finish his thoughts. Still, I think you'll find this part of interest." He pointed to a section that began on the second page of his notes. I began to read with Watson peering over my shoulder.

The demons are waiting for me. I cannot escape them. F says he alone can protect me, but I see now he's the devil himself. The mekhashef...

"*Mekhashef?*" I said.

The policeman and his wife had a brief debate in Yiddish. Then he said, "The nearest I can get is 'sorcerer' or 'wizard'. That is the title Frankall used."

"Yes, a self-selected title. I think Frankall believed it gave him an allure he might otherwise have lacked. Swindlers rely so much on the trappings."

I read on. The words rambled, but some phrases resonated with me.

There is no honour for me, no hope of redemption. The things I have done. I would escape but that would lead them to Esther and the children. I can have no more blood on my hands.

The detective tells me Esther and the boys miss me and would welcome my return. Could I? Were it so easy...

He will not talk. Despicable things the Mekhashef does but I will help no longer. We are to take him away. The fall will loosen his tongue, he says.

"He's talking about you, Holmes," Watson said.

"I was not sure about that part," Glaser said. "It did not seem to make sense: 'the fall will loosen his tongue.' What fall?"

"Not fall, in the singular," I said. "Falls. The Reichenbach Falls." I read on.

The Mekhashef is desperate. It is a strange thing to see him wrestle with the same fear that has emptied my soul these past years. Ba'al fills him with mortal terror and I thrill to see it.

"Ba'al?" Watson said. "Wasn't he a false god? I seem to remember him mentioned in the story of Jezebel."

Glaser said, "It has a number of meanings. Master, lord... In the context, though, I think he means master.

"For most of his life, Horowitz was an observant Jew. Even though he seems to have lost his way in recent years, I just cannot see him worshiping a false idol. 'I am the Lord your God who brought you out of Egypt. You shall have no other gods but me.'" He smiled. "I may have absorbed a little of it, too."

"Have you been able to determine who this 'Ba'al' is? I assume it's a man?"

"I haven't been able to decipher much more than I've given you, I'm afraid. Esther will do a better job. She'll have more time to focus and she knows her husband's ways of expressing himself."

Thursday, 25th May

This morning I picked up Mrs Horowitz and escorted her to Camden Town. She stared in wonder at the elegant houses as we neared Harrington Square. Her children will join her later.

Mrs Prentiss greeted us with her usual warmth. "It is a great pleasure to meet you, Mrs Horowitz," she said. "I always enjoy meeting other linguists. What languages do you speak?"

They were soon chatting like old friends and I was pleased to see my plan coming together so well.

I returned to Baker Street, but the rest of Frankall's letters proved fruitless. I found no reference to 'Ba'al', 'master' or 'lord' in any of them. Perhaps he did not keep the letters sent by the fellow; or perhaps they did not communicate by post.

I summoned the Irregulars. I was happy to see they have recovered their humour. These boys have a profound sense of the ridiculous, something I always find entertaining. They listened carefully as I gave them their instructions.

"I am looking for a woman by the name of Gertrude Pike," I said. "She used to be a cook for Angel Frankall in his Highgate house."

"Usual rates, Mr H?" Kevin said.

"Usual rates," I said, "And an extra shilling to any boy who gets the information to me by sunset tomorrow."

Friday, 26th May

Like cabbies, cooks have a network. They all seem to know one another. I had no doubt the boys would discover her whereabouts without much delay. However, even I could not have anticipated how quickly.

"Got her, Mr H," Kevin said.

"Already?" I glanced at the clock. "It is scarcely twelve hours since I gave you the assignment. That was excellent work, Kevin. Here's your money. So," I flicked my coat tails behind me as I sat on the armchair. "What have you learned?"

"She's working in Pimlico in an 'ouse not far from where Billy is living." He gave me the address. "Family have a rum name. Bazalgette."

"You do not mean Basil Bazalgette?" I said.

"That's 'im. You know the geezer, Mr H?"

"I've met him. He's an Egyptologist at the British museum. He helped us with the Coptic Patriarchs case last year. Well, well, that is interesting."

"Only one thing, Mr H. She ain't there."

"I thought you said that is where she is working?"

"It is. Only 'is nibs, Bazalgette, has gone off to Scotland and taken the whole lot of 'em with 'im. Family, servants, the lot. Won't be back till next Sat'day according ter their milkman."

Confound it! I do wish the middle classes would stop taking themselves off on holiday. It is really too inconsiderate. Now I must wait another week because the wretched man has taken his wretched cook away. Are there no cooks in Scotland?

Damnation!

28

A note from Esther Horowitz: She has completed the translation. Watson and I took a cab to Camden Town without delay.

Bessie answered the door. "Oh, Doctor Watson," she said, smiling broadly. "How good it is to see you, and you, too, Mr Holmes. Come in. I'll let the mistress know you're here."

We joined Alice Prentiss and Esther Horowitz in the study.

"Hello again, Mr Holmes, Doctor," Mrs Prentiss said. "Esther and I were just discussing a Russian document."

Esther Horowitz seemed a woman reborn compared with the widow I left at Harrington Square just a week ago.

"I understand you have made progress, Mrs Horowitz," I said.

"Your arrival is timely, Mr Holmes," she replied, handing me the journal and a thick sheaf of notes. "It's hardly more than an hour since I finished."

"Thank you," I said. "You completed the work much more quickly than I expected."

"Esther has worked tirelessly to complete the task," Mrs Prentiss said. "I do not think I have ever seen a harder worker."

"I knew it was important," she said.

"I greatly appreciate your diligence. Thank you," I said.

"It is I who must thank you, Mr Holmes. You cannot know what it means to me to understand Chaim's actions over these past years. He stayed away to protect us, you know. That evil man threatened to harm us, even the children, if Chaim did not do as he wished. He recovered his faith in the end. He prayed for delivery from his torment, and the Holy One sent you."

I could find no answer to this.

She handed me another page. "This is a summary of the most important points in the journal, and I have referenced the page numbers so you can find the original notations."

I skimmed through the page. "Who is 'Q'?" I said. "You say your husband makes frequent mention of someone with that initial."

"Chaim never says the man's name. He refers to him only by the letter *kuf*. Chaim also mentions 'Ba'al', but from the context, I think that may be the same person. He uses the same phrases to describe them, 'characters of darkness', and 'doers of evil'. I am sorry I cannot be more specific. He also mentions someone he calls 'the priest'. These notes are peculiar and I cannot quite decipher what he meant. Chaim wrote hurriedly and, I think, often in the dark."

I swallowed back my disappointment. "I am grateful to him and to you, for all you have done. You have more than earned your wages." I handed her an envelope. The cheque it enclosed would ensure she and her children would never go to bed hungry again. She was too genteel to open it, but she clutched it tightly.

"I am sure you are too generous, Mr Holmes," she said.

I dismissed the thought with a gesture.

"Won't you have tea, gentlemen?" Mrs Prentiss said.

"Thank you—" I began, preparing to leave, but Watson seemed to think some form of social nicety was required. With reluctance, I sat and waited. He ignored my glare.

"It is good to see you looking so well, Mrs Horowitz," he said. "I hope you will not be offended if I tell you that you seem ten years younger than you did the last time I saw you."

"I have Alice to thank for it," she said. "And you, of course, Mr Holmes, for introducing us. Alice has arranged for me to translate documents for Brahms and Co."

"That will not affect your own work?" Watson asked Mrs Prentiss.

"By no means. Esther translates Greek, Russian, and Yiddish. Mr Brahms is delighted. He has been expanding into those markets, and Esther's skills are enormously helpful. I continue to translate the German, Italian, and so forth. Between us, we speak eight languages."

"Alice is teaching me Italian. I have always wanted to learn it."

"And in return, Esther is teaching me Russian."

They were finishing each other's sentences, talking at once as only true kindred spirits can.

"And how are your children?" Watson said, adding to my torment.

"They all get along so well together," Mrs Horowitz said. "They have roses in their cheeks from the time they spend in the park. Alice and I can keep an eye on them from the window."

"I am delighted it all worked out so well," I said, rising. "You will forgive me, but I have much to do."

"Thank you again for everything, Mr Holmes," Mrs Horowitz said. "I am in your debt."

"We both are," Mrs Prentiss added.

Back at Baker Street, the evening vanished in a cloud of tobacco smoke and close reading of the translation.

"Must you?" Watson said, at some juncture.

"What? The tobacco? You should be used to it by now, Watson, after all these years."

"The tobacco is suffocating, but it was to your frequent exclamations I was referring. I am perfectly peaceful, reading my book, and then you cry out, 'Aha!' and I am startled quite out of my wits."

I chuckled. "I am sorry, my dear fellow. I shall endeavour to keep my cries to a minimum."

"Or you could explain what it is you are finding so interesting." There was no denying the curiosity in his voice.

I set down the journal and picked up a teacup that had materialised. The contents were cold. I spat them out. I do not know why people insist on bringing me cold beverages and food.

Tea forgotten, I said, "In the beginning, Horowitz had utter faith in Frankall's apparently supernatural abilities. He became a devoted acolyte. It was some time before he discovered the truth, and by then, he was so under the other's control he had no hope of escape.

"Two years ago, he tried to flee. He bolted from Frankall's home and took off into the night. In his condition – penniless, friendless – he had little chance of success. Timms found him and brought him back.

"For several days they starved and tortured him. They injected him with opium and threatened him with all sorts of evil if he did not comply with Frankall's wishes. Their main threat was to his family. He was too cowed to do anything but obey."

"Poor beggar," Watson said. He rang the bell for Mrs Hudson and said, "He paid dearly for his interest in the dark arts. By the time Frankall made you his focus, I assume Horowitz was truly lost."

"Not so. I had thought the same thing but I had not counted on the man's spirit.

"A full year before I crossed Frankall's path, Horowitz had decided on his own that his only hope of salvation was to wean himself off the drug. He tried and failed several times, but he at least managed to decrease his usage considerably. In the meantime, his loathing of Frankall grew. It was no less than the contempt he felt for himself. He became determined to destroy the man who had once been his mentor."

"I do not understand that, Holmes. Horowitz's slavish devotion, I can see. But why did Frankall keep him around? Surely Horowitz was more of a liability than an asset."

Mrs Hudson arrived, took my cup of cold tea, sniffed her annoyance, and left the room. I waited until she shut the door behind her before saying, "Certainly, at the end, but Frankall was too vain to notice Horowitz's hate. He saw only fear."

"Have you been able to decipher those references to Ba'al or Q?"

"Only insofar as to agree with Mrs Horowitz that they are the same person. Whoever he is, he has no great fondness for the Sorcerer. Horowitz never seems to have met him; he only knew what he gleaned from fragments of conversation between Timms and Frankall. I suspect they never mentioned Q by name in Horowitz's presence. They never trusted him. He records fragments. Here, for instance, 'Timms says all Q's plans are dashed and he blames the *mekhashef* for botching the Updike job...'"

"So Q did hire Frankall," Watson said.

"Yes, that much is plain. There are many other such accounts. In one, Horowitz reports that Frankall has been to see Q and returned in a foul mood. Timms wanted to kill him. Q, I mean. Thought he was becoming too much a liability, but Frankall suspected he had prepared papers to be published after his death that would condemn all of them. Besides, the man was willing to pay a king's ransom for the right information. Initially, I think, Frankall was willing to do Q's bidding, take his fee, and move on to the next victim. However, when Updike spoiled their plans, he began to see other possibilities. Why give information to Q when he could keep it for himself? It was around this time that they started to talk about leaving London."

"And when you mentioned Reichenbach, they decided Switzerland was as good a place as any. The question is who is Q?"

I hesitated before replying.

"Holmes?" Watson urged. "You have an idea?"

"There is only one man with an initial Q who knew what Updike did for a living, but he seems a highly improbable candidate."

"Quackenbush?" Watson said. "I met him once, but I cannot say he made much impression. An altogether forgettable character."

"Yes, that describes him well," I said. "He has worked with Mycroft for about ten years, I think. For a while, Mycroft thought he might be groomed as a successor."

"What happened?"

I put the notebook and the translation away. "Mycroft said he focuses on minutia and ignores global issues. What is that phrase, something about gnats and camels?"

"'Blind guides who strain gnats and swallow camels.' The Gospel of Matthew, if memory serves."

"Quite. That seems to sum up Quackenbush. Updike, on the other hand, had a brain to match my brother's."

"It is possible, then, that Quackenbush was jealous. He was disappointed at not being given the opportunity he had come to expect."

"Perhaps. He knew Updike; knows Mycroft. I cannot rule him out. All the same…"

"What do you have against the idea?"

"I suppose I resist the thought that someone who works so closely with Mycroft could have fooled him for so long. And he is such a miksop."

"But perhaps the kidnapping and torture of Updike was not planned. Perhaps Quackenbush was angry with Frankall for using such brutality. It is possible, isn't it, Holmes?"

"Yes. It is possible."

I lit my pipe and puffed. I was falling into a reverie when Watson said, "What of the priest Mrs Horowitz mentioned?"

"Hmm? Ah, I cannot make it out. From the tone, I think he used the word ironically. For instance, here Horowitz says, 'the *mekhashef* – the Sorcerer – has been to the priest and has added considerably to his coffers as a result.'"

"That is odd," Watson agreed. "Perhaps this person's name is Priest?"

"Perhaps." I studied the pages before me. My eyes were tired from the hours of reading. "It is possible. It is a difficulty with translation, Watson. In the end, so much of it is a matter of interpretation. I must say Mrs Horowitz seems to have done a pretty thorough job of translating the document, at least in terms of the elegance of her style. I cannot, of course, speak to her accuracy."

"But you will take her word for it?"

I shook my head. "I shall have Glaser double-check one or two passages, but overall I am satisfied."

"If you are satisfied, why double-check?"

"Taking pains is my business, Watson. These notes leave me with questions and no answers."

29

Thursday, 1st June

Watson and I had lunch with B. She was as intrigued as I to read Mrs Horowitz's notes.

"Priest?" she said. She looked at the original Yiddish and back at the translation.

"Yes," I said. "Does that mean anything to you?"

"It's just… Keep in mind, I am no expert, but as far as I can tell, the word Horowitz used was 'cohen'."

"That's a Jewish name," Watson said. "Are we looking for another Jew?"

"It is a name, but it is also a title. I believe it could translate as vicar or priest. Mrs Horowitz used the latter term, but it is a matter of interpretation."

"I do not understand," Watson said. "Why could the man not just write what he meant? Why all the word-games?"

"He may not have known," I said. "Frankall seems to have used a lot of nicknames and codes in Horowitz's presence. Besides, Horowitz himself does not use Frankall's name."

B was still reading the notes, her meal forgotten. "This letter, *kuf*," she said, "I see Mrs Horowitz translates that as a Q."

"Yes, is that not correct?"

"It is not incorrect, it's just… Hebrew letters do not really have direct English equivalents. The *kuf* has a sound not unlike a Q."

"Then where is the difficulty?" I asked.

"It lies in the fact that other English letters can sound like a Q, too. The K and the hard C. It may not signify, but I would be remiss if I did not point it out. You might want to ask Glaser or the rabbi. Perhaps I am wrong."

B's advice was sound. Watson and I stopped by Hatton Garden before returning to Baker Street. The rabbi peered through his glasses at the translated pages.

"Lady Beatrice is quite correct," he said. "It is a difficulty in translating a language based on another alphabet into English. The *kuf* would usually be translated as a Q, but a K or, yes, a hard C would also suffice. It made sense to Chaim, but it is difficult to know what he meant. I am afraid that you will need to have a suspect in mind and see if Chaim's comments apply to him, rather than use Chaim's writings to direct you."

"Oh."

"I am sorry, Mr Holmes," he said. "Not very helpful, I know. Looking through the rest of the translation – I am only skimming, you understand – I think Esther has done an excellent job. Not only is it accurate, but it possesses a certain elegance."

"What about the word 'cohen'?" I said. "B said it was a title."

"Yes, the word 'cohen' means one who belongs to a priestly order. It could mean the name, Cohen, or it could mean priest. I cannot guide you in either direction."

Damn!

Sunday, 4ᵗʰ June

This evening, Watson and I walked to a genteel house in Pimlico. The maid showed us into a sitting room that seemed more museum than residence. Egyptian paintings, statues, and artefacts filled every space. Most entertaining of all was the full-sized statue of a baby elephant that dominated the south end of the room, its trunk resting incongruously on a grand piano.

"Mr Holmes," cried our host, emerging from a veritable forest of palm trees. "I was so delighted to get your message that you would be calling upon me. Splendid, splendid. And Doctor Watson, too, how'd'do, sir. You will join me in a sherry?"

We assented and our host poured a healthy measure into our glasses.

"The Queen," he said.

"The Queen," we echoed, and drank the excellent vintage.

"Please, sit. Oh just move Archibald. The viper, I mean. He is not real." Watson contained his amusement with some difficulty, and placed the stuffed snake on the cramped table.

"I am afraid this is a rather cluttered house," Bazalgette said. "My wife says I should move my bed into the British Museum and live there. How can I help you? Are you searching for more Egyptian treasures?"

"I fear my visit this time is on a rather more prosaic matter," I replied. "I need to speak with your cook."

"My cook?" He blinked. "She has only been with us a few weeks. I hope she is not a woman of dubious character?"

"By no means. Mrs Pike is the epitome of virtue, Mr Bazalgette. I need to ask her about her former employer."

"A bit of a bad lot, was he? Well, that's no fault of hers. Certainly, you may speak with her."

The maid brought us down to the kitchen in the bowels of the house. The staff looked startled at two gentlemen appearing in their domain.

"Mrs Pike," I said. "My name is Sherlock Holmes. This is my associate Dr Watson. Is there somewhere we might speak privately?"

She seemed nervous. It was obvious she did not recognise the coachman who had once eaten her soup.

293

"Yes, sir," she said, "this way."

She led us into a comfortable sitting room just off the kitchen. One of the few perquisites open to the cook was having access to such a place.

I let Watson open the questioning. He began in his usual gentle manner. "We need to ask you about Mr Frankall."

"Oh," she said, "Him." Her expression said it all. "Cannot say I'm surprised, sir. He was a bad lot and no mistake."

"How so?" Watson asked.

"All that communing with the dead. Ain't natural."

"We were interested in his associates. Did you know any of them?"

"Not much," she said. "I mean, I keep to the kitchen."

"Come now, Miss Pike," Watson said in his silkiest tones. "An intelligent woman like you must have kept an eye on things. It is a wise thing to do when one's employer is the very devil."

"Well... I don't know that I would call him a devil, for all his strange dealings. He could be generous enough, and was complimentary about my cooking."

I groaned.

Watson gave me a vexed look and said, "I have no doubt your food is excellent, Miss Pike. Indeed, Mr Bazalgette was just saying the same thing. But Mr Frankall was involved with some extremely unsavoury people. He caused a great deal of suffering. Indeed, an innocent woman, a mother of two young children, died because of your former employer and his associates. Anything you can tell us would be of enormous value."

The woman looked distressed. "Oh, that is dreadful," she said, and dabbed at her eyes with the hem of her apron. She thought for a moment and then said, "Well, you could talk to

Mr Timms, although I cannot say he'd be too willing to help you. Tight lipped. But there wasn't much he didn't know about the master's business. Could have been all for show, I suppose. He was a one for the airs and graces. There was a Jewish man, too. Horowitz. He'd help you, right enough, though I'm not sure how much he knew. The master didn't confide in him. Didn't trust him, not altogether. Too decent, I reckon."

"I am afraid neither of these gentlemen is in a position to help me," I said. "Can you think of anyone else? A business partner, perhaps?"

She frowned over this question and then said, "Well, I did once overhear Mr Timms mention someone called Mr Parsons. Sounded like he was Mr Frankall's solicitor. Can't be sure, though. They hushed as soon as they saw me."

"Parsons!" I cried. "Not Priest."

She looked utterly confounded, for which I suppose I cannot blame her. "Yes, sir," she said. "I am not sure where you would find him, but he would be the only other man I can think who might be able to help you, sir."

We called upon Peter Huggins on our way back to Baker Street. He confirmed that he was acquainted with Parsons. "A bit unimaginative. A plodder," he said. "Still, as my poor friend Hardwicke likes to say, I know of no harm in him."

He went to his bookcase and leafed through a thick book. "Yes," he said. "He has an office near Gray's Inn. Here is his address."

"Thank you, Mr Huggins," I said. "That is helpful."

"Speaking of Hardwicke," Watson added, "How is he?"

"He is in a wretched state, poor fellow. He sent his children to Ireland to stay with his late wife's family. They are distraught, as you can imagine."

"Yes, indeed. If you see him perhaps you will let him know that the man responsible for his son's kidnapping and his wife's murder is dead."

"Why, that is excellent work, Mr Holmes. Can you tell me anything further?"

"The investigation is not yet complete," I said. "I am hoping this fellow Parsons will be able to shed further light on the matter."

"When do you mean to see him?"

"Tomorrow morning."

"I wonder – forgive me, I do not mean to tell you your business, Mr Holmes – but I wonder if I might accompany you? Parsons is, as I said, a bit of a plodder, but he will not readily reveal the confidence of a client. If I am there, I may be able to, ah, persuade him."

"A capital notion. Thank you, Huggins."

Monday, 5th June

This morning we met Huggins in Gray's Inn. He led us over the cobbles to a door, identical to all its brothers. We wound our way up a narrow and twisting staircase to the top of the building.

Parsons, a small, colourless man, rose when we entered his cramped chambers.

"Mr Huggins," he said. "An honour, sir, a very great honour."

Huggins shook the fellow's hand and introduced Watson and me.

"Mr Sherlock Holmes," said Parsons. "Well, this is a treat and no mistake. Please, have a seat. I am sorry the room is so small." He looked around him in dismay as if he had suddenly become aware of his chamber's deficiencies.

"Mr Holmes needs to consult with you about a former client," Huggins said. "I would appreciate your candour, Mr Parsons. The matter is a grave one."

"Who is the client?" Parsons said, blinking over his half-moon glasses.

"Angel Frankall," I said.

Instantly, the fellow was dumbstruck. His already colourless face seemed to blanch even further. "Oh dear me, no," he said. "That will not do."

"You need not be afraid, Mr Parsons," I said. "The man is dead. He cannot harm you."

"Dead? Really? Are you certain, Mr Holmes?"

Did I mistake it, or was their pleasure behind those words? No, I was not mistaken. The merest whisper of pink came into the man's cheeks and he rubbed his gloved hands together.

"He fell from the Reichenbach Falls into the chasm below," I said. "Yes, he is dead."

"Oh my, oh my word, that is excellent news! That is to say, I am glad to have such confirmation as yours, Mr Holmes. I hope you will not look upon me unkindly when I say I am not sorry to hear it. No, indeed. Not sorry at all."

"You were afraid of him," I said.

There was a brief hesitation before he replied, "Quite terrified. I am ashamed to admit it, but it is the truth."

"There is no shame in being afraid of an exceedingly dangerous and unscrupulous man, Mr Parsons. There is only good judgement."

His face glowed with pride and he seemed almost animated.

"You are good to say so, very good indeed. Now, pray tell me what you need and you may be assured I will help you any way I can."

"May I ask the nature of the work you did for Frankall?"

"Primarily it was in the form of contracts. I may add these were of a most peculiar nature."

"How so?"

"Generally, they stated that Mr Frankall was to perform a service for the client, an unspecified service, and would then be paid one month after the performance of said service one third of the individual's inheritance."

"That's pretty rum," Huggins said. "How could Frankall know the client was to come into an inheritance within that time-frame?"

"Precisely." Parsons rubbed his hands together.

"Do you have copies of these contracts, Mr Parsons?" I said.

"Certainly."

He rose and began to rummage through his cabinets. He drew out a file and handed it to me.

"Well, well, and what have we here?" I indicated the name.

Watson said with loathing, "Brian McKenna."

"Yes," Parsons said. "That one was most peculiar. In this instance, the gentleman's entire fortune, an exquisite art collection, was bequeathed to a Mr Ostap Bender. Then again, I understand the testator was gravely ill and had no heirs. Although these contracts seemed unusual, Mr Holmes, I did not see anything illegal or even immoral in them."

"No, there is nothing."

"Who is Ostap Bender?" Watson said.

I shook my head. "Another alias, perhaps."

"What I don't understand," Huggins said, "Is why Frankall would draw up a contract at all. Could he not simply have threatened the heirs? He seems to have had no scruples."

"That is true," I said, "but for a man like Frankall appearance was everything. He made everything look above-board to preserve the illusion that he was in league with supernatural powers. When the wealthy relative died, the beneficiary could convince himself it was due to Frankall's magic. No whisper of murder need trouble the conscience."

"Murder?" Parsons gasped and sank back in his chair. "Dear heavens, have I been party to so foul an act? Please, say it is not so, Mr Holmes."

"You have done nothing wrong, Mr Parsons," I said. "You were asked to draw up contracts and you did so. The nefarious activity took place elsewhere. You were not to know."

I continued rifling through the papers. A name caught my eye. "Take a look at this, Watson," I said, handing him the document.

"Carton? The fellow who defenestrated himself after changing his will and leaving his wife and son nothing."

"The very same. I understood the will was drawn up by someone called Gradgrind."

"I am not familiar with that name, Mr Holmes. I drew up the will, as you see."

"Were you present when it was signed?"

"No, I was not. Mr Frankall said the gentleman was dying from tuberculosis. He knew my fear of illness and said he would see that the will was signed and witnessed. It seemed a kindly act." He hesitated. "Now I think of it, the will was not returned to me for several weeks, and I believe Mr Carton passed away in the interim."

It was standard fare with just one beneficiary. "Do you know anything about this organisation?" I asked. "Brother Costello's First Church of Spiritual Enlightenment?"

"Yes, it was set up by Mr Frankall for a friend of his. An act of charity, I thought. I have the papers here." He handed me the document.

"Good God!" I cried.

"Holmes?" Watson said.

I pointed to the name.

"Good heavens. But, this means he is..."

"Ba'al, himself."

30

We returned to Baker Street and I spent most of the day in silent contemplation. At one point I made a comment to Watson, only to realise he was not there.

There were still elements of the case that confused me, but as the fog of pipe smoke filled my room, so the fog of confusion in my mind receded. By the time Watson returned, I had not only devised a plan, but set it in motion by sending messages sent to B and to Billy.

"How is Stamford?" I asked when my friend joined me.

He glanced at the billiard chalk on his fingers and laughed. "He is well. He sends his regards."

There was a knock at the door below and a moment later a set of footsteps crept up the stairs. "Our friend Bradstreet has had a trying day," I said.

Indeed, when the inspector entered the room, he looked thoroughly exhausted and rather the worse for wear.

"An arrest that turned into a brawl," he explained tersely.

"You should have brought more than one constable with you, Bradstreet. You know what a dangerous area Whitechapel is."

"How did you…? Oh, never mind. I am really too tired to care."

"How is your son enjoying being on the force?" Watson asked.

"Very well. He's a big lad and people don't bother him. All the same, I think he may have too kind a heart for this sort of work." He sighed and stretched out his legs. I thought it would take little or no effort for him to fall asleep right there on our sofa.

A moment later the door opened again and Mrs Hudson brought in a fresh pot of coffee.

"I hope this one is hot," I said.

"The last one was hot when I delivered it," she snapped. I cannot understand why the woman is so sour sometimes.

"Here you are, Bradstreet," Watson said, "A good cup of coffee will revive you."

We sat and drank and the spark returned to the inspector's eyes. "I wondered what progress you were making on this Sorcerer case, Mr Holmes. Any developments?"

I told him what I had learned so far.

He whistled. "Well, that was unexpected. I should go and arrest him."

"Not yet. I need to do a little further investigating before we take that step."

"I hope you are not planning anything…"

"Illegal?" Watson said, helpfully.

"Dangerous," the inspector said.

I was tempted to reply my plan was both, but I kept silent.

Bradstreet did not stay long. As he put on his hat he said, "Do please be careful, Mr Holmes. You have no idea how hard it is on your friends when you are hurt."

"Well, Holmes?" Watson said after Bradstreet left. "What are we doing?"

"Not we, Watson. I am taking Billy with me." I raised a hand at his inevitable protest. "There is nothing to worry about. We are simply looking for some more information. While I am conducting the search, I want you to stay with B. She will be expecting you. Here is the plan…"

Tuesday, 6ᵗʰ June

Even before I reached Whitehall, I surmised Mycroft might be too busy to see me. The newspapers were full of the ghastly news: Negotiations in Bloemfontein have failed. A

302

second Boer war is now inevitable. I found the air of gloom in Whitehall quite oppressive. Mycroft has been in conference with senior ministers all morning. I asked Gillespie to have him telephone me at his earliest convenience.

I continued on to the gasworks at Horseferry Road and there borrowed some equipment.

At one o'clock, Billy arrived in Baker Street. I explained the plan. He chortled. He was even more amused when we donned our disguises.

"Cor, if you don't look barmy in those whiskers, Mr H," he said.

We made our way to Warwick Square in our gear, carrying various instruments and meters, and looked indistinguishable from the genuine article. At the house, we knocked at the servants' entrance.

"I suppose it's all right," the listless valet said. "I'd be obliged if you would finish before the master comes home."

"Can't make no promises, guv'nor," I said, concealing my surprise. "It takes as long as it takes, know what I mean? Don't want to muck about with gas leaks. On my word, no."

The fellow looked as if he would stand there and watch us the entire time. Fortunately, a moment later we heard a feeble voice call, "Dillahunt, are you there?"

"That's him now," said the servant. "I'll be back in a jiffy."

"Cor," Billy whispered. "I thought that put the kibosh on it for sure. Thought you said 'is nibs never left the 'ouse."

"He doesn't. I wonder what drew him out today." I was carefully opening the jar of sulphur and ammonia that I had prepared for the purpose. I hid it behind the dresser.

303

The servant returned with his master at his heels. The gentleman was about to question us when the stench reached him. "Oh good heavens," he cried, "We shall be gassed."

"Best leave for a bit, your lordship," I said. "We need to fix the leak and let the gas clear. The boy and I will sort it, never fear."

"But I just came in," he protested, "And it's pouring rain."

"Not safe to stay," I said.

"That geezer in Richmond Terrace, he stayed, didn't he, gov'nor?" Billy said, wide-eyed. "They never did find the rest of him, did they?"

"Only those few... bits," I agreed.

"Lady Beatrice keeps asking you to tea," the manservant reminded his master. "I am sure she would be delighted to see you. Mrs Varney and I can wait at the King's Arms, down the road." To me, he added, "I suppose you can let us know when it's safe to return?"

"We can do that, right enough," I said. "Shouldn't take more than two, three hours."

In less than ten minutes, we had the house to ourselves.

"Right," Billy said. "What you want me to look for, Mr H?"

"Papers, documents, journals. Any chemicals would be of interest, too. Anything that seems out of the way. I shall start in the study. You can start down here."

"In the servants' quarters?" He rolled his eyes. "All right, all right. Don't get shirty."

I started by examining the study itself before exploring the contents of the desk. I expected nothing and nothing is what I found. This was a clever man, a man who had kept his secrets for many years. He was hardly likely to leave incriminating documents in an easily accessible place.

The wastepaper basket contained nothing but the day's newspapers.

Billy and I scoured the house from top to bottom but we found nothing incriminating.

"Does it matter, Mr H?" Billy said, wiping his brow. "I mean, you have enough to arrest him with that solicitor's evidence, doncher?"

"A clever lawyer may be able to make a case for fraud, but, equally, a clever lawyer could make the case our bird was himself a victim of sharp practice." I continued to search the study with my eyes. Billy waited, arms folded, a look of resignation on his face.

"I shall give you a note to bring to Scotland Yard, Billy. Ask for Inspector Bradstreet. If he is not available, either Lestrade or Stevens will do. Do not let anyone stop you."

"You can count on me, Mr H." He grinned.

I gave him money for a cab and he set off.

Alone in the house, I sat cross-legged on the floor and pondered. What was I missing? Think, man! There had to be something here.

What did I know of the fellow? He was a man of guile, well used to covering his real nature. Highly intelligent. Unhurried. Methodical.

You're still missing it. Don't be a fool. Concentrate.

He was very tall, imposing, even for a man of his years...

A man of his years.

Yes, he was old. He needed easy access his files. They might be up high, on a top shelf. He was tall enough to reach without any difficulty. Probably they would not be down low. His agility was poor. On the other hand, the footprints on the carpet showed he still slept in his bedroom on the first floor. So, less infirm than he appeared.

Would he want to keep his papers in the bedroom? Unlikely.

I closed my eyes and remembered the first time I met him. He was cordial. He rose with a little difficulty and shook my hand. Everything about him was unhurried, precise.

I asked for his expertise.

His eyes flickered to the bookcase.

His eyes flickered to the bookcase. At the time, I thought he was merely thinking about his reference books of arcane lore... Slow it down. See it again.

I returned to the study and stood near the door just as I had when I had met him with B. In my mind's eye I watched him. That glance.

Bookcases lined the room from floor to ceiling, except for the end southern end where a large window overlooked the garden. Beneath it stood the table that held his clock-making equipment.

I went to the bookcase and examined it. The lower shelves contained novels, classics of literature, and bric-a-brac. The books were pristine, their spines intact. Above them, from waist height and up, were large volumes that seemed to be encyclopaedias of arcane lore. These spines were worn, the shelving highly polished from frequent use. At the time, I thought this merely reflected an ardent student. Now...

I selected the largest tome, about two feet tall and five inches thick. The contents were not lore. It was a dossier on members of the government. At the back of the file was a page that read, "Mycroft Holmes." Compared with the rest, it was almost empty. It contained a smattering of information about my brother's age and general health, his relationship to me, the location of his office building. I found a newspaper clipping of a picture of the Prime Minister with Mycroft standing in the background, almost in the shadows. Not enough in the shadows.

I moved on to the next file. This was no less illuminating. It was a dossier on Frankall, exquisitely detailed and up to date. So much for our friend's poor memory. The file contained a list of the Sorcerer's known aliases as well as his real name, Ostap Bender. Well, well. The remainder of the inch-thick file was a page-after-page account of his crimes. The names of the victims were listed in meticulous detail, what Frankall had done to them and how. All the things the old man claimed not to remember.

Unfortunately, Sir Christopher did not have a telephone and so I could not contact Mycroft. I would have to wait for Scotland Yard. Well, we had enough to arrest him. There was no need of haste.

I stopped in sudden alarm.

He was out when we arrived.

He never went out.

Under the window that overlooked the garden was a table containing all his clock-making equipment. I turned my attention to it again.

It was much neater than the last time I had seen it. The smattering of cogs and wires now lay to the side. He had cleared a space for his work. What work?

I bent over the table and sniffed. The surface smelled of bananas and I felt an immediate headache. Using my magnifying glass, I detected a speckle of black powder on the wood.

Oh, God…

I grabbed a handful of tools and ran to the door. There was not a moment to lose. In my haste, I collided with Lestrade on the doorstep. Billy laughed. Stevens smirked but kept silent.

"You're in a rush, Mr Holmes?" Lestrade said.

"We must hurry if we are to prevent a catastrophic tragedy. You will find evidence of treason and murder in the study. The bird is in Wimpole Street with Lady Beatrice."

"Good heavens," Lestrade said, "Surely you did not leave the lady alone with a villain?"

"Watson is there, too. I need to borrow your carriage. Stevens, Billy, come with me."

"Oy, Mr Holmes," Lestrade began to protest, "You can't just—"

"We must make haste, Lestrade, or all will be lost. His servants are waiting in the pub on the corner. Question them. See what they know. Hurry, man, hurry! There is not an instant to lose."

"What tragedy?"

"Carandini planted a bomb," I cried. "In my brother Mycroft's building."

31

I leaped into the carriage and instructed the driver to take us to Whitehall. Lestrade nodded his consent. We galloped off with Stevens and Billy still tumbling into their seats.

"What is this, Mr Holmes?" Stevens asked. "I can better help you if I am prepared."

I could hardly find words, although I appreciated the sense of his comment.

"Sir Christopher plans to blow up the building where my brother works. He thinks if he brings down the government he can prevent the war."

"How do you know, Mr H?" Billy said.

"He cleared his table of clockmaker's stuff and it smelled of bananas."

"Bananas?" Billy said.

"Nitroglycerine smells like bananas," Stevens explained. "That's the stuff they put in dynamite."

"Cor!" Billy seemed excited rather than alarmed.

"There was gunpowder, too. Just a small trace."

There was no way to know where the bomb was located, nor when it was likely to explode.

He knew Mycroft's building, but he could hardly know the exact location of his office. At least that information was not in his meticulous dossier.

Did he gain entry to the building? There was always a guard posted at every door, but an old man... He said it himself: The old are invisible. An elderly gentleman, a retired major, in fact, carrying a box or a suitcase, no one would raise an eyebrow. I did not find the bomb in his home, therefore he had already planted it.

These were my thoughts as we clattered through the streets. And, in rhythm with the horses' hooves ran the refrain: *Please don't be late…Please don't be late…*

We gained the building. I leaped from the carriage before it halted, and bounded up the steps.

Gillespie started. "Mr Holmes—?" he began.

"There is a bomb. I do not know where, but I think near Mycroft's office. Have your men clear the north and west of the building. Let Melville know. Find out if anyone let an old man in earlier today. Hurry!"

He cried to one of his assistants, "Sound the alarm!"

Immediately, the loud bell tolled, echoing through the still and sleepy building. Gillespie fled with uncommon speed down the hallways, banging on doors and crying, "*Fire! Fire!*" as he ran. Doors crashed open and men streamed out and rushed to the exits.

"Stevens, you and Billy search the south end of the building. I will alert my brother and then search the east side."

I took the stairs three at a time and found Mycroft on the top landing with a cluck of ministers. "Good heavens, Sherlock," he said. "What on earth is going on?"

"There is a bomb in the building," I said.

"A bomb? Are you sure?"

"No."

He studied my face and nodded. "Best err on the side of caution," he agreed.

The ministers fled. Mycroft and I followed more slowly, two people wading through a tide of government officials who rushed to safety.

"Do you go outside, Mycroft," I said when we reached the lobby. "I shall assist with the search."

He hesitated. For a moment, I thought he would refuse. Then he nodded and patted my shoulder. "Please try not to die, Sherlock. I do not think my heart can take much more."

As soon as he left, I joined in the search. As I examined the hallway on the Whitehall Court side, Gillespie ran up to me and said, "This is Constable Dunlap, Mr Holmes. He let an elderly gentleman in earlier today."

The red-cheeked soldier said, "Sir, yes, sir. I'm afraid I did, sir."

"Describe him to me," I said.

"Very old he was, eighty if he were a year, sir, though his hair was still mostly black. He was tall and thin and spoke like a gentleman."

"Go on."

"He said he was supposed to see Mr Mycroft Holmes, sir. I told him he'd come into the wrong entrance, being as he came in the Whitehall Place side and Mr Holmes's office is at the Horse Guards Avenue end."

"What happened next?"

"Well, he said he'd go outside and walk back around to the other side, but…"

"But you took pity on him."

"Yes, sir. He seemed so infirm."

The soldier met my eye in shame, completely aware of his folly.

"Was he carrying anything?"

"Yes, sir, he had a suitcase."

"Just one?"

"Yes, sir."

"Did you have someone escort him?"

The shame deepened.

"No, sir. I gave him directions. Ordinarily I would have sent someone with him, but it's been so busy here today… My fault entirely, sir."

"We'll discuss this later, Dunlap," Gillespie said. "See to the evacuation of the north side of the building and then wait outside with the others."

"Yes, sir." He turned to leave and then said, "The suitcase was old, sir, black leather, and tied up with string. I don't know if that helps. I really am most awfully sorry."

Gillespie waited until the young man left before saying, "Don't judge him too harshly, Mr Holmes. He's a fine young man as a rule."

"Well, at least we have confirmation Carandini was here, and we have an idea what we're looking for. I suppose that's something."

Billy and Stevens joined us, panting. "We've cleared the south end on the ground floor. Mr Melville and his men are checking the upper levels."

I said, "The bomb will be on the ground floor, somewhere near the Horse Guards Parade end. Come!"

We clattered through offices and cupboards, searched behind statues and under benches. About ten minutes later, Stevens cried, "I found it!"

Gillespie, Billy, and I joined him in the public toilet.

The black leather suitcase, tied with string, was on the floor under the basin.

"Go outside," I said to my companions. No one moved.

Gillespie took a pocket knife and cut the string then carefully opened the case. He whistled. "Enough dynamite here to blow out the side of the building."

Stevens, white-faced but calm, said, "What can we do?"

"No need to panic, lad," Gillespie said. "We have ten minutes, yet. Mr Holmes, do you by chance have a wire-cutter on you?"

"In fact, I do," I said, handing it to him. "I took the liberty of 'borrowing' it from our bomber's own toolbox. I thought we might need it."

"How does it work?" Billy said. "The bomb, I mean."

"The clock has wire coiled around the key at the back," Gillespie said. "Once the key reaches the right place, it pulls the trigger on that gun, see?"

Billy nodded, too fascinated to be frightened. "And the gun fires into the dynamite and it explodes," he said.

"Exactly," Gillespie nodded approvingly. "We could have used a lad like you in the Engineers Corps. Now, how do you think we should disarm it?"

"Cut the wire from the clock to the gun," Billy said.

"Good lad. You want to do the honours?"

"Gillespie!" I protested, but Billy had already snipped it.

"Now," Gillespie said, "Very carefully take out that gun. Smooth movements, we cannot risk it going off."

With exquisite care, Billy removed the weapon and handed it to me.

"That was exceedingly well done, Mr Gillespie," I said. "I had no idea you were versed in bomb disposal."

He grinned. "Nice to play the soldier again. It's been a while. The credit belongs to the lad, though. Steadiest hands I've seen in a many a year."

The army arrived and secured the dynamite. Only then did we deem it safe enough to give the all clear. The staff returned to their offices, chatting unconcernedly about the day. If they only knew how close they had come to death they may not have been so cheery. Then again, what good would it do to tell them?

Mycroft brought Gillespie, Melville, Stevens, Billy, and me to his office and poured us a glass of sherry. He cocked his eye when Billy raised his glass, but I reckoned the boy had earned it. Besides, he's been drinking gin since he was seven.

"I am indebted to you all. Indeed, the Prime Minister and the entire government owe you a debt of gratitude. Your very good health."

"If I may, Mycroft, I would suggest our first toast should be to the late Augustus Updike. Without his sacrifice, who knows how things may have transpired."

32

Watson was waiting for me at Scotland Yard.

"A bomb?" he said.

"Enough dynamite to destroy half the building. Thank heaven we were on time. Did our friend give you any difficulty?"

"None. We had tea and enjoyed a very civilized conversation. Then Lestrade arrived and arrested him. He must have known that Beatrice and I were part of the plan. Still, he thanked us very politely for a pleasant afternoon and shook our hands. Lestrade is trying to question him, but hasn't made much progress, I think."

The Inspector confirmed this. "Not said a word. He refuses to talk to a 'mere underling' like myself. Cheeky devil. Says he will speak to you, though."

Carandini was sitting at the table in the cold, tiled room. He seemed to be sleeping.

"So, Mr Holmes was my gas inspector," he said, looking up at me. I was still dressed in the workman's attire, although I had removed the wig and whiskers. "You would not have fooled me when I was younger. Not even ten years ago. It is a monstrous thing to get old. So much has been robbed from me."

I sat opposite him and said nothing.

"Well?" he said. "You have questions. Ask them."

"I see no point in asking you anything. You are aware of what I want to know. I am willing to listen."

"I have no idea what you want me to tell you," he began.

I slapped the table with my fist. The sudden bang made him jump.

"There is no point in dissembling," I said. "I have recovered your secret ledgers. I have seen your dossier on members of the government and the royal family." I paused. "The bomb has been found and dismantled."

Although his expression did not change, the light seemed to go out of his eyes. "Ah," he said.

I sat back, adopting an air of insouciance. "Whenever you are ready, Sir Christopher," I said.

For several moments he said nothing. He seemed to be weighing the merits of speaking versus the value of silence.

He cleared his throat and said, "Perhaps I could have some water."

I did not move but called out, "Guard, water for the prisoner."

The guard brought in an enamelware mug and jug of water, then left. I poured and handed the mug to Carandini. He took a long mouthful.

"I was having tea with your friend Lady Beatrice when they came to take me. Darjeeling. Good china. How strange it is to go from utter civility to utter ruin in a matter of moments. She is a woman of substance. A man would be proud to have such a daughter.

"I liked her father. He was a brilliant man, you know. A polymath. He could speak several languages, had a knack for the sciences, and was interested in knowledge of every sort. For a time I thought him a kindred spirit."

"And then?"

"I misread him," Carandini said. He sipped another mouthful of water. "I thought his passion for knowledge surpassed every other consideration for him as it did for me, but when he learned of my politics, he severed all ties. In the end, I discovered he was a prosaic thinker. He could not see beyond the status quo. 'Queen and Country' and all that nonsense."

316

"I believe they call that patriotism."

"Patriotism should not imply slavish devotion, surely? Isn't the essence of good citizenship a willingness to question our leaders? To call them to task when they fail us?"

"Is it because of your son that you hate Britain?"

"Hate? Dear me, no, my dear Mr Holmes. I do not hate Britain. She disappoints me. I hate what she is becoming, but I hope for her redemption. If only government officials could see what they risk when they ignore right and do only what is expedient, what fills their pockets. Every one of them has a secret. If you have seen my dossier, you know that to be true."

"Politicians are weak, flawed," I replied, "because, in the end, they are human. That is true of every government in the world regardless of its philosophy."

"But if only they could be made aware that people are watching they would not be tempted into evil. Would heed what President Lincoln called, 'the better angels of their nature.'"

"And who decides what right is? Who is to say that one man's choices are better than another's?"

"Is that not what you do? Every time you have someone arrested you are passing a judgement, are you not?"

"I follow the law. I am not passing a moral judgement."

"Oh come, Mr Holmes. You sometimes ignore the letter of the law for the sake of the greater good, do you not? Is that not making a moral judgement?"

"How did you meet Frankall? Or Ostap Bender, I should say."

The dark eyes flashed and I suddenly saw the depths of his hate. "A vile man. An evil man. I did not lie to you about him, Mr Holmes."

"You did not tell me the whole truth. You were in league with him."

"To a point." He sipped his water. "Everything I told you that first day you came to my house was the truth, though, yes, there were some omissions.

"When my son died, I became obsessed with contacting him. My academic interest in the occult became fanatical. The obsession led me, eventually, to that creature who called himself the Sorcerer. In the beginning, I believed. I wanted to believe, you understand. He was so plausible. Often he seemed to be successful, but sometimes he failed. This fallibility, as I perceived it, seemed to make him all the more credible. I trusted him. Confided in him."

Another sip of water.

"At the time, I was in bad financial straits. I was about to lose my home, everything. The Sorcerer claimed he could secure my fortune if I, in turn, would pledge my honour to bring him more clients. I had a great many contacts in the spiritualist community and one word from me would secure his future. We shook hands on it. A month later, Lionel Carton threw himself out of a window and his wife died not long after. I was astonished when a solicitor contacted me and said I had inherited a fortune."

"How happy for you."

"No, Mr Holmes, no. I was not happy. I was horrified. I demanded to know where the money came from. No one would talk. I realised what a fool I had been. I asked my friend Barton to look into the matter. Everything I told you about his death was the truth."

"Except you did not mention your involvement."

"No. No, I confess I did not. When Barton died, I was terrified. He had discovered enough to show me what a perfidious fellow this 'Sorcerer' was. You can imagine my horror when Frankall came to see me a few days later. He was pleasant, complimentary, and utterly deadly. He told me, in the most civilized manner, that my interest in his work could not continue. Bad things happened to people who were too inquisitive, he said."

"And what answer did you make to this?" I said.

"I swore silence and he saw my terror. He knew I was no threat. So I held my secrets, but I kept a file. Then, when you came to see me, I thought you may, perhaps, be able to destroy him."

"Why did you not tell me openly about the man?"

"I was torn. On one hand, I wanted Frankall stopped, destroyed. He is – was – altogether evil. But I could not betray his secret without also betraying my own. I gave you part of the file I had compiled and then I did something of which I am ashamed: I told Frankall that you were on his trail. I hoped that he would see me as an ally. Then, if you arrested him he would have no reason to reveal my secret, but if he did betray me you would not believe him because I had helped you."

"Very clever," I said. It was not a compliment.

"I regret all my dealings with Frankall. I knew he was behind Carton's death. All I can say in my defence is I had no idea what he planned when I first spoke to him. On his matter, I hope you will not judge me too harshly. I have willed everything I own to Phineas Carton. I would appreciate it if you would make my apologies to him."

His hands trembled and the water spilled onto his shirt.

"And who will apologise to Augustus Updike?" I said. "Do you know what torment that man endured? And what of the farmer and his wife who were shot to death by Timms?"

"I am truly sorry for that. I learned of Updike purely by chance. My servant, Dillahunt, was stepping out with his maid and they gossiped about their betters."

Dillahunt... Rose's Dilly. Her young man who was working as a valet in Pimlico. Ah.

"They thought Updike was a spy," Carandini said. "I pretended not to be interested, but I paid attention. Eventually, Dillahunt told me Updike worked with your brother. Mycroft Holmes was England's biggest secret, the beating heart of the Empire. It was downstairs chatter, but I was interested enough to want to know more. I was desperate to learn more.

"I wrestled with my conscience for days and ultimately decided preventing another Boer war was worth contacting Frankall. He was the only one I knew who might be able to get the information I needed. I told myself he would simply drug the man. I had no idea he would resort to torture. He had to, he said. Updike's mind was too strong and he resisted the potion. He would not yield to Frankall's questions. Eventually, Frankall invited Updike to Devon and you know the rest. I knew none of this until later. There was no malice in my heart, Mr Holmes. My intent was honourable."

"Honourable? You have a queer notion of the word. Did you really believe you could prevent a war by killing my brother?"

"Your brother is the heart and soul of the government. You must know this. Without him, everything collapses. Remove Mycroft Holmes and this empire will crumble. 'The linchpin', Updike called him. Frankall did not learn much, but he learned that.

"War... War, Mr Holmes, is a wretched business. My son died, and for what? I determined no other man's son would die if I could prevent it. Can't you see, I wanted to do something good, to leave a legacy worth something, instead of…" he had no words. He lay his hands out in a gesture of worthlessness.

"It did not occur to you that if you blew up the government building, you would be killing many innocent people, not only my brother?"

"I set the timer for the end of the day when most people would have left. Originally, before I knew the name Mycroft Holmes, I thought to destroy the Houses of Parliament, but the loss of life there would have been immense. I wanted to keep the deaths to a minimum."

"That is your justification?"

"Casualties of war," he said. "What are a few dozen lives compared with thousands?"

He finished the last of the water and I refilled his cup. He sipped and said, "Your brother is a good man, Mr Holmes. He inspires extraordinary loyalty. I wrote to him, you know. Months ago, I sent him a letter and pointed out the danger of another war with the Boers. I told him how immoral war is. He ignored me. In the end, there was no choice. He and the government he serves must be stopped." Tears filled his dark eyes and cascaded down his cheeks. "It is all hopeless," he said. "Hopeless."

Thursday, 8th June

I called upon Phineas Carton this morning to tell him I had solved the mystery of his father's death. He listened to me in a sickened silence.

"Abominable," he cried. "How could any man behave so reprehensibly? I am horrified that my father died for nothing more than greed. And my poor mother, too."

321

"It is appalling," I agreed. "All the people involved are now dead. Carandini, himself, will hang. He asked me to tell you he regrets his actions and has left his entire estate to you."

"I do not want anything from him."

"I understand. However, most of his fortune was rightfully yours. You should have it back. I have no doubt your father would wish it."

"Thank you, Mr Holmes," Carton said. "Just knowing the truth is worth more than all the fortunes in the kingdom. I can never thank you enough for all you have done. I will consider your advice."

Friday, June 9th

Lestrade stopped by this evening. That he had unhappy news was evident in the slump of his shoulders.

"You look glum, Lestrade," I said. "What is wrong?"

"It's Carandini," he said. "We found him this morning in his cell. Heart attack."

"He died on his birthday," Watson said. "Just as Mme Bronski predicted."

33

Friday, 7th July

This evening, a group of us waited in the sitting room as Stevens kept watch at the window. "Here he comes," he said.

We listened to his footsteps coming up the stairs. I shushed their giggling. Really, you'd expect intelligent people to behave with more decorum. A moment later, Watson stepped into the room and started at our chorus of, "Surprise!"

After the dinner and the cake, the champagne and the toasts, my old friend opened his presents and described each gift in detail to the cheering crowd. A set of surgical instruments from Mycroft, a manual on billiards from Stamford, a new hat from Lestrade, a pair of emerald cufflinks from Emerald, a tiepin from our Hatton Garden friends, and a fountain pen from B.

There was only my large box left, and although he cast curious looks at it as he was opening the other gifts, Watson kept it until it was all that remained.

Stevens picked it up and placed it on the table. "It's heavy, anyway," he said.

Watson opened the box and stared in silence at the contents.

"Letters?" Lestrade chuckled. "Oh, for shame, Mr Holmes."

"I wrote these when I was... away," I said. "When the world believed I was dead. At least once a week I wrote to you, my dear Watson, about what I was doing. I thought it was time I delivered them."

"My dear fellow," he said in a choked voice. "These are riches, indeed." He wiped his eyes and said, lightly, "I do not suppose you have records of any old cases in there?"

"If I gave you everything now, my good Watson," I replied, "What should I give you next year?"

Glaser left first. "I promised Rivkah I would not stay late," he said, shaking our hands. "Thank you all for the baby gifts. You are very kind."

"Give that daughter of yours a kiss for me," Watson said. "We very nearly share our birthday. I should be her honorary godfather."

"What a lovely idea."

"I must go, too," Lestrade said. "Wait a moment, Glaser, and we can share a cab. Many happy returns, Doctor."

Emerald wiped cake off Watson's lapel and said, "Ah, Johnny, what will I do with you? Come have lunch with me tomorrow, my dear."

She kissed his cheek and followed the policemen down the stairs.

At last, only B, Watson, and I were left, sitting amid the gifts and the crumbs of cake and the dregs of champagne. Watson was still selecting letters at random from the box and reading them. From time to time, he glanced up at me and smiled or shook his head.

B yawned and said, "I am sleepy. I shall bid you goodnight, Sherlock. Happy birthday, John. I hope your day was all you wished."

"Joy beyond imagining," he said. "Thank you, Beatrice."

Left alone, we sat in our customary chairs, quiet and peaceful.

"I should go to bed, too," Watson said, but he did not move. "Such an embarrassment of riches," he said, looking at his treasure.

"I fear you shall make good use of those instruments from Mycroft before the year is out. No doubt that is why he gave them to you."

"A Savigny set. I never hoped to own something so grand. It was very generous. You are right: they shall get a lot of use."

He plucked another letter from the box and smiled as he read it.

I said, "Perhaps you should save the rest for tomorrow, and the day after."

He chuckled. "You think I shall read each only once? My dear fellow… You cannot imagine what this means to me."

"You thought I quite forgot you during my long absence," I said. "I hope you now realise that was not the case. Every time I sent a report to Mycroft, I included the most recent letters I had written to you. He deposited them in my bank. If I had failed to return, if Moriarty's men had succeeded in their lethal plans, Mycroft was to make sure all those letters came to you."

"I am delighted you were able to give them to me in person. I am a little curious, though. Why did you wait so long?"

"They were written during a period of extreme distress and anxiety. I did not wish to be reminded of them. However, recent events made clear to me the effect my absence had upon you, my dear Watson. I decided it was time to show you once and for all that you were never far from my thoughts."

"There, now," he said, "You've proved me right."

"How so?"

"You really are the best and wisest man I've ever known."

EASTER EGGS AND OTHER NOTES

Readers of my first two books, *A Biased Judgement: The Sherlock Holmes Diaries 1897* and *Sherlock Holmes and the Other Woman* will know I enjoy hiding Easter Eggs in my stories. *Return to Reichenbach* was no different. The following contains spoilers, so please read the book first.

Many of the characters names in this novel pay homage to various people who have become part of Holmes's lore. Edgar Hardwicke is named for the late Edward Hardwicke (1932-2011), the actor who played Dr Watson to Jeremy Brett's Holmes in the Granda series (1986–1984). Brett (1933-1995) also makes an appearance under his real name, Peter Huggins.

My Sorcerer uses the alias Angel Frankall. This is an anagram for Frank Langella, the American actor who played Holmes on Broadway in 1981 to great acclaim. Frankall's real name in the book is Ostap Bender. This was the name of a character played by Mr Langella in the 1970 Mel Brooks' film, *The Twelve Chairs*.

The Sorcerer's ally, Christopher L. Carandini was inspired by the late Sir Christopher Lee (1922-1915). Lee not only portrayed Holmes on film, but also Mycroft and Sir Henry Baskerville. His full name was Christopher Frank Carandini Lee.

In the novel, Watson and Lady Beatrice are accompanied to Switzerland by René Moody. He is named for the late Ron Moody (1924-2015). Though best known for his award-winning portrayal of Fagin in the movie *Oliver!* he also played Holmes in *Sherlock Holmes: The Musical* (1988 / 1989). Honest!

Lest you think the modern depictions of Holmes have been overlooked, you should know that the emerald is a form of beryl. Therefore, 'Emerald Vertue' owes her name – though assuredly not her character – to the producer of BBC's *Sherlock*, Beryl Vertue.

The true location of Mycroft Holmes's office remains a close secret. I therefore took the liberty of situating it in roughly the same spot as the War Office on Horse Guard Avenue. Historians among you will know that building wasn't actually opened until 1906. Still, its size and location made it ideal for the purpose of the novel.

The drug used by Frankall is based on *salvia divinorum*, also known as 'sage of the diviners'. A hallucinogenic, it is native to Mexico and was used by the Mazatecs for religious purposes. It wasn't mentioned in print until 1939, but it had been in use long before then. It is likely the well-travelled Frankall discovered it and adapted it for his own use.

In the Victorian era, Spiritualism was immensely popular. Queen Victoria and Prince Albert had clairvoyant Georgiana Eagle entertain them at Osborne House in 1846. Mediums were revered and feared in equal measure. One of its most famous adherents was Sherlock Holmes creator Sir Arthur Conan Doyle (1859-1930).

The tarot was a popular tool used by mediums and psychics. The Visconi-Sforza deck remains as popular now as it was then. It is actually comprised of a number of incomplete decks and named for the Italian noblemen for whom it was made.

Madame Helena Blavatsky (1831-1891) mentioned in scathing terms by Carandini, was an occultist, medium and founder of the Theosophical Society. She settled in London in 1885 Her movement spread widely and had many admirers, but she was considered a fraud by her critics.

Mycroft's colleague William Melville (1850-1918) was the first chief of the British Secret Service. He was credited with foiling a plot against Queen Victoria in 1887. He later became pivotal in investigating and preventing several anarchist plots. According to his biographer, Andrew Cook, Melville's code name was 'M'. Yes, just like James Bond. Like Conan Doyle, he was also a friend of Harry Houdini.

Until 1916, Ireland had its own time zone called Dublin Mean Time, which was 25 minutes behind Greenwich. After the 1916 Easter Uprising, the time zone was abolished by the British Government.

Today, the ferry to Dublin docks in Dun Laoghaire, but in 1899 it arrived at the city's port at the North Wall.

Kells is more built up today than it was in the late 19th century, but it remains in many respects the medieval town that once housed the famous book that bears its name. All the landmarks mentioned by Holmes still stand.

Acknowlegements

This book would not exist without Sir Arthur Conan Doyle's extraordinary creation of Sherlock Holmes, nor without the readers, publishers, editors and filmmakers who keep him alive.

I would like to thank my daughter Cara and her partner Chris for their unfailing support, and my family and friends for their encouragement.

Special thanks to Jane, Patty and Ellie for their tireless proofreading, suggestions and corrections, not to mention their friendship and enthusiasm. You ladies rock!

I am grateful to the staff of *The Kells Experience* for their invaluable information about Kells in the late 19th century.

Likewise, many thanks to Olaf, Nicole and Silvia at *Deutsche Sherlock Holmes Gesellschaft* for their invaluable comments regarding the Meiringen chapters. If Holmes or Doyle in Switzerland interests you, look for their book, *The Adventures of Two British Gentlemen in Switzerland – In the Footsteps of Sir Arthur Conan Doyle and Sherlock Holmes* soon to be published by the Sherlock Holmes Society of Germany.

Finally, much love and gratitude to my readers and to Sherlock Holmes fans everywhere. I'll see you in the bookshop.

ABOUT THE AUTHOR

When Geri Schear was seven, her grandmother gave her a copy of The Hound of the Baskervilles. She's been obsessed with Holmes and Watson ever since.

Her short stories have appeared in a wide number of literary journals in Ireland and in the US. She has contributed a tale to *The MX Book of New Sherlock Holmes stories, Vol. III*, and *Beyond Watson.*

She currently lives in Kells, County Meath.

Also from MX Publishing

MX Publishing is the world's largest specialist Sherlock Holmes publisher, with over a hundred titles and fifty authors creating the latest in Sherlock Holmes fiction and non-fiction.

From traditional short stories and novels to travel guides and quiz books, MX Publishing cater for all Holmes fans.

The collection includes leading titles such as *Benedict Cumberbatch In Transition* and *The Norwood Author* which won the 2011 Howlett Award (Sherlock Holmes Book of the Year).

MX Publishing also has one of the largest communities of Holmes fans on Facebook with regular contributions from dozens of authors.

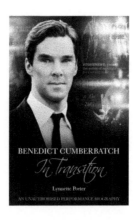

www.mxpublishing.com

331

Also from MX Publishing

Our bestselling short story collections 'Lost Stories of Sherlock Holmes', 'The Outstanding Mysteries of Sherlock Holmes', 'Untold Adventures of Sherlock Holmes' (and the sequel 'Studies in Legacy') and 'Sherlock Holmes in Pursuit'.

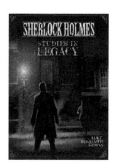 

www.mxpublishing.com

Also from MX Publishing

The Missing Authors Series

Sherlock Holmes and The Adventure of The Grinning Cat
Sherlock Holmes and The Nautilus Adventure
Sherlock Holmes and The Round Table Adventure

"Joseph Svec, III is brilliant in entwining two endearing and enduring classics of literature, blending the factual with the fantastical; the playful with the pensive; and the mischievous with the mysterious. We shall, all of us young and old, benefit with a cup of tea, a tranquil afternoon, and a copy of Sherlock Holmes, The Adventure of the Grinning Cat."
Amador County Holmes Hounds Sherlockian Society

Also from MX Publishing

The American Literati Series

 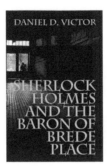 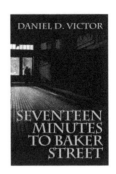

The Final Page of Baker Street
The Baron of Brede Place
Seventeen Minutes To Baker Street

"The really amazing thing about this book is the author's ability to call up the 'essence' of both the Baker Street 'digs' of Holmes and Watson as well as that of the 'mean streets' of Marlowe's Los Angeles. Although none of the action takes place in either place, Holmes and Watson share a sense of camaraderie and self-confidence in facing threats and problems that also pervades many of the later tales in the Canon. Following their conversations and banter is a return to Edwardian England and its certainties and hope for the future. This is definitely the world before The Great War."
Philip K Jones

www.mxpublishing.com

Also from MX Publishing

The Detective and The Woman Series

  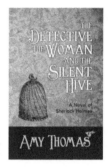

The Detective and The Woman
The Detective, The Woman and The Winking Tree
The Detective, The Woman and The Silent Hive

"The book is entertaining, puzzling and a lot of fun. I believe the author has hit on the only type of long-term relationship possible for Sherlock Holmes and Irene Adler. The details of the narrative only add force to the romantic defects we expect in both of them and their growth and development are truly marvelous to watch. This is not a love story. Instead, it is a coming-of-age tale starring two of our favorite characters."
Philip K Jones